THE BEST OF THE

Bellevue Literary Review

THE BEST OF THE
Bellevue Literary Review

EDITED BY DANIELLE OFRI
and the staff of the
Bellevue Literary Review

BELLEVUE LITERARY PRESS
New York

First published in the United States in 2008 by
Bellevue Literary Press
New York

FOR INFORMATION ADDRESS:
Bellevue Literary Press
NYU School of Medicine
550 First Avenue
OBV 640
New York, NY 10016

This book was published with the generous support of
Bellevue Literary Press's founding donor the Arnold Simon Family Trust
and the Bernard & Irene Schwartz Foundation.

Cataloging-in-Publication Data is available from the Library of Congress

Book design and type formatting by Bernard Schleifer
Manufactured in the United States of America
ISBN-13 978-1-934137-04-8
FIRST EDITION
1 3 5 7 9 8 6 4 2

Contents

COMING OF AGE

PART II: CONFLICT:
GRAPPLING WITH ILLNESS

DISABILITY

COPING

MADNESS

CONNECTIONS

FAMILY

PART III: DENOUEMENT

MORTALITY

DEATH

LOSS

Acknowledgments

THE BEST OF THE *BELLEVUE LITERARY REVIEW* IS AN ANTHOLOGY OF THE first six years of the *BLR*. The *Bellevue Literary Review* and the anthology were created from the hard work and dedication of the *BLR* editorial staff:

Danielle Ofri, *Editor-in-Chief*

Stacy Bodziak, *Managing Editor*

Ronna Wineberg, *Fiction Editor*

Jerome Lowenstein, *Nonfiction Editor*

Corie Feiner, *Poetry Editor*

Frances Richey, *Poetry Editor*

Suzanne McConnell, *Assistant Fiction Editor*

Roxanna Font, *Founding Poetry Editor*

Donna Baier Stein, *Founding Poetry Editor*

Doris Milman, *Copy Editor*

Martin J. Blaser, *Publisher*

The *Bellevue Literary Review* is published by the Department of Medicine at New York University. The *BLR* editorial staff would like to acknowledge the support of Bellevue Hospital Center, NYU School of Medicine and the staff of the Department of Medicine. We are also extremely grateful to our Editorial Board and manuscript readers for their continual hard work and devotion to this literary enterprise.

www.BLReview.org

Introduction

WE ARE ALL UNITED IN THE COMMONALITY OF EFFORT CALLED HEALING. Decades ago when the medical model was paternalistic, we were accustomed to hearing only of the relationship between doctor and patient; it stood as though alone, supreme among lesser associations that the sick form with those around them. Perhaps the doctor-patient relationship is still the keystone, or perhaps it is no more critical to recovery than those other interpersonal bonds. Either way, that ancient traditional linkage can today be best seen as part of a context of relationships that is far bigger than has, until recently, been acknowledged. The structure of that bigger context centers around the patient, his or her disease, and the perceptions of it that combine to form the experience unique to each individual. The patient has a story to tell, and so does every other participant in the calculus of healing.

This volume is an anthology of such stories. Whatever else may be its lessons, it teaches us the ways in which we are bound up together in the presence of illness. Every member of the healing surround sees people, problems, and events in ways different from every other member, and tells of them in a different voice. In this book, the rhythms and cadences of the sick and needful merge with the rhythms and cadences of those who would heal them, either with the technology of which they are masters, or the love they bring, or—far more often than might be thought—both.

I say *both* because, ultimately, the best of healing is expressed in ways that can be recognized as encompassed by the Greek word *agapē*, as used by Paul in chapter 13 of I Corinthians. Translated into Latin as *caritas* and into English most accurately as "caring love," *agapē* is recognized by Paul as being even greater than faith or hope. Healing involves all three, "but the greatest of these is caring love." There are stories of *caritas* in these pages, but there are also stories of frustration and anger and disappointment. This is because attempts to heal are so much more complex than can be appreciated except by those immersed in them. And too often, even the participants cannot recognize the emotions that whirl their turbulent way through the minds of anyone but themselves. This is not for want of wanting—we certainly all endeavor to find empathy—but for want of being able to see inside minds not our own. The stories in this book guide us toward the paths to understanding.

We write for any, and often several, of a multitude of reasons. Those who heal and those who would be healed—patients, family members, doctors, nurses, medical students, technologists, social workers, everyone—need some way to express what they are feeling. To write about feelings is to bring them forth from some inner place into a form in which they can be seen with perhaps less of the passion of the moment, and with more equanimity. Triumph and tragedy need distance, if their meaning is to become incorporated into the wisdom we hope to gain from the events of our lives. Writing about one's own or another's experience of illness is very much like the literary form it often takes, namely poetry, described by Wordsworth as being, "emotion recollected in tranquility." Yet, some of the finest of both prose and poetry have been created when the writer is not yet tranquil, and still feeling the untamed and amorphous torrent of what is being described. Once on the page, though, it becomes more a thing of substance and shape, more accessible, more governable—and therefore more a thing from which truths can be learned, both by ourselves and our readers.

To write is also to share, so that one is no longer alone with emotions whose meaning can become clarified by the telling. The process of finding words to express the feeling, and then transcribing those words onto a page is something like seeking advice from a wise friend; elucidating a chaotic thought to readers will often elucidate it to ourselves.

Writing gives power to the powerless, and who feels less power than patients and family members do, or medical personnel when their efforts fail, or when they are rejected or undervalued by those meant to be helped? We need to write in order to bring back a semblance of control, to lessen feelings of impotence, and to return to compassion when it has been dispersed by the frustration of defeat or loss of self-esteem. We need to reflect on our deepest values, especially when they are threatened. At such times, the Muse allows us to muse.

In all these ways, writing is a means of healing. Whether we need healing for the wounds caused by the slings and arrows of the illnesses that are our daily portion, or whether what needs rectifying is the pomposity and self-importance into which we so easily slip, the making of literature is a balm. The medical profession has no monopoly on self-centeredness—it is seen in patients and individual family members as well. It is an enemy of *caritas*, and therefore of healing.

The stories, essays, and poems in the following pages deal with all of this, in a spectrum of styles and voices that reveal the variety of experiences of illness and of the reactions to it. We present it as a gift, to the reader and to ourselves.

—SHERWIN B. NULAND
Yale University

PART I

INITIATION

The Plagiarist

Hollis Seamon

"WHY?" ALTHEA LEANED TOWARD THE SPLOTCHY-PALE STUDENT WHO sat in her small office chair, his wide khaki thighs overflowing its seat. "You had to know you were doing it. And you had to know that, this time, you'd be kicked out."

The boy's face flushed an unhealthy plum and tears began to roll down his cheeks. He kept his eyes focused on his boots—they were leaking slushy, salty water onto Althea's blue rug. Ever so slowly, he nodded.

Althea flung herself back in her chair. Jesus. The poor slob. The poor stupid kid. She closed her eyes. Her heartbeat was thudding in her ears again—*boom*, boomedy, *boom*, boom, boom. Her head made it into a little song, a high whining soprano melody over the imperious bass. Then, her long training forced her to scan it: dactylic, a particularly obnoxious meter. She put a hand to her chest and coughed. Coughing, she'd read somewhere, was supposed to stop it, this runaway pounding of a deluded heart. It didn't. She coughed again. The EKG electrodes, glued to her chest, jiggled. She opened her eyes.

The boy hadn't moved, hadn't wiped his tears. They were running into the woolen scarf bunched around his neck.

She leaned over her desk. "Derrick," she said. "It's so obvious." She jabbed one finger onto the first page of his paper, right under the bold-typed title he'd seemed so proud of when he submitted the paper last week: The Wedding Crasher in *The Ancient Mariner:* Why You Wouldn't Have Invited Him, Either. "Look, here are your opening sentences." She cleared her throat and read aloud, "'People got married in the 19th century, too, just like today. They had weddings then, too, and just like today, no one wanted weird old guys showing up and ruining their fun.'" She glanced at the boy's face; he had a small smile.

"Yeah," he whispered. "That's my thesis. I wanted to say that, you know, this guy just shows up and..."

She held up a hand, palm out. "Fine. But, then, here's the next line you've written here." She read the words slowly: "'The ancient Mariner, bright-eyed and compulsive, is a haunter of wedding feasts, and in a grim way he is the chanter of a prothalamium.'" She stopped, letting that grand last word linger. She repeated it: "Prothalamium."

Derrick was still smiling.

Blood thudded in her neck and throat; her palm throbbed. It occurred to her that she might have to smack him. She just might have to whap him upside his dim, tear-stained, smiling, biscuit-colored cheek. Christ. She folded her hands tightly together on her desk. "Derrick, that is not you. That is clearly not your wording."

The boy nodded.

"Derrick," she said, loudly. "Listen to me."

He jumped, his smile fading slowly away, the corners of his chapped lips drifting. His eyes were a soft spaniel brown, with no eyelashes.

None at all, she suddenly noticed. Not a lash. And very little in the way of eyebrows. No wonder he looked odd, like the Pillsbury Dough Boy. Was he on chemo? Oh God, a sick kid and she was about to ruin his life. No, no—he'd done it himself. He had cheated. Not her.

"Derrick, what's a 'prothalamium'?" She waited, knowing he didn't know. She tapped her tented hands on the desktop, in time to the beating of her heart. *Hot* diggity, *dog* diggity, *boom*, boom, boom, *boom,* boom, boom.

The damp shoulders rose and fell, once. His eyes went back to his boots and to the white-rimmed puddle gathering around them.

She sighed and picked up a book from her desk and flipped to the page she'd marked with a hot pink sticky note. "It's a wedding song. The word comes from the Greek, Derrick. You might have looked it up. If you were going to plagiarize, you might have been just a bit smarter about it." She pointed to the page and the penciled star she'd drawn on it. "It's not your sentence, Derrick. It's Harold Bloom's sentence. See? Here it is, word-for-word, page 201, last paragraph, right here in Bloom's quite famous book on the Romantic poets. *The Visionary Company.* It is quite famous. The kind of book professors have read. Did you never think of that?"

His head rose and his eyes widened. "No," he said. "I didn't. I just—I just couldn't say it like he does. I mean," he stopped and smiled again, whispering, "the chanter of a pro-thal-a-mi-um. Man, it sounds so good, when he says it. And when I say something, it sucks. Right? I don't have enough words in my brain or something, to work with, you know, and when I say something, it stinks."

"Well. Yes." She shook her head. "But you can't take Harold Bloom's words, Derrick, you know that. You can't steal words like that." She closed the book with a snap. She stared into the boy's eyes. "Why the hell didn't you just put the damn words in quotes? Why didn't you just do that, with a citation? Why didn't you do that, and save us both from going through all this? I called the registrar, Derrick. You have two previous plagiarism incidents on your record—proven, documented. They'll throw you out of the university this time. You're a senior. Four years. All that money. Jesus." She felt her voice start to quaver, grow high with despair, harmonizing with the twanging of her heart. She was getting too excited, she knew it. She was getting angry and that only made her heart rate worse. But she couldn't stop asking.

"Why? Why? Are you ill? Do you have some sort of—condition—that is affecting your work? A disability of some sort?"

"No," he said. One of his hands rose to his face, its bitten nails plucking at the remnants of an eyebrow. "No, I'm okay."

"Then why? Why didn't you just put the lousy words in quotes, Derrick?"

His lips started to tremble. "I don't know," he said. "I wanted to. I know it's wrong. It's stealing and it's wrong. But I wanted those words to be mine, you know? I just wanted them."

Her heart drummed against her ribs. Sad, stupid little fuck. And he wasn't ill. He wasn't having chemo. He just did that thing—that tripso-trichso-thing she'd read about, where people pluck out their own eyelashes. Damn.

When he'd gone, closing the office door gently behind him, his signature on the papers, confessing his crime, leaving just his salty wet spot behind on her rug, she stood up, reached under her loose jacket and shifted the weight of the portable heart monitor away from the small of her back. She swung the metal box around to her side, where she could see its digital display. Quite a thing to keep hidden, this Holter monitor—a black square buzzing box, held by a shoulder holster affair, sprouting a forest of wires that were attached to the seven color-coded electrodes stuck to her ribs and chest. The electrodes under her breasts itched. The tape, everywhere, pulled. She tried to stretch but the wires resisted. And her heart, her stupid middle-aged, fifty-four-year-old freaked-out heart that raced for no reason, that quivered in her chest like a hooked trout, kept on and on: *hot* diggity, *dog* diggity, boom.

She checked the time. Half an hour to go: she'd had the thing on twenty-three-and-a-half hours now. Surely she could find something to do for the last half hour. She turned toward her computer, but then hadn't the energy to switch it on. She just sat still, watching the digital read-out on the monitor tick away the minutes.

At 12:53, she decided she'd had enough. Twenty-four hours minus seven minutes couldn't really matter—close enough for government work, as her father had liked to say. She pulled the shade on the office window, locked the door, and took off her jacket and turtleneck and bra. One by one, she pulled the tape away from the electrodes, wincing as it tore her skin. Then the electrodes themselves—the blue from atop her left breast, the brown from her right, and so on down to her ribs: white, green, red, black, orange. Each disengaged electrode dripped a clear, bluish goo. She found a plastic bag in her file cabinet and dropped them in. When they were all in there, sliming together in a gluey bunch, she twisted the bag into a knot and tossed it in her wastebasket. She located tissues to wipe her skin. She lifted her breasts and tried to see the skin below them, where the electrodes had been glued— she couldn't see much but what she could was red and swollen, puffy, damaged. Everything burned. For one moment, her eyes seemed to drift up to the ceiling and look down: she saw herself standing there, a full professor of literature in her tasteful book-lined office, Althea Roland, PhD, naked to the waist, welts bubbling up all over her torso. As if she'd been attacked by wasps. Or subjected to a long, tortuous experiment by aliens. With a strange buzzing box and wires gripped in her hands. She smiled. Well. Just like poor dumb Derrick. We smile from the midst of the hopeless, hapless messes we get ourselves into, don't we, son?

Dressed again, Althea put Derrick's signed papers into her book bag; she would make Xerox copies and bring them to the registrar's office on her way to drop off the monitor at her doctor's office. She'd told Derrick it was out of her hands now, that the process of dismissal would begin the minute the registrar received these papers, that he'd hear from the Dean shortly. All she had to do was turn in the evidence. Like a good detective, her work was done— the punishment, thank God, was not her responsibility. Oh, he'd said. Okay. He hadn't even blinked, as he shuffled out her door. So be it. Amen. Good riddance to a bad cheater. *Que sera, sera*, eh?

She wrapped her head in her old gray scarf and hefted the book bag, grown suddenly heavy with evidence and a Holter monitor, still faintly buzzing. It was a good thing she didn't have to pass through a metal detector; some half-trained university security guard would shoot her—they were allowed to carry guns these days, a terrible irony waiting to happen. She stepped out the door. But when she got outside, into the ice-slickened aftermath of the third February storm so far this semester, it was all she could do to stand up and slither her way down the sidewalks to the freshly-salted parking lot. She wasn't risking her brittle, honeycombed bones by walking the two extra blocks to the registrar's office. So the papers that would ruin Derrick's life could stay in her book bag one more day. Big deal. Fuck it.

Maybe he'd get lucky and she'd die before she turned them in—her car would slide into a tree on the slick mile between the college and the medical center. Or she'd have the massive heart attack tonight, all tucked in and cozy in her bed, then suddenly struck by the unbelievable, undeniable first pain, a granite boulder dropping onto her chest, cold sweat springing from her skin. She would thrash in panic, trying to draw in air, terrified, alone. It would hurt, horribly, but briefly. Then she would become still and very, very quiet. Her old dog, her ancient, half-blind faithful dog, her very own Argos, her old sweet dog would curl himself beside her, whining, trying to warm her cooling body. Derrick just might get that lucky, the poor shmuck. It could happen. That kind of thing happens sometimes. That kind of last minute reprieve. It does. It could. It might.

But it didn't. She gave the monitor to her doctor's receptionist, who tossed it casually onto the counter and said, "Here's your appointment to talk over your results. Bye now." So Althea went home to her normal post-divorce-times-two routine. She ate a peanut butter sandwich for supper. She graded papers and watched television simultaneously, hoping each activity would neutralize the painful futility of the other. She went to bed and slept badly, wakened over and over by her jolting heart. But she did not die.

On Tuesday, she went to her 9:30 class—19th Century British Literature—and there Derrick was, slumped in the back row, as always. She put her books down on the front desk and opened her attendance book. She checked his name off—he'd never missed a single class. And wouldn't now, apparently, although his college career was certainly over. There are rules: Repeat plagiarists do not graduate. Have a permanent record of cheating. Don't get a refund. Don't get a diploma. It was over. Kaput. End of story. *Fini*.

But here, after all, he was. He wouldn't speak in class—he never had. But he would take notes and use his yellow highlighter to mark the passages she talked about in his Norton anthology. And when she read some poetry aloud, he would close his eyes and nod along with the beat, smiling, happy. He would. He always did. And he would, apparently, keep on doing it until someone told him, officially, that he could not. He would not leave until someone planted a big official boot on his ass and kicked, hard. No, dear Derrick would not go gentle into that good night, not at all.

Her heart dove—took a spectacular plunge into her diaphragm. Its fall left that peculiar hollowness in her chest, that empty second when there was no beat at all, that airless moment that felt like a little death—yes, and a bit like the *petite morte,* orgasm, but not really, not enough—before it thudded hard against her ribs and quivered there, trembling. Over and above all that commotion in her chest, she heard herself say calmly, "Okay, folks. Today it's Keats." She laughed a little, flipping the rice-thin pages of her heavily annotated text. "If I'm not mistaken, today we tackle Keats' sonnet, 'When I Have Fears that I May Cease to Be'."

How perfect. How stupidly divine, her timing these days. Her syllabus = her life + her death, times X. Solve for X, the great unknown. She sighed quietly and began to read the poem aloud, beating along in fine iambics, her voice strong and steady, far out of sync with her crazy heart: *When I have fears that I may cease to be/Before my pen has gleaned my teeming brain.* Oh, yes, perfect. She looked up to see Derrick's eyes closed, his face alight with his hopeless, ecstatic listening.

On Tuesday afternoons, between 2 and 3, during her office hour, Althea always emailed her best former student, the one who himself had gone on to become a professor, to teach at another college, and so on. The one she'd been in love with but had never told, because it was against the rules to love a student. Even though he'd been a grown man, even then—the one-in-million brilliant guy who came back to school at thirty-five, after being a musician, a cook, a drunk, a carpenter, a clerk in the A&P. And she'd only been forty herself back then: not so much older. A new professor herself, back then. Divorced, twice. No kids—she had a PhD instead of kids, she liked to say. So he hadn't been so very far away, and forbidden, had he? But she wanted tenure; she couldn't take a chance, could she? Instead of risking it, making a damn fool of herself, she'd gotten a puppy—black and fuzzy and utterly in love with her. The World's Best Dog, she liked to say. And, he still was.

And then, like all of the good ones, the brilliant student had graduated. He'd finished his thesis, collected his 4.0 GPA and was gone. They'd written, for a while, then not. More than ten years of not. Recently, she had Googled his name. And found that he, too, had acquired what was called a "terminal degree," as if he, too, had gotten what would be his last disease. She emailed; they caught up. He was chair of his department and, funny thing, he'd married. One of his own bright students, two weeks after she graduated and made an honest man of him. And he'd gotten tenure, as well.

So, she'd loved and lost in silence, and the world had kept on turning, as it does. But, still, he made her laugh even now, by email. His office hour was between 2 and 3 on T/Th, too. Ah, sweet synchronicity. For weeks, they'd been trading made-up slang names for English courses. She would send a name; he would define the course and vice versa. This wouldn't have entertained anyone else, perhaps, but it brought light to Althea's small days— somehow, it calmed her heart. These exchanges had started simply—he had called her Literature by Women course "chick lit." She sent back "prick lit" for his Masculinities in Western Literature course. He had come up with alternatives for the women's lit course: Clit lit. Bitch lit. It got less and less politically correct. She kept a list of all their course names so far; it made her chuckle:

> Mick lit = Irish Literature
> Zit lit = Adolescent Literature
> Hip lit = The Beat Generation
> Stiff lit = Murder Mysteries
> Swish lit = Gay Literature (Alternative: Limp wrist lit)
> Crip lit = Literature of the Differently Abled
> Gefiltefish lit = Jewish Literature
> Whip lit = The Writings of the Marquis de Sade
> Flick lit = Film Studies
> E'nit? lit = The Stories of Sherman Alexie
> Pip lit = *Great Expectations*
> Nit Wit lit = The Benjy Section of *The Sound and the Fury*
> (also acceptable: Lenny's parts in *Of Mice and Men*.)

Her fingers clicked over the keyboard; she'd had a brainstorm overnight, lying awake, listening to her heart sputter and chug. "Dickless lit," she typed. "Hint: it's not a whole course, just one book." She sat back and waited.

Two seconds later, his message came back. "Hard one. (Ha, ha.) Have to think about it. No time now, though. Have to fly to Maine; Gina's father died yesterday. Suddenly—only mid-fifties. Out of the blue. Stroke. Terrible timing: did I tell you we're pregnant?"

She sent back: "Oh no. So sorry. Write when you get back. When you have time." She turned off the machine and held her face in her hands. She could feel that she was flushed, that blood was pumping hard into the frail little vessels of her face. Her brain. She had tears in her eyes and she didn't know why. She couldn't be sorry that some girl named Gina, whom she'd never seen or met or wanted to know or even know existed, had lost her father, could she? Hell, no. She could be furious, though—furious that he'd married someone whose father was as old as herself. Someone young enough to be pregnant. Oh, yes, she could still be furious. And she was. Oh God, she was.

On Wednesday, Althea sat on the table in her doctor's examining room, paper crinkling under her. She had meant to turn in Derrick's papers on her way to the doctor, but just didn't have time. The nurse took her blood pressure, smiled, went out of the room, came back in, took it again, and went out again. Althea's heart went crazy, leaping like, like what? She thought for a minute, in search of the perfect simile. Okay—her heart was leaping like a wild deer caught in the cage of her ribs. That wasn't bad. Lines from a Marvell poem swam into her ears: *The wanton troopers riding by/Have shot my fawn and it will die.* It was interesting, wasn't it? An early word for "deer" was "hart." Surely not coincidental? Nothing was, really, coincidental. She coughed and looked at her swinging feet; they hadn't made her take her tights off and so her feet were clad in black, with a small hole beginning on her right big toe. But that couldn't matter here—in the cardiologists' offices, they only cared about the parts from the waist up. She crossed her arms over her chest and rocked, humming.

Dr. Engleman's hair was reddish today, with gold highlights. It was the most astonishing thing—a cardiologist who changed his hair color weekly. From silvery gray to deep brown to sandy blond, a constantly changing array. It was the only odd thing about him, though. He was a tiny man, near her own age, neat and thin and gentle, with round black-rimmed glasses. Today, he shook his head and put his hand on her wrist, feeling her pulse. "Althea, your blood pressure is way up. It's horrendous. We'll have to change your medication."

"Oh. Yes, okay." She never could speak well to Dr. Engleman. She lost her training, her wit, her built-in facility with words, the minute she was faced with anyone in a white coat. "Um. What did the Holter show?"

He smiled, and pulled a fat bunch of paper from her file. "Look!" he said. "If I unfolded this, it would roll across the room and all the way down the hall! Look, your heart beat 112,782 times while you had this on." He pointed to the number of the top of the summary sheet. He giggled like a child. "112,782 beats in one day! Isn't that amazing? What we ask that little old pump to do, every day." He leaned over and patted her shoulder. "You know, they used to think that everyone, at birth, got allotted a certain number of heartbeats and when they were gone, they were gone. Boom, your number was up. Literally. Isn't that funny?" He put a stethoscope on her back and waved a finger when she started to speak. "Shhh."

So she just thought what she'd like to say: Yes, I know about that heart-beat limit; that's why the poets, the sonneteers, declared that their love was killing them. If the woman they loved was so damn beautiful that she made their hearts beat fast, she was killing them, one lost heartbeat at a time. *But at my back I always hear...*

He lifted the stethoscope away. "Your heart is going like a jackhammer, Althea. No wonder you get dizzy." He dangled the Holter report in front of her. "But there's nothing really wrong. Look." He pointed to the report. "It's fine. See? It says 'normal sinus rhythm.' Some palpitations, the kinds called PVC's and PAC's. Neither of those kills you, by the way. They're nothing—I mean, I know they might feel like they're going to kill you, but they don't. Everyone over fifty has them. You must just be super-sensitive to feel them as strongly as you do. Oh, and you also had some brief incidents of tachycardia. Tachycardia just means 'fast heart.' So, sometimes, your heart goes, like 125 beats a minute. That's fast. But then it stops, on its own. So that's nothing, too."

She felt tears rising in her eyes.

He leaned closer, tapping her arm with the metal round of his stetho-scope. "Do you understand, Althea? You're fine. I think you just get scared. Your blood gets full of adrenaline and that fools your heart into going into 'fight or flight' mode, for no good reason. It feels like you're in danger, but you're not. It's a fake warning. False alarm. You get scared. That's all. We'll get you started on a new blood pressure medication and we'll recheck your heart in six months. How will that be?"

She couldn't stop the tears; words she hadn't even thought about came spilling from her mouth. "You know what, doctor?" she said. "You know what happened this morning? My dog peed blood. He's the World's Best Dog. He's 14 years old and going blind but I still believe he'll live forever. He's got to. But then today, in the snow, he peed blood. Big red splatters. And he whined the whole time." She tried to take a deep breath, but her throat was too tight. "Of course I'm scared. I'm looking straight at mortality, every fucking day. Little skeletons dancing around my head. *Memento mori.* Aren't you scared, too? Aren't you scared spitless at least fifty per cent of the day and eighty per cent of the night, doctor? Aren't you?"

Dr. Engleman pushed a hand through his hair and backed away. He began to write in her file. "And maybe something for anxiety, too."

At the desk, filling out the check for her co-pay, Althea stopped. She looked at the nurse behind the counter and said, "Do you know the term for the psychological disorder where people pull out their hair? You know, their eye-lashes and all? I think it's a kind of compulsive disorder? Part of obsessive-compulsive disorder? Tripso-something?"

The nurse stared. "No," she said. "I don't. You want me to ask one of the doctors?"

"No," Althea said. "I can look it up."

But when she returned to her office, she didn't look up the condition. It didn't matter what the right word was, did it? The perfect word wouldn't change a damn thing.

Unless… Unless that word was beautiful, so powerful that it did change everything. Like the words people used to believe in, long ago, words so full of power and mystery that they shouldn't even be spoken, words that summoned up the godhead or conjured the devil. She turned the key in her car's ignition and whispered into the dashboard: "Yahweh." Nothing happened. "Beelzebub." Nothing still. She drove home slowly over icy, treacherous roads. "Bibbity bobbity boo," she sang.

On Thursday, 9:30, Derrick came to class. And the following Tuesday, too. And the next Thursday, when she gave an exam, he came and took it, sweating over his blue book. And the next Tuesday, when he got his exam grade back—C+—he smiled. He hadn't recognized all the quotes, but he'd identified the Keats one, hadn't he? Derrick's plagiarism papers stayed in her book bag—she still hadn't had the time to turn them in to the registrar. Or the energy. She was so tired, all the time. Her heart leapt crazily, day and night. She hardly slept, afraid to be jolted out of dreams by the screeching false alarms that came knocking on her ribs like sly messengers, like telegrams from the front, like phones suddenly shrilling in the middle of the night. She didn't take her pills, any of them—not the Lotrel, not the Pravachol, not the Xanax, the Fosamax, the Miacalcin, the Caltrate, or the StressTabs. Not even the herbs: no black cohosh, no soy extract, no kava-kava, echinacea, chamomile, or rue. No eye of toad or toe of newt, either. Why should she, if all she was was just scared, for no good reason? Fuck it.

Two weeks later, the vet told her that her dog had cancer in his bladder and it would be kind, soon, to put him down. But she couldn't, she knew that. She bloody well could not destroy the World's Best Dog. It was just too much to ask, wasn't it?

Four T/Th's, 2-3 p.m., went by and she didn't hear from her former, brilliant student. He had, apparently, grown weary of their silly little game. Maybe he was too busy, supporting his young wife through her first grief. Maybe she really was that young, his wife, that fragile in her present state. That new to the world of sorrow and of death.

She sent one last email: "Dickless lit = *The Sun Also Rises*. Ha. Ha. Get it?" She never heard back.

All through March, it snowed again and again. Every morning, afternoon, and evening, her dog stained the snow red, deeper than pink now, splashes of surprising scarlet in the clean white. Often now, he cried in his sleep. Sometimes, he shuddered and groaned. Sometimes, his eyes would suddenly shoot open and wide and he would sit staring wildly into space, shivering.

One bitterly cold moonlit night, she urged him into his evening walk around the block. "Come on," she told him. "We need the air." Even her city street looked lovely in the glassy blue light of moon on snow. Her two booted feet and the dog's four padded feet crunched along together in the diamond-hard snow, a kind of contrapuntal harmony.

But then, about halfway around the block, the dog simply sat down. He lowered his butt onto the ice and just sat. She tugged his leash, gently. "Come on, sweetie," she said. "Let's go home." He sighed, and rested his front half on the ice, too. He stretched out like a flat black dog-shaped shadow, right there on the sidewalk. He closed his eyes.

Her heart flipped in her chest, then sank, fluttering and skittering against her ribs. Oh God, not here. Not now. She crouched down beside him. She held one of his silky-cold ears in her mittened palm. "Oh, please," she said. "Come on." His tail wagged once, but he made no effort to stand.

She knew she couldn't lift him, couldn't carry his weight in her arms. She held tightly to his ear and raised her face to the winter sky, a silent plea, as close to prayer as she could get. The night was still. Nothing.

Althea slid down on the sidewalk and wrapped her warmth around the old, tired dog. She lifted his ear and whispered into it, the first thought that hit her brain: "Once," she said, "there was a poet named Elizabeth Barrett— yes, yes, later she married Robert Browning and became Elizabeth Barrett Browning—that's the one!—and she had a dog named Flush, a dog she loved with all her heart. Flush even got dognapped once, you know, and Elizabeth, who was an invalid, left her bed to save him. She and her lady's maid traveled into the terrible slums of London, all alone, two trembling, respectable Victorian women, and they got Flush back. Elizabeth's brothers wouldn't go; her father wouldn't. It was silly, they said, so much fuss over a dog. But Elizabeth and her maid went. They gathered their little bits of money and they paid the ransom and they saved him. They did!" Her lips were numb now and she was beginning to slur her words, but she kept talking. "Oh, yes, it's all true. Later, long after Elizabeth and Robert and Flush were dead and gone, Virginia Woolf wrote a book called *Flush.* Did you know that, sweetie?"

The dog's tail gave another slow thud against the ice, so she went on, her voice misting the air and coating the dog's ear with frost: "Yes, and this is what the book says, how Woolf quotes Barrett, who is describing Flush. This is how it goes." Althea closed her eyes and pictured the page in the book she was teaching in her Senior Seminar. Pages glowed in her head; she could read the words right off the back of her eyelids, like magic. "Yes, I've got it. Listen: *He was of that particular shade of dark brown which in sunshine flashes 'all over into gold.' His eyes were 'startled eyes of hazel brown.' His ears were 'tasseled'; his 'slender feet' were 'canopied in fringes' and his tail was 'broad.'"* She opened her eyes. "Isn't that lovely?" She sat up, her arm around the dog's shoulders. "Come on, now. It's time to go home. I'll tell you the rest at home. It's a good story. In Italy, Flush fathers puppies and Elizabeth—in her late forties!—has a son. Really! You'll want to hear how it all turns out. Come on."

Slowly, the dog's head lifted. With a great sigh, he pushed himself into a sitting position. Althea tugged his collar and he tottered upwards until he could stand. Together, under the icy moon, they limped their slow way home.

The next morning, she called the vet's office and made the appointment, for the first day of spring break. The cheery voice of the young assistant fell into somber tones when she realized what the appointment was for.

Althea wrapped the telephone cord around her arm like a blood pressure cuff, looking at the calendar on the kitchen closet door. "He hates coming to the office," she said. "He gets so scared. Is it possible for someone to come here? He's been your patient for fourteen years and so I thought that perhaps…"

"Wow. Fourteen years." The girl's voice slipped back into cheer, despite herself. "I've only been here, like, three months. But I'll ask the doctor. I think she'll come out to your house. She does, sometimes, for, ummm, you know, that sort of thing."

Suddenly, Althea felt the urge to giggle. "Of course she does," she said. *"Because I could not stop for Death—/He kindly stopped for me."*

"Excuse me?" the girl said.

"Nothing. Poetry. Nothing." Althea pressed her hand to her chest, staring at the calendar. She wouldn't mark it down, that appointment. That was just too much to ask—she would not write those words in her kitchen.

On the last Thursday before spring break, she took the plagiarist's papers out of her book bag and, after class, she called him to her desk. He stumbled up, pale as oats. She held out the papers. "Take these," she said, "and do whatever you want with them. I won't say anything, either way."

He blushed, right up to his bald eyelids, his skin turning a soft, creamy peach. "I—what?"

She leaned over, speaking gently. "Surely you remember 'Dover Beach': *neither joy, nor love, nor light, nor certitude, nor peace, nor help for pain.* All of us, all the time, we're all just dicking around on this goddamn darkling plain. You see? There's really nothing to be done, Derrick, nothing at all. Take them."

He slipped the papers from her hand, then backed away.

"Oh, wait," she said. "You'll be so pleased. I just thought of this, just this morning and I wrote it down, right here, for you." She smiled at him, holding out the piece of paper where she'd jotted the magic word, just as it had come to her in the icy dawn as she sat stroking her old dog's silky head. *Trichotillomania. From the Greek. Tricho = hair. Tillein = pull. Mania = madness.* "Take it, Derrick. It's your word. Perfect and it's for you."

The boy's hand plucked the piece of paper from her fingers and shoved it in with the others. He gripped the whole dog-eared mess against his chest. "I have to go," he stammered. "I have another class."

She nodded. "Of course. Just don't forget to read that, Derrick. It will make all the difference." She stood up, leaning over the desk toward him. She lowered her voice. "And, Derrick, you just go ahead. Just go ahead and steal all the fucking life you can, right now." She put a hand to her pounding chest then slapped it down on the desk, hard. "Right here. If you cannot make your sun stand still, Derrick, yet you will make him run. Make him run, Derrick."

The boy backed farther away. He backed all the way to the classroom door and into the crowded hall, where he was swept from her sight, still clutching his papers.

Funny. He hadn't seemed comforted, not at all, not as she'd expected. He hadn't looked saved or even grateful, the dumb cluck. Not one bit. No, what he had looked was terrified. Yes—that was it. He looked terrified, for no good reason.

Having an MRI/ Waiting for Laundry

Jan Bottiglieri

I AM WONDERING HOW A CHILDHOOD THAT SEEMED ALMOST MISERABLE AT times can be looked back upon with such an aching love for even the smallest detail. Because the noise here inside the MRI machine is so common, so familiar, that within seconds I am leaning against the wall near the back door of my mother's house, circa 1975, listening to the green Maytag spin. The breeze does not circulate mechanically through a close, bright tube; it wafts through the open door hung with flowered curtains my mother sewed herself in the room across from mine, and they are so lovely I am afraid to touch them. It is 1975, so my father is already dead but not my grandmother, and with my eyes closed I feel her moving through the house behind me, smoothing sheets, waiting. It is 1975, so my brother may already be smoking pot in some local basement but could then run up the steps and home for dinner, having still his childhood and all his limbs. It is 1975, so I have never been in love or made love to, never almost died from cancer, never married, never carried and bore my son, never had this MRI. It is 1975 and I am twelve in a house I know so well I can tell you—that cupboard?—left to right, bleach, silver polish, Bon Ami, a china dish filled with slivers of still-good soap. It is 1975, and I am just a girl waiting for laundry, trying to help her mother. Then the nurse cuts in over the speaker to tell me I am finished just in time: because I tell you, I am certain, that in a few more seconds that bell would have rung, as clear as the sunlight through the open door, telling me the cycle was over—and that sound, circa 1975, would surely have stopped my heart.

The Road to Carville

Pat Tompkins

*T*HE BACK OF HIS SHIRT WAS STUCK TO THE CAR SEAT, AND IT WASN'T noon yet. When the road plowed through forest, Garlan Hamilton slowed during the stretches of shade. A ball game crackled on the radio. "Strike," said Gar, trying to predict the next pitch. But it was ball three. "Aw, he's gonna walk him." He favored the Sox because he'd seen them in Chicago once during the war. A fine city. But maybe he wouldn't enjoy Chicago now. He hadn't liked much since the Army.

Gar didn't particularly like his job—"Hell, that's why they call it work," he'd say—but he didn't hate it the way some people did. His job had some pluses. He traveled some, at government expense, and nobody bothered him. He listened to whatever he wanted on the radio as he guided the four-door DeSoto down dirt roads, trailing rust-colored clouds. He wanted to be left alone.

Gar rarely passed another car, and the few houses he saw were little better than tin-roof shacks. He was thinking about lunch when he saw the dead armadillo on the side of the road. Poor guy. They came out at night and had bad eyesight. To fend off predators, they could roll into a ball, but such tactics would not save them from barreling trucks. Gar sympathized with the odd-looking creatures. In his teens, during the Depression, his family had eaten armadillo for dinner a couple times a month. His father called them "Hoover hogs." They did taste like lean pork, but without their shell, they looked defenseless, more possum than pig. Gar had since learned that people could get leprosy from eating armadillo meat. Had his parents known that? You could get sick from undercooked pork, too; it just wasn't something you thought about when you were hungry.

During the third inning, he stopped for gas. Gar plucked a Coca-Cola from watery ice in a red metal locker, handed a nickel to a teenage boy, and flipped off the cap. "Yes, sir," he said after he drained half the bottle. He held the Coke against his neck, while plucking at his damp shirt with his free hand. "How far's it to Youngerton?" he asked the boy.

"Twelve miles."

Maybe it was a lingering thought of bad meat, but Gar decided not to stop at the barbecue stand he'd had in mind earlier. He bought a bag of shelled peanuts instead and chewed them as he drove, one elbow on the windowsill. A heron in a patch of swamp near the road lifted a twiglike leg and tested the water with its foot. A thick canopy of branches—sweetgum, box elder, tupelo— filtered the heat of the sun. Yes, this surely beat his last job working at the post office: two years fiddling around with stamps and small change in a dim, stuffy room. But even that job had a plus: you never took it home in your head. You might be numb from the routine, but you didn't worry about the mail that passed through your hands. Delivering the post as a mailman would have been ideal, but all that walking would have killed his feet, his left foot anyway.

At a massive oak bearded with gray moss, the road forked. A wooden sign shaped like an arrow pointed left: Youngerton. The one facing right said Rocheau. Gar considered going right, as he did at some point on every trip lately —just keep driving and never return. But he dutifully headed left and when he reached the outskirts of the town, he gripped the wheel with both hands and stopped whistling. He began looking for the McPhersons' house, 161 Cypress.

This was the hard part. No one was ever glad to see him arrive. Gar stumbled getting out of the car, partly from sitting so long, partly because of his bad foot. He stumbled more lately, it seemed, or maybe he just noticed it more. He'd lost three toes during the war. No heroic action, though. Some idiot dogface had run over his left foot with a forklift two weeks before V-E Day. The damage—a hangnail compared to injuries he'd seen—left a dull, constant ache. On the McPhersons' doorstep, he passed his hands over his wavy brown hair, then wiped his palms on his pants before ringing the bell.

A stout woman wearing an apron over her dress opened the door and stood behind the screen door. "Yes?" she whispered. He detected the fear in her one word.

"Afternoon, ma'am. I'm from the government, here to pick up your daughter." Through the dark screen, he saw her eyes shine with tears.

"Yes," she whispered again and pushed the screen door open so he could step inside.

Gar had seen many cases, so he was prepared not to flinch when he met this girl. Yet he had to check himself from reacting as the mother led her daughter forward. Eldonna was 15, with copper-colored hair and the greenest eyes he'd ever seen. Her skin was clear aside from a sprinkle of freckles.

More than 20 years before the war, the federal government had taken over Carville Hospital from the state of Louisiana. The only hospital in the country for leprosy patients was now officially named the Hansen Center, but everyone still called it Carville. If a boy in Shreveport got in trouble, his mother might say, "I'm going to send you to Carville if you don't behave."

No one who went to Carville ever left. Most of the patients Gar took to Carville lacked obvious signs of the disease. The horrible parts came later: amputations, blindness, disfigurement. He'd seen that mainly in photos, but it was enough for him.

Last week, Gar had collected another person newly diagnosed with leprosy, a 26-year-old farmer with a wife and two kids. The man's suitcase was packed, but when the time came to leave, he refused to go. Gar had to handcuff him and force him into the back of the station wagon. He'd used his handcuffs only once before. Usually he never had to touch the people he drove to Carville, although he'd convinced himself that he was unlikely to pick up the disease from them. The doctors who diagnosed them didn't catch it; the nuns who staffed the hospital in Carville stayed clean; a husband could have it and his wife would be healthy, like the couple last week. Most of his passengers were numb with dismay, numb like the patches of skin on their ear lobes or knees that first indicated something was wrong. They stared out the car window, memorizing the landscape.

It was a shame anyone had to go to Carville, a pity there was no cure, but Gar had been to war and knew how little fairness had to do with anything. Still, when he looked at Eldonna McPherson, he wanted to punch someone. Like the doctor who'd condemned her. Gar's job was part of the Public Health Service, but nobody thanked him for what he was doing. The farm woman last week had said, "What do they pay y'all to come steal my husband? You're no better than a bounty hunter."

"I'll take your grip," Gar said and picked up the girl's suitcase. He held out his other hand toward the round hatbox she held, but the girl shook her head and stepped back. "I'll be out by the car when you're ready," he said.

He leaned against a willow tree and smoked a cigarette, a habit he'd picked up in the Army. Gar glanced at the pack. Lucky Strike. What sort of name was that? Lucky. Huh. He wondered about the hatbox. What would she need a good hat for in Carville? For chapel. For funerals. Gar wanted a glass of ice water and needed a toilet, but he did not want to return to the house and ask for favors. He stepped behind the tree instead.

Gar was about to light up again when he heard the screen door open. The mother and daughter walked hand in hand to the dusty station wagon. Their chins quivered and pointed to the ground. They embraced and the woman had to force herself to release the girl. She stepped back and stared at Gar. "Don't worry, ma'am," he said. "I'll get her there safe and sound by this evening."

"Call me when you get there," the mother said.

"I'll call you tomorrow." Eldonna turned toward Gar. "I can do that, can't I?"

"Sure. You can call anytime," he said, although he wasn't certain this was true. Gar opened the back door and Eldonna got in. After waving good-bye until she could no longer see her mother, she wrapped her arms around the hatbox on her lap.

A few miles passed in silence before Gar said, "Mind if I turn on the radio?"

"No, sir. I don't mind."

"Anything you want to listen to?"

"It doesn't matter to me."

He tuned in a station of popular music, love songs, music to dance to. Years ago, he'd been a fair dancer. That's how he'd met his girlfriends, at dances. It certainly wasn't his handsome face—with its bulbous nose and acne-scarred cheeks—that won him dancers. But on the dance floor, his stocky figure turned almost graceful, moving with the music. When Nat King Cole started crooning "Mona Lisa," Gar listened to a verse, then changed stations. He glanced occasionally at his passenger in the rear-view mirror. Eldonna was a helluva lot prettier than any Mona Lisa. Eldonna's mouth had full lips, closed, not smiling or frowning. She'd probably never really been kissed by a man. Chances were, she never would. Patients at Carville weren't allowed to date or marry; men and women didn't even eat together in the dining hall. Not that there weren't ways around the rules. But if a patient had a baby, she wasn't allowed to keep it. He looked again in the mirror, noticing her breasts, then was immediately ashamed of himself.

Maybe it was better to go in young and not know what you were missing. This girl would always sleep alone, with no one to stroke her long, shiny hair or her slender neck or her soft thighs or—Jesus, man, get a hold of yourself. She was a leper; that smooth skin would become scaly, with ulcers and sores. He shrugged his tense shoulders and searched the radio for another baseball game, then switched it off.

The woods gave way to high, bright fields of sugar cane. When he'd come home on leave, Gar had seen German prisoners of war in the fields, cutting cane. Hot work; it made your back sore and your arms ache. He'd been surprised, then glad to see that the damn jerries weren't sitting on their duffs. Shit, he thought now, the cane cutters had been on vacation compared to what they did to our POWs. Helluva way to treat people. Had Eldonna seen the Germans in the cane fields when she was younger? What could they talk about? The war probably wasn't a good subject.

Gar spotted a dark, furry lump in the center of the road and swerved to avoid it.

"Mister, would you stop the car? Please?"

He glanced in the mirror. Was she carsick? He pulled over on the gravel shoulder. "What's wrong?" He turned to face her, but she was peering out the rear windshield. In a flash she was out the door and hurrying down the road. She covered 50 yards before Gar shouted, "Hey." He trotted after her. He couldn't run worth a damn anymore. That girl could outrace him easy. Was she trying to escape, hide in the forest of sugar cane?

When he caught up with her, she was bent over gray fur, a raccoon. Eldonna held her hand close to its snout. "He's still alive."

Gar crouched down. Sure enough. No blood on the road. Good thing he'd swerved.

"Maybe he's just stunned." Eldonna moved to pick it up.

"Hold on now. You don't want to be handling that. It could be rabid."

He pulled Eldonna over to the shoulder although no other cars were in sight.

"We can't leave him there," she said.

"Let me check the car. I might have some gloves."

"I know what." Eldonna ran back to the car and removed a wide-brimmed yellow hat from its box. She brought the empty hatbox back to the raccoon before Gar had even reached the car. He returned flexing his fingers in thick canvas gloves. With his hands, he scooped up the warm body.

"Be careful," Eldonna said. He meant to move it to the side of the road, but she held out the box. "Put him in here."

The animal felt lopsided. "I think one of its rear legs is broke."

"The doctors at Carville can fix that." She took the box from him and studied the raccoon, wrapped in its bushy tail. "He looks scared."

Gar saw the restless button eyes and nodded. "Probably his first time in a lady's hatbox."

Her smile—the first time he'd seen it—pierced Gar. Had he been fully awake before?

He shook his head as they headed back to the car. "I don't think they'll be wanting you to bring a pet to Carville."

"I won't keep him. When he's better, I'll let him go." Eldonna embraced the box. "He must be thirsty."

"We'll stop at the next gas station and get some water."

"Thank you."

Gar wiped his face with his handkerchief before starting the car. How was this girl going to survive in Carville?

They stopped at a Mobil station near a crossroads. While a boy pumped gas, they discussed how to get the animal to drink. He should stay in the box but a bowl wouldn't fit in it. "We need a baby bottle," Eldonna said.

Gar explained the problem to the boy who was cleaning the windshield. "Anywhere around here we can get one?"

"How about an eye dropper?" the boy said. "My mom used that with a baby bunny she found last spring."

"That sounds fine. But do y'all have one?"

The boy, Alan Hargitty, offered to phone his mother. "We live nearby. You could stop and pick it up."

While he called, Gar fetched two Cokes. He and Eldonna drank the sodas as they stood in the shadow cast by the tall sign advertising the gas station, a large red winged horse on a white background. "My Uncle Jason has horses," she said. "He lets me ride them."

Gar nodded. He'd heard lots of things about Carville, but nothing about there being any horses. It wasn't a resort. Somehow the patients filled up their days. Or got through the days. Empty days. Empty years. He stared at the Mobil sign; he'd seen it at countless stations throughout the state. But he noticed the horse's wings as though for the first time. And he began to think that he would not drive Eldonna to Carville after all.

Alan gave them directions to his house. Gar shook his hand and slipped a dollar in his shirt pocket.

"Thank you so much," Eldonna said. She started to offer her hand and then stopped.

The boy looked puzzled but said, "Good luck."

On her front porch, Mrs. Hargitty showed Eldonna how to feed the raccoon. "Just give him a dropper or two at a time. He might be hurt inside." She gave them the glass dropper with its small bottle.

"Where y'all headed?" she asked.

"Baton Rouge," Gar said.

"That's a ways. I'll get some more water."

In the car, Eldonna finished feeding the raccoon. "Why'd you say Baton Rouge?"

"It's none of her business where we're going."

"She was very nice."

"Yes, she was." She wouldn't accept any money and had offered them lemonade. She might not have been so friendly if he'd said Carville. "Has that water perked up your patient?"

"I think so."

Baton Rouge wasn't far from Carville. What if he drove there—or somewhere else? He considered the possibilities, shimmering before him like the mirages on the parched roadway. They could go to New Orleans. He could leave her to the big city; New Orleans was full of lost souls and shadowy places. But what would a country girl do there except get taken advantage of? He didn't have enough money with him to get her settled in a boarding house. He could turn around and take her back to her mother and quit this job. That would get him off the hook, but not her. The government would send someone else to take Eldonna to Carville. Perhaps she had relatives somewhere who would help her.

"Have you always lived in Youngerton?" He stretched his arm across the top of the seat and glanced back at her.

"Yes, sir."

"Ever travel any? Visit relatives?"

"I went to Mardi Gras when I was ten. And we went to the state capitol building on a field trip last year." He found out that she had an aunt and cousins near Lake Charles whom she'd visited years ago, when a cousin married.

As though confirming something he already knew, Gar nodded. Damn. There wasn't going to be an easy solution. "Do you have brothers and sisters?" He looked at her in the rear-view mirror.

"Two sisters; one's married and one's younger than me. My brother died in the war. On Guam."

Gar nodded again. "I was in the Army. Volunteered. Sent to France." Now he was thinking about going AWOL. Did soldiers plan that or was it a sudden decision? Maybe you couldn't do it if you thought too much about it. Gar remembered that one of his Army buddies was from Baton Rouge. Andy Fontaine. Guys called him Ace because he could bluff his way through any poker hand. They hadn't kept in touch, but Andy was someone Gar felt he could rely on. Maybe Ace would have an idea. He could call him. Stop somewhere for dinner. Yes, he'd phone Andy.

The sun would not set for another hour at least, but the June heat was finally simmering down. Gar turned on the radio again. Patti Page zipping through some happy-go-lucky love song. Usually, he didn't do more than stop at gas stations with his passengers. He ate after delivering them to Carville. Turning down the music, Gar announced, "We'll stop for dinner soon." He glanced in the mirror; Eldonna was focused on the hatbox in her lap. He swatted at a butterfly that had blown into the car. Jesus, this heat. I'm not much hungry, he thought, but it'll give me a chance to call Andy.

"He needs something to eat, too," Eldonna said.

"Raccoons'll eat near anything." He remembered the bag of peanuts from the morning. Still in the glove box. "Here, try these." He passed the bag to the girl.

She poured a handful in the box; the raccoon only sniffed them. He pulled into a dirt lot alongside the Ice Box, which looked more like a juke joint than a cafe. "They sure know how to fix crawfish here," Gar said. Eldonna didn't move, so he opened the car door for her. "All the iced tea you can drink, too," he said, hoping to coax a grin from the girl.

Inside, the cafe was cool and dim, as though the shade of the oaks penetrated the roof. They sat in a booth and Gar told her to order whatever she wanted—"It's on the government," which was true only because it paid his salary. Then he excused himself to make a phone call. The phone was near the bar, around a corner from the cafe. It took several minutes for the operator to find Andy's number in Baton Rouge. Gar rehearsed what he would say. He had thought to tell the straight story; that would be easiest, but that idea seemed less easy as he imagined Andy's surprise at hearing from him.

Gar, you sonofagun. Where are you? What are you doing?

I'm driving a leper to Carville.

No, it sounded like a bad joke. How could he ask Andy what to do about Eldonna? The phone rang again and again, each brrinng sounding like a bleat for *Aaaaace*. After more than a dozen rings, he hung up. Gar passed a hand through his hair and stared at the dial as though he didn't recognize the letters and numbers.

Back at the booth was a pitcher of iced tea and two tall glasses, but no Eldonna. He glanced around the room; he didn't see her. His first thought was that she'd run away. Gar poured a glass of tea and stirred in sugar. It probably meant his job; you weren't supposed to lose lepers. What was a job anyway, except something you wouldn't do unless you were paid to? The glass wet against his palm, he gulped the iced tea, as strong and sweet as dark rum. Then he played with the long-handled spoon, turning it end over end. Run, Eldonna.

His eyes were closed when he heard the whoosh of the seat cushion as Eldonna sat down across from him. Gar dropped the spoon. "Where'd you go?"

"I had to use the ladies' room," she said and filled her glass with iced tea.

He nodded as if to say, I knew that. He almost said, "What's taking them so long?" but stopped himself. They were in no hurry, but he couldn't think of anything to say to the girl with the shiny copper hair. It hung in soft waves to her collarbones. She'd only taken a sip of the tea.

"Would you rather have a Coke?"

She shook her head. "This is fine, it's just too strong."

He asked the waitress for some lemon. "Thank you," Eldonna said as she picked up a wedge from the small bowl.

"Speak up if there's anything else you want."

She squeezed the lemon over the tea. A squirt of juice hit his nose.

"I'm sorry," she said.

"It's a big target." She smiled and he smiled back. "I like mint in my tea," he added.

"Me too. We've got a big patch of spearmint by the garage."

"I put in a whole sprig and then mash the leaves with my spoon." He stopped, abashed, as he noticed the waitress approaching. What was he doing, talking about fresh mint? At Carville, you were probably lucky to get ice in your iced tea.

They ate dinner without talking, surrounded by the buzz of others in the restaurant, their utensils clinking against plates and cups. He insisted she order dessert. "Never known a girl who didn't like dessert," he said.

While she dragged her spoon around the sherbet as though peeling an orange, Gar telephoned Andy again. Maybe they could stay with Andy a few days until he figured out how to rescue Eldonna. No answer. Sure, get charged with kidnapping. As he counted the rings, a band started playing in a corner of the bar. Several couples danced to a swing tune where tables and chairs had been cleared. What was he thinking? Andy wouldn't be home on a Friday night.

When Gar returned to the booth, he noticed that most of the sherbet had melted. The girl's fingers tapped on the tabletop. "Pretty good band," he said. Except for a booth with two men who resembled bullfrogs, Gar and Eldonna were the only customers still sitting. He thought of asking her to dance. He hadn't danced in years.

He lit a cigarette and closed his eyes, picturing himself and the girl dancing. Instead, Gene Kelly intruded in a scene from "On the Town." What a dancer. Did they show movies at Carville? Would lepers want to see a musical? Gar sighed and ground out the spark in the cigarette.

Eldonna's fingers weren't moving to the rhythm of the song.

"Nervous?" he asked.

"I guess." She stood up. "We'd better be going."

Outside, the crickets shrieked. On their way to the car, Gar thought of what he'd like to say. I'm sorry. I don't want to take you to Carville. It's my job, but I'm quitting. It's a lousy job. You're the last person I'm ever taking to Carville. Another voice said, And what good will that do her? You'll feel better and she'll still be in Carville.

He opened the back door for Eldonna and circled the car, once, then twice. He slapped the roof with his palm. "Damnation." Then Gar got behind the driver's wheel. "How's that raccoon?"

"He's asleep. But the peanuts are gone."

'That's a good sign."

Soon it would be dark, with the tall cypress and pines blocking the quarter moon. This stretch of road resembled a tunnel. A blaze of headlights would bring the only light, abrupt and bright. Armadillos would wander out, awkward and nearsighted. Their armor plating wouldn't protect them from a moving car. A sudden death. Maybe they were lucky that way. Garlan Hamilton drove to Carville for the final time.

What Were the White Things?

Amy Hempel

THESE PIECES OF CROCKERY ARE A REPERTORY COMPANY, PLAYING ROLES IN each dream. No, that's not the way it started. He said the pieces of crockery play roles in each *painting*. The artist clicked through slides of still lifes he had painted over thirty years. Someone in the small, attentive audience said, "Isn't that the cup in the painting from years ago?" Yes, it was, the artist said, and the pitcher and mixing bowl and goblet, too. Who was the nude woman leaning against the table on which the crockery was displayed? The artist didn't say, and no one in the small, attentive audience asked.

I was content to look at objects that had held the attention of a gifted man for so many years. I arrived at the lecture on my way to someplace else, an appointment with a doctor that my doctor had arranged. Two days before, she was telling me his name and address and I have to say, I stopped listening, even though—or because—it was important. So instead of going to the radiologist's office, I walked into a nondenominational church where the artist's presentation was advertised on a plaque outside: "Finding the Mystery in Clarity." Was this not the opposite of what most people sought? I thought, I will learn something!

The crockery was white, not glazed, and painted realistically. The pieces threw different lengths of shadows depending on the angle of the light in each painting. Sometimes the pieces were lined up touching one another, and other times there were gaps. Were these gaps part of the mystery the artist had in mind? Did he mean for us to be literal, to think: absence? He said the mind wants to make sense of a thing, the mind wants to know what something stands for. Okay, the artist said, here is what I painted that September. On the screen, we saw a familiar tabletop—objects familiar from years of his still lifes—but the two tallest pieces of crockery, the pitcher and the vase, were missing; nothing stood in their places.

Ahhhh, the small, attentive audience said.

Then someone asked the artist, What were the white things? He meant what were the white things in the other paintings. What did they represent? And the artist said that was not a question he would answer.

My mother, near the end of her life, announced that she was giving everything away. She was enraged. She told me to put a sticker on anything I wanted to keep, but every time I did, she said she had promised the thing to someone else. The house was all the houses I had grown up in. The things I wanted to keep were all white. But what *were* the white things?

After the lecture, I tried to remember what I had wanted to keep. But all I could say was that the things I wanted to keep were white.

After the lecture, a call to my doctor's receptionist, and I had the address of the specialist. I wasn't so late that he wouldn't see me.

When the films were developed, an assistant brought them into the examination room. The doctor placed them up against lights and pointed out the distinct spots he said my doctor had suspected he would find. I told him I would have thought the spots would be dark. I said, Is this not what most people would expect?

The doctor told me the meaning of what we looked at on the film. He asked me if I understood what he said. I said yes. I said yes, and that I wanted to ask one question: What were the white things?

The doctor said he would explain it to me again, and proceeded to tell me a second time. He asked me if this time I understood what he had told me. Yes, I said. I said, Yes, but what were the white things?

Angina

Alicia Ostriker

*T*he flat field of my chest
    stretches like a drumskin

once there was a seabed here
then a swamp, the shells and weeds

skunk cabbage and cattails
bold green hieroglyphics

lie crushed in their burgeoning forms
no longer crazily trying to breathe

so help me, I am arid, arid—
and a deer steps toward me, a beauty

oblivious to anxiety, she treads
lightly across my chest,

pauses, her head turns
on the impossibly graceful neck

her gaze falls through my eyes
until the pain, too,

begins to evaporate
I would like to remain

held in that gaze, motionless
unquestioning, letting whatever

is going to happen, happen.

Cold Kiss

John Kay

I hear *dead white leaf*, off key,
when he says, *It's probably pre-cancerous.*

A dog-eared memory awakens
of hearing the word, *cancer*, directed at *me*

for the first time; then, losing my legs,
spilling like a can of paint, freefalling

through the cold architecture of death,
cold fire, cold prayers soaking my lips,

I find my son in a Star Trek T-shirt,
his eyes climbing the ladder to my heart.

We walk out, sidestepping time,
stuck with pins to this particular kiss.

Nesting in a Season of Light

Angela Wheelock

S PRING IN THE YUKON IS ALL EDGES AND SHARP LIGHT, WITH ICE-CHOKED rivers running to join the sea. After the vernal equinox, the days steadily lengthen, and by May, it is light when you go to bed at night, and light when you get up in the morning. Some people put aluminum foil over their bedroom windows, but I never did. I liked to go to sleep with the afterglow of sunset lingering in the shadows; I always felt hopeful then. Maybe that's why I was sure that May would be the month that I would get pregnant. Even though we had already lost one pregnancy, we still had the innocence of those who don't truly understand how things can go wrong.

May is called 'Eggs Month' by the Kaska because that is when birds lay their eggs and the land returns to life after winter darkness. Kaska, northern relatives of the Navajo, live in a handful of villages in the Yukon. My husband Pat and I had lived in the northernmost of these villages, Ross River, for five years the spring we were determined to have a baby.

A terraced hill looms over the village. You can hike to the top of this hill and look down to where Ross River lies at the confluence of the Pelly and Ross Rivers. Down below are the older log cabins and the newer pre-fab houses of the native village and the modest brown house where we lived. You can make the houses disappear by lifting two fingers and holding them in front of your face as you look down. It will seem as though there are no people living in that country; all you will see are mountains and trees and rivers shining in the sun.

"It is important that any woman planning to get pregnant have a good knowledge of her body's cycles," the fertility book I was reading informed me.

By spring, I had given up recording my basal temperature, after never observing any clear patterns. Instead, we relied on having sex every two days during the most likely time of month. By Mother's Day, my period was late—the kind of late that only someone obsessed with becoming pregnant would even notice. On day eight of my missed period, I felt brave enough to expose my tender hope to the scrutiny of a pregnancy test. When I arrived at the nursing station, the nurse, Babs from Ontario, was sitting outside drinking a glass of orange juice, yawning.

"It's the light," she said. "I can't sleep."

I peed into a cup and waited nervously, sitting on a stool in one of the examining rooms, as Babs held the test strip in her hand.

"It looks like it's turning positive," she said with a smile.

On the weekend, we worked up space for a garden. Pat spaded horse manure into the dark soil and I organized the plants and seeds. The soil looked rich, but it wouldn't grow anything without fertilizer.

"If insufficient progesterone is being produced in the second half of the menstrual cycle, the endometrial lining will not thicken and develop enough to support the embryo," I read. I knew that I had a hormonal imbalance. Our doctor, whom I will call Doctor Brown, loved to talk about what this might mean. For now, we were doing very little—not intervening, as Doctor Brown said.

Pat went away for a week, not long after we saw Dr. Brown. I was angry even though, as he pointed out, there was nothing he could do to control the outcome of the pregnancy. I took comfort in hanging clothes on the line that stretched across our yard. As the song of a Swainson's thrush drifted over from the nearby woods, I fitted wooden clothespins to damp T-shirts and pants and socks. In the afternoon, I buried my face in armloads of cotton, inhaling the scent of clothes dried in the open air.

In the early days of June, I began spotting. When I called Dr. Brown, I asked about the possibility of progesterone and he explained that in order for progesterone to work, I should have begun taking it before conception. Dr. Brown lived in Whitehorse, a five-hour drive from Ross River, by way of a narrow gravel road that winds up over heights, then dips down to creeks, skirting muskeg and mountains. With this journey in mind, we decided to stay in Ross and take our chances with the visiting doctor who examined me and reluctantly agreed to phone in a prescription for progesterone. Much later, I learned that a pelvic exam was exactly the wrong thing to do. But that was later. As we left the nursing station, I held onto my body and moved slowly, stepping up into our truck without saying anything.

The next morning, the fragile pregnancy fell out of my body. Dr. Brown had asked us to save anything we could in the event of a miscarriage, so Pat placed the small bit of blood and tissue into a clean glass jar as I wept.

The light, which was nearing its peak as the summer solstice approached, took away some of my grief. A week later, when light was filling the world, we transplanted wildflowers from the roadside to our yard. We dug up clumps of shrubby beard's tongue, a blue-blossomed member of the penstemon family that grows on bare hills. Flowers are like that in the Yukon, growing in the merest hint of soil. Hunkered low to the ground, they defy the subarctic climate; I didn't feel nearly as sturdy.

On the first weekend in July, we hiked up into the alpine in an area frequented by small herds of woodland caribou. We surprised one herd in a snow patch and the caribou galloped away from us, their strong legs carrying them effortlessly over the next ridge. I, on the other hand, was hesitant as I hiked, not yet recovered from the miscarriage.

As I look back, it seems as if that summer was filled with sadness. One day, however, as I was riffling through a shoebox of snapshots, I found a photograph taken that summer of my mother and me. I'm wearing a fuschia shirt and clutching a bouquet of flowers; we're both smiling. "Wasn't that a good visit," my mother scrawled on the back of the picture. I have little memory of that visit, but I do remember that in August we were full of renewed optimism. We were going to meet again with Dr. Brown and develop a new strategy. Things would work out.

In August, chinook salmon arrive in the Lapie River and other tributaries of the Pelly, having traveled thousands of miles upstream from the mouth of the Yukon. They follow the scent of home until they come to the place where they were born. There the females lay eggs and the males fertilize them. Then, spent by their marathon journey, the fish die. Biology exerts a strong pull. We decided, that August, that I would begin taking Clomid.

"Clomiphene citrate has been successfully used for many years to stimulate women to ovulate," my fertility book explained.

"But I ovulate don't I?" I asked. "Otherwise, how could I get pregnant?"

"Actually," Dr. Brown said, "it is possible to sort of ovulate."

Apparently a woman can ovulate in such a way that things won't work out. Maybe, he said, that was what was wrong with me.

In September, bull moose run headlong through willow thickets and buckbrush, maddened with the desire to mate. Pat and I hadn't reached the point-of-panic yet, but sometimes I felt panic's breath on the back of my neck and heard it whispering words in my ear: childless, barren, hopeless. We had sex whether we were in the mood or not. Afterwards, I lay still until the wet spot beneath me began to cool. Then I put on my pajamas and thought about how I might already be pregnant, even though it would be at least two weeks until I could risk a pregnancy test.

In the autumn mornings, the grass in our yard was coated in a sheath of frost. In the afternoons, sandhill cranes rode the thermals over the hill and wheeled and circled, their voices a distant clamor carried on the wind. The last of the aspen leaves clung to the trees—rustling.

In early October, we learned that I was pregnant and, for a brief moment, we were wildly happy. Dr. Brown was guardedly hopeful. By the third week of the pregnancy, I was again spotting. Spotting, I learned, was a euphemism for bleeding that was particularly cruel in its ambiguity: it might be ominous or it might be meaningless. The only way to know would be whether the pregnancy continued or it didn't.

Soon, snow blanketed the ground and the house boomed and cracked as the falling temperatures caused the walls to contract. We had done everything that Dr. Brown recommended and it wasn't enough; this pregnancy seemed as doomed as all the rest. In mid-November, we went to Whitehorse for an ultrasound. The technician had little to say during the test, but his face told us that it wasn't good news. We had to wait, he said, for Dr. Brown.

"Your uterus is empty," Dr. Brown said softly.

His theory was that I had had another miscarriage, and he seemed nearly as sad as we were with this latest setback. Two days later, after a D & C to clean the remnants out of my uterus, we were on our way back to Ross River, unaware that my body was a ticking time bomb.

Unbeknownst to us or to the ultrasound machine, one of my eggs had gotten caught in the narrow tunnel of my left fallopian tube and implanted itself there after fertilization. All the time that I thought I was recovering from another miscarriage, a trapped embryo was growing. It grew until in the early hours of the morning—four days after the D & C—the ectopic pregnancy ruptured, causing massive internal bleeding.

Somehow I managed to sleep through this life-threatening event. But when I arose, I fell back onto the bed gasping, unable to stand.

I screamed.

On any other morning I would have died right there on the bed or some-where on the way to the kitchen, where the only phone hung on the wall too high for someone crawling to reach. But this morning, Pat was late leaving for work and heard my scream. When Henry, the local nurse, arrived and took my blood pressure, the lower number was close to zero.

At the local nursing station, I was put on electrolytes and oxygen to keep my body functioning until a plane arrived to medivac me to the hospital in Whitehorse. Meanwhile, the bleeding continued and I fought to push the oxygen mask off my face.

"I'm dying, aren't I?" I asked Henry.

"We haven't lost anyone yet," Henry answered, as sweat poured off his face.

I was carried onto the plane nearly five hours after first awakening that morning. Dr. Brown was the first person I saw in Whitehorse.

"We're going to operate," he said. "Do you understand?"

I managed to shake my head yes. It was the last thing I remembered until I awoke in the recovery room, woozy from anesthesia and blood loss. Dr. Brown explained that I only had one remaining fallopian tube and that most of the blood in my body was no longer my own. Because he had missed the ectopic pregnancy on the ultrasound, I needed emergency surgery. Because he was an excellent surgeon, he saved my life. It would be a long time, however, before I had enough strength to think about this. Meanwhile, the nurses admired the stitches on my belly and injected me with morphine.

"Don't mind the fetal pig," my sister had said to me years earlier, when I opened her refrigerator to get some cream for my coffee.

Sure enough, there was a fetal pig covered with saran wrap nestled between the milk and the orange juice—homework for biology. As I lay in the hospital bed, I remembered that pig and I envied my sister the sight of intestines, heart, lungs. I wished then that my abdomen was a permeable membrane and that I could insert my hand and fix what had gone wrong.

The second day after my surgery, I stood in the dingy shower stall weeping with rage as water ran over my body. Despite the fact that I had lost two previous pregnancies, I still believed that Doctor Brown had the answers. Now, all of that had fallen away.

As the year wound down, snow fell from a gray sky—snow on snow on snow. The days were so short that I could feel the dark pressing at the back of my eyes. After New Year's, I sat for hours in the oak rocking chair that nestled beside the woodstove, looking out the front window over the mountains. I found out that grief isn't like anything you imagine. It isn't really like sadness; it is more like feeling you're going crazy.

"Make a list," the counselor I met in the hospital advised me when I found the strength to phone her. "It doesn't matter what's on it. It will give you something to focus on."

My list contained the barest elements of functioning: get out of bed, make coffee, brush hair. Most days though, I ignored my list and sat and turned the details of the ectopic pregnancy over and over in my mind, until the memories were polished as smooth as the stones you find near rushing rivers. I didn't want to see people or talk to anyone.

"Light griefs can speak; great ones are dumb," Seneca wrote nearly two millennia ago. I think he was right.

Pat expressed his grief differently. His axe connected with frozen blocks of wood in the back alley. One piece of wood became three, again and again, until there was a pile of wood ready to be carried into the house. At night, I lay awake listening to the wood in the stove talking, as the water burned out of it, wishing that I could deal with my sorrow in such a physical way.

In mid-February, we traveled to Watson Lake, a round trip of about five hundred miles. As daylight faded, we climbed the continental divide, and ptarmigan flew up from the margin of the road like ghost birds in the dusk. At nearby Frances Lake, a thin yearling moose was standing beside the road, snow falling onto its back. The yearling ran as we came closer, plowing through deep snow. Our headlights illuminated the tracks where its mother had run off. We stopped to watch for a moment with the windows rolled down and we could see the moose's breath coming in puffs of white against the gray of twilight.

Over the days and weeks that followed, the image of that young moose alone in the semi-darkness kept returning to my mind; a key fitted into a door I hadn't realized I needed to open. What was it, I wondered, about that young moose and the fact that his mother had run off into the growing darkness that kept inserting itself into my thoughts?

At another visit to Frances Lake, we discovered chewed moose bones—the remains of a wolf kill. Moose are notoriously fierce in the defense of their young—kicking out in a flash of leg and hoof. Wolves respect this fierceness, but succeed in killing yearlings nonetheless. Acknowledging that desire cannot always affect outcome—whether one is a human mother or a moose—drove a wedge of solace into my grief. For the first time, I thought about what it might mean to forgive myself, and the baby I will never know, for the intersection of events that took its life and almost cost me mine.

One night in March, I walked home from a meeting under a mostly clear sky. The moon poked out from behind a cloud and the northern lights licked at the top of the hill, and in the intake of a breath the aurora drew closer, filling the sky with shimmering light. It occurred to me then, that although isolated from the urban phenomenon of support groups during the ebb and flow of conception and loss, I didn't lack support. Starlight and daylight, raven and thrush, had been my companions on the journey. They could not speak words of comfort, but that was not a shortcoming. They say that listening is the greatest gift we can offer to one who grieves; the Yukon wilderness holds an infinity of listening.

In April, we talked about trying to get pregnant again. The one thing we were sure of was that Ross no longer felt like a safe place. On weekends, we looked at houses in Whitehorse. Back in Ross, the signs of spring seemed more poignant, with the awareness that it would be our last. Spring comes to Whitehorse too, but it is a different place. In the evenings, we picked wild crocus, whose blooms cast a purple haze over the bare hillsides. Plants leapt out of the ground, growing quickly in the cool air and long light of spring days.

Flocks of lapland longspurs roamed through the village, eating seeds at the edges of fields and lawns. When I looked up from something else, I caught a glimpse of a flock wheeling across the sky. The small birds sounded like miniature chimes turning together in the wind. My Audubon field guide told me that they are "bold in the breeding territories." Soon, they would be on the tundra. They would follow the light out to the edge of the land where the trees end and the Arctic Ocean begins. Once I found an injured lapland longspur, in the grass near the store. When I picked it up and cupped it in my hands, I felt the fierce drumming of its heart. I thought about that fierceness as I watched these spring birds eating, preparing for nesting in a season of light.

Fissure

Debra Anne Davis

"Is THIS YOUR FIRST TIME?" A VOICE ADDRESSED ME. I LOOKED UP FROM the magazine I was reading. The voice belonged to a middle-aged woman sitting to my right. She was wearing a shiny blouse with bright flowers. She was smiling broadly at me, which was somewhat disconcerting.

"Yes," I answered. I left the magazine open in my lap.

"Well, you've come to the right doctor!" she said. "Dr. B— is wonderful; he's very gentle." This was actually reassuring to hear. She opened her eyes wide when she spoke of the doctor, and she smiled confidently. "I wouldn't have let him operate on me twice if I didn't trust him," she continued. Then she told me about how she had a "wandering" colon and about how much better her life was now that she had a colostomy bag. She obviously wanted to tell me about these things, these things that are not generally discussed in polite company, especially between strangers. This would have been awkward, even rude, in a different situation. But here, she was speaking out of generosity. We were, after all, both sitting in a proctologist's waiting room.

"If you don't mind, may I ask why you're here?" she asked. There were tiny lines around her mouth when she smiled at me. Maybe she thought I, in my mid-20s, seemed too young to be here? Maybe she was just nosy? Maybe she thought I looked nervous and needed some help? It's true, I *was* nervous. I saw that she could help.

"I'll tell you, if you want," I began. She nodded for me to go on. I continued on in my customary and—as I'd already learned, in conversations with my parents and my boyfriend and my boss and my friends—completely ineffective way. She sat there still listening, her head slightly tilted, her mouth mildly smiling. "I was raped last week," I told her. "The rapist had anal sex with me, and now I'm bleeding. That's why I'm here."

Not even a pause. "I'm sorry," she said. Her face stayed mostly the same, though the little smile went slack. She didn't lean further forward or pull back from me. She didn't say "Oh!" or "I'm *so* sorry." Her calm surprised me. She *was* sorry that this had happened to me, I believed. But she did not pity me. She was wise, I felt, and her empathy came from that.

I had been noticing blood on the toilet paper, a bright red streak down the soft white tissue. *He's still making me bleed*, I thought. *Still.* The bastard. There had been a dull soreness, too, and sometimes sharp pain that seemed to shoot straight through the center of my body, pain that reminded me of the attack. Tears would well up in my eyes, though not from the physical discomfort. I felt sad, pity even, for my poor, hurt body. And so, six days after I'd been raped vaginally, orally, and anally by a complete stranger in my own home, I went to see a proctologist.

The Police Department's Victim Services counselor had made the appointment for me. The nurse had told her that I'd need to take two enemas before my exam. I'd never bought an enema before, but when I went to the drugstore, I found that there was a whole shelf of them. The brand I'd been told to buy was even on sale. I bought two of them.

I'd been staying at friends' houses since I'd been attacked. Carrying my little white paper bag, an *Rx* emblazoned on the front, I knocked on my friend's door.

"You don't need to knock," Derrick said when he saw it was me. It was both a practical and hospitable comment. Derrick lived with two other guys, a guitar player and a bass player; Derrick was a roadie. They never locked the front door of their bachelor pad. So there would be, in fact, no need for me to knock. I would be able to walk in any time I wanted to. And, I was always welcome.

After greeting me at the door, Derrick returned to his place on the couch. He took another bite of the 7-Eleven danish he was eating for breakfast. He was watching a soap opera.

I sat in the big brown recliner next to the couch. We chatted. We watched the soap opera. These were normal things that normal friends did, I knew. But this was not normal. Not at all. Because I kept thinking, I really should go do the enema thing now. But I sat through a set of commercials, and then another set. I didn't want to do what I had to do. But what choice did I have? As usual, none.

"Uh, Derrick?" I forced myself to say as the third set of commercials began. "I need to go use the bathroom for a while, if that's okay."

"Sure," he said.

"I have to go take an enema," I said and rolled my eyes—can you *believe* it? He pushed a button on the remote and the TV screen went blank. He turned to face me.

"I have to go to a proctologist this afternoon," I told him. I had been avoiding telling him because I'd thought I would feel embarrassed when I did. But instead I just felt sad. This was yet another in a seemingly endless series of humiliations, burdens, traps I'd had to endure since I'd been raped. A weight spread across my chest, heavier than a lead vest. I knew I'd have to act, though, in spite of it.

Derrick did not seem disgusted by my revelations, was not squeamish, as I'd feared he'd be. "Sure," he said. "Go ahead." He turned the sides of his mouth up, trying to make a little smile, but his eyelids, the true mirrors of his soul, drooped lower. "Do you need anything?"

"No," I answered.

I went into the bathroom and locked the door behind me.

The bathroom was small. There were beard hairs in the sink.

I set one of the green and white boxes on the edge of the counter and looked at it. *Fleet* in large white letters, *Comfortip*® in small black letters. I read the sides of the box. The comfortip was "soft, prelubricated." Lovely. "Anatomically correct *Comfortip*® assures ease of insertion." "Easy-grip, easy-squeeze round bottle." On the back, an outline drawing of a man, with no expression on his face (his mouth a single straight line), is first lying on his side, one arm and one leg bent, and then below that, he is up on his knees, his cheek resting on the floor, his arm crooked beside his body and up against his face. In each drawing his other hand is inserting the enema.

I read through the instructions. "With steady pressure, gently insert enema with tip pointing toward navel. Squeeze bottle until nearly all liquid is expelled. Remove tip from rectum."

I broke the tape sealing the top and opened the box.

I pulled my pants and my underwear down. I picked up the bottle of solution and got down on my knees. Holding the bottle in my right hand, I pressed my head down onto the bathroom floor. There were smears of white shaving cream, globs of green toothpaste stuck in the fluffy rug. I poked the tip of the bottle inside me. I was sore, the tip was cold, I was naked and on my knees on a dirty bathroom floor, squeezing this liquid into me—all I wanted to do was cry, but instead I kept gently squeezing.

I'd been told I had to take two full enemas before my appointment. I only took one.

The proctologist's office was in a medical center which I'd driven past dozens of times since I'd moved to Austin, but I'd never been inside before. I arrived at the appointed hour, took the elevator to the appointed floor, opened the appointed door. I walked to the reception desk and checked in with the nurse. I was met with a knowing nod and a sympathetic look; she knew who I was. She asked if I could fill out some forms. I told her I'd try.

After I'd been sitting on the pastel floral-patterned couch for about twenty minutes, holding a magazine in my hands and pretending to read it, I saw the nurse walking towards me. She asked me quietly if I'd like some Valium. Her offer surprised me. Did I look that upset? I'd thought I'd been putting on a pretty good show, blending in with the crowd. But, yes, I realized, I'd love some Valium. I tried to smile up at her. She left but instantly returned with two little white cups, one containing a small peach pill with a "V" cut out of the center, the other containing water. I took both cups and thanked her.

As I relaxed back into the cushions of the comfortable, pleasingly-colored couch, I lost myself in *People* magazine. The office door opened and closed without my notice. Patients were called by the receptionist. I floated around in the world of Hollywood stars and the problems the rich and famous face.

"Is this your first time?" The voice addressed me.

By the time the nurse called my name, I was feeling much better than I had when I'd first sat down. The friendly woman's enthusiasm for the doctor had reassured me some, and the Valium was taking care of the rest. I was led into a small office crowded with heavy oak furniture. A fifty-year-old man in a white coat sat at the large desk. He rose to shake my hand and introduce himself, though I already knew this was the famed Dr. B——. I sat in the chair that was facing his desk.

He looked directly at me and said, "I'm very sorry to hear what happened to you." I nodded my appreciation for his comment. "Would you mind if I got some information before the exam?" he asked. I tensed my shoulders, raised my eyebrows, and thrust my head a little to the side; this was supposed to convey *okay*.

He asked questions about my medical history, about my present symptoms, about the rape exam in the hospital. I listened carefully and tried hard to answer his mundane questions. I was feeling almost too relaxed from the Valium, but I knew these questions were important so I tried to get everything right. After a couple of minutes he called the nurse on his intercom and then led me into another room.

The examination room of course. The nurse held out a paper robe to me and instructed me to strip from the waist down. Once again, I did as I was told.

There was an exam table, but instead of asking me to sit or lie on it, the nurse told me to kneel at the foot of it. I stood still. She looked at me, wondering if I'd understood. I had understood; I wasn't moving because I needed all my strength, at the moment, to keep from screaming. I told myself to breathe, to try and forget; but this had been the position I'd been raped in, against the foot of my own bed. I knew she was a nurse, he was a doctor. I was here because I was hurt and they were going to help me, but why, why, did I have to keep doing these things? I moved one foot and then the other one, bent my knees and pressed them down on the little platform at the end of the table, leaned my body over the examination table, and pressed my face down on the thin, shiny paper that covered the vinyl pad.

The plastic gloves, the K-Y jelly, the metal instrument strategically inserted into the body cavity under question...a proctology exam is much like a gynecological exam in reverse. That nurse in the waiting room was a genius. If I hadn't needed the Valium then, I definitely needed it now. It fogged my brain just enough to keep me from bolting out of the room. The doctor and nurse went about their jobs.

The exam itself was fairly brief, though it was as much as I could stand. When it was over, the doctor stood up and told me I could get dressed and then asked me to meet him back in his office.

I returned to my seat in front of the large oak desk. The doctor was waiting for me. There was a stack of papers in front of him. He smiled at me. I either smiled back at him or just stared blankly at him. My mind was stopped up with cotton and nails. The Valium numbed my nerves, knitting for me an outer helmet of fuzz; the terror of being once again on my knees, exposed and penetrated, this terror pricked relentlessly at the false calm, threatening to tear through. The doctor was talking to me.

He told me that I had something called an "anal fissure." He handed me a little slip of paper. I looked at it. The paper had his name and address at the top and then the title in capital letters, "ANAL FISSURE," and under that an explanation: "A fissure is a cut or tear in the lining of the anal opening."

> Fissure: a narrow opening or crack of considerable length and depth usually occurring from some breaking or parting
> *Webster's Ninth New Collegiate Dictionary*

The rapist had shoved me against the foot of my bed, torn my clothes off of me, and rammed his dick in my ass. Again and again, harder and harder still. The force of this, these thrusts that had caused me more physical pain than I'd ever felt before in my life, pain so extreme that I actually forgot for a while to be afraid, the repeated stabs of his body into mine, the way he slammed with all his strength, as if I were an enemy, as if *I* were the monster. This, this he'd done to me and this is what it had caused, a "fissure," this medical term, a rip, a tear, an abyss. The rape was over, I'd thought, but now six days later, I was finding out that it wasn't. I was torn, still bleeding, still bleeding from the barrage, the violence, his incomprehensible rage.

The small slip of paper the doctor had handed me contained a surprising number of instructions. "It is important to continue all the treatments until instructed to discontinue them." "Insert one suppository morning and evening." "Keep suppositories in refrigerator. Lubricate with Vaseline or K-Y Jelly before inserting into rectum." "Sit in hot tub morning and evening for 15 minutes."

The doctor handed me another slip of paper, a prescription for the suppositories. When I had the prescription filled later at the pharmacy where I'd bought the Fleet enemas earlier that day, I got back a short, fat orange plastic bottle with a label taped on it.

> Davis, Debbie
> Anusol
> Insert One Suppository Rectally Every 12 Hours.

This was not who I wanted to be. This was not what I wanted to do. More slippery K-Y Jelly, the suppositories wrapped up in foil so they looked just like little silver bullets, all doctor's orders, all humiliating and disgusting, my knees bent, my hand thrust up inside me, I inserted them into my body, morning and evening.

Once a day, I filled the tub with warm water, at just the perfect temperature, and slipped in. I love taking baths. I hated these.

The doctor gave me more papers, some reprints of articles to read, a list of foods to eat and foods to avoid. He explained each piece of paper carefully before gently handing it to me. I had no idea what he was talking about. I accepted each slip and packet of papers, hoping I wasn't missing some very important information.

In college I'd taken two terms of Japanese language classes. I listened carefully to everything Chiyoko-san had said, but understanding even the most basic words and phrases was a challenge for me. I now felt the same way, except that the doctor was speaking my native language. *Sumimasen. Wakarimasen.* And why was he talking so fast?

After the doctor had explained everything to me, and I'd nodded my good-bye, I went back to the waiting room. The kind woman who'd spoken to me earlier was no longer there. I sat on the gaudy couch, holding in my fist the papers he'd given me.

I watched as a dark-haired woman walked out of the doctor's office and past the reception desk. She walked halfway across the room and then stopped and leaned against the wall. A middle-aged man with skinny legs and a big belly sprang up from his chair and went to her. He stood facing her. She rested her head against the wall, closed her eyes, and told him something. His eyes were open; he listened without speaking. The doctor, I thought, had given her some bad news. She needed the wall for support, not because of her medical condition but because she had to deliver the news to this man.

Was she dying? I wondered. The man reached out to her, put one of his hands on each of her elbows. Did she have colon cancer, and was it taking her away from him? They were both seeing the same future, I thought; she would leave him, he would be left. Is this what there was in life? Breakings and cuts? I'd thought it was just me. But now I saw it was all of us. The problems may be different, but the pain is, mostly, the same: ubiquitous, unavoidable, engulfing.

I went home and did as I'd been told. I took the medicine, and I sat in the warm water. The medicine healed my wound, and the water soothed it. The fissure, though, deep and long, remained.

She Makes the First Cut

Linda Tomol Pennisi

My daughter's hands
enter their rubber gloves,
remove an instrument
from its blue plastic case.

I whisper from one hundred miles
away: Remember Bach's sonata—
the way you learned to curve
your fingers to lift the beauty

from the keys? Remember me
curled inside the dark
red chair behind you?

Have I told you
how what your hands were doing
moved the delicate bones

inside my ears? Tell me,
when you learn, how those tiny bones
are capable of such a miracle,

how their movement reached far
into my heart's tight chambers;

how today my mind's eye
finds you, though you have entered
another city, where your hands

tremble a bit as you cut
into the cadaver's back,
as they trembled at recitals

when you were small,
till they found their way inside
the music, and the music gathered

all around them, and waited
for the touching.

I Want to Tell My Daughter Not to Name the Cadaver

Linda Tomol Pennisi

*B*ut on this first day
in order to slit the skin from the back,
she needs to remove the person
from the body, so I only ask,
Who? And she answers,
*An old woman, with little muscle
and no fat.* And I leave it at that,
entrust the body's
sacredness to the pauses
along the line—those delicate synapses
between her nerves
and mine.

MUD

Thomas McCall

Chicago, 1967

3 A.M. THE OPERATOR SAID, AND THERE WAS A MUD, A MEDICALLY unattended delivery, a dead baby, on the West Side. She didn't know how long the mother had carried the pregnancy. The nurse who would meet him there was Darlene Phillips.

He pulled on his clothes and left his room, half-asleep, wobbling slightly. The hallway lay empty and still, all doors closed, everyone asleep who wasn't out on a delivery. A ceiling fixture cast gray light. In the big bathroom with its row of sinks, he washed his face and brushed his teeth, the watery noises bouncing off porcelain and tile and echoing back. He looked into the mirror and decided not to shave until he returned. He studied his face for a moment, its color and features, the wrinkles of sleep. This assignment should be easy, no pressure, this baby already a goner. Not like the one yesterday whom he couldn't resuscitate, the handsome boy whom he'd wrapped in a towel and had to present to a wailing mother. A mother who, when she saw what he lifted in front of her, howled for him to do *something*. And all he could manage was to shake with fright and wrap his arms around the dead child, clutching the cold firm body to his chest.

These were the weeks he was assigned to the Maternity Center, a free, home delivery service for the city's most impoverished women. It was a stint required of all the senior medical students, ten at a time. With the help of the nurses who accompanied him—practiced veterans, more midwives than nurses—he'd delivered indigent babies of every race and mix. And they usually came without effort, most births happening so naturally that he couldn't spoil them if he just stood by and did nothing.

Of all the school's rotations, the Maternity Center was the one most given to mythic stature; it had all the right ingredients. Daily forays into neighborhoods painted as too dangerous to ever visit otherwise. Low-tech obstetrics as practiced by the ancients. And the prohibition against students returning to their homes until the two weeks were up. The students occupied an aged, broken, freezing hovel just off Maxwell Street, an abandoned gas station on one side, a whorehouse on the other, and a buttressed, eight-lane slab of the Dan Ryan Expressway which soared overhead and blocked all sunlight.

It was the sixth floor of a housing project, a building designed to accumulate black poverty and stack it so high that it might, like ether, vanish into thinner air. Darlene Phillips met him at the curbside. They'd been together on routine deliveries twice before. She was a petite, round-faced, matter-of-fact woman.

The elevator didn't work. Darlene in the lead, they scaled a debris-filled, outdoor staircase decorated with wisps of snow caught in its corners. High up, the wind whipped through the stairs' chain-link side. Below, a few dark cars wheeled through the night.

A scarecrow answered the door at 606. She was gaunt-eyed, young, and black. Her head was bony and stark, a shaved field of dark stubble. She wore a white gown, torn and thinned from wear, bloodstained from her waist on down. No slippers. No socks. Long toes.

"We're from the Maternity Center," he said. "You called."

"Yeah." Her head pitched submissively downward. She scratched a cheek with fingers so gracile they reminded him of a spider crawling a wall. She shuddered.

A drop of blood fell from somewhere under her nightgown and hit the floor.

"Let's get out of the cold," he said.

They entered a living room of sorts, the air warm and stagnant. Darlene referred to a notecard. "Your name is Leslie?" she asked.

The girl nodded.

"Where's your baby, Leslie?"

She turned and led them to a bedroom whose only light came from a table lamp consigned to the floor. A lone window was smeared with filth. On a double bed they saw two pillows without cases, a snarl of banked sheets and no blankets. Near the head of the bed, the wall showed a gaping hole edged in torn sheetrock and looking as if it might have been fashioned by a small bomb. It was an opening large enough for a person to stoop and walk through into the blackness of the next apartment. Apathy or anarchy had joined one unit to its neighbor.

Leslie motioned to the bed's center. He stepped closer and saw a dismal heap at the bottom of a well of sheets. His breath caught.

The baby, a girl, was very small, a pound or two. In death, she curled against her placenta, her reddish skin and the blue-black afterbirth blending into a thick, bloody stew. Her face was turned in profile to show a tiny, perfect chin and eyes so tightly shut they seemed glued.

Sulky Leslie folded her arms across her chest. The lamp cast her looming shadow against a wall.

"When did it come?" Darlene asked.

"Maybe a hour ago."

"How far along were you?"

Leslie lifted a shoulder in ignorance.

"Had you been having any pain? Any warning?"

"Nope."

"Did the baby come hard?" Darlene asked.

"Jist flopped out."

"Did you do anything to yourself? To get it out?"

"Fuck off," Leslie snarled.

Darlene had dead-ended.

He asked, "How old are you, Leslie?"

"Sixteen."

"Is anyone here with you?"

"You got eyes?"

He pointed to the hole in the wall. "Or over in there?"

"Nobody in that shithole, honey. Musta moved out."

"Will someone be staying with you?" Darlene said.

"My man," Leslie pronounced without hesitation. "He out somewheres."

"Does he pimp for you, girl?"

Leslie craned her neck forward and scrimped her eyes. "Shut you mouth, pussy! Or you and the pale mutherfucker gonna drag you asses outa here."

"You have other children?"

No response. Darlene gave up and walked to the doorway where she stopped, her back to them.

He stepped to the bed and covered the baby with a fold of sheet. The smell of clotted blood and amniotic fluid hung in the air like contagion. He considered walking through the hole in the wall. He ached for the sight and touch and smell of his wife.

"Where's the phone?" he asked.

"Kitchen," Leslie said.

"We have to call the police to come pick up the baby. Because she's stillborn."

Leslie showed no reaction.

Darlene left for the kitchen. Leslie went to a corner of the bedroom and crouched on the floor, her gown pulled taut over her knees.

He removed his coat and pulled on latex gloves. He loaded the baby and the still glistening placenta into the plastic sack they kept in their instrument bag. Everything felt chilled in his hands. This palm-sized corpse might be the lucky one, he thought.

Darlene returned and they stripped the bed of its wet, bloody sheets. He asked Leslie to lie down, so he could examine her. She did so without argument. No expression. No tears.

She'd passed all her afterbirth and bleeding was nil. It didn't seem as if she'd done anything to herself to abort the pregnancy.

Darlene brought a clean nightgown from a closet. She handed it to Leslie, then told him he could go. She'd wait with Leslie for the police.

He shut the apartment's door behind him. Relief came from the cold, clean smell of the air. Traffic had picked up. From this elevation he could see the dawn burning a chink, nascent and purple, into the eastern sky. In the west, a waning moon hung low and defeated. He put his forehead to the freezing chain-link wall of the staircase and thought about what he'd left behind in 606. A dead baby. A bitter, life-already-ended teen-ager, a near mother. An exploded wall. A hellhole of an apartment that didn't grant its inhabitant a whit of physical comfort. An amalgam of overwhelming gloom.

How did these people do it every day—put one foot in front of the other?

He pressed his forehead to the chain-link as his brain swirled and his breath plumed white in front of him. He was discouraged and feeling faintly sorry for himself. Nothing reconciled. Somehow, as miserable and hapless as these people seemed to be, they'd made him feel puny in their midst. He needed to leave the Leslies and their staggering poverty behind and re-enter his world of privilege. To regain balance. Besides, he'd left no mark on anyone he'd met on this rotation—it was they who had marked him.

He descended the staircase. On its first landing, a vision of the diminutive, nameless baby girl suddenly flared in his dark brain, her body incandescent. Heaven's light.

The Initiation

Alicia Ostriker

I was still a kid
  interning at Bellevue
It was a young red-headed woman
looked like my sister
When the lines went flat
I fell apart
Went to the head surgeon
a fatherly man
Boy, he said, you got to fill a graveyard
before you know this business
and you just did
row one, plot one.

Love Is Just a Four-Letter Word

David Watts

*T*HE WARDS OF THE GENERAL HOSPITAL WERE LARGE BARNS, PATIENTS lined up along the walls like cows in their stalls. Flimsy off-white curtains on rings created a semi-permeable privacy. The gaps, the absent rings, made it all relative.

Sounds and smells knew no boundaries, bed to bed, stall to stall. They who were there shared a common experience. I saw a black-and-white photo once of the "old days." *Old,* old days at the General Hospital. No curtains then. An all-pervasive whiteness in the room, radiators lined up in the center aisle of the barn floor in what must certainly have been a room overwhitened and overheated.

We rounded at 8 o'clock. Every morning. Old patients got updates. New ones got complete clinical histories, presented by the intern on call during the previous night. I was the neophyte, the medical student who could not be expected to know much and whose half-opened eyes blinked from stall to stall, having already learned to expect the same old faces, old bodies, still there it seemed, past death.

That morning I saw in the distance, a distance usually approximating infinity between Bed One and Bed Twelve, a young Latin woman whose drop-dead beauty was visible even from afar. Her presence there gave me great difficulty concentrating on the updates of the old crones, wondering what disease she had and why such a spectacular jewel would be lying in our hospital.

Standing, finally, at the foot of her bed, the intern recited her history: third admission, all of them for gonorrhea septicemia.

I noticed the IV running. A piggyback infusion bag marked Penicillin dripped methodically.

Why septicemia? the resident asked.

She disseminates, the intern said.

Why does she? The pelvis has a spectacular defense mechanism, evolved over centuries of survivalism. A girl just never knows what she'll come across in this world.

The resident paused for the expected sniggering, then went on. The pelvis protects against most anything.

Not pelvis, the intern said. Pharynx.

It took a couple of beats to catch what was just said. I'd grown up in the conservative South, "Christian" family, and all that—the girls I knew wouldn't let me kiss them much less offer me a blow job.

The intern went on. She has some kind of localized susceptibility to this organism. The lymphatic system of her throat is selectively deficient. It allows the gonococcal organism, and only that organism, to slip past and gain access to the bloodstream. She doesn't disseminate from any other source or with any other infection.

But why three times?

She's monogamous. Same boyfriend with each infection. The boyfriend refuses to get treated.

The intern continued. She has the Snow White syndrome, he said.

Part of the job of the intern is to one-up everybody with facts or diagnostic pearls that no one else knows. It's a little game that keeps everyone on their toes. We suspected he made this one up.

Only in this case, the poison apple is the boyfriend.

The resident was unimpressed. Seasoned. Less inclined to be moved by romantic eponyms. Why does she stay with him? he asked.

Or why does she keep going down on him? said the intern.

In that moment we became acutely aware of her presence. Everyone knew she had heard our discussion. Others in nearby beds, if they were conscious, probably also heard. Privacy was a luxury none of us could afford. But there was something more to this extravagance of information at her expense. To be sure, most of the patients didn't care or wouldn't remember five minutes later. But we all knew she was different. Maybe we hoped this unflinching frankness, bringing her story out into the objective light of a medical teaching exercise, might give her a new perspective.

I was busy being in shock. First to be spellbound by her beauty and then the knowledge, entirely new to me, that a beautiful woman, knowing the consequences, would give herself so completely. It gave me goose bumps.

Ask *her*, the intern said.

We did.

She said nothing. Just turned her head to the pillow.

The resident stared at her with hard, knowing eyes. Love is just a four-letter word, he said with a shrug, and then moved on to the next bed.

All day I watched her out of the corner of my eye. Her willingness, her vulnerability made her beauty more striking. It was too much to bear. I reflected on my own ordinary love experience and decided I had wasted my life. I could spring for her in a moment. She was the kind of woman who "needed protection." Someone who would keep her from harm. But I was a student, white coat and all that. Professional. We were in different worlds.

I went to her bedside. I said, you could die from this, you know.

Her round eyes misted. But she said nothing.

He should get treated...the words had no impact. Or get arrested, I added with unexpected gusto.

She looked down at her hands.

I was overstepping but I rationalized it was out of concern for her and pressed on. If he really loved you, I said, he would get the cure.

He *does*, she said. He *does* love me.

I realized this was the first time I had heard her voice. It was mellow, softer than I had imagined, but angry and insistent against my sharp cry of criticism.

You don't understand, she said. He just can't admit it's his fault.

Too much guilt?

No…he's…he's the kind of guy that believes nothing's ever wrong with him. So it's always my fault.

I felt rage for the creep who, because of his own behavior, kept putting her life in danger. But I knew to say so would be a waste of time. I thought I saw her sob gently. And I realized that if we were in the same world, I could love this woman.

Snap out of it, I told myself. And then to her, so what are you going to do? You can't keep doing this.

The mist became a tear, brimming the deep well of her eye. She rolled to the side, turning away from me and everything I stood for. She drew her hair back with two fingers, snuggled into the pillow and closed her eyes, squeezing the tear into the space between us.

Close the curtain when you go, she said.

Field Trip, Ypsi State

Roy Jacobstein

We didn't want the middle-aged females,
      their steely-stringy mental hospital hair.
            We wanted our *peers*. Psych 402: *Psycho-*

Pathology of Human Deviance.
        And the woman I got didn't groove
            on me, either. Was it her fault that poster

in the Arcade had pointed straight
       at her heart, that thin man in the navy
           blue coat and long white beard telling her

Come to New Orleans.
       When I asked *Why, Madge?*
         What would induce someone to fly

two thousand miles to a place
       she knows no one?, her Thorazine-
          dulled eye fixed me like a marshmallow

On a charred brazier. Lord, Lord,
       have you ever created a bigger dolt?
         That's where the Mississippi River flows

into the Gulf of Mexico.

Ask Him If He Knows Jesus

Clarence Smith

A PAIR OF SNAKES COILED UP THE SHAFT OF A CROSS. THIS IMAGE APPEARED on a flyer in the student lounge—an advertisement for a medical clinic in Venezuela. "Volunteers needed for a rewarding experience in international health." I kept it folded in my pocket and a few days later, while studying pharmacology, used the back side to list the adverse effects of aspirin—thrombocytopenia, ulcers, hepatitis.

It wasn't clear to me why I called the phone number on the flyer. Since the death of my grandmother earlier that year, I'd begun to feel a kind of detachment. At times in the pathology lab, I had the somber but not unpleasant notion that the hands inside my latex gloves belonged to someone else. The two years of facts I'd learned so far in medical school had swelled into a leaking abscess.

The clinic in Venezuela, having received donations from a wealthy American church, would provide airfare and lodging for volunteers. I had to fill out an application which asked me to sign a statement affirming my belief in the infallibility of scripture. I signed because my grandmother had been a beach-lover and a Baptist, and I wanted her in Heaven searching for seashells. But in the margin beneath my signature I wrote an addendum explaining that contradictions precluded infallibility. The religious nature of the application attracted and repelled me at the same time. For years I'd been making occasional visits to various churches. I was beginning to realize that I enjoyed being ankle-deep in religion.

My application apparently found favor among the missionaries, and they sent a letter inviting me for the month of July, all expenses paid. As much as I'd hoped for some kind of rebuttal, the letter included no mention of my stance on the infallibility of scripture. It occurred to me that these missionaries might be more interested in practicing religion than discussing it. For a while I was almost embarrassed for having written the note.

After two planes and a three-hour cab, I arrived in the city of Merida, where the roads were clogged with decrepit American cars. Standing in the hotel parking lot, I had my first view of the Andes Mountains. I turned in a full circle, my head tilted back. In a nearby tree was an exotic bird with fiery colors. Uniformed gardeners were trimming foliage at the edge of the parking lot, some of them strapped with sawed-off shotguns.

There were twenty of us—physicians, medical students, nurses, dentists, and an optometrist. We boarded a red and white school bus that resembled a crumpled aluminum can that had been painstakingly straightened back out. The clinic itself was in a small mountain town half an hour away, and as we drove, encroaching verdure scraped the sides of the bus. We passed a settlement with dirty children in the shade of banana leaves, and huts made of corrugated steel, cinder block, and chicken wire. I saw a boulder that had been painted to look like a giant frog with purple and green spots.

I glanced at the white-haired man sitting beside me. His nametag read "George Mitchell, MD." He looked to be in his fifties, had blue eyes and a face sunned to the color of a grocery bag. When he gripped the seat-back in front of us, the sleeves of his scrubs tightened around his bulbous, vein-wrapped biceps. He had a leg stretched across the aisle.

"David Price," he said, reading my nametag, and I realized I should have introduced myself earlier. And then, as if resuming a long conversation, he said, "Only five percent of the people here are Christian."

"I thought this was a Catholic country."

"I'm not saying a devout Catholic can't be a Christian, but when you get to know these people, you'll understand they have no concept of God's love." He drew a penlight from his shirt pocket and flashed yellow circles on his palm. "For a lot of them, Jesus is just another statue."

Our bus heaved itself up an uneven road, past a motorcycle repair store, a grimy cafe, and an elementary school where the kids wore white shirts and blue pants. This road was like a cable keeping the town from sliding into the river. Stray dogs ran alongside our slow-moving wheels.

"Have you been here before?" I asked.

"No, but I went to Mexico last summer." After a pause he said, "When did you become a Christian?"

The question made me uncomfortable. "My dad was a serious believer, and my grandmother—my mom's mother—she was a Baptist."

"Tell me about your father."

"He took off when I was eight." I laughed before he could tell me how hard that must have been. "I see him now and then, and he's really happy I'm in med school."

The bus came to a stop, and across the street a crowd of maybe fifty waited outside what appeared to be our clinic. The older members of the crowd sat on a low, crumbling wall, and the rest formed something akin to a line on the narrow pathway running alongside the road. A group of children gazed curiously at our white faces in the bus's windows.

I watched as the first physician off our bus, his stethoscope around his neck, smiled his way into the crowd. A little girl reached out and touched his pants, as if there were communicable power in the blue scrubs.

The clinic was a converted church. The pews had been replaced with semi-private stalls. I worked with Dr. Mitchell, who, it turned out, was a nephrologist. He insisted on praying aloud with each patient. He seemed to believe that God shared his interest in the kidney.

Late in the afternoon, he let me conduct an interview. The patient,

Miguel, was an older man with a flannel shirt stretched tight over his paunch belly. A depiction of horses adorned his large belt buckle. He often felt thirsty and had to wake up at all hours to urinate. We didn't have the equipment to test his blood sugar, but I guessed he had diabetes, and Dr. Mitchell agreed.

"Can we pray for you?" Dr. Mitchell said as he balled his stethoscope between his hands.

The patient listened to the translation and said, "*Sí.*"

"David," he said to me, "why don't you pray for Miguel." He sounded like an anatomy instructor challenging me to make the first incision.

"All right," I said. I'd listened to Dr. Mitchell pray with four patients since morning, but I wasn't sure I knew how to do it. I had a distant memory of recitations at the dinner table when I was little. My father, before absconding with the preacher's wife, used to have me and my two brothers on our knees every night while he begged God—whom he called Daddy—to electrocute our family with the idea of eternity. After he left, my mother married a martial arts instructor.

Dr. Mitchell closed his eyes, waiting for me to pray. I stared at the top of his head. The sparse, evenly spaced strands of white hair reminded me of soil furrows after a light snow. I was nervous but, when I thought about it, the format of Dr. Mitchell's prayers seemed fairly straightforward. Thank God for something, apologize to God for a sin, and then ask God for something pragmatic.

Miguel wore a blank expression, and his calloused hands were folded between his thighs. His back straight, he sat in a cheap plastic chair. Our eyes met, and I quickly looked down at my sweating palms. I remembered learning all about the sympathetic nervous system. I recalled the biochemical pathways involved in sweating glands, dilating pupils, and various other features of anxiety.

"Lord," I said.

"*Dios,*" muttered the translator.

"Thank you for Miguel. Please forgive us for..." I paused, cudgeling my brain for a sin, and said, "Forgive us our great pride in medicine. And please lighten the burden of Miguel's polyuria."

"Excuse me," said the translator. "I will need a dictionary to translate that."

"Amen," I said. When I opened my eyes, Miguel was watching me. I'd made a fool of myself; Dr. Mitchell would give me a failing grade in prayer.

Miguel stood and hooked his thumbs through his belt. He told us about a man in town who needed to see the American doctors.

"He should come to the clinic," Dr. Mitchell said.

"But this man cannot walk," Miguel said through the translator. "He has no one to carry him."

"He needs to come to the clinic like everyone else." The nephrologist leaned back. The legs of his plastic chair bowed and scraped against the floor, on the verge of collapsing.

"The man's legs do not work. He was in a car wreck two years ago."

"We can't play favorites," Dr. Mitchell said, draping his stethoscope around his neck. "You saw the people out there." He gestured toward the front of the clinic. The crowd outside had grown since morning.

"He lives with his sister, but she works all day. She is…" The translator and Miguel discussed the meaning of a word. "The sister is a witch."

"He can ride to the clinic on her broomstick." Dr. Mitchell said this with a straight face, but then seemed relieved when the translator didn't understand. The doctor put his elbows on his knees, and his spine curved like a coastline.

Dr. Mitchell was the chief of medicine at a hospital in Atlanta. I could tell he was frustrated by the clinic's primitive methods of diagnosis. He was an expert in electrolyte physiology, but we lacked the technology to consider such things. There was no laboratory for analysis of blood and urine. His only sources of information were a translated interview and a physical exam. He caressed skin, palpated masses, and listened to organs through his stethoscope. He scrutinized every patient's fingernails. Our first day I watched him diagnose, with varying degrees of certainty, plantar fasciitis, diabetes, renal cell carcinoma, Goodpasture's syndrome, and four urinary tract infections. Urinary tract infections gave us a sense of accomplishment, because our meager pharmacy at least contained antibiotics. When a patient came in with bone pain, Dr. Mitchell asked questions about urine.

A few days later we saw a seven year-old boy without legs or testicles. When he sat in your lap, he wrapped his arms around your neck. His sun-wrinkled grandmother watched him with almond eyes while he walked around on his hands. We took pictures of him, and he smiled for all our cameras. He was a fraction of a person but he made legs seem cumbersome.

That afternoon, when the clinic closed for lunch, Dr. Mitchell and I sat in our cubicle. He told me we were going to visit the paralyzed man Miguel had mentioned.

I remembered how Dr. Mitchell had scoffed at the notion of a house call. "What made you change your mind?" I said.

"I'm happy to visit the man in my own spare time," he said, almost defensively, and I decided not to press the issue.

"If he's paraplegic, he'll probably have an indwelling catheter," Dr. Mitchell continued. He gazed at the pharmacy on the far side of the waiting area. He leaned forward in his chair and squinted, as if, from this distance, trying to read the label on a vial of pills. "We might need some Bactrim." He yawned, a fist covering his distended mouth, and I had the fleeting impression of a man hoping to mitigate his boredom with an afternoon adventure.

Dr. Mitchell didn't seem to mind when another physician and medical student joined us for the house call, but I found myself vaguely resentful of the extra company. The four of us followed our translator up the steep hill.

This translator was Raul, a thin man with mirror sunglasses and hair that went from widow's peak to pony tail. His black boots were adorned with jangling spurs. He'd been converted by a previous group of medical missionaries, and now carried a small Bible in each back pocket. He looked back every so often to make sure we were keeping up. The climb was nothing to him.

Dr. Silas, a resident in dermatology, liked talking about the latest research. He said, "You can induce nerve tissue regeneration in adult lampreys."

"The lamprey's a good animal," Dr. Mitchell said. There were patches of sweat under his arms and down the middle of his back. He'd changed his nametag from "George" to "Jorge."

"And they've done it with rats at Johns Hopkins," Dr. Silas said.

"Amazing things are being done there." This was Todd, a medical student from Emory. Last night he'd shared his testimony with the staff, describing how he converted during his first year of medical school. He realized, while dissecting a cadaver, that he knew everything about his anatomy but nothing about his soul. When he began preaching to his classmates, the dean insisted on a psychiatric evaluation.

Some Mormons were walking in the opposite direction, and we exchanged tense greetings. They in their ties, and we in our scrubs—all of us fighting for the souls of Catholics.

"Forty-two people came to Christ yesterday," Todd said when the Mormons had passed. "The angels are celebrating in Heaven."

"It seems like they'd be sad," I said, "about all the people who didn't come to Christ."

The paralyzed man lived in a cinder-block hut at the end of a dirt trail. There were no buildings beyond it. A garbage heap seemed ready to subsume the small, dilapidated structure. It reminded me of phagocytosis, the process by which a cell engulfs surrounding debris.

Raul kicked a sun-bleached aluminum can and said, "You are a long way from laptop computers and that snake-charmer Marilyn Monroe." He gripped the bars of the hut's single window in which a bedsheet had been hung with duct tape and called, "*Señor* Camilo."

We could hear muffled words from within. The sheet fluttered—a flaccid sail briefly animated. Then a hand appeared and deposited a key on the windowsill. Raul took it and, before opening the door, peered around the side of the hut.

"I sense witchcraft," he whispered. He grabbed me by the wrist and flattened my hand against his chest.

"I have a gift," he added, "for detecting evil." I felt his racing pulse and almost believed him. He released my hand, just as the reflection of a mangy dog slithered over the silvery lenses of his sunglasses.

Inside, Camilo lay shirtless, his legs shrouded in bedsheets. He had acne scars and a dainty, well-trimmed mustache. His slack lips neglected a bead of saliva rolling toward his chin. Hanging from one of the bedposts was a plastic receptacle half-filled with watery urine. The catheter tube snaked down the bedpost and disappeared between the mattress and wall.

"*Hola,*" said Dr. Mitchell. "We're doctors from the United States. It's nice to meet you."

Camilo nodded without making eye contact with any us. There were damp spots and crushed insects on the cement floor. A wheelchair was parked in the corner, but there was a step in the door and the terrain outside was rocky and overgrown. In an adjoining room was an unmade bed where his sister apparently slept. Raul said she worked all day and cared for her brother in the evening.

Dr. Silas looked at Raul and asked if Camilo had bedsores. I remembered my grandmother's bedsore, as deep as the nurse's finger.

"No," said Raul. He took off his sunglasses and slipped them into a breast pocket.

Dr. Mitchell asked if the catheter had caused an infection.

"No."

"Is he Catholic?" Todd asked.

"He has not gone to church in many years."

"These guys at Johns Hopkins," Dr. Silas said, looking at me and Todd, "their idea was that myelin induced regeneration, so they took this rat and cut its optic nerve."

Raul stepped into the sister's room, his nose twitching like an electrified frog-leg in a science experiment. I watched him through the doorway while Dr. Silas talked about the regeneration of a nerve at Johns Hopkins. Raul dropped to a knee and looked under the sister's bed. Closing his eyes, he mouthed a silent prayer.

"They wrapped it in the myelin of a sciatic nerve," Dr. Silas said, "and it grew back into the brain." He used his fist and index finger to illustrate the rat's nervous system.

At the end of the bed, Camilo's toes were curled and his feet were pointed downward like a ballerina's. With a slight jerking motion, one of them rotated outward.

"His foot moved," I said.

"It's normal to have muscle spasms," Dr. Mitchell said.

He scraped the tip of his penlight along the outer edge of Camilo's foot, which prompted the tendons to tighten reflexively, pulling the toes upward. Then he looked Camilo in the face and asked, "Does it hurt when your foot moves?" He repeated the question for Raul, who had just returned from the sister's bedroom.

"*Sí,*" Camilo said.

Dr. Mitchell placed his fingers on Camilo's wrist and, after feeling the pulse, stood beside the bed with his hands on his hips. There was a period of silence. I wanted him to give Camilo a thorough examination. He represented the best of modern medicine, and I believed he would somehow make Camilo's life better.

Camilo reached for an envelope on his bedside table. He held it in a trembling hand and spoke briefly to Raul.

"He's saving money for a trip to Cuba," Raul said. "The surgeons there will cure him."

In the envelope was a passport substantiating Camilo's plans.

"Many great doctors are in Cuba," Raul said with a hint of pride. "You heard about the Americans putting razor blades in Castro's breakfast? The surgeons stitched up his tongue with silk thread."

"I don't know of any research coming out of Cuba," Dr. Silas said.

"They do all kinds of research," Dr. Mitchell said, "and ethics are a top priority, I'm sure." He cleared his throat, coughing up the residue of his sarcasm.

Camilo nudged me with his passport. He wanted me to look at it. It was brand new, and probably the only object here that he valued. Someone was going to stamp a cure onto one of its pages. I passed it to Dr. Mitchell, who bent it by its edges until the pages fluttered back into place.

Looking at Raul, Dr. Mitchell said, "Ask him if he knows Jesus."

Raul explained that some Jehovah's witnesses had come just last week.

"He needs to stay away from Jehovah's witnesses," Dr. Mitchell said. "They're morons."

Raul said, "Is a moron the same as a son of a bitch?"

"No," said Dr. Mitchell.

Todd told Camilo a story from the Bible. A group of believers brought a paralytic to see Jesus. A crowd blocked the doorway, so they lowered the man with ropes through an opening in the roof. After Jesus healed him, the man triumphantly carried his mat into the street. Some day, Camilo might carry his wheelchair.

Raul paused in his translation, looked thoughtful for a moment, then added, "Wheelchairs are very heavy."

"Just tell him," Todd said, annoyed.

I wished Todd had chosen a different Bible story, something more ambiguous, like the part where Abraham nearly murdered his own son. For some reason, I was embarrassed to hear about Christ healing a paralytic.

"You'll walk in Heaven one day if you accept Jesus Christ as your personal Lord and Savior," Todd said. "Would you like to do that?"

"*Sí.*"

Todd seemed as if he would preach for hours, promising Camilo an alternative to Cuban surgery. It was easy for him to evangelize, being insulated by language. While Raul translated, Todd stood there mapping out his next sentence. I remembered how, when I was young and going to church with my family, religion had suggested a comforting mystery. Now the words were worn out, as if they meant something different to everyone who used them.

"Streets paved with gold," Todd intoned, "and you walking around."

"*Sí.*"

Dr. Mitchell checked the time. His watch glinted in a beam of sunlight coming through a small hole in the roof. On the wall a broken clock was illustrated with a nativity scene. The paralyzed second hand divided Mary's head and nimbus.

Todd moved closer to the bed. "Would you like to accept Jesus as your personal Lord and Savior?"

"*Si.*"

"He's just telling you what you want to hear," I said. My voice echoed strangely, as if it were searching the room for a place to lie down. "Can't you see that? He'd commit his soul to Notre Dame football if you asked him to."

"Camilo," Todd said, ignoring me, "do you acknowledge that you're a sinner?"

"Maybe we should pray," Dr. Mitchell said sharply, laying a hand on Todd's shoulder.

Stepping back from the bed, Todd had a look of despair, as if suddenly realizing, after countless chest compressions, that his patient was long dead.

Dr. Mitchell stared at me, and I feared he would request another of my untranslatable prayers. But instead he said, "Is there anything you'd like to tell Camilo before we pray?"

I looked at Camilo, whose gaze was directed somewhere safe. After a moment I said, "No."

Dr. Mitchell's eyes swiveled over each of us before targeting Camilo. "What we're going to do is lay our hands on this poor man's legs."

His nostrils flared, as if relishing the scent of Christ's blood on Camilo.

We knelt around the bed. The stone floor was cold against my knees.

Dr. Mitchell began, "Gracious, almighty, heavenly Father."

"*Dios,*" said Raul.

"Thank you for our brother Camilo. He has shown us our limitations. If we had one iota of faith…"

"I'm having trouble translating that."

"It's something really small."

"I will say the faith of a mustard seed." He said it.

"I just want Camilo to know that even a small amount of faith is enough to make him walk."

"I see," Raul said. "Perhaps I should pray as well?"

Our hands were draped over Camilo's dead legs. The patient looked me in the eyes for the first time.

As Raul prayed, he squeezed his eyes shut, perhaps to see God better. I didn't understand anything he said, but I felt as though his prayer contained something more than the meaning of its words. I became uncomfortable and shifted my weight from one knee to the other.

Camilo's leg twitched beneath my hand. I'd hoped he would stand up, but then, after the prayer, I was actually relieved to see him still paralyzed, to see that things were still the same even though we had prayed. We left one of Raul's Bibles on the bedside table, amid canisters of antiseptic.

On the way back to the clinic I caught up to Raul and asked him what he'd seen in the sister's bedroom. He said a pentagram was painted under the bed, sprinkled with blood, probably that of a chicken. "You see," he said, "there are demons everywhere."

That night I went to fill my canteen with potable water from an outdoor dispenser, and as I strolled back to my room, I saw a pair of Catholic priests, heads bowed, pacing the lawn. The one closest to me fingered a loop of rosary beads. I passed a rusty swing set which, incongruously, had been built in the hotel's parking lot. The slide ran directly into the grill of an old Ford. Dr. Mitchell sat in one of the swings, its chains squeaking. His slight motion suggested a settling pendulum, but his bare feet kept him moving.

"How did you feel about Camilo today?" he asked.

"I wish he'd gotten up and walked." Sitting in the next swing, I felt the chains tighten in my hands.

"What would you have done?" Dr. Mitchell said. A hotel employee slouched across the parking lot with a shotgun. "If he'd walked, it would have been a miracle. You can't just ignore a miracle."

"That's not something I'd ignore." I nodded toward the priests on the nearby lawn and said, "Maybe I'd become one of them."

"A real miracle destroys your faith," the doctor said, "because when you see one, you have no choice but to believe."

"I'm not sure I even know what a miracle is."

"A miracle is a club to the back of the knees."

One of the priests, having finished praying, walked into the well-lit hotel entrance. Though I couldn't see his face, something about him told me he was smiling.

The next morning, Camilo's sister, the witch, came to the clinic to thank us for the modern medical treatment that had restored her brother's legs. She said he wriggled his toes not long after waking. He slid one foot to the floor, and then the other. He tried to stand, but his atrophied legs weren't strong enough to carry him. When we explained we'd done nothing but pray, she crossed herself and announced a miracle.

We didn't believe her. But then Camilo himself arrived with two neighbors supporting him under the arms. Todd dropped to his knees shouting praises to God. Tears began spilling out of his eyes. He crawled across the cement floor, gripped Camilo by the ankles, and kissed his feet. Apathy had been chiseled into the smooth granite of Camilo's face, but I could discern the beginnings of a smile. The smile came in parts, as if each facial muscle had to remember its role.

Dr. Mitchell and I had been interviewing a teenager one month pregnant when Camilo arrived. The three of us stopped to watch Todd embrace his way up Camilo's body. It seemed as though he wept from desire, from wanting more than anything for the miracle to be real. I could tell that Todd was trying desperately to incorporate the miracle into his personal Venezuela story. After releasing Camilo, he stood up straight, wiped his tears, and then, in a courteous fashion, shook Camilo's hand as if to welcome him back into the ambulatory world. The two turned and presented broad smiles to their audience.

Dragging a chair from our cubicle, Dr. Mitchell invited Camilo to sit down. He rapped Camilo's legs with the bell of his stethoscope, eliciting normal patellar and ankle reflexes. Then he removed Camilo's shoes and socks to inspect his bare feet. Dr. Mitchell concluded his exam with a shrug. This man's legs are normal, his expression seemed to say, just withered by inactivity.

One of the nurses pulled out her guitar and began singing "Hark the Herald." Other members of the staff joined in. I saw Dr. Silas place his arm around the optometrist's shoulders and, swaying side to side, the two of them poured their voices into the mix. The Venezuelans who couldn't sing in English hummed along with the tune. The staff aggregated around Camilo, who smiled and said nothing. I saw Raul leaning into the music, his hands in his back pockets. His mouth was clenched shut, as if resisting an urge that threatened to overwhelm him.

I slipped out the back door. There was an enclosed space behind the church, where some dogs were nosing through a pile of garbage. I wanted to believe the miracle had been a hoax. I could hear the celebration building inside. After a while the door opened, disgorging Dr. Mitchell with a surge of music. We stood there and watched a dog jam its snout into a greasy paper bag. Dr. Mitchell's stethoscope was clamped to his neck, the bell dangling over his belly. "It's a miracle," he said, and I wondered if God was mocking us.

Shobo
(Pyrexia of Unknown Origin)

Dannie Abse

*H*e hardly knew a single English word
and was too much in pyrexial sloth
to throw 16 kola nuts from his right hand
to his left. The interpreter grumbled
that he worried about my clay-red tie.
This colour, it seemed, invoked the wrath
of Shopanna, Lord of the Open Spaces.

I was not trusted. I knew nothing of
his gods, their shrines, those tall pillars of mud,
nor of the dread power of the earth-spirits.
He felt himself to be perversely cursed
and could not send for the babalawo
—the priest who kept water in his house
but preferred, sometimes, to bathe in blood.

I was too rational in my white coat,
unable to offer analgesic words
in the right order. Rational? Less so
I agree at night, mystery's habitat,
where a man may think he hears a footfall
on the stairs becoming faint, fainter,
ever more distant, till not heard at all.

Of his near dead whom had he offended?
Whose brooding ghost-moans hurt his head?
Far from home, stricken, insolubly alone,
he lay there resigned in imagined thrall
to some strange malignant eidolon.
I read the negative lumbar puncture report,
nodded, smiled, uneasily moved on.

Prisoner

John Stone

In the prison of his days
Teach the free man how to praise.
—W. H. AUDEN

T his is the house of Anopheles
  in the city of malaria
that infects 500 million souls a year
in this reeling world
and kills a million, so many of them children.
I hear them crying, not here in Atlanta,
but in Africa. In Vietnam.

* * *

I have never before been a prisoner.
But in 1965, I was ushered down the footfall
halls of this federal penitentiary.
Claustrophobia walked beside me
as the great doors clanked open,
then shut behind me.

* * *

This is the room where we commit malaria.
This is the inmate who has volunteered.
For his pains, he will get not only malaria,
but money for cigarettes, time off his sentence.
In this room he becomes
an honorary veteran of the Vietnam War,
whose jungles bred the malaria
now ready to assault his blood.

* * *

The prisoner jokes: "You're gonna adopt me, now,
ain'cha, Doc?" He rolls up his sleeve. "You gonna
get me outa this place, right?" Out comes the vial,
inside it a single single-minded mosquito.
The Anopheles walks his arm.
The prisoner in the next bed reminds him
that he has about two weeks left in which to pray.
That he should smoke while he still can.

* * *

Leeuwenhoek made a microscope and looked
and saw the red blood cells, the spermatozoa.
Had he looked at teeming blood, he would have seen
malaria, too, riding the red cells to the reaches
of the body, malignant spirits, terrorists by land, sea, sky.
Animalcules he would have called them. As for
spermatozoa, they are not officially discussed behind bars.

* * *

The prisoner's disease announces itself: headhammering;
then chills, then rigors that shake south Atlanta.
The prisoner writhes like an epileptic, grinds his teeth.
He expects worse: it comes. His fever spikes to 104.
He boils in his skin in the valley of thirst.
He is a burning man. He is sick. Low sick.
He suffers.

* * *

The soldier in Vietnam suffers, too,
wounded in battle, reeling with malaria.
The drugs for his malaria no longer work.
The soldier bares his arm and his blood flies
to Atlanta stopping only for fuel.
He has three weeks left before his malaria
rises up again, wanting more of him.

* * *

During the past 40 years, I have thought often
of that prisoner, who volunteered to breathe
the bad air of this world, who sickened
with the mosquito, but did not die.
Nameless, unpraised, he became a hero
as surely as that first physician who passed
the catheter through his own quaking heart,
a hero as surely as the soldier still pinned down
by the gunfire of the ages,
who has also borne our griefs,
who has carried our sorrows.

First Born

John Grey

You want to tell everyone
that your wife's not sick
she's having a baby.
She may not feel great
but goddammit if she's not healthier
than anyone in the entire hospital,
every doctor, every sad sack
fidgeting anxiously in a waiting room.
"It's a miracle" you want to
cry out to the woman whose husband's
downstairs having radium treatment,
the guy whose girlfriend is in a coma,
the old man whose bride of fifty years
no longer speaks his name.
You know enough that for every miracle
on this earth, there's at least three
that are grinding their marvels in reverse,
so you keep silent.
Eventually, the nurse struts down the corridor
two steps behind her smile,
declares that "It's a boy."
All heads look up.
For a moment there, a tumor,
a dead brain, a blank look,
are, each in turn, a boy.

Breathe

Caroline Leavitt

S HE WAS SITTING IN THE DARK, AT THE KITCHEN TABLE, WEARING HER
flowery blue nightgown, when Sammy and his dad came downstairs, both
of them dressed and washed, Sammy in his favorite blue and red striped jersey.

"What are you doing in the dark, silly?" his father said. He snapped on
the light and then they both saw the smudges under her eyes, the wobbly
line of her mouth. "No sleep again? Boy, you're a mess today, honey," he said,
bending to rub her shoulders, but she jerked away. His hand floated in the
air. "What's the matter?" he asked.

"Can't you ever say, honey, you're the loveliest woman in the world? You
do so much? You make our lives so easy?"

"You know I think that."

"Then say it. Would it kill you to say it?"

"You're the loveliest woman in the universe, never mind the whole
world. And I love you. And everyone knows it."

She stayed mad, cooking them breakfast, slamming the pots, so that she
burnt the edges of the French toast and spilled the orange juice in a pool on
the table. Nothing tasted right that morning, as if she had put a spell on it that
made the food turn to metal in their mouths, and the whole time they were
eating, she didn't take a bite herself. She just leaned against the counter, her
arms folded about her, and watched them, not moving even when his father got
up to leave for work. He leaned forward to kiss her. "I said I was sorry," he said
in a low voice, but she turned slightly from him and he kissed the air.

"If you feel like smiling, you'll know where to find me," his father said.
He bent and gave Sammy a huge hug and kiss. "You be good, sport," he said.

After his father left, the house seemed quieter. Except for his mother's
anger, simmering, about to boil over, like one of the pots on the stove, and
now it was directed at him. "Why are you taking so long with breakfast?"
she snapped, pointing her finger down at his plate of French toast. "Eat. The
doctor says you need protein." He didn't want to tell her he couldn't eat
the toast that tasted like rubber tires, the juice that had too sharp a tang. She
tapped her fingers on the counter, rifled her fingers through her hair. "It's so
bloody cold in here," she said, but she didn't turn down the air conditioner,
which was always set on high because it helped him breathe better, espe-
cially when it was humid. Instead, she wrapped her arms about herself, then
went and got a sweater and put it on over her flowery nightgown. "I said to
finish," she said, and he heard something hard and ungiving in her voice that
scared him.

He gathered up his lunch and his books, and went to the door, sure he had remembered everything. The school was so close he could walk, and because there were safety patrols all along the way—kids he knew with criss-crossed white straps across their back and the shiny silver badge—his parents sometimes let him. He turned for his goodbye, but his mom was standing with her back to him. Maybe it was better to just go. Maybe it was better not to say anything. He opened the door so that it creaked.

"Wait just a minute, buster," she said. He turned and there she was. She kneeled down beside him and looked deep into his face, almost as if she were searching for something. Her breath smelled dark like coffee. He patted his pocket and felt the metal lump of his inhaler. "I have my inhaler," he told her, because she always asked.

She studied him for a moment and then shook her head. "I'm sorry," she said quietly, "Sammy, it's not you. Or your dad. It's me. It's just me. Sometimes I can't stand myself." And then she hugged him so tightly he thought his ribs might crack. "Goodbye, Sammy," she said and then she stood up and opened the door for him. As soon as he stepped outside, he heard the air conditioner go off. The house would soon be blanketed in heat.

He didn't know why he decided to go home early from school that day. It was just after lunchtime, and he was on his way to the bathroom. You had to be responsible about it, not dilly-dally, and come back to class. He wasn't really a dilly-dallier, but that day, he took his time, going the long way, exploring the bulletin board of Masks of the World, reading some of the essays about "What I would do if I were Robin Hood today," but most of the kids said things like they would get a better costume instead of those stupid tights, or they'd steal candy instead of money and they'd keep all the candy for themselves. He stopped reading and idly walked past the long glass doors to the outside. He didn't know why, but that day, he walked to the front door, and experimentally pushed it open, without even stopping at his locker first to get his things. You weren't supposed to go outside by yourself, not even the sixth graders were allowed to do that. He didn't know why, but he always thought if you did, a bell might go off. Ms. Patty, the principal, might run out and then you'd have to listen to one of her lectures about good behavior. He stepped out into the morning heat and then he was suddenly running, heading home, exhilarated and delighted with himself because there were no safety patrols to make him march right around and go back to school. Who would have thought he could do this?

He was very careful. He knew how to cross streets, to stop and look both ways and then look again, and not to turn toward any beeping cars. He knew if anyone spoke to him, he should just keep on walking, and if anyone touched him, he should kick and bite and yell "fire" because more people would respond than if you just yelled "help." He had already had four lessons in school at the Safe Kids program. He had six lessons of karate in gym so he knew just the places to kick, how to break free of a grip, and how to find your power, deep in your belly like heat in a furnace. No one was going to kidnap him or hurt him, not if he could help it. There was only one thing that could hurt him and that was his asthma. An accident of the genes, his mother told him, and it always made him think of a car crash because of the sad, furious way she always said it.

Right, then left, and then left again and there was his street, and that was when he started to feel anxious, to worry that he had done something wrong. What would his mother say? She'd have to call the school, or maybe she'd take him back there and make him apologize the way she had when he had taken some bubblegum at the market, not really thinking. "All thinking is thinking," his mother told him. "That's no excuse." And his father had said, "Give the kid a break, for God's sake." They argued furiously, the way they always did about him these days, and then he started to wheeze. "Great, just great," said his father.

"You think this is my fault?" she asked.

He knew where the extra key was, tucked in a fake rock, hidden in the hydrangeas, because his mother was always losing her keys, but when he got to his house, to his surprise, he saw his mother's car out front, the blue of it shiny, as if it had just been washed, and the front door wide open, like a mouth talking to him. She worked every day at the dress shop, so how come she was home? For a moment, he stood perfectly still, balancing himself on his heels, halfway between the front door and the car door. Down the street, he heard a motorcycle backfiring. He headed for the car, and when he got closer he saw there was a big suitcase in the back, which startled and disturbed him; as far as he knew, no one was going anywhere, and if they were, surely they would have told him. He jumped into the back seat and tried to open the suitcase, but it was locked. He glanced towards the house, waiting. Where was she going? And when would she be back?

The car was getting warmer, the air felt heavy with rain, which usually meant he was going to wheeze. Experimentally, he took a breath. It felt all right, but you could never tell. He was at the mercy of the weather. The winter chill could send him to the hospital. The summer heat wasn't good for him. His doctor gave him something called a peak flow meter, blue plastic, with numbers in red and green. He'd breathe into the mouthpiece as hard as he could, and his breath would push a little arrow up towards the numbers, and if the arrow went up to the green numbers, he was fine, but if they moved to the red, then he'd have to see the doctor and no one was happy about that.

He crunched down on the floor of the car. There was a light cotton blanket folded there and he drew it over him. He'd surprise her, jumping out and calling "Boo." And he'd ask her about the suitcase.

It seemed like a long time. He turned around twice, changed his position, and wished for a drink of water, or one of the biographies he loved to read, but that would spoil the game. He liked stories where people had something wrong with their bodies that they overcame, like Helen Keller. But when he said so in class, Bobby Lambros hooted, "Big deal, she got famous. But she's still *blind* and *deaf*, dummy!" Then Bobby shut his eyes and waved his arms around and made grunting noises, saying "wa wa" like in that movie they made about her, and Sammy turned away, disgusted.

He tried to jimmy open the suitcase with a hanger he found on the floor, but all that happened was he bent the hanger out of shape. Yawning, he curled up in the corner of the car, the blanket tented over him, and then, despite himself, his eyelids began to droop, his muscles lightened, and there he was, on the floor of the car, rolling into his dreams.

The car was moving. Sammy heard the rivery sound of the road under him, and he sat up blinking, pulling the blanket from his face, and there outside was the highway. There were cars zipping past in a blur of color. And there was his mother in front, singing along to some song on the radio. "You are my spec-i-al someone," she sang, her hands shaping the air. Her voice sounded bright, as if it had bells in it. The air seemed full of her happiness. She picked up the cell phone and dialed. "I love you, too," she said in a voice that seemed both strange and wonderful to him. "I'll be there around dinnertime." Then she put the phone away.

His neck hurt, his legs hurt and he was now deeply thirsty, so sluggish with sleep still that he didn't feel like saying "boo" anymore or playing any game. "Mom?" he said, and he saw her start, slamming on the brakes, pulling over to the side of the road and then jumping out of the car, tugging open his door, and making him get out, too. Her face was white.

She grabbed him roughly by his shoulders. "What are you doing here?" she demanded. "How did you get into the car? Do you know how dangerous this is? How stupid?"

Her eyes were bright as mica and she was wearing a blue dress and long hanging earrings he had given her for her last birthday. Her mouth was red with color and she looked different to him, as if the old Mom had been scrubbed clean. "Why aren't you at school?" she said.

"Where are we going?" he cried.

She was quiet for a moment. She took a step toward him and wobbled and then he saw she was wearing high heels instead of her usual flats. "Honey," she said, "we have to get you back to school, right now." Her voice sped up, like one of his father's old 78 records. She glanced at her watch and her face drooped. "It's nearly three," she said in amazement. "How did it get to be nearly three already? Maybe we can call Cheryl," she said hurriedly, reaching for the phone. "Maybe that would work out."

"Why do I need a sitter? Why can't I stay with you?"

She dialed, cocked her head. "You can't come with me," she told him and then she turned back to the phone. "Come on, come on, come on," she said, and then she finally hung up. "What am I going to do?" she said, and he heard the panic in her voice.

"Why? Why can't I go with you?"

"Because you can't," she said sharply. She paced back and forth. She picked up her cell phone and then put it down. Her lower lip quivered.

"Mom," he said. "Are you crying?"

"What are you talking about?" she said. She pointed to her eyes. "Dry. See that? Dry. No one's crying here." She stared down at her watch and then back at him, as if she were deciding something.

"Mom?"

"You'll have to come with me," she said finally. "We'll figure something out later."

He nodded doubtfully. "Where are we going?" he asked.

"Never you mind. Just get in the car and buckle yourself up." He started to get in the back but she stopped him. "Sit in the front where I can see you," she said.

"I thought I wasn't supposed to. I thought I can't sit in the front until I'm 15 or something—"

"Just do what I say and don't argue," she said. "Everything doesn't have to be by the goddamned books. Sometimes the goddamned books are wrong." He flinched, hearing her swear. She got in and snapped on her seat belt and took a deep breath. He tentatively got in and pulled on the seatbelt, and the whole time she made this restless tap with her fingers on the steering wheel. Being in the front seat felt so funny, so wrong, as if the world was upside down and he was hanging on by his fingertips.

Usually his mother drove carefully, checking the lights, keeping within the speed limit, always waving another car forward. Now, though, she drove like a crazy person, winding in and out of lanes, beeping her horn, and checking her watch every five seconds. The radio was off and all he could hear was the highway and his mother's breathing, and his own, which was beginning to feel a little jumpy. His mother passed a car that beeped at her and the driver shouted something. "Oh, hush your horn," his mother said.

Breathe, he told himself. Breathe slowly. Doctor Michaels was always telling him he had to relax. That learning to breathe right helped kids with asthma. Don't hold your breath, he said, and all Sammy could think of was the time he had asked his mother for a pet—something that wouldn't make him allergic. A turtle. A frog. "Don't hold your breath," she had said.

It felt to him as if they were driving forever. It didn't feel like any of their usual drives, when she would encourage him to sing along with the radio (singing, the doctor had told him, opened your lungs), when they stopped at every little place for ice cream, always ordering whatever flavor seemed the most exotic. They sometimes played a game where they were outlaws on the road. They took different names. She was Gladys and he was her son Pete. She was Annie and he was her nephew Simson. They lived on a farm in Oklahoma, a high rise in New York, and once in a traveling circus. They would walk into diners and talk about their lives, making up details as they went along, introducing themselves to the waitresses or anyone else who might listen, who might want to play along with them. "Isn't this lying?" he asked once and she laughed. "Honey, it's educational. It's like language immersion, you know what that is? You sink yourself in a whole different world and then it becomes real to you. And what we're doing here is life immersion. Studying geography." She was better at it than he was. She was always someone exotic: a lion tamer, an actress, an opera singer. He was always just a boy who didn't have bad asthma.

"Where are we from today?" he asked.

"What?" She glanced at him and then, distracted, peered back at the road. He smelled something. Perfume. He was allergic to perfume. Stores were minefields for him. Before she could even read a magazine that came to the house, she had to check it for perfume cards and throw them out.

"What state are we from? Who are you? I think I want to be Carl."

She was silent for a long while and he was about to ask again. "I don't know," she said and then she beeped the horn angrily.

He saw the blue sign that said a fuel stop was ahead. "I have to pee," he said, but instead of taking the exit, she pulled over along the side of the road. "Come on, you can go here," she said.

"Why can't we go to the rest stop?"

"Because there'll be way too many people. There will be lines. And we don't have the time."

"Why not? Where are we going and why do we have to rush?"

"Pee," she ordered.

Cars were whizzing by. Reluctantly, he stepped out onto the grass. "Go there, behind those trees," she said, tottering on her heels. "No one can see you. I won't look." She looked past him at the road, the blur of cars. "Quick before a cop comes," she ordered. "It's all I need, getting arrested for your indecent exposure."

He stepped back from the road and unzipped his corduroy pants and then quickly peed and zipped himself up again. When he came out, she had a bottle of water. "Hands," she said, and splashed the water on them like a fountain.

She shooed him into the car, and then got in herself.

"I'm hungry," he said. She dug into her purse and gave him some cheese crackers.

"I don't know what we're going to do with you," she said, resting her hand on the top of his head. She got that worried look which made him feel smaller than he already was. "Don't look at me like that," she told him. "You know this doesn't mean I don't love you."

He flinched and looked at her, but she was staring straight ahead at the road.

"I played endless games with you," she said. For a moment it seemed to him that she was talking to someone else and not to him, that she was reeling off a list. "I let you play hooky and took you out to movies that weren't age-appropriate." She glanced at him and then looked back at the road. "The whole time I was pregnant with you, I sang you the same song every day, 'Got to Get You into My Life' by the Beatles. I rubbed you through my belly and talked to you as if you were there. You were small as a minute and I loved you. I did. And I do. How many times did I take you to the emergency room? How many nights did I sleep on the floor beside your bed and argue and plead with all your doctors? But don't I deserve a life, too? Don't I deserve happiness?" She turned the wheel.

He knew enough not to ask too many questions. Especially not now, when she had that look on her face. He watched the road ahead, the world turning into something unfamiliar.

He studied the clock on the control panel. One hour passed, then two. They had been driving more than two-and-a-half hours when the fog came in. "Damn," she said, craning her neck. "How am I supposed to see through this?" He opened his window, letting the fog in. "Don't do that!" she said, and he shut it, but the cool air collected and his lungs tightened.

He sat up straighter, stretching his chest so that his lungs could take in more air, the way the doctor had told him to do. He couldn't help it. He coughed and his mother turned toward him. "Take your inhaler," she said automatically, and he reached into his pocket, pulling out lint, two pennies, and then he reached for the metal in his pocket but found, instead of his inhaler, a big metal math puzzle. He glanced at his mother in horror. She was frowning again, hunched over the wheel, then turned to him.

"You don't have it?"

That morning he had checked for it, he had felt the metal in his pocket, but it must have been this puzzle. Instantly, he felt panicky. "You didn't take your inhaler?" His inhaler was supposed to go everywhere with him. The school nurse had an extra one locked in her cabinet, but he avoided her at all costs because he didn't want her embarrassing him by asking him loudly "How's the old asthma today?" as she did the last time, when all the other kids had laughed. "How's the old asthma?" they asked him, as if the asthma were a person. Extra inhalers were in the house—in his room, in his parents' room, even in his mother's dress shop. They were everywhere and nowhere because he'd never let anyone see him use it; he never gave anyone the chance to mock him about it. If he felt wheezy, he'd tell the teacher he had to pee and then he'd go into one of the stalls in the bathroom and, even if no one else was in there, he'd flush the toilet to mask the whooshing noise that the inhaler made. Some kids outgrew asthma and so what if he was trying to help it along by leaving his inhaler in school, hidden under his sweater in his locker? He folded his arms across his chest.

"Are you sure it didn't fall out? It isn't in the back seat?" She slowed the car and felt around in the back seat with her free hand, bringing up fistfuls of air. "It's all the fog, the damp," she said. "I'll turn on the air conditioner and you'll be able to breathe again." She shut all the windows and turned the air conditioner on, but all it did was make them both cold, and this time, when he coughed, the wheeze was louder.

"Can you hold on?" she asked him. "We can call your doctor and get a new prescription phoned in somewhere, how about that? Can you wait?" She glanced at her watch. "It'll be fine," she said, "it'll be just fine. I'll call your doctor, have him phone in a prescription."

He coughed again, felt his lungs narrowing, which always made him panic. "Mom—" he said.

"We'll find a hospital, then. We'll go to an ER." She made the car go faster.

"I can wait," he said. He hated the emergency room. You never knew if they were going to make you stay overnight, and they fit in an IV and there you were attached to it and the medicine they gave him always made his heart speed like a bird wildly flapping in his chest.

"I'm fine—" he said, but he could barely get the words out. They both heard the accordion sound of his lungs, the thin gasping wheeze, and she suddenly seemed to deflate.

"You're not fine," she said.

She wrenched the car around, startling him, making him bump back against the seat. "Okay," she said. "Okay. We'll circle back and find a town. We'll come back. There's still time." She picked up the cell phone and dialed. "Pick up, pick up," she said and then she clicked the phone shut and looked at the map again. Suddenly she was spinning the car around, changing direction, and all they could see was the fog. "If I could just see a bloody sign—" she said, and then he coughed again.

The fog was so heavy now he couldn't see any signs along the road; he couldn't see the road in places. "Mommy," he said, "I'm sorry!" and then he coughed, and it was like breathing through a straw.

"I'm sorry, not you," she said. "I'm the one who's sorry." She grabbed her phone again, she punched in some numbers. 911, he saw. The numbers he was supposed to call if he was in trouble. She put one hand on his shoulder and shouted into the phone. "If I knew where we were I could drive to a hospital!" she yelled and then suddenly stared at the phone and threw it out into the fog. "Okay," she said, drawing herself up. "Okay." She looked at him. "Someone will be here," she said.

"Who?"

"Someone," she promised.

They both heard the car. She leaped out and he started to unbuckle himself but she shook her head. "Stay in the car," she ordered. "Don't get out until I tell you to," and when he moved to the door, she jerked his hand away. "I said, stay in the car! Don't make yourself sicker!"

Then she drew herself up, as if she knew what she was going to do, and for one moment he couldn't see her. She was swallowed up in the fog. And then she moved closer and looked back at him and then there, coming toward them were headlights, and she lifted up one arm and waved and waved.

There were two men in blue uniforms who put him in the ambulance, in the back, on a cot. There was a battery-operated nebulizer for him to breathe into, the familiar bubbling sound of it, and he felt his lungs grow bigger. "That's it, breathe," said one of the men, and Sammy did. And even though he felt better, they said he had to go to the hospital.

"Where's my mom?" Sammy cried.

"She's following us in the car," one of the paramedics said. He lifted Sammy up and tapped at the window. "See? See the car?" But all Sammy saw was the fog.

"You'll be fine. Good enough to pitch a little league game."

"I don't play baseball."

"What? Now that's a crime!"

"Rest easy," they told him, and they said he just had to see a doctor at the hospital, to make sure that he was all right, that his father had been called and was coming right away. "Just a little asthma attack," said the paramedic. "Happens to the best of us."

"Does it happen to you?" Sammy asked, but the paramedic shrugged. "My cousin," he said.

Sammy lay still and thought about the fog, and how it could fool you, how it was like all those stories he and his mother told in all the diners they had ever visited. He thought about what he could tell his dad when he came to the hospital, when he saw Sammy all alone, when he wondered where she was. Sammy would say he bet she had gotten lost and would be there any moment. He'd say probably the car had broken down and she had to wait for help. He'd say he felt clear-lunged and healthy now, and he had ridden in the ambulance without her because it was a big adventure.

He wondered what his dad would say back.

"Is she behind us?" he cried and the paramedic gave Sammy his hand and let him hold it tight.

"Of course she is," he said. "Of course."

If Brains Was Gas

Abraham Verghese

I TURNED THIRTEEN THAT WEEK. I ASSUMED THAT IT CAME WITH SOME NEW liberties, but no one had specifically said so, and I was too uncertain to ask. Still, the night after my birthday, Elmo and me made plans to go out. I washed and conditioned my hair when I got home from school, then dried it and combed it out. Usually I wore my hair in a French Braid, but for that evening I left it loose. When I looked over my shoulder into the mirror, I liked the way my hair reached to my low back.

I came out to the living room and sat on the edge of an armchair. My uncle, J.R., lay on the sofa where he had flopped down as soon as he came home from work, his jacket and boots still on, watching an *Andy Griffith* rerun. Mamaw—my grandmother—was sitting on her recliner, a cigarette sagging on her lips, the smoke above her head looking like the blurb of a cartoon, her hands busy with her puzzles. She glanced up at me and I knew she had me figured out. I had been about to ask Mamaw for permission to go out, but now I pretended to have come out of my bedroom to watch TV.

Mamaw let off a resonant fart and then settled back into the recliner, as if she were momentarily airborne.

"Sheba, Sheba," Mamaw grumbled looking round her chair, but Sheba was in the kennel behind the house and could not be blamed for this one. J.R. and I exchanged glances; "power farts" was what J.R. called them and he claimed they were the cause of the trailer being so loose on its foundation and the brick skirting starting to come loose. He wrinkled his nose, and pushed his front teeth halfway out his mouth. A laugh—though it sounded more like a hiccup—escaped me; I couldn't help myself.

Mamaw glared at me. "Missy, I guess you done done all your homework? Or ain't you got none again?"

"Mamaw!" I said, knowing I had just blown my chance of going out, "It was J.R.! He made me laugh. He pushed his teeth out!"

"Junior Hankins!" She put down her puzzle. "Tell me, son, why did I pay an arm and a leg to have your jaw fixed so it wouldn't stick out like a lantern? For you to scare people half to death?"

J.R., not looking at her, raised off the sofa and leaned towards the TV as though something of the gravest importance had caught his attention: Bill Gatton of Gatton Ford-Hyundai-Mazda was dressed as an Arab and talking about a tent sale. Mamaw's eyes bored into J.R., but his own eyes became little slits as he studied the TV and tapped his temple with a thoughtful finger; he nodded as he listened to Arab Bill. I tensed up. Now I was in trouble with both of them.

"Thirty-one year old and act like a four year old," was all Mamaw said. She turned back to her puzzle. J.R. kept his eyes on the TV. I had been holding my breath, and now I let it out. There was a step I felt I was missing, rules that no one had explained to me.

In a minute J.R. caught my eye and he did it again: his upper lip bulged, became pale as it stretched, then turned out to reveal the denture. It slid out like the head of a snail, came to a rest perching on his chin, pink, wet, and in a perpetual leer. When I was a baby, J.R. had stuck his teeth out at me and made me terrified of all men—this is what Mamaw told me—and I was two years old before I would go near my father who left soon after anyway. My mother (J.R.'s only sister) had disappeared soon after. Mamaw had raised me. J.R. had lived with us ever since I could remember. When he married Onesta, she joined us, which I always thought was one too many people to be living decently in a double-wide, but nobody had asked for my opinion.

"Missy," J.R. said, heaving off the sofa, "let's you and I go to Kmart. I need motor oil. Just run out." He shook his key chain with the big-boobed mermaid. Jingle, Jingle, Jingle.

"She ain't going to Kmart or nowheres this time of night," Mamaw said without looking up from her puzzle.

"Mamaw!" I said, sure that my date with Elmo was off, but hoping at least I would get to go with J.R.

"Ma," J.R. said, "we're going to Kmart, and she is plenty old enough to go out, and it's only seven-thirty, and Onesta ain't back from work yet, and supper ain't ready, so quit your whining, and think about dining..." He walked over behind her and bent over and kissed Mamaw noisily on the side of her face. When he raised up, he grimaced for my benefit, as if he had slammed into the stink wall behind her recliner.

My coat was on, my pocketbook was on my shoulder, and I was shining the door knob with my sleeve, avoiding Mamaw's eyes, waiting for J.R., hoping Mamaw would say nothing to stop me.

I climbed into J.R.'s pickup and shut the door. "Lock and load," he said, just as the engine came to life. With one fluid, practiced motion—I had never seen anyone else do this—J.R. flipped the heater on defrost, the fan on high, the radio on WJHW 104 FM, the headlights on high-beam, the parking brake off, the gear in reverse, pushed the cigarette lighter in, let the clutch out, and it seemed we were rolling before the 351 big block completed its first cycle. J.R. looked at me while he did all this, to show me that he did this entirely by feel and because he knew I appreciated this sort of talent. Elmo couldn't do nothing like that.

Sitting Big-Foot high in that cab, the night dark around us, the unlit gravel road crunching beneath our wheels, only the instrument lights glowing, I felt we were in the cockpit of our private plane, off on a secret mission. Only J.R. could make me feel this way. With his short beard growing high on his cheekbones, his close-set blue eyes that always made it seem as if he could see right through me, and the brown hair parted in the middle and longish like Jesus Christ, I thought he was the handsomest and sexiest man I knew. Kind of like the Alabama lead singer, though J.R. had done that look first. It was strange how I could be with Elmo, him smelling of hot water and soap, the Pinto giving off Pine Sol fumes, ten-dollars in Elmo's pocket to burn, but never feel as good as I did with J.R.

At the first traffic light within the city limits, J.R. pulled up next to an old couple in a blue sedan and yelled through closed windows, "Hey Stupid!" and then stared straight ahead. The old man, thinking he heard something, looked up at us. J.R. turned to the old man as if to say 'What in the hell are you looking at?' The old man looked away. I wished I had peed before we left the house.

We pulled into Kmart and parked in a handicapped spot. A lady with giant curlers under her scarf and a shopping cart half-full of Alpo and paper towels, scowled at us. J.R. put on a limp and let one hand curl up in front of his chest, spastic-like, and stumbled in her direction. She muttered and her little steps got faster and faster as she tried to skirt J.R. When J.R. stepped on the rubber mat and the door swung open, he was miraculously healed. His back straightened, his arm unfolded, his chin was held high, and he strode in as if he were Stonewall Jackson in Levi's, boots, and black bomber jacket. And he knew I was behind him, watching.

We walked the aisles; I looked at the shelves while J.R. looked at the women. The place was full and Christmas music was still playing. The customers seemed relaxed and happy, while the store clerks looked harried. J.R. asked a brunette with a "Let Me Help You" button whether condoms were sold in the hardware section. She gobbled and her eyes got goldfish big before she fled. "Happy New Year," J.R. called after her.

My heart was racing. Was it just coincidence that he asked about condoms? I started to check my purse, and then snapped it shut when I remembered the cameras above. They might think I was shoplifting. The speaker above my head blared "Attention Kmart Shoppers," and J.R. stopped in mid-step and yelled: "Yo!"

In Household Furnishings, J.R. sneezed his "accshit" sneeze. People stared around aisles and between shelves. J.R. sneezed again, a double sneeze: "accshit, aaaacshit," leaving no doubts. He pushed his teeth out at an old lady who seemed hypnotized by him. I stood there. I knew people looked at me and thought I was J.R.'s girl. There was nothing I could do about that, and besides, it made my feel good. I wondered if J.R. felt the same way.

In the parking lot we ran into a guy J.R. knew. J.R. was fixing to buy dope. The guy's hair was extra long and he pushed it behind his ears, first one side then the other. His fingers had gnawed-down nails with clear polish on them and he had letters tattooed in the webs between his fingers. I studied his face to see if he felt stupid about any of this. I heard J.R. say, "Don't worry about her. She's fine."

We went to the guy's car and drove to the far end of the parking lot, near the dumpster. He and J.R. lit up a fat joint and passed it back and forth, ignoring me. I sat in the back seat, looking out the side window, trying to breathe in as much of the car air as I could without drawing attention to myself. When they were ready to leave the car, I stepped out and almost fell on my face, grabbing the door. Back in the pickup, J.R. said, "You high, Squirt? I seen you trying to suck up all the air in the car."

I shook my head, trying to look bored, but I was smiling and could not control it. I closed my eyes and leaned my head to one side. This was my test to see if I was high: if I was, my head would feel like a large boulder rolling down the side of a mountain. It felt that way now in J.R.'s pickup.

Elmo pulled in to Kmart just as we were pulling out. I made J.R. stop and roll down the window. I leaned over J.R. to hear Elmo. Elmo stuck his head out and twisted it up to talk to me. He had gone to my house looking for me, he said.

"I'm with J.R., tonight," I replied, leaning against J.R., squishing him.

"So?" Elmo said. But his voice lost confidence. "He's your uncle, right?"

"Damn!" J.R. said to Elmo, "you really *should* go to college. Missy, he is *not* as dumb as he looks." Traffic was backing up behind Elmo. A car honked and even though it was dark, I knew Elmo's face was turning beet-red. We pulled away.

"*If brains was gas,*" J.R. began, and I joined in, "*Elmo wouldn't have enough to prime a piss-ant's go-cart around a Cheerio.*" When we reached "Cheerio" we were both rolling with laughter. I felt sorry for Elmo but I couldn't stop laughing. Everyone in passing cars knew we were stoned. They were looking at us. Everyone knew. I was glad we were heading home.

J.R. looked down at a couple in a Corvette next to us at a traffic light. "Holy mackerel, Missy," he said, "look at the cock-box on that young'un." I didn't get a good look at the woman, just an impression of long legs and lipstick. "Fuck her, buddy. I did," J.R. shouted

"What's a cock-box, J.R.?" I asked for no reason, thinking of how Elmo squirmed when I had wanted to study his hard-on. Elmo hadn't minded if I touched it, but he didn't want me to *look*.

"You *know* damn well what a cock-box is, Squirt. Get fresh with me and I'll tell Mamaw all about you smoking dope and fumbling with Elmo in the burley shed."

I felt my face turn red. J.R. laughed his 'Hee-Haw' laugh and said "Fumblefumblefumblefumble," his lips a'splutter. I slapped at him. He can read my mind, I thought. The lollipop condom, floating in its juices and burning a hole in my pocketbook—he knows. Since I got the condom, I hadn't been with Elmo. Mamaw, and then J.R., had seen to it.

"I *control* Elmo," I said to J.R. for no particular reason. "That's what I like about him. I *control* him."

J.R. looked at me strangely. "Control this," he said to me, sticking his middle finger in the air. I tried to break his finger, but my laughter made me a poor enforcer.

"You know something, Squirt," J.R. said in the pickup, as we rode back, stoned, from our Kmart, motor oil mission, "I have found my true love. I have found the person who can satisfy me sexually, spiritually, and in every other way."

"Yeah, I like Onesta too," I said, lying through my teeth.

"Hell with Onesta. I don't mean Onesta."

Does he mean me? My mind worked like slow treacle and no words came out. I felt tingly all over. My face was burning. I knew in the last year I had blossomed. My tits in profile were every bit as good as Cher's. And J.R. had seen me once when I had put on make-up and heels when Mamaw was out shopping, and he had given me a wolf whistle. I didn't have slut eyes like Daisy Nunley, I didn't have knockers like Juanita Clayber, I didn't have a brother who pimped for me like Wanda Pearson. But I guess I had *something*, I knew that, and it was a good feeling. Mamaw knew it too and it made Mamaw extra surly and made her keep close tabs on me, and warn me about "turning out like your dang-fool mother."

"I don't know why I am telling you this, Squirt," J.R. continued, "but I sure as hell don't mean Onesta."

My stomach tightened. I felt like I had been in a car like this before and some other man said these same words. I looked around at the field whizzing by. I told myself: *I must remember this moment clearly.* I focused on a field on my side of the car, but the field had no boundary and as we drove by it went on forever.

"Me?" I blurted out. "Do you mean me?"

J.R. laughed for a long time. He looked at me with admiration, as if he didn't know I could be so funny. A little girl inside me began to weep, even though I knew I should be relieved.

"Someone else, Squirt. Not you. The love of my life. The reason for my living," he said.

Did this mean J.R. would leave home, I wondered. The thought of being alone with Mamaw—without J.R. or Onesta—crossed my mind and was painful. I thought of Onesta: Onesta from Oneida, raven-haired Onesta, pretty Onesta, dumb-as-a-coal-bucket Onesta. Yet, J.R. had always acted like he knew what he wanted from Onesta. And what she was—pretty and dumb—was exactly what he had wanted.

I found myself speaking: "What the hell do you get married for in the first place? If you're just going to..." I was surprised at the half-sob in my voice. I turned away so he couldn't see my face.

J.R. gave this careful consideration. "When I met Onesta, 'This is it,' I said. 'This is it.' So I got married."

"Well you were dumb as shit for not knowing better." The look of surprise on J.R.'s face reminded me of Elmo's face in the parking lot. "*This is it, you said?*" I continued, taunting J.R. "*This is it?* So what the hell happened? What happened to, *This is it?*" A part of me felt as if I were Onesta.

"Things happen," I heard J.R. say. "That feeling you have when you marry someone, when you love someone...it's great for a while, but it doesn't last.

I met someone else now, Missy. She gives me that feeling again. It feels so good, Squirt. I can't control it."

"Same thing can happen again, J.R." I said softly.

He didn't say anything for a while. We were into fog again and he slowed the pickup. He lit up a fat roach that had been in his pocket and took in a deep drag. His eyes bugged out. "Hell, I know that," he said between his teeth, holding the smoke in. I snatched the roach from him. The pickup swerved as he tried to get it back. I leaned against my door, out of his reach, my feet raised, ready to kick him in the face. He backed off. I took deep leisurely drags, holding them in as long as I could.

"You're something else, Missy," he said. Now, give that back . . ."

"Fuck you, Uncle," I said. "Fuck you, you big dummy. You can be so . . . funny, so . . . brave. But you're a *stupid shit* on top of that."

I saw him flinch. He got serious, his eyes mournful, and I sat up and was just about to say I was sorry when he stuck his teeth out. I threw a punch at him, but he slipped it and it buried itself in the shoulder part of his jacket. He held his fist out, ready to bust me if I tried to hit him again. He was bobbing on the seat now, like Ali, jiggling his eyebrows up and down, a big grin on his face, stealing glances at the road, waiting for me to punch. "The greatest of *all* time!" he said. I was still glad I didn't ride with Elmo.

When we came down our driveway it was almost eight o'clock. A car without lights came roaring out of the driveway and took off up the hill. I looked back and could see it was a Chevy hardtop.

"Who the fuck . . . ," I said.

I didn't recognize it, but J.R. seemed to and was subdued. I could see that the car had stopped near the main road and now it waited, the engine running. Onesta's car was in the yard. J.R. sat in the pickup for a while and I waited with him. Something told me not to open my mouth.

J.R. entered the trailer through the kitchen door and I followed. Mamaw and Onesta were at the kitchen table, facing each other, smoking. Onesta's eyes were red. Mamaw had her bottle of Jack Daniel's on the table and was sucking on ice chips at the bottom of her glass. She looked mad. Maybe she had found out about the condom. Maybe Elmo came back and spilled the beans. Maybe the pickup truck was bugged. Maybe that car was the FBI and we were going to the slammer.

When Mamaw opened her mouth I thought she would ask me why my eyes were red. But she was looking right through me at J.R.

"It's about time you brought the young'un home," Mamaw said softly.

"Missy, sweetheart, would you go to your room?" Onesta said, not looking at me, but staring at the table.

"What are you, her mother?" J.R. asked. His voice sounded funny.

Mamaw hissed: "What are you, her father?"

"Could be," said J.R., looking at Onesta.

Mamaw reached up and slapped J.R. across the cheek. The anger in her eyes was like nothing I had ever seen. My body felt heavy; I could not move.

"You tell Mamaw about your girlfriend?" asked Onesta in a quiet, restrained voice.

"*You* tell her, Onesta," he replied, glancing at the door that led to the living room.

"You tell Mamaw how she's married?"

"She ain't . . . married," said J.R., a quaver in his voice that gave away his lie. The second hand of the kitchen clock was the loudest sound in the room. We all looked at him. I thought to myself: this is not real, this is not happening. But for the first time since we walked in, it dawned on me that this might have nothing to do with me.

Mamaw grasped J.R.'s shirt, almost fondling it, and slowly pulled him down so his face was inches from hers, She whispered, "Read my lips, dummy. *She* is married. *You* are married. *Her goddamn husband is in the living room waiting to talk to you.*"

"She ain't married," J.R. said. His voice had cracks in it.

The swinging door from the living room opened and a man I had never seen before walked in. I was sure he would have a gun in his hand. I wanted to pee in my pants.

He was squat and carried himself very upright so as not to waste inches. He was wearing a cream shirt, jeans, and black loafers with white socks. He had red hair that was pulled from behind one ear in a sweeping arc to cover his baldness.

"Are you J.R.?" the man asked, pushing his glasses back on his nose. His teeth were even, with spaces between them. They were clearly his own teeth. His eyes were blue and clear.

I stepped away from J.R.

J.R. stepped behind Mamaw.

Mamaw sighed, her head bent over the table, and then she ground out her cigarette. J.R. looked around the kitchen—as though seeing it for the first time—and his Adam's apple bounced like a yo-yo. Mamaw poured a big dollop of Jack.

"I am Katherine's husband," the man said.

J.R. seemed about to say something, his hands moved, but no words came out.

"Katherine done told me all about you and her," the man said. "She asked for my forgiveness and I've given it. She done confessed in front of the whole church. God has forgiven her. She confesses of her own free will."

J.R. tried to look at the man while he spoke but could not hold his gaze.

The man continued, his voice rising in pitch, but very clear. "I done forgiven you, too. I don't appreciate what you done to my family but I've forgiven you. I sure hope your wife can do the same."

Onesta began to cry. J.R. tried to glare her down but she was not looking at him, and besides this was not the time for it.

"I will ask that you stay clear of *my* wife. I don't want to see you anywhere around her," the man said.

J.R. looked at the wall behind the man's head. The man turned to go out through the swinging door. He stopped and bowed his head as though about to add something, and then, thinking the better of it, left. We heard the Chevy pull into the driveway and then drive out.

No one spoke in the kitchen.

J.R. took a deep breath as if to compose himself, to ready his explanation.

Onesta took a long sip from Mamaw's glass. Neither Mamaw nor Onesta would look at J.R. He looked at me over their bowed heads. He tried to get the mischief back into his eyes but they appeared shallow and shifty. He tried to smile, but his cheeks were quivering and the smile threatened to degenerate into a sob.

I waited.

J.R.'s eyes pleaded with me.

As if with a will of its own, his denture came pushing out at me—an offering. Under his sad eyes, he gummed the denture. It glistened with saliva. His upper lip was flabby and sunken. It was pathetic, like an old man's nakedness.

Then, in what I think now was the cruelest moment of my life, I yelled at him. "You big dummy!"

Mamaw and Onesta looked up, surprised at my outburst, but I continued, "You big dummy! If brains was gas . . . you, you . . ."

I walked out. My eyes were blurry and my feet slipped on the gravel road. I took deep breaths. I took the condom from my purse and ripped its cover off with my teeth. I chewed the condom, tasting the oily lubricant, hearing it squeak as I ground it to a pulp. I felt a calmness, a sense of who I was, a sense of completely inhabiting my body. It was like nothing I had ever experienced.

See Photo Below[1]

Rick Moody

*T*here are large individual variations among young people

    All characters held up to reprobation in the Old Testament
    are worthy of veneration

Better a dry morsel

    Than the most persistent
    Principles of the universe—

    accident and error

Insist on total liberation:

    A decorated table reserved for ninety minutes,
    with party hats and balloons

    People free of venereal disease should marry

I am not able to analyze this section
    without further information

    Subjects are not allowed to eat food
other than that provided in test meals

    Your protagonist's occupation is
    a spotter in a dry cleaner

The Board deems it desirable to induce uniformity in this matter

    Acts prohibited include idling away time and
    the dropping of the final "h" in the termination "burgh"

That name in common local use at present should be adopted

    All three of us are more excited than ever

    The town hussy gives good advice once you get beyond
    the tough exterior

    Driven by passion, he and his sweetheart drive to a neighboring state
    whereupon they lie down gently

---

1. Roman laws gave the father a power of life and death over his children. We must not allow the pendulum to swing. Minors are subject to numerous restrictions of their freedom

PART II

CONFLICT:
GRAPPLING WITH ILLNESS

The Facts

Mark Rigney

*O*CCASIONAL LAPSES IN TASTE OR DISCRETION WITHIN THIS NARRATIVE ARE entirely intentional. They serve to damn the innocent and punish the guilty, all of which the media, in their infinite fourth-estate wisdom, failed to do through the omission of facts, spirit, and other vagaries. So, if it seems inappropriate to interrupt a tragic drowning with observations about the nesting habits of local birds, then consider this: Lewis Kohler knew even less of those birds than they did of him. It is a stone-cold fact that he never once opened a book on birds or enquired after the name of a species he did not already know, which amounted to three: cardinals, blue jays and sparrows— and the sparrows he lumped into one large group, completely ignoring the ten-odd variants flitting through the Olentangy valley.

Further, if it seems callous to contrast Lewis' unhappy death with two small pony-tailed girls on silly bikes, then remember: small pony-tailed girls on silly bikes are everywhere in this country, as is death, and thus the two are inseparable. They go together, hand in hand, and on occasion they meet, scythe and sickle versus Barbie and bells.

Not that life is always such the proverbial vale of tears, but honestly— drowning just isn't any fun. Might as well liven things up.

Newspapers of the day described the drowning of Lewis Kohler in quick, definitive terms, using sentences like "Mr. Kohler, of 104 Schuyler Street, had been confined to a wheelchair since a 1998 car accident." They correctly appre-hended both his age and the fact that he was a regular visitor to Antrim Park Lake, a placid, kidney-shaped pond encompassed by a looping, mile-long bicy-cle trail. They gave his address and noted his former occupation, the sale of hardwood flooring through Kohler's, founded by his father—but bankrolled by his diminutive, ambitious mother—in 1947. And, when it came time, they offered a perfectly factual obituary, dry and depressingly efficient:

> Lewis Kohler, 68, of Clintonville, died Saturday morning, May 6, 2000, at Antrim City Park. He is survived by his son, Edward, of Akron, and his sisters, Lottie (husband John) Felson and Shirley (husband Josh) Lutz, both of Marysville. Mr. Kohler was a 1960 graduate of Whetstone High School and attended the Ohio State University, majoring in Business. Arrangements are pending through the Robert October Funeral Home in Worthington.

None of the papers bothered to note how odd it was that all of his remaining kin made their livelihood, in one fashion or another, from the auto industry—Edward for Goodyear, and the sisters, both secretaries, for Honda. Editors deemed ephemera of this sort as irrelevant to the matter at hand, that matter being Mr. Kohler's sudden and terminal immersion in Antrim Lake.

Lewis Kohler often asked his in-home caregivers, Maurice and Kaylie, to load him into his Delta 88 Oldsmobile and lug him up to Antrim. It was among the few city parks easily accessible by wheelchair from beginning to end. The fact that traffic on Highway 315 (an interstate by any other name) buzzed by at speeds exceeding seventy-five miles per hour did not put him off sufficiently to explore other options.

"I'm used to the roar," he'd tell anyone with whom he might strike up a conversation, usually dog owners. He liked to borrow sticks and hurl them for Yuppie Labradors. Not surprisingly, both the Yuppie Labradors and the sticks (mostly box elder and cottonwood) escaped the newspapers.

So, in a descriptive sense, did Lewis Kohler: not a single article ever mentioned what he looked like.

Well, to be fair, one paper did run a small single-column black-and-white photograph, very grainy and very out-of-date, as evinced by Lewis' nearly full head of hair.

Maurice, meanwhile, received no fewer than five photographs over a one-week period, all of which revealed in no uncertain terms that Maurice, full name Maurice S. Myles, was black. In print, no one ever mentioned Lewis Kohler's ethnic heritage, but, just to be absolutely certain, the newspapers identified Maurice's racial status nine times, three times in articles that also contained redundant photographic evidence. These self-same articles went on to mention how Maurice had worked for HomeHealth for five years, and Lewis Kohler—wonderful, helpless, world-class Caucasian Lewis Kohler—had been only his second assignment. Maurice Myles had large hands, proclaimed one writer, which caused most readers to assume Maurice was a giant, the sort of hulking menace that causes God-fearing white parents to lock their daughters inside after dark. In fact, Maurice was a small man, lightly built; in his hip-length caregiver's jacket, pressed and whiter than polished bone, he could not have been more unassuming.

To the credit of the profession at large, at least one reporter sought to capitalize on Maurice's meeker side by describing how Maurice wept when relating the events to police officers—and he cried not once, not twice, but even days and days after the initial event. "It's my fault," he whispered, speaking only to himself. "All my fault."

When these words hit the paper, letters appeared suggesting that Maurice S. Myles be prosecuted, as swiftly as possible, for criminal negligence, reckless endangerment, and a host of far less applicable charges, including littering.

One of those letter writers turned out to be Kaylie Linderbuck, Lewis Kohler's weekend caregiver. Recall: Lewis Kohler died on a Saturday morning, a day which usually would have been Kaylie's watch, starting at midnight

Friday. She and Maurice had agreed to the switch in advance, so that he would work Saturday for her—and draw lucrative overtime pay—and she would cover for him on Monday. Readers of newspapers, especially grumpy early-morning pre-coffee readers, promptly found fault with both. Kaylie Linderbuck appeared lazy and shiftless, a woman who would do anything to avoid the duties of her thankless but easy job of pushing, on demand, a wheelchair-bound codger around a lake. Maurice S. Myles, whose middle initial invariably appeared together with the rest of his name, struck these same readers as over-tired, greedy, and possibly incompetent. The truly avid fans who followed the story into its second week, were not, therefore, surprised to find that Mr. Myles lost his job, that he was fired by HomeHealth after a summary and previously unscheduled employee review. Ms. Linderbuck retained her job, albeit with another patient, but the article covering Maurice's dismissal didn't bother to mention Kaylie's status. Nor did it mention her consistently ignored middle initial, M for Monique.

The actual events of the day, while straightforward enough, became surprisingly slippery once police and reporters determined to pin them down. Here is what they settled on:

At nine-thirty sharp, Maurice bundled his charge into the aforementioned Delta 88 (copper-brown), and after a short drive of precisely three point six-five miles, they arrived at Antrim's lower parking area, where, after a ten- or possibly eleven-minute struggle with the chair and the Delta's recalcitrant seatbelts, Maurice and Lewis eventually departed for the lake. The paved walkway led first through an underpass below Highway 315, a hybrid of a tunnel and a bridge which stank constantly of river muck and dead fish from the Olentangy River's regular floods. The Olentangy, which chugged along on the far side of Antrim Lake, tended to pool and collect under the bypass thanks to an engineering gaff with a drainpipe which, rather than helping a small local stream enter the river, instead allowed the river to enter the stream, sometimes for weeks at a time. Lewis often griped about this, since the residual layers of mud also gummed up his wheelchair and left dust prints of the river on his immaculate golden oak floorboards. "Rivers," he was fond of saying, "are not good indoor pets."

At nine forty-seven, Lewis said, or so Maurice explained it later, "I'm a big boy now, and I can damn well get around a one-mile trail on my own, thank you very much. I know I'm ready, you know I'm ready. The question is, are you going to let me do it?"

"No," said Maurice, and continued to push.

Did we mention it was a gorgeous day, with alternating sun and shade, puffy clouds, low humidity, and a cheeky, water-ruffling breeze? Or that "Olentangy" is an approximation of the original Shawnee, meaning, simply, "muddy river"?

No matter. The distance between the parking lot and the far side of the underpass, where the bike trail came in from two sides to create a T-junction, was and is exactly fifty-five point three-seven meters, plus an additional ten point three meters tacked on for the particular spot where Maurice had parked the Delta 88. This is not a lot of space in which to frame a convincing argument, especially one so radical as what Lewis Kohler proposed that day. As he well knew, no caregiver, or at least no care-giving employee of HomeHealth, was supposed to let his charge out of either sight or hearing range.

"Maurice," Lewis griped, staring straight ahead and eyeing, not unkindly, a pair of spindly pony-tailed girls riding pink training-wheeled bicycles, "what was all that therapy for if not to give me a little independence?"

"Don't know," Maurice said.

The girls rode off and Lewis frowned at his useless feet. "If you don't let me go, I swear to God in Heaven that I will make up the worst, most insidious lies about you. I'll tell them you never wash me, you leave crumbs all over, there are cockroaches crawling out of my bed sheets, you smoke in the house—no, you mainline in the house—and you never, ever, come when I call. You'll lose your job before I'm even off the phone."

"No," said Maurice. "Capital N, capital O."

Lewis changed tactics. "Not only will I get you fired, but I'll give you a hundred bucks, right now."

Maurice leaned around so he could see Lewis' face. "You serious?"

Lewis dug into his left trouser pocket and hauled out a rumpled wad of green. "Two twenties and a fifty," he said. "I'll give you ten back at the house."

"Can't do it," Maurice said, accelerating the wheelchair for emphasis. "Sorry."

"I'll make the call. I'll tell 'em about Sarah Selzer."

Maurice hesitated for one full rotation of the chair's wide rubber wheels, and then he took the money.

He gave in, not, as he told the press and a gaggle of detectives, because he felt sorry for Lewis and wanted to do something nice for him, but because of Sarah Selzer. While Maurice had only been with Lewis for six short months, he had made his living as a caregiver for five years, and most of those five had been spent in the household of Ruth Selzer, an ill but irascible woman with knitting-needle eyes and a flirtatious, slightly unstable teenage daughter, Sarah. When the convalescent mother, formerly Jewish but now a devout born-again Christian, caught the pair in flagrante delecto on the floor, she opted to forgive —but only on the condition that Maurice never again fail to do anything less than his finest work. Ruth promised she'd be watching, following his career with private investigators if necessary, and while Maurice had never doubted her, now he had the proof: Lewis knew. If he told, Ruth would back him up. He'd wind up a security guard in a parking lot kiosk, freezing in winter, sweating in summer, no tips, no perks, no future.

"Second chances," Ruth had said to him, pointing a brittle finger in his direction as if applying a curse, "that's what Jesus is all about. But third chances, no, sir. The Lord giveth, and the Lord taketh away. Don't make me do the Lord's work, son."

Maurice had never forgotten, not even for an hour, that single pointed finger. Worse, he found he could barely remember Sarah and how she'd felt, naked and squirming beneath him, how she'd slid her fingers inside his pants and brushed his ear with her tongue. All he was sure of was that she hadn't been fat. She'd been small, young. She'd been unbelievable—and thus, apparently, forgettable.

Maurice hadn't realized how heavy a really fat woman could grow until he met Kaylie Linderbuck, who, despite her winsome name, was easily the widest, stoutest mortal he'd ever encountered, a sort of human building, soft and squishy. Kaylie heaved from place to place, crippling the floor joists of every home she entered. She never walked: she lumbered. By comparison, Maurice was emaciated, almost skeletal; predictably enough, they despised each other, although both enjoyed their mutual charge, Lewis.

The one thing Kaylie truly disliked about Lewis Kohler were his wheeled walks around Antrim Lake. She hated these with couch-potato passion, indolent and furious all at once. A mile, to Kaylie, required a Herculean effort from her knees, ankles, heart, and lungs. All three—Kaylie, Maurice, and Lewis—knew full well why Kaylie had begged off Saturday. It was Lewis' favorite morning for a walk—"walk" being a term he used with cynical satisfaction—a walk he would do his level best to take come rain or shine or melon-sized hailstones.

Facts such as these never entered the public ledger, at least not through the newspapers. Nor did the papers ever publish a photograph of Kaylie Linderbuck, so most of those who tracked the events following Lewis' death pictured her as lazy, yes, but also as some sort of track star, lithe and quick, the picture of health. Pony-tailed, in all likelihood, a grown-up version of the bicycle girls. Nothing could have been further from the truth. Her actual hair rose in piles off her head, it wound into dark balls, and then dropped down her shoulders and over her forehead in great curly moplets. Her father was mixed Dutch and Zuni, her mother a French emigrant born in Quebec City; their forbears were no more pure than she, and traced their roots to Shanghai, Botswana, and Mirenburg.

Thus the cast: Kaylie Linderbuck, mutt; Maurice S. Myles, skinny black American male; Lewis Kohler, who finally won his battle for independence with a timely threat plus ninety dollars, dead.

Maurice kept the two wrinkled twenties and the equally ratty fifty in a Mikasa flower vase, and he placed the vase atop his television in the dark spare bedroom of his dim, unloved apartment. Thomas Jefferson stared at him nightly through the criss-crossed cuts of the glass. Some nights, Maurice thought about getting rid of Mr. Jefferson by spending him. It's only money, he thought, but he couldn't bring himself to touch the bills, and so they sat there, three stern little judges, eating him up by degrees. Only money: to Maurice, it was blood money.

At the exact moment that Maurice and Lewis separated, a fisherman, standing on the newly emplaced concrete wharf just past the T-junction of the trails, caught a crappie. Whether it was a black crappie or a white crappie, he could not be sure. He knew that both species lived in the Olentangy, and that both, thanks to the very same ingenious overflow pipe that flooded the underpass, could occasionally swim out of the river proper and into Antrim Lake. Unfortunately, all crappies tend to look more or less identical, the one being ever so slightly darker, or blacker, than its lighter, whiter cousin. The fisherman, despite feeling vaguely inferior for not knowing his catch's exact identity, was, overall, quite pleased. It marked the fifth crappie he'd landed in three hours, which was not such a bad rate of return, considering he was inside the city limits, and besides, crappies made for excellent pan-fry—or so he told his wife and his three young sons. In the strictest sense, this was something of a fib, since crappie, like most fish, tend to taste much like the waters they swim in, but the fisherman had, over time, convinced himself that crappie, pan-fried, made a tasty meal. So, of course, it was true. Factual. Printable, even—except that nobody bothered.

Until now.

Traffic on the highway was light that morning, which allowed Lewis to overhear snatches of several conversations as he wheeled himself clockwise around the pond, including a few snide remarks about "some damn fool" who'd "caught another crappie." Lewis looked forward to reaching the far side, where the highway receded and the woods took over, where it was quieter, where there were fewer fishermen and he could catch occasional glimpses of the meandering Olentangy through the trees. Maurice had hurried away in the opposite direction, counter-clockwise, and Lewis correctly surmised that Maurice would try very hard to catch him well before the halfway point, just to make sure that everything was all right. Which, as Lewis knew, it would be. What on earth could happen?

The odds are good that as Lewis mulled those thoughts, a red-winged blackbird called. Antrim in the early summer is home to many red-winged blackbirds and so, while it may not be an absolute front-page fact that a blackbird sang just at the point where Lewis Kohler arrived at the curve—the only sharp curve on the entire circumference of the lake—it does seem entirely probable that a blackbird could have done so, and that it very likely did.

Lewis, meanwhile, whether by accident or design, hit the curve at a good clip. First one tire and then the other rolled off of the pathway. Did he fight to get back on? Did he curse or mutter? Ah, too late! On to the next stage, over and across the steep, grassy banks, then down with a messy splash into the shallows of the lake. Now he cursed; he must have, because those steep, grassy banks turned out to be just steep enough to give his wheelchair the requisite momentum to plow right through the shallows. Another curse! Or was he just wide-eyed? He knew what was coming: the submerged lip of what Antrim had formerly been, a limestone quarry.

The lip was hidden, precipitous, dramatic. It took only a moment: Lewis Kohler tipped forward—did he call out to God? Was he composed? Frightened? Surprised?— and then, with only the smallest of ripples and a few heavy bubbles, he was over the edge and gone.

* * *

In point of fact, he was not actually gone, since he remained just below the surface for some time, and in any event he never truly vanished so much as he merely departed from obvious view. It is also a fact—or at least very likely—that a large number of crappies saw him there, and that one or more red-winged blackbirds flew overhead, looking not for him, and not for crappies, but for each other, probably to fight—if they were males—or to nest, if one was male and the other female. Female blackbirds rarely fly simultaneously, perhaps because they are constantly browbeaten by their gaudy husbands into staying with the eggs.

The papers missed all that, of course. It's their job to miss such things.

Kaylie Linderbuck, middle name Monique, woke up at about that time in her apartment, and she rolled over in her bed, a bed with a sizable dent in the center where her body came to rest each night. She then rolled up and over the lip of the mattress, shed a mountain of bedclothes, and placed both feet, gingerly, on the floor. She burped. She went back to bed.

Lewis, meanwhile, began to sink. All the air pockets in his clothes had escaped, and now there was nothing to stop him from finding the bottom. First he floated out of his wheelchair, and the chair sank beneath him, banking slowly off the vertical quarry walls and leading the way deeper and deeper into the bowels of the ink-dark lake. Lewis kept struggling, and spurts of wobbly bubbles flooded out of his nose, then out from the corners of his mouth. He waved his arms and tried to swim, but his clothes and the dead weight of his legs conspired against him. Very much against his will, a single enormous bubble of air escaped him, rising skyward like a special effect, and Lewis felt the lake rush into his lungs and throttle his final gasp for breath.

It hurt more than he had expected, as if someone had stuffed an anvil into his chest and now the anvil was suddenly and dangerously expanding.

On the far side of the lake, Maurice, jogging now, passed two teenage boys trying their hand at fly casting.

"I thought you said crappies didn't like flies," said one to the other.

"They don't," said his friend. "That one must have been starving."

Maurice ran on. He had never admitted it to anyone, but he was hopelessly near-sighted, and he couldn't tell, not for the life of him—so the saying goes—whether Lewis was still on the path, or even on the planet. All Maurice could see of the far side of Antrim Lake was a kind of shimmering blur, the merry sparkle of the sun glancing off wavelets on the water. He became more fearful with every jogging step.

It is a fact, recorded by various witnesses, that when Maurice reached the halfway point, he was already out of breath, but when he did not find Lewis waiting for him, he proceeded to run at a dead sprint all the way to the single sharp curve, a bend where a small crowd had gathered to point and whisper at a stew of objects drifting in the water: a cheap pocket address book, a blue Clippers billcap, several receipts, and a nearly empty bottle of SPF 45 sunblock, all of which had floated out of an open pocket on the back of Lewis' chair. Two gawky girls on Barbie-pink bicycles informed Maurice that they'd seen a man in a wheelchair crash into the water just about there—"There," said one, pointing afresh—and wasn't it gross and sick and disgusting?

"Someone," said someone, "should call the police."

Maurice himself performed that duty, from a small callbox near the underpass. "Hello!" he yelled over the roar of the highway. "There's been an accident!"

He later reported that he couldn't hear anything on the other end of the line, and the Parks Department sent a team that afternoon to fix the phone. They went home in a sullen mood after making a terse note in their log, Phone in perfect working order.

The police arrived promptly. They appraised the situation and summoned a diving team to return Lewis Kohler and his wheelchair to the surface.

End of story. On to the epilogues.

Kaylie Linderbuck continued her stint with HomeHealth for another seven years, during which time she applied for disability leave on five separate occasions, four of which were granted. She died of a heart attack while bobbing unhappily through a water aerobics class at HomeHealth's private health club. Seventy-three mourners turned up for her funeral service, sixty-three more than had attended the memorial for Lewis Kohler.

Maurice S. Myles, thinking of Sarah Selzer, wracking his brains to remember her touch, sank into a fierce and crippling bout of depression, a lonesome struggle which saw him move through three Ohio cities in less than two years, always one step ahead of Sarah and two steps behind his mordant sense of guilt. He tried churches, he tried dating, he tried drugs. For a time, he was addicted to painkillers, sleeping pills, and caffeine, all at once. He took up bowling. He participated in the making of an amateur X-rated movie, but felt nothing, neither joy nor revulsion, and he quit before the lunchtime break was called. He joined a cult and became, for a period of almost three weeks, Shining Star, Master of His Own Destiny, Blessed Child of the Cosmos. He developed a liking for canned pears, and it was this, more than anything else, that drew him back to the world, to a world stuffed full of miracles, miracles like lakes and joggers, white and black crappies, girls on bikes with clackety training wheels and women so fat they could buckle a floor.

Maurice moved one last time, to Alaska, a fact the newspapers missed, for they were on to the next scent, something about abuse in the public schools and how someone would have to pay and heads would roll—and it happened, too, but only after a Special Crimes Unit took charge. In Alaska, we lose sight of Maurice, for the papers there are different, consumed as they are with local road conditions and the forty-thousand names for snow. It wasn't hard for Maurice, a grim black man in a snow-white uniform, to blend in to Alaska's hospitals and background checks, as if he had always been there—as if he had always been faultless in his work.

For Lewis, there can be no epilogue, except to remember that for all the details added here, for all our pathetic attempts to do justice to his life, we have only begun to discern the steps of his dance, the pattern of his music, and the marvel of all that we must miss.

Forgettery

Rachel Hadas

When a voice is silenced,
    the language goes on talking.
The language from however high it falls
lands on its feet, stalks gracefully away.
Nor does a recently vacated space
fail to fill. Replacements
lurk behind every bush, are never shy
about stepping forth to take up the tale again.
Everything conspires to make us oblivious
to our own obliviousness.

This train skims pleasantly enough along.
See me gazing vaguely out the window
in expectation of what I don't remember.
Gleaming green behind its tattered promise,
a line of trees divides the visible
from something else. The view clears: no more trees,
little hills instead, fields, slice of river.
What was that flicker, that
quivering of attention
as if at something hidden?
The impulse to discover is that strong.
I could have been in search
of nothing and have found
just what I was looking for.

The Absolute Worst Thing

Seth Carey

*E*VER SINCE KINDERGARTEN, I'D WAIT AT THE SCHOOL BUS STOP WITH MY best friend Chris Kelly. To kill the time we'd invent games. 'The absolute worst thing' was a real favorite. We'd dream up the worst situations we could think of and progressively build upon them until they were as dreadful as possible.

No matter how we tried to outdo it, the absolute worst we could come up with was always trumped by one particular scenario:

"What if you could still think and feel but you weren't able to move?"

We agreed—this was The Absolute Worst Thing.

That was about thirty years ago, and I still think it's the absolute worst thing.

I was diagnosed with Lou Gehrig's Disease (ALS) December 14, 2001—no problem remembering that date. The doctors who diagnosed me were careful to explain that this meant a death sentence. I was thirty-nine years old.

When they suggested one more blood test, since "maybe you're lucky and you just have AIDS," I knew that the absolute worst thing was for real, and it was happening to me. I knew things were going to get ugly, so I told my good friend (and recent girlfriend), Shannon, that she should run from me. Luckily for me she ignored sound advice and asked to get married instead.

We got married that March.

In the last two years, seven months, and eight days, this disease I'd never heard of has been busy kicking my ass. I've gathered way too much info on ALS (all of it depressing) and can rattle on about it. It boils down to this: ALS kills motor neurons, the signal pathways to voluntary muscles. Those are what you use for things you want to do, like petting the cat, rolling over in bed, holding your head up...you get the idea.

Those muscles are also used in breathing, something I do regularly, and very much hope to keep on doing.

I have bulbar onset ALS, whose symptoms include uncontrollable outbursts of laughter and weeping, sometimes both at once. Fortunately for me, most of my outbursts have been in the more socially acceptable form of laughter. The slightest humorous thought, or the dreaded heart-tug of a Spielberg moment, so popular in phone commercials, and I wave goodbye to self-composure. It makes it tough to act macho. It's not as bad as it was initially but I still cry in my oatmeal most mornings.

I miss being able to do everything I used to do. I thought I understood what I'd miss and could sort of stockpile experiences to keep from missing them too much. It worked better with some things than with others.

I knew that I'd miss fishing, so I did a butt-load of it. But how can you stock up on hugging your wife?

We have three cats I can no longer pet. Shannon, my wife, sometimes takes my hand and runs it over the fur of one that's nearby. The cats start purring and, usually, I end up sobbing.

Mosquito season has now become its own special form of torture. I watch the mosquitoes land on me. They walk about a bit searching for just the right spot to drill. I try to explain to whomever is around, what's happening. My voice is hard to understand in the best circumstances, but when you add frustration and impending doom, I'm reduced to undecipherable yowls. They only know I'm upset, but not why.

I know all too well there's nothing funny about ALS. It's stripped me of the use of my body and voice. It has been an endless source of frustration and humiliation.

But there's already enough depressing crap written about ALS. Laughter and denial are the tools that make living with this nightmare possible.

I credit my approach to dealing with ALS to the many hours I've spent stuck in highway traffic. When you find yourself in a traffic jam, you are faced with a choice. You can get all mad, flipping the finger to everyone, banging on the dashboard. Or you put on your favorite CD, rummage around for a roach, and sing along with the guitar solo.

Either way you're going to end up at the same place.

Sentence

Barbara F. Lefcowitz

A moon approaching fullness
the round black lacuna
that will replace forever
the middle of this page
waxes invisibly each moment

a presence I've suspected
since first awareness
of an uninvited guest
at the door of one eye
perhaps the other

long before I knew
the word thief
or implications of the sentence
they robbed them blind

Pain

Stephen Dixon

*H*E HAD A PAIN, AT FIRST DIDN'T PAY MUCH ATTENTION TO IT, THOUGHT IT
came from something he ate, then from too much coffee, or vodka or
wine, or exercising, but it was almost always there, constant for hours some-
times, bothered him at night, he didn't tell his wife about it, but after a week
of this and when he couldn't sleep and was turning over in bed a lot and had
gotten up and taken something for the pain, she said "Anything wrong?" and
he said no and she said "But you've been squirming around in bed," and he said
"Oh, a slight pain in my stomach," and she said "Where, upper, lower?" and
he said "Or maybe not even the stomach; the right side below the ribcage," and
she said "You take anything for it?" and he said "So far nothing's worked;
aspirin, ibuprofen and just now some antacid liquid," and she said "So it's been
going on for a while. How long?" and he said "It's nothing, it'll go away on its
own," and she said "But how long have you had it? It's obvious, not just
tonight," and he said "A few days," and she said "Does it ever let up?" and he
said "A little," and she said "You should speak to Denkner," and he said "You
know me; I hate seeing doctors except for my annual physical," and she said
"Call him, just as a precaution, and he might even give you a simple explana-
tion for it and solution over the phone," and he said "I'll see," but he didn't call
and the pain seemed to diminish the next two days and disappear entirely for
longer periods than before and he thought "Good, it's going away, I wrenched
something and now it's healing. I made the right decision not to call Denkner,
because he would have asked me in for tests, wouldn't have found anything and
the pain would eventually disappear," but the next night when his wife was
asleep and he was reading in bed, the pain returned worse than ever and so as
not to disturb her he took one of his pillows and got a quilt out of the linen
closet and slept on the living room couch, or was able to sleep for about an hour
because the pain at times was so great, and when he came back to the bedroom
next morning to get his things, his wife said "Where were you last night? I
reached over several times and you weren't there," and he said "On the couch.
I felt a little congested in the nose, couldn't sleep because of it and didn't want
to disturb you," and she said "You take some cold medicine?" and he said "That
stuff always gives me a pain in my penis later when I urinate, so I just don't
trust it. But the cold, or whatever it was, seems better now," and his stomach
pain, now that he thought of it, and "stomach" because about half the times
the pain seemed to shoot across it and the other times seemed to stay in the
same place, right below the right side of the ribcage, was gone, but that day in
class he nearly doubled over when the pain suddenly hit him and he told his

students, all in their seats around the seminar table and some of them, he could tell, wanting to get up to help him, he was calling the break twenty minutes before he usually did because his stomach was upset but he'll be back the second half, so nobody leave for the day, went to his office, sat in his reclining desk chair, closed his eyes and clutched his midsection and said "Pain, please go away, please go away," canceled the rest of the class and his office hours afterward and drove home and his younger daughter said, when he walked in the door, "Daddy's home early, Mommy," and she said "Yes, what's wrong, you look awful," and he said "Damn pain down there again but this one almost killing me; I gotta get into bed," and she said "Oh darn, you didn't call Denkner, did you, and I never reminded you," and he said "I forgot, or I didn't want to go, but please, I have to lie down," and she said "Listen, I know, lie down, I'll get you something for it; and it's probably nothing serious—we get ten scares for every real disorder—but you have to find out what's causing it," and he said "You crazy? Not right now," and went into the bedroom and lay on top of the covers, pain went away in an hour and he came back into the kitchen and said "Look at that; gone; I'm even smiling. I hope that's the last of it, for it was the worst pain I ever experienced, and I'm sorry for yelling at you," and she said "Don't get mad again but I made an appointment for you with Denkner tomorrow—ten a.m., only slot he had open; I didn't even check with you if you were busy," and he said "I don't see why I should go. I feel fine, as good as ever, so only if the pain comes back," saw the doctor three days later, was examined, put through tests, couple of days after that the doctor called to say the lab results and sonograms indicate something quite serious could be wrong and he wants to refer him to a specialist, specialist said he had to be operated on as soon as the hospital could fit him into its schedule, operation wasn't successful and treatments after that didn't work and he had to take a leave from teaching, he felt nauseous a lot from the medication, pain got worse, they had to hire people to take care of his wife almost all the time now because he was too weak to get her off and on the bed and other things, they were starting to be short of money, his medical leave ended and he had to retire and go on pension and Social Security, things got worse all around, he thought Damn life, everything's going okay, nothing great but he was at least able to move around freely and enjoy life a little and take care of things: his wife's illness, paying all the bills, his work at home and school and his writing and looking after the kids, and now nothing it seems but pain, weakness and fatigue and everything else that's bad or comes with serious illness and he hates it, it's all so goddamn hopeless and he sometimes feels like doing away with himself but knows he can't because of what it'd do to his wife and kids and he's still able to help out at home a little so doesn't want to leave them completely in the lurch and also maybe some new drug will be discovered to relieve his condition somewhat, his doctors say researchers in various places around the world are working hard at it, so he has to hold on, nothing else he can do, got worse and more discouraged and depressed and almost every night after the woman who got his wife into bed had left and lights were out and they were in bed, he thought of times before he was so sick, nights after he got his wife set for sleep, covers over her, he'd stand on her side of the bed and lean over to kiss her on the lips good-night and every few nights would say, if they hadn't already done this soon after he got her from the wheelchair to the bed, "I know you're all set for sleep, but do you want to?" and his face would say what he meant and she almost always smiled and said something like "Sure, why not," or "I was hoping you'd suggest it, and if you didn't, I was going to," and they did it and then he got her ready for sleep again, shirt and booties back on if he had taken them off, head and shoulder on two pillows, bottom leg stretched out, doubled-over pillow between her knees, cushion between her feet, covers over her, kissed her on the lips goodnight, shut off her night table light, washed up and got into bed naked beside her, laid his handkerchief over his bed lamp so there'd be less light on her, made sure his watch, glasses, notebook, pen and book he was reading at the time were on his night table, would read for about half an hour or till his eyes got tired and then would try to read some more even though it was usually late by now, he'd only get five hours' sleep, broken up by his having to turn his wife on her other side once or twice, before his younger daughter got up for school and he'd get out of bed ten minutes later, brush his teeth, wash, shave, and do calisthenics in his bathroom, pushups on his bedroom floor and dress and go into the kitchen and get food out for his daughter's breakfast and some things out for his wife's more elaborate breakfast later on, push the button of the coffeemaker which he'd prepared the night before, get the two newspapers from the driveway and sit and read the front page of one of them and drink coffee for about five minutes and then take a short run on the same streets almost every time, get back and start the van so the engine would be warmed up, take his pills which he had set out the previous night in a jar lid alongside one with his wife's, cut some fruit and put an English muffin or bread or a bagel in the toaster for his daughter and go out and turn the ignition off and she'd come into the kitchen around now and get her lunch ready and school stuff together and say "We should leave, I'll be late," and he'd spread cream cheese or butter on whatever he'd toasted for her and pour another coffee in a special mug that fits into the van's cup holder and she'd eat her breakfast and drink a glass of water in the front seat while he drove and sipped coffee and he'd say somewhere along the way "Main or side entrance or trailers?" and she'd tell him and he'd say "Pick you up regular time today?" and she'd say yes or "Can I call you after school?" and sometimes she'd kiss him goodbye but mostly she'd just get out of the van and wave and from there he'd go to the Y nearby and work out in the weight room for about twenty minutes and quickly shower and feel great as he left the place and walked to the van and drove back the same route unless he needed gas and at home fill the kettle with water, if he hadn't already filled it that morning or the previous night, and put it on the stove and go into the bedroom and say as he pulled one of the curtains open "Time to get up," or "Ready to get up?" and she'd say something usually muffled under the covers over her face and if he didn't hear something like "A few more minutes" he'd open the big-window curtains but leave the other side-window curtains closed because that window was the only one his neighbors could see in, and take her covers off one by one and fold them and put them on a chair and remove her booties if she hadn't kicked them off at night and stick one inside the other and put them on the folded-up covers and take away the rolled-up towel from beside her back and the pillow and cushion from between her knees and feet and put them on the same chair and get her on her back if she hadn't already managed to get on it and if she had, then straighten her body out, and exercise her feet and legs and then help her turn over on her stomach and she'd try to do pushups and stretch exercises while he went to the kitchen to turn the burner off under the kettle and prepare her soup, tea and liquid concoction she drank down the pills with every morning and go back and help her to her knees so he could get behind her on his knees and exercise her thighs, and sometimes, maybe once a week, more like every other, he'd pull down the pad she wore at night and say "All right?" and she usually said yes, and stroke her down there from behind and then try to penetrate her and sometimes, in anticipation of penetrating her after he exercised her from behind, he'd go into the bathroom and pee and put lubricant jelly on his penis, but coupling in that position almost never worked because he couldn't keep her steady enough to get his penis in, so he'd get her on her back and do it from on top or the side and then wheel her shower chair out of the bathroom to the side of the bed, lock the wheels, pull her by the ankles till her legs were over the side and then sit her up, make sure her feet weren't twisted and were flat on the floor, put his arms around her and say "At the count of three," and lift her onto the chair, straighten her up, buckle her in, unlock the wheels and pull the chair from behind into the bathroom, slide it over the toilet and take the bucket out from it, put a folding chair beside her, stick the pills into her mouth and hand her the liquid concoction, set the tea, soup, some fruit on the chair along with two slightly toasted rice cakes or lightly toasted rice bread with cream cheese or butter or egg salad on them, put her tape player by her feet with a tape already in it so she could listen to books on tape, go back to the kitchen and pour some of the kettle's boiled water into an extra-large mug with miso, grated ginger and dried seaweed in it, drink it while reading a newspaper for about fifteen minutes in the living room easy chair or, if it was warm out, on one of the plastic patio chairs outside, and then go back to the bathroom and pick up whatever dish she was done with and say "Everything all right" or "okay?" and she'd say yes, or could he get her glasses and book or a certain numbered tape from the green Library of Congress or blue Princeton Recording for the Blind box on the bed in her study, one she's listening to is almost finished, and he'd do that and say "Anything else?" and she'd say no, "I'll yell for you when I need you," or "just check in on me in half an hour," or "My portable phone," for he almost always forgot to give it to her when he gave her the rest of the stuff, and he'd get that and hand it to her or set it on the chair and close the bathroom door and sit at his table in the bedroom, put some paper in and begin to type.

Revelations

David Shine

*B*efore he died,
the man with the new
artificial heart

sat, mantis thin,
in his striped hospital robe
and spoke in a whisper:

The hardest part, he said,
is not having a heartbeat,
just a whir.

But no one asked about
being afraid, how it felt
without the pounding.

If his joy was tempered
by the resolve of the device,
never racing or skipping a beat.

Or whether in sadness
an ache gripped his chest
like pain in a phantom limb.

The Little Things

Joan Malerba-Foran

S HE STANDS SIDEWAYS IN THE MIDDLE OF THE HALLWAY, HER BLOATED
backpack blocking traffic from both directions. Today, however, I am in
no mood. I'd spent the previous night grading eighty-one essays and, when
I finally did make it to bed, it was for a slim six hours crammed between leg
cramps and Technicolor nightmares.

"Shaniece." I wave her toward our door: Room M059.

The rule of conduct for freshmen confronted by a homeroom teacher
rarely varies. Shaniece chooses the most common move, which is the one-
quarter pivot-away followed by the half-glance toward the ceiling. Students
and teachers favor this maneuver because it allows for the maximum flexi-
bility of interpretation: I could use cooperative pretending (act as if the stu-
dent didn't hear me and repeat the name), conciliatory patience (hold the
door like an anxious host), or common spite (close the door). On this partic-
ular morning, repeating the name and/or holding the door are not options.

I close the door. Most likely Shaniece now has the impression that I hate
her. The fact that the late bell has rung or that the principal's froggy-voiced
morning warning has already blasted over the PA is irrelevant. In the tiny
sphere of her world and the gigantic universe of her emotional needs, none
of that will matter.

Sighing, I reopen the door and lean out.

"Shaniece, come on. I thought you were in here." An obvious lie, but like
all fiction, it is designed to reveal a truth. Shutting the door will be a
metaphor for her life and, as small as that gesture is and as right as I may be,
it will only add to *my* nightmares.

I've never been what you would call a good sleeper. I make it through
the night about twice a week, and those nights are never consecutive. I've
been to counselors, therapists, and psychologists, but always for ancillary
issues: a marriage that was on the rocks, a job that was on the rocks. The
truth is, at forty-five, my world is on the rocks because (according to my ex-
husband) I drink too much and too often. Whether this is true or not, my
preference is—literally—for my whiskey to be on the rocks; at least it was
until I had to sneak drinks. My husband detested the sound of clinking ice
cubes coming from the bathroom or a walk-in closet. The solution, though,
was simple enough: drink straight from the bottle. Of course, long term I'm
left—like every misunderstood drinker—to grapple with the impossible
dilemma of where to dispose of the empties. There aren't enough recycle bins
in any town to handle the yearly refuse of one heavy drinker.

"You don't look good, Miss."

Ah! My morning was now complete. Students may fail to notice a chalk-board filled with detailed directions on *exactly* what homework is due tomorrow, but they will never miss a sign of weakness in a teacher.

"Just tired. Get your seat. I have to take attendance." I tallied them: 8 out of 15 were present. That was about right, since two were recently incarcerated and four were scheduled for court this week. Actually, I'm not supposed to know those details, but the kids tell me. They don't want me thinking that they've skipped school. "I'm gonna give it to you straight, Miss, 'cause I'm no chicken-head," and they come right out with it: "I didn't cut yesterday. I was with my lawyer." Or, "I was coming to school but the Sheriff came for me." Brash as it sounds, it is a tender offering; for an instant, something soft and virtually invisible peeks from behind the determined eyes and set jaw. It's a flash—as rare as a hummingbird in the city—but at that instant, everything is straight: no hidden agenda, nothing personal.

I count heads once more. And then again. And then once more. I'm a fanatic about attendance, since it can mean more than a "P" for present or an "A" for absent; in some cases, it might supply an alibi; in others, it might register as a violation of parole or of group-home rules.

Standing on tiptoe, I turn on the overhead TV for the morning announcements. "Pay attention, people." Shaniece and Tamarra flip their cell phones shut. "Fellows, du-rags off." Michael, Lyonel, and Jerrad look up, confused. They can't hear over their earphones, buried and buzzing like fat-tened bees in their ears. I swirl my index finger over my head. They unknot their rags with practiced fingers, slide them off, and sink back into their music. I nod and give a thumbs-up. I check the table next to the door, mak-ing sure everything is in place: Kleenex, hand lotion, scotch-tape dispensers, a pair of scissors, the daily newspaper, and flyers announcing writing contests or department news. I'm ready.

My left temple throbs; my tongue has acquired its own flavor. I slip a square of mint-flavored gum into my mouth and bite down. The coolness bursts open like a storm cloud, making my eyes tear. They notice.

"Miss, you got any more gum?"

I gingerly shake my head, trying not to arouse the sodden bulge of pain purring in my sinus cavity. "Just this one." They don't necessarily believe or disbelieve me; I'd come to understand that wasn't the point of these exchanges. During my first year of teaching I'd never lied. One, I am honest by nature. Two, I will never lie when the truth will do, unlike some of my drinking buddies. If I was going to have a piece of gum, I made sure that I had another 140 pieces—one for every student plus homeroom. This isn't, however, about fairness, honesty, or approval; it's about survival. It isn't the commodity but the transaction that matters. Students know that a new teacher doesn't make much money, certainly not enough to satisfy the never-ending requests of growing teenagers. What they don't know—and need to figure out—is a particular teacher's biases. As the saying goes, "Guilt buys good presents." Just how guilty are you, Teacher? How much do you pity the inner-city child? You know the one—he's walking around with more electronic gadgets being confiscated by security than a teacher will ever own; she's walking around in a new outfit, her nails shellacked and cornrows redone every two weeks. My last haircut was four months ago. I tell everyone that I'm letting my hair grow out. Grow out from what? No one asks, thank God. No one cares.

I can feel the buzz from last night's binge slipping away. It's getting harder to keep the alcohol in and the pain out. How had my mother done it? In the past few years I'd reconciled myself to her dying drunk, but I'd never considered what living drunk had been like. Was this it? The wait for the next little thing that might—if just for a moment—make the day bearable? I glance at the clock over the door. It reads 8:45, which means it is either 7:43 or 7:47. The clock is off one solid hour, but I can never remember if it is also two minutes plus or two minutes minus that hour. Then again, the first period bell hasn't rung so it must be 7:43 . . . now 7:44 . . . meaning the bell will—

The bell blasts and they drift out the door, lugging their sagging backpacks. They bounce against each other, crushed in a nimbostratus of overinflated coats. I'd often wondered why they kept their coats on all day, since there is a rule against it, since every other classroom is hot as an August attic, since their clothes underneath are pristine. All I had to do to find out was ask. The coats don't fit in the slender lockers, and there is no other safe place to leave them. I don't mean that they are stolen, but all the coats look alike— it doesn't matter if the bulbous, midnight-blue down jacket is a Tommy Hilfiger knockoff or the real thing. Among the boys, there is one other jacket of choice, which is the camouflage style. Those jackets may replace my original "Irony Award," something I haven't reissued since 1976. I'd originally created it to bestow upon those women who rigorously shop in our local vegetarian store while nonchalantly wearing fur coats. I can't get my mind around that concept. If memory serves, this particular irony was the focal point of my first drunken monologue; at least, I'd like to think it was. Call me elitist, but some things are more important than others to drink over.

Now, several decades later, I'm considering bestowing this award on those who intentionally wear camouflage clothing *indoors*. Ten years ago, I'd almost given the award away for this very reason. Newly divorced, I was working in the produce section of a supermarket while getting my bachelor's degree. I was reloading a sale item: *Buy one bag and get two free!* The produce section was empty except for a couple of elderly women, when a man in his mid-thirties strode through the door. His hat, shirt, jacket, pants, and gloves were all camouflage patterned. He was completely drenched in the spattered colors of a summer forest plunged in four o'clock shadows. He strutted past me in perfect posture, utterly confident. In my slightly soused state, I couldn't resist.

"Hey," I called out. He turned, a puzzled look on his face. I had broken one of the unwritten commandments of aisle-etiquette: grocery clerks are to be ever-present but silent. Contact is reserved for fetching.

"Yeah. You." I pointed at him, wiggling my index finger up and down to take in his entire outfit. "I can see you." He started to frown, and then I saw the pink stain spreading up from his camouflage collar to the camouflage flaps of his hunting hat.

I had to explain myself to my manager after the hunter/military/shopping man complained. Mr. Yagos tended to categorize employees as either mildly incompetent or stunningly stupid. I knew this was a problem for him, in my particular case, because I wasn't either one. Over the years, I'd suggested to him that the tendency of Western philosophy to classify in binary categories was too limiting and that if he couldn't fit people into just two columns, why not make more. I reminded him about this while he was reprimanding me about my "uncalled-for comment" and my "sassy demeanor." He still wrote me up, blemishing an otherwise flawless work record.

Now, watching students swagger past me in full fatigue regalia, I make a mental note to rethink the Irony Award at a time when I am far less dry; most likely, I won't even attempt it until I'm fully soused.

"Miss. Miss. Please. Miss."

To my right is the ever patient and pleading face of Shamaylia. She is a sweet girl plagued by congenital tardiness. Her parents have yet to attend a single meeting that they have scheduled for their own convenience. Shay always needs the same thing: sign her into homeroom even though she is late. And, as always, the roster is on its way to the collection point.

I shake my head. "I sent the attendance sheet down already." I have to catch myself and not offer to run down the hall after it. However, she must have noticed my upper lip twitch because I see hope flicker in her eyes. My throat tightens against a sudden welling of emotion. *How is it possible for a fifteen-year-old kid to look younger?*

What am I thinking, anyway? I'll never get through the crowd. The halls are so packed that students move in a shuffle-hitch, as if shackled. "I can't. Mr. Marken is watching." The light in her face dims and goes out. She turns away.

I can't help her because I have a job. Like all the other teachers, I have to supervise the area surrounding my doorway entrance between the ringing of the bells. It's a vague space, a zone that only the principal—watching the monitors from his office—can accurately judge. If I look left, then I'm not noticing the crunch of students to my right. If I look right, then something is sure to happen on my left. Looking straight ahead seems to elicit the least number of undirected complaints over the PA.

"Teachers," comes The Voice. "What is it you don't understand about keeping our students moving? I see congestion in 'The T.' We must move quickly to our classes. We can't teach an empty seat."

"The T" is the cross section at the head of the third floor. The elevator and the stairway funnel all the students coming for English, History,

Reading, or the Library at that point. Imagine sharing your driveway with the entrance ramp for several highways and you have "The T." There isn't a teacher in the world who can unknot that mess, unless you count Ricardo— a brassy mass of dedicated Mexican muscle. He commandeers one wing of "The T," and he takes personally anything that comes between him and an orderly hallway. It isn't a pretty sight or sound, and it sure as hell isn't for anyone with a hangover. Fortunately, I didn't meet Ricardo until my ability to have a hangover was two years in my past. There comes a point in a heavy drinker's life when all one can do is stay wet. There isn't anything else—no buzz, no high, no low—only the need for a steady supply. If drinking such large and frequent amounts didn't kill a person, it would all be rather routine. People make a bigger deal of it than it is. As long as you don't drive, sign a contract, or do math, the problems are minimal—at least, for the drinker. To be fair, the observer—such as someone's boss, or friend, or maybe a daughter—does have some legitimate complaints.

I see it on the first student walking into Period 1. I put my hand on his chest and stop him at the doorway to get a closer look. Several students plow into his back. He doesn't flinch. Raveius is a seventeen-year-old wall. He's the student who has to sit in back or along the side because no one can see around him. He is also as kind-hearted as he is large.

"Did you know him?" I ask, peering at the tiny newsprint. My head is moving back and forth like a hen searching for millet. He is standing in the zone that my bifocals can't quite cover. "Who was he?"

"Terrell. His name *is* Terrell. He *is* my cousin, Miss."

Had I used the past tense? Damn! I had, and I know better. "Wearing the obits" is done on the first day. After that, it's the large, pin-on buttons. Buttons—hundreds of them—the size of small sunflower heads, pinned to the straps of backpacks, banging against books, clattering like cicadas as the student-sellers dip into their manila envelopes and pull them out. On each is the smiling, disembodied face of an obscenely young person who was walking home on a Monday and dead on a Tuesday; or at work on a Wednesday and dead on a Thursday; or on a date on Friday and—you get the idea. The cause could be anything from a heart attack to a gang fight, from an innocent bystander to a big-mouth asking-for-it. The buttons are made in the high school print shop and they cost a dollar. The money goes to the mother to help her cover the cost of burying her son. Always a son. Little girls are the victims of hit-and-runs, and those happen only about once a year.

The first time I'd witnessed this kind of behavior, I didn't know what to make of it. None of my experiences in suburban schools had prepared me for this reality of urban life. I've since learned that this expression of mourning is what folklorists, anthropologists, and sociologists label "the phenomena of spontaneous memorials." Raveius has cut out his cousin's obituary and scotch-taped it dead center on the substantial expanse of his solid red tee shirt. The long column hangs like a grotesque tie. The photo is thumbnail size; the closed-mouthed smile of the young boy—seventeen at most—is probably last year's school photo. By the end of the day, most of my students will be walking billboards for the deceased. They will lean in my doorway to ask hesitantly, "Miss, can I use some tape?" Others will borrow the scissors, and I'll watch as they meticulously clip out the article. I have homeroom students who refuse to start the day until they can check the newspaper. "I got to know if somethin' went down last night," is the way that it's been put to me.

Initially, I thought they were being superstitious. That was before attending eight funerals in one year, where the average age of the deceased figured at 14.875 years. I don't know how I know that number, except one morning I found it scribbled on the pad I keep next to my bed. An empty bottle of Jack Daniels was on top of it. There was also a sheet of yellow legal paper inside the bottle. Try as I might, I couldn't tap the paper free from the tacky inside. As the morning wore on, I became apprehensive. What had I written? And to whom? I didn't want to break the bottle until I rediscovered my stash, because even an empty liquor bottle is usable; swish a quarter of a cup of warm water around in it for a minute and in a pinch—like on Sunday—the residue will hold off the shakes. It's more psychological than physical, but it does offer a cushion until the pharmacy opens and I can get NyQuil and Benadryl.

I knew that I'd stumble upon my stash eventually—under the folded clothes in the laundry basket, behind the radiator, inside a boot at the back of the hall closet—all the regular places Mom had used, plus a few I'd thought up while evading my husband's search and seizure. Around noon, I found a full pint tucked inside a half-used box of Kleenex. I slugged back a couple mouthfuls, then grabbed the empty fifth and wrapped it in a towel. I placed it in the center of the bathroom floor and whacked it with the bathroom scale. Of course, I sliced several fingers picking through the shards and then bled like a newly tapped maple; there's always enough alcohol in me to turn a bruise or cut into a blood bath. When I spread open the sheet of paper, there was a scrawl of loopy words in what must have been my handwriting: *Oh that the everlasting had not fixed his canon against self-slaughter.*

Shit. Why can't I quote Shakespeare when I'm awake, when it might do me some good? I crumpled the paper in my bloody fist and lay curled on the floor for a long time. Truth-be-told, the reference made me queasy. Pick any act from *Hamlet: Prince of Denmark*, it doesn't matter which one, thinking like Hamlet is *not* a good sign.

It seems that, lately, I've been spending more and more energy trying not to notice that my Drunk Self is depressed and making noises about wanting to die. My Dry Self has some issues with this, although not as many as Sober Self would like. Sober Self never gets involved but then, she rarely appears and, like any infrequent guest, is never asked to do any real work. Drunk and Dry watch as Sober tries to clean up the mess that happens in her absence, gets frustrated, and hastily retreats.

When I finally stood, the dried blood had glued the paper to my fingers. I ripped it off, watching with satisfaction as the blood re-blossomed in ripe, red drops from my fingertips. It hurt, and it felt right. I never complain about pain that's earned. Raveius, Camillia, Theira, Xavier, Carl, and so many more . . . they don't have the solace of earning their pain. It comes with their territory. Losing family members and friends to disease or violence isn't something they are shielded from. What's the point? It'll be on page two of the newspaper; page one if the police are involved. Yet, they never complain.

Raveius walks past me to his seat and his classmates stream by, button by button. Using the past tense is a small thing, all told, but it's the little things in life that make a drunk. It's the nick, not the amputation. Raveius is bunched in his seat, carefully tucking the strip of newsprint between his bulk and the edge of the desk. He's just fine; right now, I'm the problem. Somehow, my pain always ends up center stage. Nearly-Dry Self hisses in contempt: *How are you going to fix this one?*

I look at Raveius, head hanging over his warm-up ditto, studiously filling in the blanks. He isn't judging me. I scan the room; all heads are down. The only face I see full on is Terrell's, a perpetually young face set in a perpetually patient smile.

I've yet to drink while in school, but I've come close on two occasions. The first is nobody's business; the second, however...Ah! There's the rub. The second came during what is called "a teachable moment," those extraordinary moments that occur when students take a carefully planned lesson in an unplanned—but far, far better—direction. One student starts by hurling questions sharp as a pitchfork's prongs, and if I let them prick their fertile imaginations, I can't miss. There is nothing I can do that's wrong if I trust them enough to turn them loose in that orchard, ripe with . . .

. . . but the bell is going to ring and there are standardized tests to prepare for, and it will take us off task. What I miss most since becoming "a professional" is being able to explore those moments with abandonment. There's no time to play. Learning translates into objectives that are assessed by measurable outcomes. All my students come and go; not one speaks of Michelangelo, or anything else having to do with art. And that makes me want to drink almost as much as the first thing does, which is no one's business. Except maybe my mother's.

I make it through the next two periods flawlessly. My temples have taken on a familiar and welcome sensation of tenderness. An amateur would complain. He'd ask the first person he saw, "Did you get the number of the truck that hit me?" To the friend gingerly asking *Are you all right*, she'd reply, "Stop shouting at me!" For me, it is an important marker in my personal desert. I won't be drinking for another four hours. The pulpy feeling hanging like a deflated halo over my skull means I'm good for only about two hours more. From years of experience, I can white-knuckle it until I get home. I'll just pop a few aspirin and keep looking at the clock for reassurance. It's the two minutes plus-or-minus the one hour that worry me. Which direction do I go? I can never remember. Such a little thing, but I can only do this if I know *exactly* what time it is.

I'm doing the calculation on my way to the teachers' lounge when Marcus catches me in the hall.

"Miss! Jarritt wants you to know that he didn't cut class. He had went to court."

If Shakespeare is right—that all the world's a stage, and we're all players performing our bit parts—then Marcus is a true professional. "Will he be in tomorrow?" I obediently ask, since I'm well aware of my part in all this. "We have a quiz." He allows just enough hesitation to give the illusion of being caught off-guard.

"He said he'll be back as soon as he can. That's all I know."

Marcus has what he needs for Jarritt. He'll relay the information that there's a quiz tomorrow and I won't see Jarritt for a couple of days; at least, not in class. I'm certain to catch sight of him hanging around in the hallway, waiting for his friends. He'll nod as I pass by. I'll ask, "Jarritt, when will I see you in class?" He'll answer, "Tomorrow, Miss." Even on a Friday, the answer will be, "Tomorrow, Miss."

Most likely, Jarritt isn't going to do any time and he can be in school today, right after court recesses for lunch. But he'll take the day off and come tomorrow, not for class but to tell his friends exactly what happened. He won't exaggerate; he'll even do his best to capture any rumors and squash them. One of the greatest survival skills here is rubbing and refining a detail until it is no more noticeable than a smudge. That way, everyone can go to sleep at night. Unlike me, they can go to bed, and get up, and go to bed, and get up, and go to bed. Something that I haven't been able to do in a long time.

It's an English teacher's dream to encounter irony in life. Paradox is for the science department, oxymoron is for the math and history departments, but irony belongs to those who barter in language—and alcohol. I drink to make the small things look big, while most everyone else stays somewhat sober, hoping to make the big things look small.

For example, take the obituary column and those buttons. It all comes down to the littlest thing after *Here lies so-and-so: Born then — died now*. An entire life is represented by that dash. Everything a person has ever done is perfectly balanced on the thinnest thread of ink. Shouldn't we at least get to choose the length and heft of it? I'm thinking I'll ask the math department to work out the proportions. I'll give them something easy to start with: maybe a ninety-year-old grandmother with 23 grandchildren could get a quarter-inch thick line that is six inches long. We can make that the maximum and work down from there. What people need is a visual, something to make them pause and not skim through with a cup of coffee in one hand

and a crumpled section of newsprint in the other. Granted, my coffee has a couple of thick fingers-worth of Lord Calvert in it, but *I'm* not the problem. I look. I notice. I take my time. *They* need to take time. *They* need to notice all those little things.

Better yet, I'm going to tell the math department to tilt the lines. Let them lean like fishing poles propped along an endless shore. And make it so that the more a person has done for others, the higher the tilt. Make it so it points right toward heaven. Yeah, as Frost wrote in *After Apple-Picking*. It goes something like, "My long ladder's sticking through a tree, pointing toward heaven still..." Something like that. I can't remember it exactly right now, but I will later. It'll come right after the first fifth. Once again, irony in English and alcohol.

Right now, the only way I know to make up for any of the pain, any of the injustice, any of my cowardice, is to be strong. And that means I have to surrender my drinking time; my precious alone time, when it's me, my bottles, and a few memories.

I'll have to give that over to someone else and not drink for me. Tonight I'm going to do a planned drunk, the second hardest thing any professional drinker can attempt. I'm thinking it probably comes closest to feeling like an alcoholic. That, I really wouldn't know, but I'm guessing I'm as close to being right as a person gets. I'm going to pace myself and hold off the blackout. I won't vomit to get the poison out and grab a buzz. I'll hang onto the feeling of disease, not allow myself that pale shimmer of a high that comes with the purge. I'll make the whole thing hurt and I'll think about Terrell the entire time I'm conscious. I bought a button so that I can lie on my bed and hold it up toward the west-facing window. Moonlight is all the light I'll need; after all, he is dead. And as I drink and drift, I'll spend the night stretching that dash farther than my eyes can see, or my arms can reach, or my legs can run, and Terrell will have all the time he needs to live his life. That's the best I can do right now. And I won't stop until the alarm clock goes off and it's time to get up and start doing the little things all over again.

Writing Poems on Antidepressants

Nikki Moustaki

Writing poems on antidepressants
        is hard. You can appreciate the difficulty
by reading the previous two lines.
Metaphors are easy
to come by when you're aching
or pining or wounded in love,
which scientists have proven is a type of madness
and madness can be cured with a pill.
Not everyday
is Paris. Not everyday
does a bird come winging
out of a carpet to give you a free metaphor,
especially if there are oranges on the table
and you're on your meds.
Each day offers some little irony or a dream
or a blind albino woman
sitting next to you on the train
with eyelashes like white silk threads
attached like broom-straw to her one closed eye
as she taps her cane against the window
and you, the poet on antidepressants,
thinks: look at that, hmmm, interesting.
Did I buy dog food? Here's my stop.

The Bald and the Beautiful

William Bradley

*G*ENERAL *HOSPITAL* WAS PARTICULARLY GOOD TODAY. THE TRIAL OF BRENDA and Jason for Alcazar's murder began, but Brenda did not appear in court. They are both innocent, of course. Framed, most likely, by one of Sonny's enemies. Maybe a foe from the past, back to settle a score. Only one thing's for certain—I'll be tuning in tomorrow.

Ostensibly, these soap operas are just on for background noise, something to fill the silence of the apartment while I write next semester's syllabuses or dust the bookshelves or make notes for my book. But as I do these things, I find my gaze wandering towards the television, where dark, chiseled men have their arms around the waists of slim, gorgeous women and say things like, "You taught me what it means to love." And I find myself ignoring the important, mundane tasks of real life, preferring, instead, a world of mobsters, secret agents, teenage lovers, and evil twins.

And later, as my fiancée and I sit on the couch, watching a documentary or a foreign film, she tells me something she read earlier that day about the roles women played in Middleton's city comedies, and I respond with, "You know, I'm pretty sure that Cameron is Zander's father, but he doesn't realize that he's right there in Port Charles."

Emily is fairly easygoing, and she puts up with a lot of inane comments, but at this she sighs and says, "How can you watch those things?"

"They're da bomb," I answer.

She doesn't say anything. Just tries not to smile. In our graduate student relationship, it is generally understood that she is the serious one, and that I'm the fool she puts up with. She plays the straight man, rolling her eyes and groaning at me. Deep down, though, I think part of the reason we get along so well is that she finds me charming in my goofiness.

So I elaborate. "I like soap operas because the actors get to say things like, 'I will destroy you.'"

"Uh-huh," she says, raising her eyebrows and folding her arms across her chest. "And that appeals why?"

"Well, I mean, it's funny. How many times have you told someone you were going to destroy him?"

"Never."

"Exactly. Me neither. But they say it all the time on soap operas. 'I will destroy you.' It's awesome. I'd love to be able to say dialogue like that. Also, I like it when the guys on the shows are all dark and seductive. They glare out of the tops of their eyes, really intense. Like this." I lower my head slightly and gaze at her with the most smoldering intensity I can muster. Lowering my voice, I say, "I can see the light of a thousand stars in your eyes."

"Ooookay," she says, pushing against my chest and rising from the couch. She walks out of the room, towards the kitchen.

My mother is really the only person I can talk soap operas with. When I was 21 and diagnosed with Hodgkin's disease, I had to move back into my parents' house. My mother and I would spend our afternoons in the living room watching adulterers and blackmailers scheme, while the heroic characters struggled to overcome the obstacles these villains placed in front of them. And the amazing thing was, the good guys almost always did overcome. Sure, the villains might gain a temporary victory or two, and—if an actor decided to leave a show—a heroic character's plane might crash into the Pacific or something.

But the thing about soap operas—and this gets left out when people criticize them—is that virtue is always rewarded, and vice is always punished. If you cheat on your wife, she will eventually find out and leave you for your brother. If you fake your child's DNA test, the real father will eventually piece things together and raise the kid with his new, good-hearted wife. If you try to use your weather controlling device to freeze the entire town of Port Charles—and all of its citizens—in an effort to conquer the world as a power-mad dictator, the device will eventually be turned on you and you will wind up being frozen alive.

I think we can all learn a lot from that.

More important, though, it seems to me that soap operas offer a type of permanence, something you can count on. Actors may change, super-couples may ride off into the sunset, heroic characters may eventually be replaced by younger, hotter bodies that look better shirtless or in a bikini, but you can usually turn on a soap opera—any soap opera—and figure out what's going on pretty quickly. The good guys show their teeth when they smile; the bad guys smirk. The eyes of the villainess will dart about nervously, while the heroine's gaze stays fixed and constant. Storylines may end, but they're guaranteed to reappear a few years later. One character's evil twin will be taken care of, but someone else will have a doppelganger soon enough; the popular couple will face a grave threat to their relationship, but they'll emerge stronger than ever; the character who dies will somehow come back, if he's charismatic enough to have left an impression on the viewers.

As I watched while chemotherapy devoured my cancer—along with the lining of my stomach and my hair follicles—I was struck by the feeling that these shows will go on forever. Many of them—*The Young and the Restless*, *Days of Our Lives*, *General Hospital*—started long before I was born, and will, presumably, continue long after I am gone.

As my condition deteriorated, my mother and I moved from our living room couch to the sterilized furniture of a hospital room (perhaps a dying room) in Ann Arbor. But those beautiful people still appeared on the glowing box, alternately pledging eternal love and planning corporate takeovers.

In that hospital room, handsome men made love to beautiful women, while I vomited up mouthfuls of bile, my intestines burned with painful diarrhea, and the lining of my mouth dried and cracked. Things got worse and worse for me, until, until . . .

Until, at the very last moment, a crack team of medical specialists arrived to administer one last, experimental treatment. Drs. Monica and Alan Quartermaine, Dr. Rick Weber, and Nurse Bobbie Spencer arrived from Port Charles' General Hospital; Dr. John Hudson and Dr. Jamie Frame were flown in from Bay City General; Dr. Ben Davidson came all the way from Llanview, Pennsylvania. "You'll be fine," Bobbie whispered to me as the doctors tried to work a miracle. Fighting back tears, she said, "I won't let you die."

"He's coding!" Ben exclaimed.

"No," Alan shouted as he worked above me. "I won't lose this one. Not him. Not him!"

"Don't you die on me," Monica pleaded. "Don't you die on me."

And suddenly, at the last possible moment, the machinery started beeping rhythmically.

"His cancer!" Jamie exclaimed. "It's going into remission!"

"It's a miracle," John replied, clenching his jaw.

Okay. That's not exactly how it happened, but that's close enough. There wasn't actually a beeping machine, but my doctors did work diligently, and I survived as a result of their efforts. My continued survival—it'll be six years this December—could indeed be considered miraculous, considering how close to cancellation the days of *my* life actually came.

These days, I find soap operas comforting. Cars blow up, pregnancies are faked, lies get told, and people are shot. But none of it is surprising. No one has ever watched a soap opera and said, "My God! I can't believe that happened!" No one's life has ever been changed by something he or she saw on a daytime drama.

This, I think, is why Emily is so surprised by my fascination with these shows. We both study literature for a living, and we both believe in the transformative power of art. We have long conversations about how the works of Montaigne, Shakespeare, Beethoven, Andy Warhol, Joan Didion, David Lynch, and Tobias Wolff challenge our perceptions, and provide for an enlightened understanding of the world. And we both turn up our noses at movies and television shows that pander or simplify—particularly when they seem to aspire to profundity.

But I still love soap operas. They don't pretend to have any amount of depth, as shows like *E.R.* or *The West Wing* attempt to. The most they can offer is predictability and stability. In a world where wars get launched for dubious reasons, where my livelihood may be threatened by a fickle state legislature's cutbacks in education, and where a 21-year-old is forced to realize that his life can—and will—be snuffed out, probably without much notice, that type of predictability can feel like divine intervention.

I often wish that life were more like a soap opera. It's not that I need more melodrama in my life—I had quite enough six years ago—but their simplified world seems easier to live in. For example, several months ago, when my grandmother died, Emily and I had a conversation about our future, and I had to tell her—as gently as I could—that I will die much sooner than she will; my medical history guarantees it. I will die before her; I will leave her alone. "I want you to be happy," I promised her. "Even when I'm gone."

It was hard for us both, but it was something that had to be said. I didn't feel that we could commit till death do us part until we had discussed what exactly that might mean. I was afraid that she was unaware of the risks, that my own positive attitude and goofy charm might have given her the impression that there was nothing to be scared of, in terms of my cancer and the chances for a relapse or damage from long-term side-effects of treatment.

It turned out I needn't have worried. She tearfully assured me that she understood the risks, the likelihood that she would go on without me someday. That getting married means that, when the relationship ends, rather than divide up the CDs and the books, one person buries the other in the ground. She put her face against my chest and cried, and I reminded her that we are both in perfect health, and would likely live for a long, long time.

And I wished that life were a soap opera. I wished that, instead of sitting on the couch offering weak reassurances, I could lift her up in my arms, kiss her neck, chin, and lips, and tell her, with certainty, that things would always be good.

"There's never anything for you to worry about, ever again. When I'm thoughtless or cruel, it's not me; it's my evil twin. If my plane goes down, my car blows up, my cancer comes back, or for some other reason you have to order my headstone, don't despair. It's okay. I will be back, a few years later, in a dramatic, triumphant return. Love never dies, and nor will I."

But since life isn't a soap opera, I just kept my arm around her shoulders and kissed the top of her head until it was time to go to sleep.

In the Hospital

David Lehman

*I*n the hospital there was time
to read to dream to act
to read Freud's dream book on his couch
and how his best thoughts came to him
in the hospital during
World War I for example when
he invented a new way of opening
a vein while sitting in front of
a typewriter the wound
survived him but in the hospital
he knew only the words glory
and honor and country
rhymed with story
and malheur and the country
matters Hamlet lauded
in Ophelia's lap when mad
or pretending to be mad
and Denmark wasn't a prison
or brothel it was a hospital

How Suffering Goes

Melisa Cahnmann-Taylor

I sit. The ache in my calves and ankles is severe.
I watch the monkey scratch my mother's head. Mother says
she has a headache. The monkey is laughing.
She says she has a sharp pain in her eardrum where the monkey
has pinned his long pink finger and stuck out his tongue.

From the far right corner of the room someone sneezes. I hear it.
A car engine, a cough. There are needles in my toes.
The Insight Meditation leader says to name your feelings.
I had car rides with my mother in mind. Naming
and holding herself one part at a time. She punctuated silence
with *stomach, stomach, stomach* and *neck, neck, neck*.

An abbreviated story of two failed marriages and a childhood
of bandages. Self pity like a cool, wet rag pressed to her forehead.
The meditation leader says it's best to catch the pain early,
when the unpleasant sensation arises, to come back to breath.

I am in the car with her and the unpleasant sensation arises.
I remember her beached body under afternoon blankets and bottles
of prescriptions willing to concede she was *sick, sick, sick*. The leader
says to name feelings three times before we scratch an itch, lift
a numb leg, or brush a stray hair from our face.

I sit in the car and say: *pain* again and again. Still it's there
where my face is *aversion* and *suffering* in the side-view mirror.
We climb stairs to our destination, and she cries
three times about her knees. Her chant is a haunt that echoes
from closets of old clothes, old minds

like old monkeys, always moving, scratching, knocking on glass.
I hear them. Their laughter, a group of girls running through
the apartment hallway. Rain falling over the porch. A change in light.
A small tremble of breath across the upper lip,
again and again and again.

Postoperative Care

Arlene Eager

Glad to be alive,
I look in mirrors
with detachment
I study my seams.
My belly looks like
a garment taken in
by a tailor's apprentice,
the crazy one
he had to fire.

Midnight in the Alzheimer's Suite

Floyd Skloot

*L*ost in the midnight stillness, my mother
rises to dress and begin another
chilly day. She crosses the moonlit floor.
There is too much silence beyond the door,
and a lack of good cheer, so she breaks
into song. But the coiling lyric snakes
back on itself and tangles in her throat.
She stops long enough to see a cloud float
along the hall, but somehow the cloud speaks
in the voice of the night nurse. Someone peeks
from a doorway. Now someone starts to moan,
someone else coughs and my mother's stray song
returns for a moment: *oh you belong
to me!* If the audience would quiet
down, she would remember. Opening night,
that's what this must be, and the curtain parts,
and the spotlight is on, the music starts,
but there is too much movement, too much noise,
yet she cannot stop, must maintain her poise,
smile and keep on singing. Then it must be
over because the night nurse is there, she
embraces my mother and leads her back
offstage, whispering, bringing down the dark
again. Tired, but pleased with her last set,
my mother lies down for a well-earned rest.

Flu Shot

David Watts

S HE STANDS IN MY EXAMINING ROOM UNABLE TO SIT, PACING, THEN stopping tensely, as if paralyzed by the urge to pace. Three times she has made this appointment, three times a no-show. My secretary raised her eyebrow when she came in. But I have nothing to say.

Now her eyes touch and glide, touch and glide over me like the scan of an electron microscope, programmed for the penetrating search.

I fetch the vaccine, rend the silver packet for its sterile pledget, swab the red nipple of the rubber disc at the top, then plunge and withdraw just the right 0.5 cc. amount. I have anticipated this visit.

I ask if she's ready. She says yes. And now the killed virus I inject into the dense fibrils of her shoulder will evoke from the rangy lymphocytes their molecules of protection. She winces, turns to go, then turns back.

Why did he have to die? And as she says this, her body gives a little seizure-like lurch. Couldn't you have prevented it?

I gather the detritus I've left behind: the silver crimps of packet walls torn open, the needle guard, the soiled pledget with its spot of blood in the center, the dangerous needle I will place in the red plastic carton marked hazardous. I remember his last office exam: 62 years old, healthy. A few small problems with his cholesterol medications that we focused on. As a part of his general check-up I might have ordered a screening sigmoidoscopy. I did not. In my ear I can hear the admonitions of hospital lawyers cautioning me not to say too much. Don't commit yourself, they might say. And I feel— what is it?—something like the shame of being caught doing something wrong. But in the cavity of that humiliation, finally exposed, I feel no desire to waffle or dodge. She deserves better than that.

Yes, I say. The cancer might have been prevented. And then there is just she and I and the truth in the room.

Strange, she says. All those years with you and with the doctor before you, nobody ever recommended a sigmoidoscopy. If that had been done the year before, would you have caught the cancer in time?

The detritus has been removed. The needle is in its safe place. I have no urge to fidget in the face of her question.

It's possible, I say, if it were still a polyp. Or if it hadn't spread too far. And I realize that though this was true, it is a manner of deflection. I am drawn to return to the unadorned answer. It's possible, I say. It's possible it could have been prevented.

She is silent.

I am silent.

She waits. I have no one. No children, no family. He was all I had.

I nod.

She reaches for her overcoat.

You'll probably have to do something about this or let it go, I say. All this hurt will come to no good.

I would never do anything, she says. I like you. I think you are a good doctor. I want—I think I want—to continue to come and see you, but it will be hard.

I'm sorry, I say. And I want you to know that I believe you should do what you need to do even if it means...

No, no. Well, maybe. I don't know.

She leaves. And returns for her flu shot the following year, and the year after, never mentioning her husband, and then, eventually, for her own screening sigmoidoscopy, well in advance of its time, a request I honor like an obedient pharmacist filling the unusual prescription, knowing it is too early, but conscious of the fear she is facing, conscious of the forgiveness she brings, coming to me for the help I might give, the test that might have saved her husband.

The City of Light

Sandy Suminski

*P*ARIS HAS BEEN PULLING ME; THIS VOLUPTUOUS MYTH HAS CONSPIRED with my unrecognized bipolar chemistry, my havoc-wrecked body clock, and my weary spirit to bring me here. It begins with my first shower.

My friend Ann has decided to go sightseeing for the day and I've declined, wanting to explore on my own. I'm in the shower for a very long time, and when I step out the steam hangs in the air. One of my legs is clean-shaven, extremely so; my skin has never felt cleaner or smoother. It is miraculously new skin. The steam has been hanging in the air now for an unnaturally long time; a miracle is occurring. I take things slowly, methodically, in exact inversion to the thoughts and images rushing through my mind. I am filled with wonder over my skin. I sit down on the toilet and gaze at my feet. They are moist from the shower and the perpetual mist. The skin starts to redden, each foot creating half of a heart that becomes whole when I place them together side by side. The heart begins to swell and beat red, then the upper left lobe breaks off. This smaller fragment turns white with death as I realize that it's Jesus communicating to me about His love and sacrifice. The heart fades away as stigmata appear on both feet. They don't actually bleed, but the vessels redden in a pattern of dark blood trickling down the arches. They heal and the heart returns whole, throbbing bright red. I am not afraid; I am filled with awe.

I linger in the bright white golden glow of the mist, crippled and stunned by this majestic occurrence. I am suddenly compelled to go outside for a walk. I toss on some clothes, a denim shirt from the Gap. Jesus stands in the Gap for us. I am wearing "For Joseph" jeans. Joseph, Jesus's earthly father. My shoes are a pair of black heeled mules whose label bears a crown; I am divine royalty.

I'm walking quickly towards the Seine. I am suddenly aware of being not necessarily at the center of the world, but being in the simultaneous center of everything. I see that every point in the world is an axis, that everything intricately turns on itself in elaborate interconnection like a million whirling spinning jacks, each shooting electrons, every point click-click-clicking and spinning in a harmonious square dance, the Virginia Reel times a million in circular formations. I am not the catalyst, rather it has always been going on and only now can I see it, only now have I been let in on the secret.

I see all the cog-like symbols and signs and wonder how much of it I can possibly take in, all of this gorgeously ordered information, the universe as one giant system of timed traffic lights. *Click* comes the man with the dog down the street, *click* passes the bird, *click* comes the waiter, *click* the cloud passes over the sun and cues the bus and now comes the taxi as the woman in the red skirt trades curtsies with the red scarf in the window and the dog at the café table laughs and the street clown twirls his cane to the beat, two three, one, two, three then *switch* I enter dipping and weaving through the flow of the feet on the pavement as *click* the man pulls on a jacket and *sweep* the woman lifts the newspaper then *crack* go the butcher's knuckles then *pbe-bpeep* goes the car's auto door lock and then *zweep* the sign says stop and I wait and *rush* goes the traffic, the leaves wave "hooray!" then *click* "come!" says the sign and I cross the street to the bridge that crosses the river.

The sparkling breathing rushing fresh river is lined with the rippling leaves of the trees full of light and the wind. Jesus starts talking to me in the voice of Manfred, the German doctor I'd met earlier in the trip. Manfred. Man-friend. Friend of man, like Jesus. He asks how I'm enjoying my birthday trip. It is easy, strolling talk, like that between long-separated friends who've met at last, like pen pals. And from now on we'll never be apart and I see that this is how it was always meant to be.

As we approach the opposite shore, glinting sculptures beckon us. I walk between the sculptures in their park as Sunday families play among them, unaware of their significance. Tall, slender silver pieces with moving parts that spin in the softest breeze and flash against the sun. A stone mosaic in the shape of a crown grounds the largest of them to the walkway. They flip and spin and move together, enmeshing with the wind and the elements, apart and above mere civilization, secret devices of communication planted amid normalcy as agents for the union of the physical and the spiritual. I am at home among them.

I sit and look out on the Seine. It is the most real I have ever felt. Only in this intense light can I truly now live. Yet I realize the price of this—a certain isolation from the merely earthbound, which I will, from now on, somehow have to manage. As I look out on the river, I notice how it splits around the point of an island. It forms the forked path of a peace sign, and the island is the pivot point. It is peace. Like the name of our hotel, Hotel de Paix. Three sections of a peace sign like the holy trinity. I have just turned thirty. It is three days after my thirtieth birthday here in the third city of my trip. This is peace. This is the Point of Peace.

I am terribly lost, terribly distraught. And I've hurt Jesus. He shows me, on a small side street when we are walking back to the other side of the river. I am floating, feeling glory, then suddenly humbled by the sight of a picture of Jesus in a small shop window. His hands pull aside his garment to reveal a burning, glowing heart, pierced with pain. I look away, down to the cobblestones. They undulate below me in heaving groans of sorrow. This is my folly—this is His sadness—that all my life I've looked straight past him to God and don't I know it's *He* whom I should look to for understanding, for love? I have broken His heart.

* * *

I walk past a movie poster, filled with men, that is posted on a kiosk. The names of past boyfriends, past mistakes, leap from the credits below. One of the men in the background of the poster glares at me with damning eyes, alive. He hisses.

The people in the street see me in my damp hair and high heels and they whisper. I left my money at the hotel, so not only am I lost, I am poor. I enter an elegant cheese shop gleaming with marble and ask the ladies there for help and they look at me with disgust and turn me away. Only Sammy, like my name Sandy, helps me. He is working at the produce stand next door. "Pommes Des Terre" says the sign, fruit of the earth, back to the earth, back to simplicity; give up your worldly objects and fine clothes and beautiful shops; turn back to those connected with the earth, who walk the earth and work the earth, as you walk the earth, as Jesus walked the earth. Only Sammy helps me. He gives me money for a taxi and helps me find the address of my hotel. When the taxi delivers me to the hotel, I leave my fancy worldly crown shoes on the floor of the cab. I walk the earth, barefoot, back to my room.

I rush to the bathroom to wash out my mouth. I brush my teeth and spit out dirt. I keep rinsing my mouth, and dirt keeps pouring out. I take another shower. I hear noises in the room. I open the door and there is Satan. A hotel maid is in the room with eyes pulsating deep, black and evil. They are windows to Hell itself. I scream her out of the room and demand she empty her pockets and laundry bin. She will not check the laundry bin. Still only in the raincoat I've grabbed to cover my nakedness, I run into the hall and yell for anyone to help me. A handsome young Russian named Nikolai comes down the hall.

He is about my age, tall and strong with perfect masculine features and slightly tousled reddish hair. He speaks no English, but is earnestly dedicated to understanding me in spite of all language barriers. I pull out my pocket notebook and try communicating with him through drawings. He understands. The doors of our minds have now opened to each other. What is language? Everything has opened today.

Once I sort things out with the hotel manager, Nikolai comes back and invites me for tea in the room of his traveling companion. Viktor is about twenty years older than Nikolai and a very Russian-looking Russian, with a stern expression and robust complexion. Viktor speaks about ten words of English. Each of the three of us speaks perhaps fifteen words of French. We draw, we gesture, somehow we communicate. This primitive cobbling together of symbols thrills me. I'm convinced I've been called to create a new language.

I learn that Nikolai and Viktor are professors at a university in Minsk. Minsk, like my nickname in high school, Minsk, short for Suminski. They are professors of political science. I show them how, as an advertising writer, I type on a computer to write scripts to sell cheese and shampoo.

The room is long and narrow, with high ceilings. There is a single bed against the wall and a small round table where we have tea. Right behind us, next to the bathroom, is a little hot plate warming a teapot. Most of the time, Viktor stands at the window, smoking, looking out at the sunny Paris after-noon, fiddling with the shutters, controlling the light that enters the room. The room becomes a cool, dark sanctuary against the sun and noise and dirt of the city. Viktor looks out the window, turning frequently, then less and less so, to join us in communication. Below, Nikolai and I sit across from each other. He on the bed and I on a chair next to the table. Our knees are almost touching. We lean in with each word and drawing and gesticulation until our most powerful communication is our nearness. Viktor recedes fur-ther and further from the circle, standing by as a sentry to guard this most holy meeting. Viktor, like victory, stands and looks off in the direction of the Arc de Triomphe, from the Hôtel de Paix, the hotel of peace, in the Bastille, incarceration, then mad freedom. Nikolai and I kiss.

The kiss is passionate. The sex is not. He insists I stay on the bottom and any move I make to be more active is distasteful to him. But it seems to move him deeply. All the while Viktor keeps his sentry at the window, staring out. After we're done, Nikolai goes to the bathroom and then leaves, motioning that he'll be back. On the way out, he offers me the condom packet as a memento. It's a small silver foil square with the word "Flirt" on it and some shiny red lips. I decline.

I don't understand why he's left or where he's gone. I ask Viktor to explain. He says something to me about Nikolai very much wanting chil-dren, and when the child-creating act is not for that purpose, he becomes very sad.

When Nikolai returns twenty minutes later, we leave. He apparently has another room on a higher floor and we must go through several doors and a split-staircase entrance to another part of the hotel to get there. It's very con-fusing. I feel lost.

Earlier, when the hotel manager had helped me with the business with the maid, he'd asked to look down my shirt at my breasts and I showed him sure why not. Now I feel he is watching us or following us and this is why we must go through all these doors and there are phones ringing from the rooms that follow us along our path and he, the manager, is now very angry that I am with Nikolai and not with him. And the truth of it is that Nikolai is God. Not actually God, but the representation of God, just as Manfred's voice is the representation of Jesus, and they are both here on this earth at this time to play out this drama of the divine trinity with me. And the Holy Spirit comes variously in the guises of Viktor or the hotel manager or Sammy as facilitator. And what is so amazing today, right now, that just as this morning Jesus revealed to me the lifelong error of my ways in looking straight past him to God, he has granted me this gift, this audience with

God. And God, sequestered from a fallen world even as his son is an ambassador to it, deigns to share this one earthly moment of human love.

In Nikolai's room, we lie down on top of the bed covers and hold each other silently in holy and forbidden bliss.

The phone rings. Fearing the hotel manager, I won't let him answer it. It rings again. And again. Tired of not answering, Nikolai picks up the phone and hands it to me. It's Ann. The holy audience has ended, as it was always meant to.

I begin to leave and Nikolai doesn't understand why. He tries to make arrangements to meet me later but I make no promises. He asks for my passport and jots down my information. We kiss. I leave to face the maze of hallways.

I wander, go in and out of different doors, up and down sets of stairs. I hear Ann calling my name. I call back, but I can't find her in the maze. More calling, more doorways, more stairs. At once her voice is below me, next it is above me. Hallways and doorways and stairs pile up in front of me like blocks, until finally, there's Ann. I rush up and hug her.

I tell her about my afternoon, about Nikolai and that I am very afraid, that the hotel manager is trying to get me. Though we are not scheduled to leave for two more days, Ann says it's time to go back to Chicago. The reality of the situation has passed out of my hands for the moment, and now I have a role to play, and Ann has one, too, and she says it is time for us to go back to Chicago, so I agree.

She goes to the hotel office to arrange our early departure, as I pack. Fearing the hotel manager's retribution, I bring everything I own with me into the bathroom, including the large painting I bought in Prague. I close the door and sit on the toilet surrounded by all my earthly belongings and wait for her to return.

Once we've gotten a taxi and have loaded everything in, I start telling Ann about Nikolai and the hotel manager and she asks me to please just be quiet. I am quiet but she can't stop what's going on in my head. I am in another world now, floating high above the confines of the world to which Ann belongs, where I used to live, too. As we drive out of Paris the web of communications only grows denser and richer as all of the street signs and traffic signals and changes in shadow and sunlight speak to me, giving me their messages, celebrating my arrival to their world while bidding me a fond *a bientôt*. As we merge onto the highway toward the airport I'm quiet as instructed, but rapture and wonder and occasional small laughter continue to pass across my face as the light within me and outside me intersects and recedes, intersects and recedes. I look up at the clouds; they form the shapes of cartoon characters. Some of them laugh for me. Only one or two are menacing. My face radiates glowing, burning, and glorious white light. I can feel it.

Bellevue

Julia Alvarez

My mother used to say that she'd end up
at Bellevue if we didn't all behave.
In the old country when we disobeyed,
she'd drop us off at the cloistered carmelites
and ring the bell and drive away. We sobbed
until the little lay nun led us in
to where a waiting sister, whose veiled face
we never saw, spoke to us through a grate
about the fourth commandment, telling us
how Jesus obeyed His mother and He was God.

In New York, Mother changed her tack and used
the threat of a mental breakdown to control
four runaway tempers, four strong-willed girls,
four of her own unruly selves who grew
unrulier in this land of the free.
I still remember how she would pretend
to call admissions, pack her suitcase up
with nothing but a toothbrush, showercap.
I'm going to Bellevue, do what you want!
She'd bang the front door, rush out to the car.

Who knows where she went on her hour off?
She needed to get away from her crazy girls,
who wanted lives she had raised them not to want.
So many tempting things in this new world,
so many young girls on their own, so many boys
with hands where hands did not belong!
Of course, she wanted to go to Bellevue
where the world was safe, the grates familiar,
the howling not unlike her stifled sobs
as she drove around and around our block.

Shaking the Dead Geranium

Harriet Rzetelny

*I*WAS SITTING IN MY OFFICE STARING AT A COLUMN OF TRAVEL EXPENSES when the call came in.

"This is Marushka." Hearing her voice on the phone for the first time, it sounded harsher than I remembered it. "You'd better come. Your brother's very bad."

My stomach lurched. "What happened? What did he do?"

"Just come."

I closed my eyes and took a deep breath. Then I went into Ellen's office and said, "I have to go. It's Ben."

Ellen is a dynamic-looking blond who, at forty, is only a few years older than I. She owns the small but successful consulting firm where I work as her executive assistant. She shot me a look full of questions she knew better than to ask, and said, "Keep me posted, Molly."

Ellen's willingness to let me go when Ben needs me is the main reason I work for her. In return, she gets an efficient, college-educated person who comes in early, stays late, and is willing to work for far less money than she's worth. In the beginning Ellen would invite me out for drinks and was full of curiosity and well-meaning advice. But I've gotten very good at evading people's attempts at friendship. There are so many things I can't talk about, I've learned over the years that it's not worth even getting started, no matter how well-meaning people may be.

The last time I'd seen Ben was two weeks ago. I'd gone to check up on him as I do regularly, especially during these times when his mind loses its mooring and he stops taking care of himself. I'd let myself into his tiny two-room apartment and walked through the cramped kitchen into the bedroom-cum-living room. He was stretched out on the daybed with his back to me and his head on Marushka's voluminous skirt. Marushka, a widow with several grown children, must have once been quite beautiful. She was sitting propped up against the wall, her face framed by a mane of rust-colored hair, like an edging of autumn foliage around a crumbled bouquet. Her neon-purple blouse was open and he had one of her still magnificent breasts in his mouth. Our eyes met; hers were full of defiance. I guess she thought I wouldn't approve.

Marushka was one of a large tribe of Gypsies who lived on the first floor in my brother's Lower East Side tenement building. She was usually out on the stoop when I visited him, and occasionally we passed the time of day. I had never seen her talking to Ben, so I was quite taken aback when I walked in on them. I didn't know why I thought Ben's mental illness had wiped out his sexuality along with his ability to balance a checkbook. I also didn't know how she'd gotten past his pervasive mistrust of people that kept him so isolated, I being the exception. But I was grateful he had a connection with somebody, anybody other than me, and that he was getting at least a modicum of pleasure in life.

Ben was eight years older than I, tall, with hair that curled tightly around his head and a hawk's nose always poking into something. When we were younger, Ben had been my friend and protector, my buffer against the world. But that was before the illness began ravaging his brain. Back then, the spotlight of my mother's love had focused on him, the brilliant son; she had little to spare for me, the quiet child, nor for my father who had finally stopped coming home. I kept hoping she would discover in my secret self something unique and special to love; it never seemed to happen. She died ten years ago from lung cancer, still mourning the son she'd lost, hardly aware of the daughter who sat dutifully at her bedside.

Ben was dazzling and fierce. He fought my fights for me and taught me how to look beyond the surface and see beauty. I adored him. By age sixteen, he'd won awards for his poetry and a full scholarship to Emory College. By the end of his eighteenth year, he'd had his first psychotic episode: convinced that my mother was sucking the life fluids out of his brain, he went after her with a bread knife. By thirty he'd been hospitalized three more times. He was now forty-three. He never graduated from Emory. He never held a job, published a book, fathered a child. Between hospitalizations, he lived as a minimally functional, oddly brilliant, but always reclusive eccentric; a kind of semi-life made possible by modern pharmacology.

All the men in my life—with the exception of my brother—come and go rather quickly. One of the men I dated briefly once asked me where it was written that I had to be Ben's mother. I couldn't explain it to him; my feelings about Ben are only a part of the story. I was the one who called 911 that first time, when Ben tried to attack our mother. I was ten years old. After the police wrestled him to the ground, and he was chained up like a dog and carried, kicking and screaming, out of the house, I locked myself in my room and cried for so long that the doctor had to give me a sedative. After that, my mother faded away, little by little. Mostly I remember her hunched over the kitchen table, cigarette in hand, playing solitaire. The doctors diagnosed it as depression, but I knew what it really was. The one person she truly loved had hated her so much he tried to kill her. She never forgave me for making that call, for telling the world about it, although I don't know what she thought I should have done. That day—my brother's murderous attack and my revelation of it—lives in me like a jagged wound that won't heal. It was so gut-wrenching for both Ben and me that it forged an unbreakable bond between us and he's come to rely on me as the one constant in his otherwise erratic existence.

After that, I took a vow of silence. I'd betrayed my mother once and I would never do it again. Throughout my childhood, I found it easier to say nothing than to possibly say the wrong thing. And her death hasn't changed that fact. It's left me isolated and pretty much alone, except for Ben.

Fortunately, I truly like my brother and enjoy spending time with him—when he's not actively psychotic. His mind is like an old suit of once-excellent quality, that has been patched and re-patched with odd pieces of material that don't quite go together, kind of like a crazy quilt. Some people might think it belongs in the rag bin. But not me. I've always been drawn to the odd and unusual in life, and I find Ben's mind endlessly fascinating.

The next time I tried to visit Ben, after the primal scene I'd witnessed between him and Marushka the week prior, he was out, probably on one of his long rambling walks. I knocked on Marushka's door and thanked her for being kind to him. Her eyes flashed, undoubtedly at my choice of words. I realized then how hungry I was for someone I could talk to about him, someone who already knew him and needed no explanations, and who might understand what it means to love him. But she didn't have much to say, or if she did, she wasn't going to share it with me. I scribbled down my phone numbers and told Marushka to call if Ben ever got to be too much for her. She took the scrap of paper and tucked it somewhere inside her blouse.

I wasn't really surprised when she called. It's always just a matter of time. But it was the tone of her voice that made the decision for me. I took a deep breath and dialed Tony Baretti. He was the intake social worker at Marble Heights, the small, private hospital in suburban Westchester where I decided to hospitalize Ben, if and when the time came. Tony had been the speaker at one of the many group meetings for families of the mentally ill I'd attended over the years, and we became friends—sort of. At least I trusted him. And he did share my amusement at some of Ben's wilder delusions—such as the one in which he decoded a fortune cookie that told him Billy Collins, our little known Poet Laureate at the time, had blown up the World Trade Center to prove that poetry still mattered. Also, Tony doesn't tell me I need to get a life.

As I waited for Tony to answer, I began to hope that I was over-reacting. Maybe I had read the signs wrong. Or Marushka had. Or something. But I didn't want a repeat of that terrible first time. Or the ones after that. Altogether, Ben had been hospitalized five times. Each time he'd been taken by the police to a city psych ward. The last one was a horror show. The building looked like a fortress and the entranceway into the unit was through a dark, narrow corridor with filthy, scuffed walls that smelled like the public bathroom in a bus station. Someone—one of the inmates, I supposed, but it could easily have been one of the staff—kept screaming "I'm not gonna take it anymore" over and over again, until I was afraid I'd start screaming myself.

Tony finally answered and I explained the situation.

"Perhaps he needs to have his medication adjusted," Tony said. "Has anyone been following him in aftercare?"

"Ben's stopped taking his medication," I said. "The most recent one they gave him was fogging his brain out so much he insisted they were shooting guacamole in through his ears."

"Okay," Tony said, as though guacamole in the ears was a normal, everyday occurrence. "We'll get the paperwork started."

My resolve evaporated again. "Maybe he doesn't really need it yet. Maybe I should try to reach the psychiatrist at the aftercare center." But I didn't even know who the current psychiatrist was—they flitted in and out of the center like fireflies on a hot summer evening. The last one I'd met, who was gone now, had been a young, well-meaning Pakistani who viewed Ben's long, rambling discourses which were full of historical, philosophical, and poetic references as a symptom that needed to be extinguished by increased medication. He didn't understand that these discourses were all that remained of my brother's once fine mind; destroy them, and you leave him with nothing but his illness.

"Molly," Tony said gently. "I know this is hard for you." When I didn't say anything, he went on: "I wish you would talk to me a little more."

Oh Tony, I thought, sometimes I wish I could, too. But the habit of silence is so hard to break. The words just disappear off my tongue like snowflakes melting on my hand.

"Well," he sighed, "it will all be in the works if you decide to bring him here. But remember that this is a private hospital, which means *you'll* have to get him here. City cops won't bring him."

"I know, Tony. But Ben hates hospitals."

"It's a tough call, Molly. But if you let him go without help too long, it'll be worse for both of you." When I didn't respond he said, "Well, if you don't do it now and he gets really bad, you may just have to let the police take him in to one of the local hospitals. Maybe after he's stabilized a little, we can have him transferred."

No, I thought, the images of his earlier commitments in the city hospitals flashing through my mind like scenes from the theater of the damned. Not that. "I'm going over there now. I'll let you know."

A thin afternoon sun filtered down from the autumn sky as I climbed the stairs from the subway and turned the corner onto Ben's block. The rundown tenements lining the street leaned into each other like a row of old alkies trying to hold each other up. Marushka stood outside the building waiting for me, her arms hugging her chest. She wore a thin sweater over a low-cut blouse, and was shivering a little in the chilly air.

"Couple days ago, he came into my apartment and started accusing me of being the devil's harlot," she began before I could get my mouth open. "When I yelled at him to get out, he got wild, threw a lamp at the wall, made a hole as big as a soup bowl. Now why does he want to go and do that?" Two curved lines, like parentheses, appeared above her eyes. "Niclos had to chase him out with a baseball bat." Niclos was the brother of her dead husband. "He's been locked in his bedroom since then. He won't come out or answer me. I don't think he's eaten. I hear him mumbling through the door. Niclos is up there."

"Oh, Marushka, I'm so sorry," I said, wishing I could just shake some sense into my crazy brother. "Of course, I'll pay for any damages."

I'd genuinely wanted to take Ben's relationship with Marushka as a sign that maybe the slow, steady decline of the past couple of months was miraculously reversing. I was always ready for a miracle. I searched for positive indications in his behavior and appearance. Failing that, I pounced on his daily horoscope for possible portents in the stars. I didn't want to have to hospitalize him.

Now I was angry at him; despite his fear and terror of hospitals, he was incapable of staying at least minimally sane. And I was angry at myself because my love was inadequate to protect him, as if love could be equated with some amulet—a cross, a Star of David, a crystal. I knew this was irrational. Chemicals were exploding in his brain and blowing out his synapses. The power or potency of my love couldn't change that. But I felt as though it should.

I called Ellen on my cell phone to tell her I'd need the rest of the day off, and then started up the stairs with Marushka following me. The door to Ben's apartment was open and Niclos was standing in the kitchen, baseball bat in hand. He watched us come in without saying anything, but his face clearly said, "You're both crazier than he is for not putting him away a long time ago." Remembering the force of Ben's terror-driven rages, I was just grateful Niclos was there.

The bedroom door was closed. I knocked gently and tried to turn the knob. It was locked. "Ben, it's me, Molly. Please let me in."

Nothing.

I knocked again, a little harder. "I'm worried about you, Ben. I just want to see that you're okay."

"The voices are coming in through the walls." Ben's voice. "The walls are the stalls where they keep the words. Molly it's not. It's the words of the voices that say Molly, but how can you know evil from the mouth of a sister?"

My heart, hammering in my chest, pounded so loud I wondered if Ben could hear it through the door. "Ben, I don't want you to be hurt. Please just open the door."

"I can only live by dying."

"He's been talking a lot about dying," Marushka whispered sharply. I hadn't even realized she was behind me. I could see this was no easy decision for her, either. "Niclos can break the door down," she said, her voice catching a little. "Maybe you better call the police."

No. Not the police. "I'll be back soon," I said to Marushka and hurried down the stairs.

Instead of going home, turning off the phone and burrowing under the covers, which was what I felt like doing, I headed towards a car rental agency I'd noticed on the main street, a couple of blocks away. After signing what seemed like an endless number of papers, I picked up a car and drove back to my brother's building, pulling up in front of a no-parking sign. Two older black men sat on the next stoop arguing with each other and drinking wine out of a bag-wrapped bottle. They looked up as I got out of the car. The curtain in Marushka's first-floor window flicked, and in a moment she was out of her door and following me up the stairs. Niclos, still holding his baseball bat, sat on a chair in Ben's kitchen. Everything in the room was black, including the sink, the refrigerator, the stove, and the window—a kind of tenement Hades. Or the eternal midnight of a lost mind. The only spot of non-black was a dying geranium in a small green plastic pot on the windowsill, its drooping flowers the color of old, dried blood.

Midnight shakes the memory as a madman shakes a dead geranium. Who wrote that? My brother, the madman, was always flinging lines of poetry around as if they were perfectly reasonable explanations for his irrational behaviors. I took a yoga breath to calm the trickle of anxiety that always hit me in the stomach whenever I behaved in any way that might be an indication that I, too, could be crazy. I knocked on his bedroom door again. "Ben, it's me, Molly. Please let me in."

Nothing.

"So should I tell Niclos to break the door down?" Marushka whispered.

"No," I whispered back. "That would frighten him even more."

"So what are you gonna do?"

I thought for a minute. "There's a fire escape around back. Maybe I can get in that way and talk to him."

We retraced our steps down to the first floor. The hallway stank from old garbage and the unwashed bodies and stale urine of homeless people who used the stairwell for shelter. The back door leaned crazily on one hinge. I went out into a rear courtyard full of stained mattresses, abandoned furniture, and discarded food containers.

Ben lived on the third floor, which meant climbing up two flights. I wondered briefly whether the rusted, crumbling fire escape would hold me. Then I forced myself to think about the dozens of neighborhood burglars who used these fire escapes, quite successfully, as their personal accessways.

By the time I reached Ben's landing, I was filthy from the grime and flakes of rust. I wiped my hands on my skirt and looked in the window. Ben was sitting barefoot on the floor in half-lotus position, surrounded by burning candles, like someone about to be sacrificed in a primitive ritual. I was shocked at how old his body looked—stooped and scrawny—although it was only two weeks since I'd seen him last. When had his hair gotten so gray? He was dressed bizarrely—never a good sign—in a checked shirt and dirty striped pants. An old orange beach towel, patterned with a big starfish in the middle, was tied with a cord around his waist. He sat watching the door, so he didn't notice me out on the fire escape.

The wooden window frame was so rotted I could easily have removed it, but a metal gate covered the window. Without any real hope I pulled it and, wonder of wonders, it slid open; my paranoid brother had forgotten to lock it, another sign of his increasing derangement.

As I was attempting to slide the window frame out of its track, the glass suddenly came out in my hand and went tumbling down into the courtyard below. At the sound, Ben shot his head around, his face shiny with terror. We stared at each other, and for a moment I could see the scene through his eyes: some filthy apparition who had taken on the visage of his sister was trying to climb through his window to do God knows what to him.

I felt a quick stab of fear; after all, I knew full well what he was capable of. But, I reminded myself, in all the years of his madness, he'd never tried to hurt me. At least, not so far. I just had to convince him that I was who I said I was.

"Ben, it's me, Molly." I tried to smile. "I climbed up the fire escape because you wouldn't let me in. That's why I look so dirty." It sounded lame, even to me.

Ben yanked two candles off the floor where they had been attached by, I assumed, melted wax and sprang up to face me, a candle poised like a fiery sword in each hand.

"Ben," I said, trying to sound enticing and a little mischievous, "I have a car. Remember how much fun we used to have when Daddy would take us for car rides? Put down the candles and let's go for a ride."

"The lies shine through your evil eyes," he said, jabbing the candles toward me.

I should have known that lying to him was not the way to go—he was too smart. I searched my mind frantically for some way to calm his fears and convince him of who I was.

"Do you remember the song you used to sing to me when I was a little girl and would have nightmares?" I began to sing:

> Rock-a-bye, don't you cry
> Go to sleepy little baby.
> When you wake, you shall have
> All the pretty little horses.

The candles wavered and he thrust his head forward to peer at me, as if a tiny flicker of recognition might have penetrated his psychotic haze. Not because I knew the words to the childhood song—an evil imposter would certainly know that—but because I sang it in the atonal, off-key voice that he'd always teased me about.

"Ben, I want to get you some help, so you'll be safe." My voice sounded eerie and hollow to me, like a ghostly echo in empty house. "I'm worried about you and I love you. You're my big brother." As I said the words, I suddenly felt them so powerfully that my body began to shake. I grabbed the sill so I wouldn't fall off the fire escape.

By now, he was staring at me intently. I knew him so well that I could almost read what was going on inside his head, or I thought I could. He was desperately trying to hang onto whatever ability he still had to distinguish what was actually happening from the jumble of voices in his head that were telling him crazy things. Was I really Molly? It must have been terrifying for him not to know.

"Ben, if you just come with me, I promise not to let anyone hurt you." I hoped it was a promise I could keep. "If you won't come, I'm going to have to call for help."

I never got to find out whether or not he understood me because at that moment a blob of hot wax plopped onto his bare foot.

He jumped back and dropped the candle. As he did, the candle in his other hand went out. I climbed in through the window, murmuring in a gentle voice, the way you would calm a frightened animal.

"Come on, Ben," I said. "Come with me. You can take your candles with you if you want. Marushka and Niclos are in the kitchen. I'm going to tell them to move away." The words from one of the Family Skills group meetings I'd attended flooded into my mind: approach gently, but with assurance. Tell the patient exactly what you are going to do before you do it.

Ben's eyes were full of suspicion as he tried to plot the plots that would protect him from a world he could no longer cope with. But after stooping down to pick up an unlighted candle, he straightened up and moved in my direction. I knew better than to try and touch him. I simply murmured in the same calm voice, "That's right, Ben. Come with me." I could almost smell the fear radiating from him, but I could also see the lines of strain running down his face. He wasn't nineteen anymore; perhaps he was just too tired to fight anymore. Whatever it was, he let me lead him to the bedroom door.

I unlocked it, gave him a reassuring smile and said, "Marushka and Niclos, please move back. My brother and I are going out for a little while." I shot a quick glance over my shoulder. Ben was watching Niclos and the baseball bat like a child watching the closet where he knows the bogeyman is hiding. Continuing to murmur reassurances at him, I stood back and allowed him to precede me through the kitchen door and out of the apartment.

When we got to the stairs he stopped. I waved him on, wondering if he would bolt. But where could he go? Niclos and the baseball bat were in back of him. He started down the stairs with me trailing along behind him like the rear guard. We must have made a strange spectacle—Ben in his bare feet and his ridiculous beach towel, still clutching his candle, and I, the filthy betrayer with bits of rust clinging to her clothes. I was still trying to convince myself that I was doing the right thing, still telling myself that he would never hurt me. All the while I continued to murmur calm reassurances at him.

Everything was moving along until we got onto the street. I don't know whether Ben had planned all along that it would be easier to get away from me once we were out of the apartment, or whether the noise and activity on the street were just too much for him, but he gave a yell and started running up the block, his skinny legs pumping as hard as they could under the flapping of his orange beach towel.

Like a fool, I stood there and shouted, "Ben, come back!"

"Girl." One of the two elderly wine drinkers looked up at me with a big grin on his face. "Man don' want you? Find one who do. Plenty of us around." The other old man laughed, slapped his bony knee, shook his head and said, "You listen to my man here. He be tellin' you the truth. Don't be chasin' him up no street. Ain't dignified."

But chase him I did. I heard a motor jump into life behind me. A black Lincoln driven by one of Marushka's sons roared past me. Marushka had her family in readiness.

With a screech of brakes, the car pulled up with one wheel on the sidewalk in front of Ben just as he got to the corner, effectively cutting him off. The kid jumped out of the car and rounded the corner so that Ben couldn't run that way. With me coming up behind him, he didn't have too many options besides jabbing at the air with his candle.

Once again, I approached him with gentle reassurance. I guess he decided I was the better of the choices he had right then, because he let me lead him back to the rental car. But his eyes watched me with low cunning.

I heard a *vroom-vroom* and saw the taillights of the Lincoln, now in reverse, pass me as it backed up the block. For a moment, the fear came back and I had a flash of Ben going after my mother with the knife. I pushed the thought away. He won't hurt you. He's never hurt you. He's your brother Ben.

I unlocked the passenger side door of the rental car and told Ben to get in, wondering what I would do if he didn't. To my surprise and relief, he did. I dragged the seat belt over the faded starfish on his beach towel and buckled it as one would do for a small child. My clever brother, however, had been making his plans. By the time I got around the car to get into the driver's seat, he was out of his seat belt, had jerked the door open and was sprinting down the block.

"Some women just can't take no hint." The voice of the first wine drinker.

"Yeah," the reply came. "What you think so turrible 'bout her that he got to get away so badly, can't even wait to put his shoes on?"

The kid was out of the Lincoln and about to tackle Ben by the time I pulled the car around again. Once my big brother would've fought like the devil, but I guess he truly was burning out as he got older, because after I gestured the kid away and said, "Ben, you have to get into the car," he stopped resisting and climbed back into the car. Maybe he'd decided I was really Molly after all.

The trip to Marble Heights went surprisingly smoothly, but my fear was that Ben would open his door and run out into the parkway and there would be no way I could save him.

He didn't. What he did was look at me out of accusing eyes and ramble on about "lying sister words" and a plague of dead rats, dead frogs, and dead vermin that he claimed were crawling around in his body.

As soon as we pulled up in front of the hospital, the accusation in his eyes turned to alarm. Ben had never seen Marble Heights before, and I hadn't mentioned where we were going, but he could spot a mental hospital at one hundred paces anywhere on this earth.

"You go in," he said, shrinking back from me with one of those rare moments of lucidity that are completely unexplainable. "I'll wait here for you."

I coaxed him into the building and murmured reassurances while Tony and the admitting psychiatrist were being paged.

Marble Heights didn't look like your typical psych hospital. It was a low, gray-stoned structure that sat on a beautifully landscaped lawn surrounded by trees and bushes in early autumn shades of yellow and burnished red. The lobby and reception area were carpeted in forest green; the walls were beige with matching green and rose trim and were hung with attractive paintings. Upholstered chairs and low tables with magazines added to the air of quiet normality. But you couldn't fool Ben. His crafty eyes darted around the room as if he was ferreting out the fiend that he knew was hiding behind one of the walls.

Tony was good with Ben, asking his questions in a calm, friendly way and simply accepting Ben's strange and disjointed answers. I'd just begun to relax when a short, dried-up looking man in a starched white coat entered the room.

"I'm Dr. Koster," he said.

His eyes had the slightly bulging look of a toad, and he tended to punctuate his sentences with a clearing of his throat which, unfortunately, gave him a slightly accusatory tone.

"Ehrm! And you are Benjamin Lewin?" he asked. A look of alarm came into Ben's eyes and he stood mute. Not a good start.

"And you are...?" he asked me. I looked down at my filthy, disheveled self and wondered if he was determining whether I, too, was there to be admitted.

Before I could answer, he glanced at the papers in his hands and said, "Molly Lewin, sister."

"I apologize for my appearance," I said. "I had to climb up a fire escape."

He nodded as if this was a perfectly normal occurrence in the lives of his patients' families. Then he turned to my brother. "Hello, Ben," he said in his nasal voice. "I have some questions I'd like to ask you, okay?"

He paused for a minute, but when Ben didn't answer, he went on with the standard list of questions. "When were you born?"

I knew the doctor was trying to assess Ben's mental state, but I also knew how suspicious it would sound to Ben. My brother didn't want people to know the date of his birth because he thought it allowed them to have power over him.

"Birth...the birth of vipers in the raging torrents of the mind battles." As Ben spoke he watched Dr. Koster through narrowed eyes and began to swing his arms back and forth, a sure sign of his increasing agitation.

Dr. Koster stepped back and took a very visible breath. Then he cleared his throat again. "Do you know why you are here?"

Another bad question, one I could have kicked myself for not realizing he would ask. This was, after all, supposed to be a voluntary commitment. Come on Ben, I thought desperately, say something at least halfway normal. But even as the thought crystallized in my brain, I felt a sinking feeling in the pit of my stomach.

Ben stared back at the doctor and started to mutter. He hunched his shoulders forward and his hands became fists. Swinging them, he began to pace around the floor. This interview was going downhill fast.

Dr. Koster turned to Tony and said, "I think we're going to need some back-up to get the patient down on the unit. I'm going to radio for Code Team."

He pulled a small walkie-talkie out of his pocket and spoke into it. Looking back at it later, I realized that the black box with its strange, crackling noises was probably the match that set off the tinderbox. It fed right into Ben's paranoid delusions. Behind me, the Admissions people began to clear out the area: receptionist, visitors, other staff were all being herded away. The hospital was readying itself for the violent outburst from my brother.

And my brother did not disappoint them. He was emitting small, growling noises from his throat which sounded eerily similar to the ones made by the good doctor. The hair on his head stood straight up, as if his terror had set off voltages of electricity in his body which were charging through him like lightning.

As Dr. Koster backed away, he beckoned Tony and me in the direction of the door. "Why don't you take Ms. Lewin into your office?"

Tony took me firmly by the arm. "Come on, Molly. The Crisis Team is trained to deal with Ben. It would just upset you to see this."

"Mind vermin, rats and frogs!" Ben shouted, making a lunge for the walls, banging and kicking against them in his rage to get out. Since he had no shoes on, I was afraid he would break his toes. I wanted to run over and put my arms around him and stop him from destroying himself yet again. But I knew he was over the edge, and that I had become part of the hostile, terrifying world against which he had to protect himself. And there was nothing, nothing, I could do about it.

"Patient rapidly decompensating." Dr. Koster continued talking into the walkie-talkie as he hurriedly left the area. "Seventy-five milligrams of Thorazine, I.M...." The rest was garbled as Tony pulled me away. Four burly men were running up the hall towards us pulling a Reeves stretcher on which to secure the dangerous patient. The Four Horsemen of the Apocalypse. A woman with a stethoscope around her neck trailed after them.

I collapsed into a chair in Tony's office as he ran back to help the staff begin an involuntary commitment of my brother. What I'd been hoping to avoid was happening after all. I had been through enough psych hospitals to know that even in the most private and presentable of them, there would be no carpets and pictures on the walls of the room where they would be taking Ben now. He would be wrapped in a "camisole"—a pretty word for a straitjacket. There would be a mattress on the floor and four bare walls. And he would be alone, screaming in rage at his demons and his terror, until the medication took hold.

The lights were off in the room and I sat staring into space, enveloped in a world of gray fog, hearing and feeling nothing. Gradually I became aware of the slanted rays of light filtering in through the window. For a long time I sat exhausted, demolished, watching the late afternoon sun mute the autumn sprays of yellows and reds on the birches and maples dotting the lawn. The autumnal equinox was past and the sun was low in the sky. On the windowsill in Tony's office stood three pots of geraniums, past their prime, but obviously well-tended. *Midnight shakes the memory as a madman shakes a dead geranium.*

I shuddered, as if a cold wind had suddenly blown through the room. A small pulse started up in the corner of my eye, like the slow beat of a dying heart. Behind the geraniums the leaves drifted lazily down from the trees as if they had all the time in the world to reach the ground. It struck me then that my brother was in the midst of a long, slow autumn, and it wouldn't be long before winter settled in for good. I started to cry, first in giant, gulping sobs and then more quietly, the tears running down my face and off my chin like water dripping from the trees after a heavy rain.

Tony walked into the office. He handed me tissues, waiting patiently until I sopped up my face. The medication had taken hold, he told me. Ben was quiet now and I could visit him. Did I want Tony to come with me?

I said no, I'd be okay. I'd done this lots of times before. Tony told me where to find Ben, and asked me again if I was okay. I nodded. After giving me another quick look, he grabbed his jacket and left.

I sat for a while longer, thinking about my brother. I knew exactly what I would see when I visited him. They would have transferred him to a bed with raised sides, like a metallic crib. He would still be in restraints, his wrists tied to the sides of the bed, and he'd be lying on his back staring up at the ceiling out of vacant eyes. The quirky, sly, fearful, funny, suspicious guardian of the last remnants of his mind—my brother—would not be in that room. My heart was breaking from the loss of him.

You can't bring back the geraniums once they're dead, no matter how much you shake them. Suddenly I saw my life laid out before me, like a diorama in the planetarium: Ben in his crazy paranoid brilliance was the sun, and I was the moon, revolving slowly around him, living in his reflection, with no light of my own. I was thirty-five years old, and the most important relationship I had in my life was with a brother who, on his best days, believed that mad King Ludwig of Bavaria spoke to him through the drainpipe in his sink. Shouldn't I have more than this? Did I still owe my mother the vow of silence I'd taken as a very little girl? Even nuns, dedicated to a life of service, have been known to leave the convent. For a long time I just sat, watching the shadows on the lawn lengthen and flatten until it became so dark I could no longer distinguish their shapes.

Finally I took a deep breath, got up, and walked out into the hall. My heart still felt as though it was breaking, but whether for Ben or for myself I couldn't say. After the gloom of Tony's office, the sudden glare of the fluorescent lights made me blink. It was late and the area was deserted. I should check on Ben and see how he's doing, I thought. But my legs felt heavy, too tired to move. Another poetry fragment, another one of my brother's favorites, came into my mind. *Over the tumbled graves, about the chapel / There is the empty chapel, only the wind's home.* Whichever way I looked, I faced an empty room. Not knowing where to go or what to do, I pulled my coat tightly around my shoulders and walked out into the night.

Thanksgiving: Visiting My Brother on the Ward

Peter Schmitt

*B*ehind the thick, crosshatched glass of the cruiser,
  my brother, back for the holiday, breathes
more slowly. A phalanx of uniforms
cloaks the open door, murmuring to him
where he sits. The carving knife is somewhere
out of reach, none of us so much as scratched.
Inside, the bound bird cools on the butcher block.

Later that night I move through many doors, each
locking behind me, each inlaid with the same
heavy glass as the squad car. Through the last
I see my brother's face, fixed as on a graph,
ordinate, abscissa. When he sees mine
he retreats from the common room to his own,
a bare cell he shares with a narrow bed.

He will not speak to me, at first. His fingers
move in perpetual chafe, like a mantis,
his lifelong nervous habit, the edges
of a newspaper shredded on the bed.
This time, his eyes say, we have betrayed him
as never before. This time, he seems to say,
he cannot find a way to forgive us.

At last I persuade him to join the others
finishing the meal, their plastic utensils
working the meat, their low voices broken
by stray whoops of inappropriate laughter.
We sit, though, in a separating silence,
my brother's hand already eroding
his napkin, eyes distant with medication.

If only he were faithful to himself
and took his daily pills... But what is the point
of such a constancy when the world itself

has so profoundly turned away? As tonight
I will leave him here, leave all of them here,
the psychotics and depressives, my brother,
to lie on their beds and stare at their ceilings,

and I know that for at least this visit
he will not come home, where our parents now sit
in darkness, their faces streaked and damp. And when
we drive him to the airport, an unmarked
police car following as an escort,
he might be a foreign dignitary
bearing developments back to his country...

For now, though, it is just two brothers, beneath
a glaring bulb. The expression on his face
would ask, *Have you gotten what you came for?*
And again I have no answer for him.
But there, at the floor of the bed, all around
the room, are crumbs of paper, as if he were
leaving a trail by which he might be found.

Overblown

Hal Sirowitz

What's hopeful about
  your problems, my
therapist said, is they're
just typical anxieties.
You don't have any I
haven't seen before. But
what concerns me is your habit
of enlarging them until they
become almost unrecognizable.
Luckily, you have me to recognize them.
I'm familiar with all your anxieties.
I can tell which ones are coming.
In a few moments we're about to be
revisited by your worry of taking up
too much of my time. But that's
why I schedule my patients
one after the other, so they can't.

Songs from the Black Chair

Charles Barber

A THOUSAND MEN EACH YEAR SIT IN THE BLACK CHAIR NEXT TO MY DESK. I am a mental health worker at the Bellevue Men's Shelter. These men are between 18 and 80 years old, usually black or Hispanic, usually with a psychiatric problem and a substance abuse history (crack, heroin, and alcohol), often with a forensic history (usually released from prison that day), and quite often with a major medical illness.

At some point during the interview with these men, I get around to the questions: "Are you hearing voices?" "Have you ever seen things that other people didn't see?" "Have you ever tried to hurt yourself?" A few times a month I hear responses like, "I thought about jumping in front of the subway," or "I can't tell you whether I'm going to hurt myself or not." Or I am shown wrists that have recently been cut, or bellies and limbs and necks with long scars. At that point, I calmly tell my client in the black chair that I think they need to go to the hospital in order to be safe. Almost always they agree without complaint.

I call 911 and write a note addressed to the Attending Psychiatrist, Bellevue Hospital Emergency Room, detailing my observations and my assessment of their mental status. Fortunately, the hospital is only one block away. Within ten minutes, the police and EMT's arrive. "Good luck," I always say to the men as they are taken away. To my amazement, they almost always say "thank you."

The staff and I are instructed to classify the men we see into one or more of the following official categories of disability or distress, as promulgated by the New York City Department of Mental Health:

SPMI [seriously and persistently mentally ill]
MICA [mentally ill chemical abuser]
Axis II [personality disordered]
Medical
Forensic [released from jail or prison]
Over 60 Years Old
Mentally Retarded/Developmentally Disabled

Immigration
Physically Disabled
Vocational
Domestic

It's a nice list of nice bureaucratic categories, but it means nothing, really. I've created my own list. These, I've learned in my two years of sitting next to the black chair, are the far more descriptive and pertinent categories:

The Travelers and the Wanderers
Guided by Voices
Vietnam Vets
Waylaid tourists, usually recently robbed
Criminals
"No English" and no papers
Various persons destroyed by alcohol, crack, heroin or some other substance
Alzheimer's patients and other victims of senility
Manic in America
People who choose to live underground and in darkness
The truly weird, for whom we can find no category that fits

But all this I keep to myself. I sit at the computer and duly check off the city's official list.

In truth, they are *all* travelers and wanderers. They come from Jamaica, Georgia, Colombia, Kuwait, Poughkeepsie, Italy, Oregon, Taiwan, Wyoming, Poland, Detroit, and Bosnia. And it is Manhattan—not Brooklyn, Queens, or the Bronx—that they want to come to.

Countless times I've found myself in the following exchange:

"*Brooklyn*! That's all the beds you got tonight! *Just Brooklyn*! Shit!!"

"Yes, that's the only place that there are beds tonight."

"Shit. I ain't going to no *fucking Brooklyn*! You sure that's it? Nothing in Midtown, or maybe the Wall Street area?"

"No. That's it. All we have is the shelter in Bedford Stuyvesant."

"Fuck, if that's all you got, I'm leaving. I gotta be in Manhattan, man. Maybe I'll come back tomorrow night."

And they get up and leave, back to the streets or park or wherever.

I've learned that homeless people prefer to be in Manhattan, just like everybody else. At first I was indignant—these people are *choosy* about where they're going to stay? But I thought about it, and realized the sources of their livelihood, such as they are, are far more lucrative in Manhattan. Panhandling goes much better in Times Square than in Far Rockaway. The men tell me that if you do it respectfully, and look decrepit enough—but not so decrepit as to scare people—you can make between twenty and eighty dollars an hour panhandling in a prime location in Midtown. They may be mentally ill, but they're not crazy: it is Manhattan that the voices tell them to go to, and not, for example, Staten Island.

"So, why did you come to New York . . . that is, Manhattan?" I almost always ask the people in the black chair.

Some of the answers I've heard over the years:

"Because Jesus told me to."

"Because someone was trying to kill me in Las Vegas."

"Because where I was staying they only let you stay in chairs, and I want a bed."

"Because when I got out of prison in Baltimore, I read that Giuliani had brought the crime rate down so I decided to return to New York."

"Because this is where the bus brought me."

"Because I can get better health insurance here than in Puerto Rico."

"Because I can't find my way home. I left my house on Walters Street in the Bronx ten years ago and I can't find my way back."

"Because I'm John the Baptist—a truth serum given to me at Trenton State Hospital in 1969 proves it—and can you get me a bed near the St. John the Divine Cathedral because I have to go there and tell them I've arrived."

"Who said I was in New York?"

"Because when I was working on the chicken farm in Georgia last week, a voice told me to come here."

"Because I always wanted to see the Empire State Building."

"Because the people here are less crappy here than they are in Florida."

"To compete in a Karate championship."

"Because I want to open a blacksmith shop in Queens."

"Because my so-called best friend stole everything I had."

"Because I always wanted to go where no one would find me."

But even among the travelers, there are the prodigious and ceaseless ones, the ones who are committed to motion as a way of life. Traveling around America—which in this case means visiting one shelter and soup kitchen and church basement and subway station and bus depot and abandoned building after another—is their profession. In the warmer weather, and even in the colder weather, a lot of them camp out, whether it is in Central Park, the woods of upstate New York, or the beaches of California. It doesn't seem to matter really where they are, as long as they can move away from it quickly. A lot of them are actually offered permanent or semi-permanent lodging— half-way houses, community residences, and the like—and they invariably turn them down, to move on to the next city. Their destinations are much like those featured in travel advertisements: New Orleans, Las Vegas, L.A., Hawaii, and New York.

There is a specific look to the professional travelers, instantly identifiable; there is almost invariably a certain healthy and woodsy glow about them, no matter how high or drunk or crazy they are. They tend to have long straggly beards and wild eyes and dusty backpacks and sleeping bags. In the summer, they wear as little as possible, and sport dark tans, and hair bleached blond from the sun; in the winter, they wear layers of sweaters and their cheeks are rosy pink. They are usually lean. A few of them, self-consciously or not, adopt the romantic trappings of the old hoboes; one night, a man plaintively played a harmonica in the waiting room, entertaining his fellow wayfarers. Once I walked past Central Park and saw a group of hoboes sitting around and roasting marshmallows at a campfire, like something out of *The Treasure of the Sierra Madre.* The parallel universe of Central Park West and its fabulously expensive French restaurants, celebrity apartment houses, and endless medical—and typically psychiatrists'—offices, was just thirty feet away.

The shelter staff came to me one night, exasperated, saying there was a white guy somewhere in the building who had been eluding them for hours. The shelter workers had been trying to take his photograph and his fingerprints —submission of which is required to enter the shelter—but this person, whoever he was, had been stealthily moving from chair to chair and room to room all night long. In other words, he was a traveler even within the confines of the shelter.

"Where is he now?" I asked the security officer.

"In the bathroom—we think," he said, and led me there.

The bathroom was a predictably dingy, rank affair, distinguished only by the curious fact that the dividers between the stalls were made of marble, with beautiful gray swirling patterns. On the marble was written, in magic marker: "Bums never have a nice day," and "Suck my homeless dick." The man sitting on the toilet had tousled reddish blond hair—lots of it—and a thick beard. He was rocking back and forth on the toilet, with his pants on. He looked, I thought, like a psychotic Viking.

"Excuse me," I said to the psychotic Viking on the toilet. "Would you mind going to have your photograph taken in the screening room? And when you're done, would you mind coming to my office down the hall?"

"Oh yeah, sure, sure, sure," he replied.

And I left there as quickly as possible, thinking that I had done my job for the night and that I would never see him again. But when I turned around a moment later, back in the office, the Viking was sitting quietly in the black chair next to me.

"What's your name?" I said.

"Leif," he said. It sounded Nordic or Danish or something, confirming my Viking theory. He probably would have been a great Viking, I thought; a few thousand years ago his wildness would have served him well. As I was contemplating this, he began doing a kind of dance in the chair—arms and legs and hands and neck bouncing away, all of them flowing to different beats—and embarked upon this rushed monologue:

"In case you wanted to know, I'm Norwegian, Ukrainian, Swedish, Danish, Irish," he began. "I've lived in Florida, Hawaii, Alaska, Oklahoma, all over Canada, and Cheyenne, Wyoming, but mainly I grew up in South Jersey.

"The malls there suck, you know? I slept under a car last night. I was in jail for a rape I didn't commit of my half-sister. What else do you need to know?"

"Have you been in the shelter system before?" I asked.

He looked directly at me. "I need help. I need help! No one's helping me after I got out of detox," he said, and as he said it I noticed for the first time that his breath stank of liquor. "I didn't have nowhere to go. That's why I'm here. But not for long. Thinking of going back to Cheyenne. That was my favorite place. Happy there. That's where I got convicted of the rape I didn't commit of my half-sister"—I noticed he used the exact same phrasing to describe the alleged crime—"and I want to clear my record. Clear my name!"

"Have you been in the hospital recently?" I said.

"I have very bad nerves," he said, not exactly to me, but, it seemed, to something beyond me—a general statement to or about the world. "*Very bad nerves*," he added for emphasis. "You know who helped me? The nuns helped me. The nuns were fucking *awesome!*" he shouted to the ceiling, and then smiled broadly.

"Do you take any medications?" I asked.

"I brought it all on myself," he said. "Nobody's fault but mine." He stood up and produced from his pockets a series of smudged and torn-up hospital papers. The papers said that he had been in a hospital in Maine, and before that a detox in Providence, and before that a psychiatric hospital in Kansas, and before that a rehab in Oregon, and that he had severe diabetes, a seizure disorder, and bipolar disorder. The medical diagnoses surprised me: he had that healthy look of the travelers, that unworried and rural look that made it seem that, at a moment's notice, he could set off on a fifty mile hike in the woods.

Suddenly he lurched forward in the chair and thirty syringes fell to the floor. They seemed to have fallen out of his red sweatshirt, but from where exactly, I couldn't tell. He picked up the syringes, one after the other, and stuffed them into his pockets and what seemed like a pouch in his sweatshirt. As he picked up the needles, he kept on talking, not stopping for a second, about nuns, disputed rapes, Cheyenne, and bad malls in Jersey. At one point he took out a thick wad of bills, again from some mysterious place on his person. "See this!" he said, waving the money close to my face. "It's chump change, and it means nothing," he said, and immediately went back to picking up syringes. Finally he was done, and I got him to sit down again.

"When was the last time you took your meds?" I said.

"The physical shit is nothing. It's a test, a test! I wish I woulda died after the seizure, I wish I woulda never woken up. Then I wouldn't have to deal with the *hassle*. The physical shit is nothing. It's a test by Jesus Christ, a test by God to see how much you can take. The only thing, man, is I gotta keep moving. Death is being static, dude."

I was about to ask him more about tests by Jesus Christ and hassles and nuns, because I liked him and was interested, when he jumped again—as if electrically shocked by something in the chair—and ran out of the room. By the time I got out into the hallway, he was gone. A few syringes had fallen out of his pocket and were bouncing on the hard shiny floor of the shelter. Fortuitously, the security officer hadn't been at his post, and Leif, the psychotic Viking, the adventurer, was able to leave undetected, free to re-enter his world.

Last January I was asked by the security staff to go to the entrance of the shelter to assess a problem case, some guy in a wheelchair. Security would not let him into the building because he didn't have papers to prove that he was medically cleared to enter the shelter system. When I saw the guy in the strangely ornate entry foyer (it has marble floors and a hand-painted ceiling), I knew why. He was in a wheelchair, had no arms and no legs, and wore a loose cotton hospital gown that was open to the waist, revealing a still oozing stomach wound. He was distressingly thin, had black curly hair, and looked Italian. A teddy bear was in his lap. A sparkly heart-shaped balloon, with the words "I love you" printed on it in expansive letters, was attached by a string to the back of his wheelchair. "I'm Richie Vecchio," he said, smiling at me. He appeared to be in no distress.

I wheeled him down the dark hall to the waiting room. The security guards looked at us dubiously—all they knew was that he wasn't authorized to come in. I looked closely at his hospital bracelet. It indicated that he had been an inpatient at Bellevue for the last four months.

"Which unit?" I said.

"16-North," Richie said. "I was in an accident," he added, happily.

I told him that they wouldn't let him into the shelter unless he got a form from a doctor stating that he was medically stable.

"You better go back to the hospital. Then you can come back here," I said.

"Oh, I'm not going back there," he said. "I've been there for four months."

As a legal matter, I said, they weren't going to let him in.

"Oh that's okay," he said, reassuring me. "I'm just happy to be out of the hospital."

"Did you sign yourself out?" I asked.

"Yup," he said with satisfaction.

"But where will you go?"

"Oh, I'll figure something out," he said.

I started in on the legalese I'd been trained with: "It is, of course, your right to leave the hospital, but I strongly urge you . . ." when he interrupted me.

"It's all right, man, I'm just happy to be free," Richie said. "But I was wondering, do you think you could let me stay in the building long enough so I could recharge my wheelchair? The batteries don't last long in the cold."

He had spotted the electrical outlet in the corner. He pushed his chin down into his chest, and engaged a button on a metal plate that lay on his collarbone. The wheelchair whirred forward.

"See the cord in the back? Could you plug it in?" he said. "It takes about forty five minutes to charge up," he said happily. I plugged in the cord.

"Is your wound okay?"

"Yeah," he said, looking down at it as if for the first time. "Jeez," he observed. "I guess it is oozing a little."

"What happened to you anyway?" I said.

"Lost my limbs in a motorcycle accident. My fault," he said. "I'm an addict. Heroin, coke, everything. Now I'm just on methadone, and a ton of medications." It was as if he were talking about varieties of ice cream.

He directed me to a pouch on the back of his wheelchair. In it was a hospital paper stating he had hepatitis and HIV, along with fifteen bottles of medications.

"Are you *sure* you don't want to go back to the hospital?"

"No way!" he said almost violently. "Four months is enough. They won't take me back anyway."

"Let me see if I can find anything for you," I said.

There are, in New York City, strange entities called "drop-in centers." They are intended to work as adjuncts to the city shelter system. They are meant to assist those who aren't medically cleared or not deemed "appropriate" for the regular system. That is, they serve those poor souls who have been rejected even by the New York City shelter system. The drop-in centers are usually a couple of basement rooms in a church somewhere. Contractually they are not allowed to provide beds. The clients of the drop-in centers sit on chairs all night long.

I called the four drop-in centers in Manhattan. I made my usual mistake, which is to ask if they have beds.

"You mean *chairs*," said an annoyed voice at the first drop-in center.

"Yes, chairs," I said.

"No chairs," the voice replied, and hung up the phone.

I called the next drop-in center. "Do you have any...er...slots?"

"You mean chairs," said the voice. "No, didn't you notice? It's cold outside. No chairs." Click.

No chairs were to be had at the other drop-in centers either.

When I returned to the waiting room there were three more clients waiting. Normally the guys in the waiting room never talk to one another, sitting silently with their heads down, avoiding eye contact at all costs. But these three were all talking to Richie. One was sharing his sandwich with him, and another was reading him a story from the newspaper.

"I'm sorry, I couldn't find anything for you. Do you have any money?" I said.

"One hundred and thirty dollars," said Richie, precisely.

The last resort for shelter were the Bowery flophouses. They charged $10 a night for a "room" with walls made of chicken wire. I called The Palace,

The Rio, The Sunshine; none of them had beds. "It's cold outside," the voices on the other end of the line said.

My last call was to the YMCA, ten blocks away.

"We have a bed, but you gotta get here quick," said the attendant.

"How much?"

"Sixty five dollars a night." In New York, even the Y's are expensive.

"Oh that's fine," Richie said, after I told him about the Y. "I'll go there."

"But you only have enough for two nights."

"It's okay. Don't worry, man. I'll figure something out." He depressed his chin, engaged the button and rolled out of the waiting room. "See you guys later. Thanks a lot," he said, nodding to his instant friends.

I left the shelter with Richie. Smoke or steam or whatever it is that emanates from the city's innards was billowing up through an open manhole to the surface of First Avenue. The wind had picked up and it must have been twenty degrees. Richie told me he had a jacket in his pouch. I pulled out the flimsy windbreaker and settled it over his shoulders. All he had on underneath was the cotton hospital gown.

I pointed him in the direction of the McBurney YMCA. "Do you think the wheelchair will make it?"

"We'll see," he said, laughing. "It looks like it's downhill." He headed out onto the street.

Then he stopped and shouted back to me. "See ya later! Thanks a lot, Charlie, I mean it. I really appreciate everything you've done for me. You're a great social worker or doctor, or whatever you are."

Richie crossed First Avenue, nearly colliding with the M15 bus. He whirred unsteadily down one side of the avenue, in the precarious slip of pavement between the parked cars and the oncoming traffic. The last I saw of Richie was the back of his wheelchair, the heart-shaped balloon bouncing in the wind, as he cut through the cloud of steam escaping from the city's netherworld.

Homelessness doesn't stop on holidays, but it does slow down. I've worked most holidays at Bellevue: Independence Day, Thanksgiving, Christmas, Labor Day. I think even the clients know it's a little tough to be in a homeless shelter on Christmas, and they stay away.

I watched the millennium come in at the shelter, saw the digital clock turn to 12:00:01 am, 2000. Here at the shelter, nothing changed. No one celebrated. Homelessness in the new millennium seemed to be just about the same as it was in the last one.

But the holiday I'll always remember was last July 4th. The shelter, about fifty yards from the East River, is a great spot to watch the fireworks. The explosives are set off by Macy's in barges in the middle of the river. The city closes down the F.D.R. Drive for the night and the crowds arrive two or three hours before the display to get a good view. At Bellevue, we have a front-row view all to ourselves.

That night I watched the fireworks from the shelter waiting room. There was nobody there but me, and I looked down upon the vast, noisy crowds, nearly fifty yards thick, packed in behind police barricades on the streets. After watching the psychedelic explosions for half an hour, I returned to my office.

Out my window I could see the massive residential wing of the building. A hundred turn-of-the-century casement windows faced me across the garbage-strewn courtyard. As the fireworks continued, I noticed a few faces quietly, tentatively peering out of a few windows. At first everything was murky, but as the side of the building lit up for a few seconds in the startling pink or green or purple aftermath of the explosions, I could see that there were dozens and dozens of faces—almost all of them black—peeking out of the windows. It was like a delayed strobe: every twenty seconds or so, I could see those heads, each time lit with a different color. As I stared long enough, and my eyes adjusted to the strobe, I could read the expressions on the faces. They all wore the same expression, an odd look, one that I'd never seen before at the shelter, where most people try to be as numb as possible: it was an expression of shy longing, a wish to be a part of something that was unavailable to them. America, it seemed, was a party that they could observe, but not attend.

All of them, I thought, every single one of the residents of the black chair, wanted to embrace the pink and green and purple light, to merge into those streaming lights over Manhattan. All of them possessed songs, songs sung in the midst of despair—songs about mythical places like Cheyenne, or about bobbing red balloons, songs proclaiming there is something much greater out there somewhere, songs hopeful that perhaps somehow, some way, someday... In a moment, I realized how strangely and cruelly exhilarating, how terribly and punishingly great it is to spend my nights listening to songs from the black chair.

Psychotherapist at the Landfill

Lou Lipsitz

—for Bob Phillips

1—

On an early morning in my seventy-first year
   it is a mixed thing
      to come to the county landfill
and in the piercing yellow light inter
these scribbled notes of bewilderment,
attentiveness and odd, interminable hope.

To bury them among garbage heaps
and old appliances: one hundred twenty-two
boxes of records, manila folders
filled with my writing—
    forty years of dreams taken down
    forty years of dilemmas,
      visitations from the archetypal powers,
forty years of human beings
talking out loud to themselves and to me,
pages, an unbelievable accumulation now;
evidence of how we humans struggle and ruminate,
trying against so much training,
so much fear, to dig
through the long, heavy dark and raise the dead—
    accomplish the slow, uncertain resurrection
    of becoming ourselves.

Because I could not bear to have them shredded
I now carry the boxes out
amidst the debris and dust of the landfill
and lay them here thinking somehow
they will be left alone to decay and vanish
in their own time, decompose under the stars.

Only I am wrong.
The bulldozer appears so quickly;
snorting and shoving things aside
burying the pile in efficient sweeps of its yellow plow.
    Then they're gone, pushed under—
    the fine attunements, the record of all
    I was able to make sense from—

gone into the garbage
—forty years worth in forty seconds.
Instant burial!

2—

And then for a week
    I can't sleep in peace.
    I wake every morning
    and know something is wrong, unfinished.

And finally, I grasp it and go back.
I have the smudge stick with me this time
and the sage and fragrant cedar.
This time, I go up to the bulldozer,
silent, unattended now, and mark it
with my stick.
    This time, I create the fire
    and speak my makeshift
    native american/modern man
prayer:
    Commit these writings, these
    scribblings half understood, memories
    of spirit struggles, to the Great Mystery.
    May they find their place,
    a breath of our strange journey,
    often obscure to us, that nonetheless,
    we yearn to know.

The smoke rises and I think of the road
I have taken myself: seventy now,
retired detective of dreams.
A mixed thing to be here with prayers and endings.
My soul feels its damp exhausted
exhilaration—
    letting go of all that was healed
    and not healed—
my long initiation through the comradely, lonely,
stinging sweat lodge of the years.

The Caves of Lascaux

Miriam Karmel

*I*T ISN'T EASY BEING THE BEARER OF BAD NEWS. STILL, LAWR MARKS PRIDES himself on knowing which patients can handle the unadulterated truth, and which ones would prefer being left in the dark. He knows how to dole out information in increments, giving his patients time to process a new reality. He offers statistics only when asked, and he always tries to make the patient sitting in front of him feel as if she is the one the odds will favor. But when he broke the news to Nora Hill, he felt as green as he had the very first time he'd looked a woman in the eye and said, "You have breast cancer."

He wanted to tell her, "You should be out dancing the samba until the sun comes up." Instead, he informed her that her left breast would have to go.

He remembers the way her thick, black hair was pushed back with a simple tortoise shell headband. Other than a splash of red lipstick, her face was unsullied by makeup. To conceal such beauty would be a waste, and he was grateful that she seemed to know that.

Lawr won't easily forget the date, which was two years ago, and not just because it is recorded in a medical chart, or because on October 15, after nearly twenty years of practicing medicine, he lost his professional bearings. It happened also to be the day he drove right past Angie's Stems and Vines without stopping to pick up the primrose bouquet he'd ordered for his wife, Selma, for their eighteenth anniversary.

He remembered the flowers only after he walked through the front door, smelled rosemary and garlic in the air, and saw a bottle of champagne chilling in a silver ice bucket. The table had been carefully laid out as only Selma, a gourmet caterer, could do. While she had been preparing a celebratory dinner, he'd been wondering whether Nora Hill was aware of how beautiful she looked without any makeup.

Lawr tiptoed back out the door and returned to Angie's to pick up the flowers, calling Selma from the car to say he'd been detained. He told himself that anybody could have forgotten, even the president of the Lincoln Park Hosta Society, even Dr. Green Thumb, as Selma calls him. Besides, hadn't he remembered that primrose, nearly impossible to get at this time of year, was Selma's favorite? But hard as he tried to picture his wife's pleasure as she arranged the bouquet in a crystal vase, he could only see Nora's face, hear the sound of her voice.

"I guess it's my turn now," Nora had said. Lawr kept a box of tissues handy for such occasions, but it was clear she wouldn't need them. Her posture remained erect; her hands stayed folded in her lap as she absorbed the news.

"Nobody should have a turn at forty-three," he'd wanted to say, but experience had taught him that silence was often better than rushing to fill the void.

It wasn't until Nora said, "So now what do we do?" that he sensed he was in trouble. Never before had the first person plural sounded so much like foreplay. This wasn't the first time that Lawr had to confront a patient with such grim news, but it was the first time he stumbled over his own desire. That's when his eyes moved to her left hand, searching for a band of gold. So there is a husband, he thought.

The truth was, in a case like Nora's there wasn't much that could be done, and he had to press his hand into his thigh to keep his foot from shaking. Then he tried to calmly lay out the game plan, which included a six-month course of chemotherapy, followed by radiation treatments. Lawr didn't say that within six weeks she'd have no need for the tortoise shell headband, and that by eight, she would have to pencil in the arch of her eyebrow, the one he so desperately wanted to touch. The rosy color would drain from her cheeks, and dark hollows would appear beneath her eyes. Her blood would thin and her appetite would wane, though food was the very thing she would need the most. After all that, she would die anyway.

Now, two years have passed, and she's still alive. But as Lawr taps on the examining room door, he knows that Nora Hill won't live long enough to acquire cataracts or osteoporosis or any of the other ordinary diseases of aging.

Nora is perched on the table, draped in a flimsy paper gown that rustles as she looks up. She looks good today. Her cheeks have color, though that could be a sign of nothing more than a few deft strokes with a makeup brush, something the hospital teaches, along with the artful tying of scarves.

Nora is a long way from needing the tortoise shell headband, yet enough hair has grown back that it looks deliberate, even chic. For a moment, Lawr fools himself into thinking that she has rounded a corner. When her hair grows long again, he will buy her the red velvet headband he saw on a mannequin in the window at Marshall Field's.

"*Bonjour!*" he booms. The greeting, which sounds hollow today, has become part of their routine ever since Nora announced that she was going to France. She and her husband had planned the trip when her cancer was in remission, and during checkups, while he palpated her remaining breast, searched for lumps under her armpits and around her clavicle, she talked about going to see the prehistoric cave drawings at Lascaux. There would be a side trip to Bilbao to the new museum everyone was talking about. "The one Frank Gehry designed," she'd explained. She planned to eat *foie gras* and walnuts. "The region is famous for walnuts, Dr. Marks. I bet you didn't know that."

By then, her flesh hung from her skeleton like a loose-fitting silk kimono. Still, when he warned her in his most authoritative voice to watch those calories, her eyes lit up, as if at last she had an ordinary health concern. But despite the remission, he knew she wouldn't have to watch her weight. He'd seen it before. The cancer was taking a time out, gearing up for its final assault.

"*Bonjour*," she croaks back. Her voice is weak, but he's glad to see that her toothy smile hasn't changed. How many times had he pictured her sinking those perfect teeth into a freshly picked apple? At what point had he imagined her transferring such affections to his lower lip? Was it before or after he'd met her husband?

William Hill, a quiet, gangly man, has never looked Lawr in the eye or questioned him about his wife's condition. When Nora reported that William had dropped out of the cancer center's support group, after just one visit, Lawr wanted to take her in his arms and console her. In a fatherly way, of course, though they were about the same age. Once in his arms, their lips would meet. No harm in a simple kiss. Then he thought of Selma. In all these years, he's never strayed.

Now Nora hands him a piece of paper. "What's this?" he asks.

"The trip is off," she replies.

"And this is some sort of proclamation?"

She attempts a smile. "I bought trip insurance. You have to tell them why I can't go."

He glances at the paper without reading it. What would he write? Patient is too weak to travel? Patient is dying?

He looks up and sees Nora's eyes fixed on him. They are as green as the hostas he propagates in his spare time. Eyes like hers were meant to feast upon the wonders of the world. This is a test, he thinks. You can lie to me, her eyes are saying. But you cannot lie to Lloyds of London.

"Why wouldn't you go?" he asks, as he returns the form. Only this time he avoids her gaze.

At lunch, Lawr runs into Jack Robinson in the hospital cafeteria. Jack is sitting alone wolfing down the remains of a cottage cheese and canned peach salad. Lawr looks at the cheeseburger and fries on his own tray and wonders if he can escape unnoticed to another table. He should be the one eating the fruit plate. Selma has been testing new recipes on him and it's beginning to show. Last night, after they made love, she gently tugged the roll of flesh around his waist. "Look, Lawr," she laughed, as if she were pleased in having produced a bit more of him. "Love handles." Then she kissed him there and said she would love him no matter what. He started to say he would always love her too, but stopped short and wondered what was happening to him.

Let Jack raise an eyebrow, Lawr thinks as he sits down. Today he needs the comfort of a cheeseburger, a balm to soothe the uneasy feeling that has settled over him.

There is something different about Jack. It isn't the starched white shirt with the monogrammed cuffs, or the expensive gold watch. There is an air about him. Rumors circulate from time to time. Stories involving nurses. Jack has the kind of bad boy reputation that follows some men through life.

"Going somewhere?" Jack leans over and taps the travel brochure on Lawr's tray.

"Oh, this." Lawr slides it across the table, but overshoots and it lands near Jack's feet. "Just something I found in the waiting room. Gives me ideas, though."

In fact, Lawr picked up the brochure on a day when he'd resolved to spend his lunch hour walking. He stopped at a travel agency, telling himself that he wanted to surprise Selma with plane tickets to some exotic destination for their twentieth anniversary. The truth is, they only spend two weeks every summer at an A-frame on the North Carolina coast. Lawr doesn't like sleeping in strange beds. And he doesn't like to be away from his plants for long.

Suddenly, he has a desire to blurt it all out, as if Jack were a priest, not a retinal surgeon. Lawr wants to ask Jack if he's ever fallen in love with a patient. "Not a nurse," Lawr would say. "Ten minutes in the linen closet with a woman who isn't your wife doesn't count." Instead he says, "Ever been there?"

"Where?" Jack pops the last of the peach in his mouth, then consults his watch.

"South of France. People go to see the caves."

"I've heard of those. Prehistoric, or so they say. Could be a hoax." Jack points to the brochure, to a picture of a bison painted on a cave wall.

"Hoax?" Lawr says, though now he sees that it's a crude rendering, like a child's crayon drawing. "Why would anyone want to do that?"

"Why do we do anything?" Jack shrugs. "Money."

Lawr hates Jack at that moment. "Love, too!" he blurts.

"Say what?"

"Love," Lawr insists. "People do things for love, you know."

Jack checks his watch again, then rises.

"Hey, Jack! One more question, before you go."

Jack starts to set down his tray, but seems to think better of it. "What's that?"

"Ever fall in love with a patient?"

Now Jack does set down his tray, as if the question demands all of his energy. "Against the rules," he says, his voice tinged with remorse.

"But it could happen? Right?"

"Anything could happen." Jack sounds impatient. "The sky could fall."

After lunch, Lawr's nurse greets him with a sigh and a nod toward the crowded waiting room. Ignoring her, he shuts his office door, slumps in his desk chair, and riffles through a pile of pink message slips without reading them.

He looks up at the closed door. The faithful await him. They are too trusting. They are too willing to follow his advice. They consume whatever he prescribes. Poison. That's what he offers, like some sicko who laces Milky Ways with arsenic at Halloween.

"Faker," he whispers, looking at his hands, which are beginning to shake. "Charlatan." If only his patients knew how little he understood, they would be rushing across the border for laetrile. "Go to Mexico!" he wants to shout. "Consult a faith healer. Try that shark cartilage they sell over the Internet."

Lawr reads the pink slips. Selma has called three times. He starts to dial the number, then puts down the phone. He picks it up again and dials Nora. He has dialed her number before, only this time he lets it ring.

If she picks up, he will apologize for lying. But did he really lie? Why shouldn't she go to France, to see the Caves of Lascaux? And why shouldn't he accompany her? The Queen of England travels with a personal physician. He imagines an entire team on alert, waiting to defend against the slightest fibrillation of the Queen's heart, the shallowest breath. He will do the same for Nora, only he will make it seem like a chance encounter.

He is about to hang up when Nora's voice apologizes for not being able to take the call. "We." He's sure she said, "we," the very word that first triggered his desire. He dials again. "I'm sorry we cannot take your call."

Had he really forgotten about the husband? Or was he deluded by his own fantasy that William Hill was dead, the victim of a botched mugging or a drive-by shooting? Lawr has even imagined the mourners whispering, clucking, reveling in the delicious irony of the situation: the dying wife attending the healthy husband's funeral.

There is a knock at the door. It's his nurse, once again using her head to indicate a packed waiting room. When she leaves, he calls Selma, who asks him to stop off for a loaf of bread on his way home. She launches into a lengthy explanation as to why she can't do it, only he isn't listening. Then he redials Nora's number, pleased to know that he can conjure the sound of her voice whenever he wants.

Lawr pecks Selma on the cheek and offers to run back out and pick up the bread.

"Don't bother," she says, returning his kiss. She smells good, like burned sugar and lemons.

"*No problema.* Honest," he says, raising his right hand. This may be the truest thing he's said all day, he thinks.

"*No problema,*" she protests. "I don't even know why I asked. There's plenty without it." She brushes a shock of hair off his forehead as she expresses concern for his day. She's letting him off the hook, though she called three times.

If only Selma knew that he had been too preoccupied with thoughts of France to remember a "silly old loaf of bread." If only she'd get angry. They could argue. He could storm out of the house. Then he could begin to build a case for taking a trip alone. A medical conference is what he has in mind.

Dinner is superb. Selma has prepared pumpkin soup, a new version of chicken marbella, and fennel salad with figs and oranges. He tells her the truth, that she could offer this meal to her clients and they will clamor for more. She tells him that the contents of a caterer friend's refrigerator is on the cover of *Chicago*, as part of a feature on the city's hottest caterers, a status that Selma aspires to as well. And she tells him that his mother called. "She wants us to visit. 'A week in Boca will do you good,' she said. And I said, 'You know Lawr doesn't like to travel.'"

He takes a sip of wine and clears his throat. How can he propose a trip now? But a medical conference is different. He will reassure her that he'd love to have her come along, but he understands this is her busy season.

Selma doesn't give him a chance. She wants to discuss his hosta. "I think I know why it's dying," she declares.

"Nothing is dying," he snaps.

"It is, Lawr. Don't you remember? You told me. Last week."

"You misunderstood. I said it *could* die, if I don't nurse it along." The truth is, it is dying, despite his best efforts. *Reversed*. It's a jokey name, given to the plant that seems to get smaller by the year. It's hard to germinate and even harder to keep alive. Selma knows it's his pride and joy. He refuses to admit that he can't make it grow.

"I stand corrected." She sighs, pushes the food around on her plate with a fork, a habit that drives him crazy, especially since she brings so little of it to her mouth. "In any event," she continues, "I think I know why it *could be* dying." Then she launches into a discussion of feng shui, her latest passion. She has already told him that according to feng shui, the proper placement of doors and windows, and even the arrangement of everyday household objects can bring health, wealth, and happiness. "Your plant is facing the wrong direction," she declares.

"That's ridiculous. Why don't you just stick to the cooking, and leave the ailing plants to me?" He drains the last of his wine, refills his glass, offers to fill hers, but she has already jumped up to clear the dishes. Her voice bristles as she tells him to stay put. Gone is the wife who forgave him for arriving home empty-handed.

Yet she's given him an opening. One pointed remark and the hurt on both sides will escalate, until he has his excuse to storm out the door. But he'd planned to head downstairs after dinner, to check on his seedlings, adjust the grow lights. Maybe he will even move the *Reversed* to a different part of the room.

He hears Selma humming as she clatters around the kitchen. She is incapable of holding a grudge, and he remembers how he loves her for that. Perhaps this is all I need, he thinks, as he pours the last of the wine. Even the love handles he's been fretting over don't seem so bad. Consider them ballast, he tells himself. Selma's cooking is keeping him grounded, on an even keel.

When Selma returns, she sets a picture-perfect dessert before him. "*Voila!*" she chirps.

"What have we here?" he asks, leaning toward it, as if to inhale a summer bouquet.

Selma shrugs and offers a close-lipped smile as she pierces the glazed surface with a silver knife. She will make him guess. She expects him to know the difference between a torte and a tart.

As he takes the first bite, her eyes are fixed on him, much as Nora's were when she tried to discern the truth about her condition. His feeling of contentment evaporates. He must say something now; a mere "delicious" won't suffice. If that's all he offers, Selma is likely to say, "The crust is a little on the tough side, don't you think?"

The dessert has a nutty taste, though he doesn't know what to call it. "You've outdone yourself, Selma," he says.

"You don't think it's too sweet?"

He imagines Nora sitting across from him in some cozy French bistro, unapologetically scraping the last crumbs of a walnut tart from her plate, telling him her plans to start baking when she returns home. She will joke about entering a bakeoff. "And I'll win!"

"I got the idea for the torte from the brochure I saw on your desk in the study," Selma says, breaking into Lawr's thoughts. "The one with the picture of the French caves. It said the region is home to an annual walnut festival. Then I was flipping through the latest *Bon Appetit* and *voila!* A recipe for walnut tart."

Lawr doesn't know if he can take one more *voila!* Is she taunting him? Is she letting him know that she can read his mind? The walnut tart now strikes him as a rebuke of sorts.

Of course she can't read his mind. But there she is, leaning across the table, saying, "Are you planning a trip, Lawr?" as she sticks her fork into his tart.

"A trip? What gave you that idea?"

"The brochure. With the caves. On your desk. I figured maybe you were planning something. Are you?"

He reaches across for her wine. He feels her eyes on him. She is waiting. He will tell the truth, but first he sips some wine. One more drop might drown out the reverberating sound of his own lies. *But why wouldn't you go? Medical conference. Nothing is dying. A trip?* Faker. Charlatan. Liar.

Selma is mashing the tart on her plate with the back of a fork. Waiting.

What can he say? The truth is, he can't keep his plants alive. He poisons his patients. He has nothing to offer a dying patient but permission to see the world before it's too late.

Selma is still staring at him. She looks beautiful. The flickering candlelight highlights her perfect cheekbones. Her elbows are propped on the polished table; her chin is propped in her hands. He has an urge to move to her side and rest his head in her lap. He wants her to stroke his hair again, push it back off his forehead, express concern for his day. But she is waiting.

"I don't know," he whispers. "I just don't know." That's the best he can offer. That is the truth.

Surgeon

Sharon Pretti

S he guides the drill through
the skull of my father,
inserts the probe below
his glistening cortex,
steers it to the spot where
blood pools like fierce
rain in the grooves of a field.
She works at the crown
of his six-foot frame,
fingers urgent as insects.
Her eyes lock on the
heave of his chest,
the hue of his cheek
as fluid speeds from his brain.
He could have sprung from her
the way she watches a twitch
flutter his lip, listens for air
to surge through the tube
snaking his throat.
She seals him, scrapes bits
of blood that grip
his skin like bursts
of sea stars clinging to rock.
When she returns him,
she stays with us longer
than she has to, taps
her thumb on the
stethoscope's disk—lingers,
as if she wants to say
where she's been, the part
of him cleaved to her palms.

The Levitron

Robert Oldshue

*L*ET ME TELL YOU ONE THING: THESE KNOW-IT-ALLS WHO COME AROUND hawking computerized this and that to make Shady Rest work like the Holiday Inn have never worked in a nursing home. They've probably never even been in one and figure they never will be, which is why they're so sure they can help us. In the million years I've been a nurse here, Mr. Hofstedder, our director, has fallen for gizmos that do everything from medicating to exercising our patients. He even got one to *visit* our patients: a box that made life-size holographic images of any visitor a patient wanted, however frequently and for however long. A busy loved one would pose for an image and record a set of nurturing phrases that could be updated by telephone as needed. A nurse who'd completed the required in-service would program the box and place a control within the patient's reach. And like most of these gizmos, it was a perfectly reasonable idea. But Mrs. Wembly dialed up a vision of the welcoming Christ that strolled to the nurses' station, causing a general tumult on 2-West, and Mr. Johnston managed to dial up a Playboy Bunny.

Then there was the flying vital-signs machine. To save us the trouble of going from patient to patient taking blood-pressures and temperatures, this little wonder zipped around Shady Rest, identifying patients by sonographically determined skull shape until it tried to take a temp on the guy fixing our elevator and he beat it to the floor with a crescent wrench.

But the worst was the Levitron, what Mr. Hofstedder called "an end to all our troubles." He was beaming the day he called us to the training room and introduced a Ms. Somebody who had a little too much hair, a little too much smile, and clicky little heels that made her satin bosom jiggle when she walked. As if me and the other girls would be impressed. As if we needed to be told that falls were a big problem for our 'clients'.

"And then there's *you*," she said as if she spent all her free time just worrying about us. She pointed to a machine we would have been looking at and wondering about if we hadn't seen so many machines of so many shapes and sizes. This one looked something like a Zamboni, the thing they clean ice rinks with, only smaller, more the size of a sit-on lawn mower, and she said you could ride it and drive it around but that was just for applications in the field.

"The military designed it to move casualties out of battle. They had no idea it would revolutionize patient care," she explained. "*Think of it,*" she kept saying, as if none of us thought until instructed to do so. "You've got a patient with vomiting or incontinence, or the patient's demented and spills all their food. The patient's a mess and so are you if you have to wrestle him to the shower and into a new set of clothes. But what if you could make the patient float? What if you could push a button and the patient would rise from the bed and stay there until you changed the bed and changed the patient? What if you could float the patient down the hall to the shower, then float them back to bed?" She switched on the machine, pushed a few buttons, and to our collective astonishment, Mr. Hofstedder began to float, an inch, and then a foot, and then several feet. She pushed another button, turned a dial, and he rotated slowly from an upright position to lying on his back, and then his front, and then his back again, and then she steered him around the room, around the cabinets and the light fixtures, before returning him, upright, to his chair.

"How was that?" Ms. Somebody asked.

"Wonderful!" he replied. "Very educational!"

"You can set the Levitron for any height you want," she continued. "The patient will feel nothing until he or she falls, which they won't because they can't. They'll simply float until you find them and gently push them back again."

She said the Levitron would be placed at the front desk and anytime one of us wanted to float a patient or to activate the round-the-clock Fall Guard feature, we'd simply come to the desk, input the patient's name, date of birth, social security number, and, of course, billing information, and everything would be perfect, which for several months it was. Our fall rate went to zero, as did our rate of fall-related hip fractures, scalp lacerations and less important injuries, so we were pleased, and Mr. Hofstedder was pleased, as were those family members who were initially somewhat dubious.

And some benefits were unexpected, like for Mrs. Bergstrom. She was so stiff, her family couldn't walk her or move her or do anything but sit beside her bed and look at her, but with the Levitron they could float her down the hall to the dining room and enjoy a Sunday meal. Yeah, it looked peculiar: there were her son and daughter-in-law sitting at a table, acting like nothing was wrong, and there was Mrs. Bergstrom, her head at the table and the rest of her sticking out half-way across the next table, but it was the first time she'd eaten in the dining room in over a year. It meant a lot to her, and it meant a lot to her son; it meant a lot to all of us.

And dear Mr. Claymore. When was the last time we'd heard him laugh or seen him smile? When was the last time his teenage grandsons had looked anything but surly when their parents dragged them in for a visit? But once we explained the Levitron, the boys floated him to the solarium and used him for a game of catch. As horrified as we were, you should have seen Mr. Claymore. He called himself the first talking football. "Claymore has Claymore in the end zone and throws Claymore!" he said, grinning as he spiraled from one grandson to the other.

And the Levitron worked outside the nursing home almost as well as it worked inside. Families could take their previously immobile parents and grandparents out to the front garden or for a walk around the block. The anti-gravitational effect lasted for several miles. With the patients appropriately tethered—and the appropriate permissions signed and witnessed—families could stroll along the waterfront or through our city's parks, acknowledging the surprise of passersby with a healthy and often long-lost sense of humor. "This is mom," they'd say looking up the rope to a hovering elder as if they'd won her at a carnival. "She just flew in from Ohio." Or, "This is Uncle Ethan. He does this when he drinks a lot of soda."

And *we* felt lighter too, which in this line of work is the most anyone can ask. So often we trudge from one mess to another, from one multi-faceted and slow-moving disaster to the next and the next. Sometimes our legs feel like lead, our bodies feel like they're six times bigger than they're supposed to be, and all we can do is stand there and gape, and sometimes even that's a lot to ask. Try showering an eighty-pound woman who kicks and scratches you. Try doing it without breaking her osteoporotic bones. Try doing it without tearing or abrading or even bruising her paper-thin skin. Try changing a bed that's full of stool again an hour later, and the next hour, and the next, because the patient's not adjusting to the tube feeds that his doctor keeps insisting that he will.

For the first time, our jobs seemed doable, the patients and their families seemed agreeable and appreciative, and Mr. Hofstedder started calling us by name, which was nice even though he usually got them wrong.

"How about that Levitron, girls?" he'd say. "I think we're really on to something here."

But just as he was starting to discuss a raise, just as we were starting to feel that we weren't nurses because we'd made a mistake, or suffered some small but irrevocable accident of fate, there was trouble with the Levitron. First a little, then a lot, and then all of us were remembering just how horrible fate can be.

It started with Mr. Overstreet. He couldn't sleep, and the aides said he was tossing all night, but he insisted he was bouncing, bobbing like a cork in water, and several other patients said they felt the same, and while some of them liked it, most of them didn't. They asked if the Fall-Guard was set a few inches too high. We looked and didn't find anything, and didn't wonder until the first head injury. After months without an incident at Shady Rest, we were floating Mrs. MontLuis to the shower when she hit her head on the ceiling so badly she needed half a dozen stitches, and the family was upset. They complained about the Levitron, and we explained that as far as we knew, it was working as it had always worked.

But then Mr. Rosselli lost weight, and then Mr. Townsend and Mrs. Torres. All the patients were losing weight, and they weren't all malnourished, cancerous or hyperthyroid, or harboring another of the bodily wasting diseases. But the weights kept dropping and the patients kept floating in their sleep, and pretty soon they were all getting hurt on the way to the shower or the dining room or church or physical therapy. Still, we tried to fool ourselves. Still, we told the patients and their families that everything was fine: we'd looked at the Levitron, we'd looked at the instruction book, and the Levitron was fine. Everything was fine.

And then it happened.

I walked in one morning and found all the patients on the ceiling. There they were, bouncing along like so many birthday balloons. Many of the patients were frightened or upset, and we had to do something. We called Mr. Hofstedder and got the number for Ms. Jiggly Bosom, but the response was just what you'd expect: for Domestic Sales press one, for International Sales press two, for Service please hold for the first available incompetent. By the time we had him on the phone, he claimed to work for the company but hadn't heard of the Levitron, and the next guy thought it was a heat pump, and the next guy— a woman actually—said we were calling the wrong division, health care was at a different number, would we like to dial it ourselves or would we like her to connect us? Finally we reached a technician who'd heard of the Levitron and knew what it was and had a screen that told her what to tell us. We told her what was happening, and over and over she said the same thing.

"You've got the blue switch up?"

"Yes."

"You've got the yellow switch down?"

"Yes."

"And you've got the dial turned as far as it can go?"

"That's right."

"Then it really should be working. It shouldn't be doing what you're telling me."

You're wondering, of course, why we didn't simply turn the Levitron off, or pull the plug. Picture 78 old people falling from the ceiling to the floor. Picture them landing on linoleum, even if we padded it. So catch them, you say. Pull them down one by one and tie them to their beds until they're all down, and then turn the machine off. But this state, like every state, has laws against tying or restraining patients in any way, under any circumstances, including this one. Believe me, once word got out, Shady Rest was crawling with inspectors and officials of every type, but they wouldn't give us the slightest help and they wouldn't give us a variance, not without a hearing, and that would take thirty days, expedited from the usual ninety days. All they could allow was manual restraint which required enough people to pull each patient down and hold them, or lie on them, or sit on them, or what-ever. But in most cases this required three or four people, and the Levitron was so severely hyperactive that several patients needed a half-a-dozen or more people. And you can't let just anyone touch a patient. It has to be a licensed professional or someone from the family or someone the family has specifically agreed to. We didn't have the staff and couldn't hire any on the spot even if we could have afforded it, and both the police and the fire department were called and looked around before saying they couldn't help us either. It would take the whole force. It would tie them up in one emergency and pose a threat to public safety.

We were left to call the families, which we did, and aside from the anger and worry we had to handle, it was hard to get them all in the same place at the same time, particularly since a lot of them were from elsewhere in the country. It was several days before we had it all organized, and by then there'd been the catastrophe we'd been hoping to avoid.

A delivery man brought a load of diapers and left a door open, and the day was hot, and the air-conditioning made a draft from the home to the street that carried out several residents. In a matter of minutes, they were the merest specks, high in the blue, summer sky, and we had to wait until they floated beyond the Levitron's influence and came to earth, hopefully slowly and safely, which, against all odds, is pretty much what happened. Mrs. Ventura floated to an adjoining suburb and landed in a garden party meant to commemorate the 35th wedding anniversary of a Mr. and Mrs. Gottlieb who were really very nice about the whole thing. Mr. Sullivan settled at the ball game which was fine except that some of the fans were less than responsible. I was too busy to be watching, but apparently he was batted from one part of the stadium to the next as will sometimes happen with a beach ball. And poor Mr. Alvarez stayed up until after dark and came down on an outdoor rock concert, and the audience thought he was part of the light show. Ironically, the one who fared the worst was the one who landed perfectly. Mr. Dworken floated to his son's house, and the next morning, when his son was making waffles for his wife and three children, he opened the window to cool the kitchen and in came his father.

"Hi, son."

"Hi, dad."

There was nothing else to say. They'd said it all already, and a lot of it they'd said at Shady Rest with everybody listening. It was the sort of thing we hear all the time. The son didn't want his father in a nursing home any more than his father wanted to be in one. But Mr. Dworken had been failing, his mind had been failing, and then his balance, and then he was walking around the neighborhood in his bathrobe. He was getting to be more than his wife could handle unless their son came over everyday and sometimes twice a day, but their son has the three kids, and his wife is involved with the older people in her own family, and I guess she's got something wrong with her stomach or maybe bowels or maybe she said it was uterine fibroids. Anyway, they'd put Mr. Dworken at Shady Rest but he'd been upset, and his family had felt guilty, and floating in the window that morning was like pulling the scab off a burn. When the son called, we apologized and said we'd be getting the place back to normal as quickly as possible and would readmit his father then. We explained that the spectacle of Mr. Sullivan being swatted around on national television had mobilized the rest of the required family members and authorized volunteers, and the next day was really quite a scene.

Relations who hadn't seen each other or spoken to each other for years were suddenly having to share ladders, climb on chairs and sometimes each other to reach the patients who, often enough, they also hadn't seen. Predictably there was a lot of complaining and several sprained backs and twisted ankles and knees but also some surprises, particularly when the time came for the head nurse on each floor to give the all-clear and Mr. Hofstedder finally turned the machine off.

It was like when a patient died. A family might have been complaining about the food, about the laundry, about the sweater or the slippers or the dentures they were sure we'd lost, which we should find or pay for. Sometimes a family would get so difficult, we'd start to feel resentful, even threatened. And then the patient would die, and we'd expect even worse, but it was almost always the opposite. No longer tortured, the family no longer snapped but instead brought us cards and flowers and chocolates and food they'd prepared. I'd seen this about-face in any number of families, but I'd never seen it or imagined it in all the families, all at the same time.

Once the Levitron was off, once the patients were back to being patients and the families were back to being families and we were back to being the nurses they were always complaining about but not yet—not for at least ten or twenty minutes—there was a wonderful and precious human moment. There were handshakes, hugs, thank-yous, fond stories, and apologies. There was some recognition, however brief, that whoever and wherever we are, we all live and we all die, although in between things can sometimes get discouraging.

But as soon as he was back in bed, Mr. Tomaczek turned on his television, and Mr. Halpner said it was too loud and turned his own television even louder, and Mr. Levin pinched Mrs. Hanratty, and Mrs. Hamamoto threw her lunch on the floor. The next day, Mr. Sherman punched one of the other nurses in the face and the family refused to believe it. She must have been provoking him, they said. What's the matter with you nurses? Don't they train you? Our father's not the kind who punches people for no reason so whoever he punched probably had it coming.

Within a few days, life at Shady Rest was back to what it always was, but after what had happened we weren't about to complain. We didn't complain when the inspectors came through with the variance we no longer needed. We didn't complain when a number of families took their loved ones to other facilities and then demanded emergency readmission when they learned about nursing homes being nursing homes and pretty much the same everywhere. We didn't even complain when Mr. Hofstedder said that he'd gotten through to Ms. Jiggly Bosom, and she didn't know about the Levitron, that she'd been reassigned to another product—Once-A-Year-Feeding—and she hoped we'd consider a presentation. "We'll hold it in the training room," said Mr. Hofstedder. "I think we're really on to something here. How about it, girls?"

And when you think of all the damage there could have been, when you think of all the patients who could have been injured either at the home or out floating around the city, there was really only one person who ended up any worse than he had been, Mr. Dworken. Last I heard he was still at his son's house causing problems. Several times, his son has tried to bring him back. He's loaded the old troublemaker into his car, strapped him in, and gotten as far as our parking lot, but he can't get his father to leave the car, can't carry him by himself, and under the circumstances, we don't feel comfortable helping him. Oh, we're willing to come out and tap on the windshield. We're willing to smile and say, "Hi, Mr. Dworken. It's wonderful to see you, sweetheart. Why don't you come in and play some bingo? Why don't you come in and let us make some hot chocolate?" One time, the son asked if we could use the Levitron to get his father from the car. We told him we no longer had it, we'd returned it, we were sorry but the two of them were on their own which was a hard thing to say and, I'm sure, a hard thing to hear. Not surprisingly, the son said what so many of our families say: you'd help us if you cared.

As if we don't care. As if we don't help. As if the Levitron would have helped. Believe me, we do what we can here at Shady Rest, but things are what they are, are what they always have been and always will be. As much as we might want to change them—as much as we nurses might wish *a lot* of things were different in the first place—bad enough like good enough, we've learned to leave alone.

Miss Erma, Private Duty

Madeleine Mysko

*F*rom Mrs. Carlisle's window I can see
   across the jumbled roofs and tree-tops, all
the way downtown. South Street I cannot see,
and yet I know on my back stoop the rain
is watering the pink geranium
I bought on Saturday, and pouring down
the walk and underneath the alley gate
to where the row of beat-up trash cans shine
like baptized sinners standing in the river.

But I must get to Mrs. Carlisle now.
She's waiting for her breakfast, gazing toward
the light, although she hasn't sight for more
than shapes—the dark that's me against the panes,
but not this view of Monday morning rain.

Biofeedback

David Milofsky

THE APPOINTMENT WAS AT THREE AND, AS USUAL, SYLVIA WAS RUNNING late. After dropping the kids off at school, she had spent the morning in her office seeing patients. Then she had gone to the University to conduct grand rounds. After discussing transient ischemic episodes with an earnest group of medical students, she visited a patient who had awakened with partial vision in one eye and was being worked up for a stroke. He was a bald, overweight man of 55 with small, determined eyes. With some surprise, Sylvia noticed that his chart had identified him as a poet.

"This is it, isn't it, Doc," the man said.

Sylvia was standing behind the patient at the time, listening to the back of his chest with her stethoscope, hidden by his bulk. "What, Mr. Marvin? This is what?"

"I had a stroke. I'm going to die, right? You can be honest with me."

"I don't think so," Sylvia said, wondering if she was being honest. "Not right away anyhow. Maybe later."

She had intended levity so was grateful when the patient laughed, his slow growl coming like thunder through her stethoscope. "Sure," he said. "We're all going sooner or later. But this isn't what you'd exactly call a good sign. Am I right? I mean, this isn't really a very positive thing?"

Sylvia smiled. Intelligence was a rare gift among patients in her practice, as was humor. "No, I wouldn't say that going blind is a good sign," she agreed. "You're right about that. But the thing is that, in itself, it's only a sign. We have to figure out what it's telling us. I'll see you tomorrow."

That was her morning. Now she was working her way through the maze of buildings at the Medical Center, looking for Dr. Nygaard's office. He had told her over the phone that it was in the basement of the day care center, which seemed like an odd place for the biofeedback laboratory, but when Sylvia finally found it, the center was empty of children or staff and she descended the stairs with a mixture of anxiety and anticipation.

The ostensible reason for her visit was to consult with Nygaard about a patient with migraine headaches whom she had referred to him, but that could as easily have been done over the phone. Nygaard's specialty was pain management and, though he had a national reputation, he was a psychologist and was viewed with suspicion by the medical community, or at least that part of it in residence at the medical school. Which accounted for the out-of-the-way location of his office. Ironically, it was the fact that he was a pariah that had brought Sylvia here this afternoon. She identified with Nygaard because both of them were outsiders. Though no one at the hospital had said anything to her directly, in her experience separation and divorce made everyone uncomfortable and she imagined that her colleagues and patients were all aware that her husband had moved out of their house and taken a two-bedroom apartment on the edge of campus.

In the dim light of the hallway, Sylvia could barely read the sign: Anders Nygaard. Knock First. For some reason she read knackwurst and was immediately aware that she was hungry. This made her laugh and she was still smiling when the door opened to reveal a stooped man with thinning hair, wearing a green visor that bisected his forehead. Now he looked up at her curiously.

"Yes?"

"Oh, God," Sylvia said. "I'm really sorry. Dr. Nygaard, I'm Sylvia Rose. We had an appointment."

Nygaard smiled now, as if he wondered why she had been laughing but didn't want to ask. "Ah, yes," he said. "Dr. Rose. Ah, I think I remember you from medical school. You were one of ours, weren't you? Very bright, as I recall. Many honors. Ah, yes."

Sylvia thought his speech patterns were odd, as if he had once stammered and had adopted the habit of saying "ah" as a strategy for getting into a sentence. She had heard of such things. She nodded. "I did medical school and my residency here and I often heard of you but I don't think we've ever met."

"Ah, yes," Nygaard said. "And now we have." He waited, apparently, to see why she had come to see him in his basement sanctuary.

This made Sylvia self-conscious. "I'm really sorry," she said. "My husband just moved out and your sign struck me as funny."

Nygaard nodded as if this conjunction made sense. "Ah, yes. The sign. Won't you come in?" He stood aside and gestured toward a table piled high with journals and off-prints of articles. Sylvia took one of the straight-back chairs and Nygaard joined her at the table. When he stood up, she noticed that, contrary to her initial impression, he was tall and thin with a small brush moustache. His tie was tucked into his shirt in military fashion and he wore short ankle boots, which irritated Sylvia for no good reason. Still, his gray eyes were intelligent and had a calming effect on her. Now he laced his fingers together and leaned back in his chair. "You know, coincidentally, I recently saw one of your patients, a Mr. Mankwitz."

Sylvia shivered involuntarily. She felt as if Mr. Mankwitz were following her around campus, to her office, now even here. "He's not really my patient," she said quickly. It was a sore point because she had already gone through this with the M&M, but whatever she might think, the rest of the world seemed to consider Mankwitz to be hers. Besides, she was curious. "How did he happen to come to see you?"

"He had been in the ER and they noticed his pressure was elevated. I also do the blood pressure lab for the University, so they sent him over." Nygaard hesitated. "An interesting man, but very nervous, hm. He had his books with him, do you know about his books?"

"Oh, yes," Sylvia said. "You mean the ones from Mount Sinai?"

Nygaard smiled but he didn't laugh, as if he had learned to respect all opinions, no matter how unlikely they might seem. "Yes," he said. "Those."

"And did his pressure come down?" Sylvia asked.

Nygaard shrugged. "In the lab, but that's not surprising. I doubt that he'll come back. He seemed to think it was all a bit weird." He indicated the ramshackle room and shifted in his chair as if to signal that this topic had been exhausted. "Now how can I help you, Dr. Rose?"

Help. It was a simple word, even a concept. They were in one of the helping professions, after all. Yet no one had offered Sylvia help for a long time, and without meaning or wanting to, she started to cry, tears leaking from her eyes and onto her black dress, as she looked directly at this strange man in this stranger place. "Damn," she said, because she hated this, hated the predictability of it, hated being the weak little woman crying on the first available shoulder, but she couldn't help it. She dabbed at her eyes with a handkerchief and said, "I'm sorry, Dr. Nygaard. I'm just tired. Really, it's nothing."

Nygaard's expression gave away little. She didn't know if he believed her, but it didn't seem to matter, and she found this comforting. It was as if people often cried in his presence, for various reasons, and he had learned to feel neither alarmed nor surprised. It didn't appear to make any difference to him at all. He didn't repeat his offer of help but rather maintained a respectful silence, his gray eyes unwavering. He didn't seem in the least embarrassed, didn't turn away. He waited.

Sylvia blew her nose and straightened in her chair. "I came to see you about another patient of mine," she said. "Mrs. Lindstrom. You remember Mrs. Lindstrom? I referred her to you. The woman with arthritic pain?" Sylvia had sent her patient to Nygaard because there was little else she could do for her. And while she didn't endorse the holistic approach, she wasn't opposed to alternative medicine, if it worked. But Mrs. Lindstrom had been skeptical and only agreed to come because Nygaard was Swedish.

Nygaard nodded, apparently content to go along with this fiction. He looked up at the ceiling and without thinking, Sylvia mimicked him, as if his notes on the case were pasted on the soundproof tiles. "Mrs. Lindstrom," Nygaard said thoughtfully. "She did come in. Twice, in fact. But she had a reaction to the lab and so it was difficult to work with her. Some people have problems with biofeedback. It's kind of a Dr. Frankenstein thing, I think." This seemed to please Nygaard and he smiled wickedly at her, a devil-may-care look that Sylvia supposed was intended to reassure her.

"What was the problem?" she asked. "With the lab, I mean. Maybe I can talk to her." Sylvia was sincere but the basement office gave her the creeps and she couldn't really blame Mrs. Lindstrom or Mr. Mankwitz, for that matter, if they felt the same way.

Nygaard shrugged expressively. "I doubt she'll be back," he said. "I wouldn't bother trying to coax her in if I were you. The training isn't easy; it takes time and dedication. People have to be willing to accept the treatment if it's going to have any chance for success. Some aren't."

This seemed like a reasonable position to take. At the same time, Sylvia wondered if Nygaard had any regular patients. Everyone she referred seemed to look around and run. Still, he didn't seem at all defensive. Perhaps because he really believed in what he was doing and didn't feel the need to persuade anyone of its efficacy. For a moment they sat silently in their chairs, thinking of Mrs. Lindstrom. Then Nygaard said, "Perhaps you'd like to see for yourself?"

"What?" Sylvia said, imagining he had Mrs. Lindstrom sedated somewhere in the dark reaches of the basement.

"The lab," Nygaard said. "If you're going to refer people, wouldn't it be a good idea to know more about the treatment?" Without waiting for an answer, he rose and Sylvia followed him down to the end of the dark hallway, where he unlocked another door and stood aside to let her enter. The hallway was empty, indeed the whole building was quiet. There seemed to be no other offices here except the deserted day care center upstairs. She hesitated for a moment, remembering the comment about Dr. Frankenstein, but there was something comical about Nygaard in his green visor and ankle boots. She didn't know what mad scientists looked like, but she doubted they looked much like him. Besides, he was on the medical school faculty so how dangerous could he be? "Excuse me," she said, and walked into the lab.

After the build-up, Dr. Nygaard's laboratory was somewhat disappointing, consisting only of two small rooms that communicated with one another through a large window. In the main room was a machine that looked oddly like three stereo receivers stacked one on top of the other. A desk and chair were next to these and blinking red lights gave the small room the appearance of an airport controller's booth.

The other room was smaller and furnished with a large easy chair, a recliner, Sylvia thought. She tried to hide her disappointment, but Nygaard was apparently inured to the reactions of others. He ducked his head modestly. "I know it doesn't look like much," he said. "But it's big enough. I have everything I need."

Sylvia had seen enough and was anxious to get back to her car. She thought she might have time for a cup of coffee before picking up the children. Still, courtesy demanded that she show minimal interest and, after all, she had gone to the trouble of coming here. "What exactly do you do in your lab?" she asked.

The question seemed to energize Nygaard, who answered with his peculiar hiccoughing speech. "Ah, yes, what do we do, that's the question, isn't it?" He laughed silently, enormously amused with himself. Then, "Ah, yes, well, I could explain, but it's much simpler just to show you. Please." He held out his hand, gesturing toward the lounger and Sylvia sat, feeling unpleasantly small and vulnerable as the cushions gave way to accept her. Nygaard produced some headphones and placed them on her ears. He attached a blood pressure cuff to her right arm. Then he took conducting jelly from a jar and smeared some on her forehead and arms. Finally, he attached small rubber suction cups to her brow and forearms and connected these by wires to the headphones.

Nygaard inflated the cuff and then let it deflate. "Your pressure's a bit high," he said, but when Sylvia started to protest, he nodded his head. "No worries," he said. "It's just a baseline reading." But it made her feel as if she were going to have an attack right here in this basement room with the mad doctor. She wondered if it had all finally gotten to her, Philip, Mr. Mankwitz, the myriad demands of each crazy day. She wondered if she should medicate herself and then what she would choose. She knew almost nothing about blood pressure medication and had no time to go to a doctor herself. Her mind was racing and she knew it, but it was hard to slow down; it had always been hard for her and it was no easier now. As if he intuited what she was thinking, Nygaard patted Sylvia on the shoulder. "No worries," he repeated. "I'll be just a moment." Then he disappeared from the room leaving Sylvia alone.

Sylvia wanted to scream. No worries indeed. Her husband had moved out, her children were climbing the walls, her practice was out of control, and here she was in a basement room with leads extending from every part of her body and Dr. Frankenstein next door. All she had were worries. And now things had gone farther than she intended, but she felt gripped by the chair and was afraid that she would electrocute herself if she tried to move her arms. Given no choice, she sat back and almost immediately felt her limbs go heavy. She thought she might fall asleep; it had been weeks since she'd slept soundly, and now she felt oddly secure and cared for in this strange place. "Ah, yes," Nygaard's voice came through the headphones. Metallic, she thought, but not uncaring. "Just relax. In a moment you'll hear some clicks in the earphones when I start the program."

Sylvia heard crackling, but it sounded as if it came from inside her head rather than from the headphones. She had trouble separating herself from the sounds that now seemed to surround her. Her arms felt very heavy. Yet the primary feeling she experienced was not of panic but warmth. And she thought she had never sat in such a comfortable chair. Quick tappings followed the crackling and seemed to originate in her ears, traveling across her brain from one side to the other, and were then succeeded by more tappings with greater intensity and rhythm. Then the tappings were chasing each other around inside her brain. Each set seemed in turn faster and more insistent than those that had gone before, but the effect was exhilarating somehow, and now Sylvia realized that the sounds were actually tracking the impulses of her brain; she was witnessing the kinetic shower of thought that occurred silently, constantly, and which she had always taken for granted if she thought about it at all. She was strangely impressed with herself, with this thing that was happening to her. It was a kind of entrancement and, uncharacteristically, it made Sylvia slow down and marvel at it all, as if she had accomplished something, reached a new kind of awareness, which in fact she had. This feeling persisted for an indeterminate period until Sylvia became aware of Nygaard's presence in the room. She wondered how long he had been there, and was suddenly embarrassed by the abandon with which she had taken to the workings of her mind.

"Ah, yes," he said. "You heard those sounds, the tappings?"

There seemed to be no need to answer, so Sylvia just nodded.

"What we want to do," Nygaard said, suggesting that this would be a mutual effort, "is slow them down."

"Slow them?" The tapping had sounded like hail on a tin roof, rapid and furious. It seemed to have a life of its own. That was what was so amazing. "How?"

Now Nygaard sat in front of her on a stool. "I can show you some exercises," he said, as if she had already agreed to a course of treatment and in the process had become a patient rather than a fellow practitioner. "Rapid response is associated with anxiety; slowing is associated with relaxation. Just as warmth is." Nygaard raised her manacled hand to her cheek in a surprisingly intimate gesture. "You see?"

Sylvia's fingertips were like brands from a fire, warm and comforting. She looked at Nygaard who was smiling slightly, though not in an unkind or mocking way. "That's incredible," she said. "Really, I had no idea."

"No one does," Nygaard said modestly. "Everyone over at the medical school thinks I'm a crackpot."

Sylvia started to object, but the fact was that what he said was true. She was ashamed now that she had had similar preconceptions. She thought perhaps Nygaard was a genius, though she supposed the two weren't necessarily mutually exclusive. Now Nygaard broke into her thoughts. He re-inflated the cuff and let it deflate. He nodded and said, "120 over 80. Perfectly normal. And while you've been in here, your temperature has risen from 81 to 90 degrees," he said. "The temperature of your extremities, that is."

Her extremities. Philip had always considered Sylvia to be a person of extremes, which seemed unfair to her, but that wasn't what Nygaard meant. He was a scientist and spoke with precision. All he was saying was that her fingertips were the extreme limits of her body. None of this seemed to touch Nygaard who sat at her feet, thin lips pressed together, a deep line of concentration cutting through the center of his forehead. She marveled at his self-confidence. Nothing in him seemed to question the truth of his conclusions or the efficacy of his procedures, and Sylvia envied him this for she questioned herself constantly. Yet it was undeniable: something had happened to her in that little room. It was measurable: her blood pressure had gone down, her fingers were warmer now and the rat-tat-tatting in her brain had slowed perceptibly. "It's slowing down," she said, as much to herself as to Nygaard.

"Ah, yes," Nygaard murmured. "You seem to be a good subject."

This pleased Sylvia inordinately, but then she thought of the time, her children, her life. "I've got to go," she said abruptly. "Can you unhook me?"

"Of course," Nygaard said, neither pleased nor displeased it seemed. "It's just a demonstration," he said diffidently. "If you want to come back sometime, I'll show you the exercises I was talking about."

At dinner, the kids were studiously quiet; despite their youth they were trying to make a point. No food fights, no tears, no distractions. They seemed to be saying, "You should think about what you're doing. You should look at yourself." Yet even though she agreed with them in the abstract, Sylvia couldn't help being glad Philip was gone. She had imagined she would feel abandoned, but in the actual case it was like leaning against an open door, an enormous relief. And though she felt ashamed to admit it, she knew that for the past few years she had dreaded coming home at night. Now that he was gone, she no longer had to feign interest in Philip's convoluted stories of academic intrigue or, if she had indicated weariness with the subject, tolerate his labored sighs or hurt silence. If she were going to hurt someone, she wanted to do it on purpose, and she wanted it to matter. She knew she had hurt the kids, knew it was unavoidable, and she knew it mattered; it was something she'd have to live with for the rest of her life. But she couldn't have cared less about their father.

Around nine the phone rang. Sylvia debated ignoring it and letting the machine pick up, but it might be a patient. She had given Mrs. Lindstrom her home number. It was Philip. "We need to talk," he said, a wheezing sibilance leaking through the receiver.

"I don't need to talk," Sylvia said, and hung up.

Then she waited, wondering what she would do if he called back. It would represent more motivation than he had shown in five years, more urgency. But she waited fifteen minutes and the phone did not ring. So that was how it would be, she thought, and discovered that, except for the children, she had no regrets. It seemed odd that twelve years with a man could be so unimportant, but there was no point in denying the obvious. Besides, it was late. She turned off the phone and went upstairs to bed.

When Mrs. Lindstrom came in, Sylvia mentioned that she had met Dr. Nygaard, though she didn't tell her patient that she had been in his lab or submitted to a demonstration. The treatment had had an effect, however. For the past two days, she had been aware of an unusual warmth in her hands and arms and she had experienced a new feeling of contentment. She wasn't happy exactly, but at peace, a term she would previously have suspected and which was, in any case, unique for her. She told herself that it could simply be the result of finally getting Philip out of her life, but she had begun to wonder if Nygaard's techniques were actually working.

"That guy's weird," Mrs. Lindstrom said now.

"In what way?" Sylvia said, trying to sound neutral.

Mrs. Lindstrom looked at her as if she were demented. "You saw him, right? That little moustache and the way his nose twitches like a bunny rabbit. Then that contraption he hooks you up to, them earphones, and all. You didn't think that was weird? I felt like it was something out of Alfred Hitchcock."

Sylvia smiled at the reference. Most of her patients had no idea who Hitchcock was but Mrs. Lindstrom watched televised reruns in the afternoon. "But did he help you?" Sylvia asked. "Is the pain better?"

Mrs. Lindstrom hesitated before answering. She was a large woman with ludicrously swollen knees and ankles. Alone since her husband's death, she was trying to remain independent but her son and daughter-in-law wanted to place her in a nursing home, as much for their convenience as for her own good. They all agreed that Sylvia would be the final arbiter of Mrs. Lindstrom's fate. "A little," she admitted now, reluctant to praise someone as strange as Dr. Nygaard but equally unwilling to lie to Sylvia.

"Then he helped you," Sylvia said. "And if he helped you, if he made the pain less intense, then maybe it doesn't matter quite so much if he's a bit unusual." She looked up, but Mrs. Lindstrom didn't seem convinced. If you want to stay out of that nursing home, I'd do everything possible, she thought, but when she spoke, Sylvia said, "I can tell you he's harmless. And there's nothing dangerous about his treatments."

"Oh, I'm not worried about that," Mrs. Lindstrom said. "I can take care of myself. I just don't like all that glue he puts on your forehead." She stopped for a moment, her face twisted in thought. "There isn't anything you can give me?"

"You said that the pain medication I prescribed made you sleepy. I could give you steroids but you wouldn't like the side effects. I'm afraid there's no cure for the kind of arthritis you have. I know it's hard."

Mrs. Lindstrom waved her off. She had no interest in explanations or sympathy. She had worked making blenders for thirty years until her hands stopped cooperating and she had to quit her factory job. "I know all that, okay?" she said, resigned. "I'll go back to Dr. Strangelove." She flexed her fingers. "It just doesn't seem like he's really like you, you know. More like some kind of witch doctor. I half expected the guy to do a rain dance or something. But I've got to admit it hurts less than it did before. Weird."

There was a message from Philip on the machine and listening to it, Sylvia noticed that he cleared his throat three times in thirty seconds. In most people she might have assumed this was caused by anxiety but in Philip she knew it was only an affectation, the way he imagined sophisticated people talked. It was sad that he was still making himself up at 38, but she was determined to stop feeling responsible for his limitations. "Since you refuse to talk to me," he began, and then cleared his throat. "I think perhaps we should talk in front of a third person, someone who is objective. I've a few names and will ring them if you agree. Then I'll let you know when they have time and you can follow up directly." It annoyed Sylvia when Philip used Britishisms he had picked up on his trips, not only because they never sounded like him, but because they didn't sound like anyone. It was as if he were imitating characters in a B movie. "Right," he said and cleared his throat with finality, signing off now. "I'll wait to hear from you then."

Sylvia shook her head. It was the most effort Philip had put into the marriage. She wondered if it would have made a difference if he had done this earlier, but she doubted it. Philip would still have been Philip, counselors or not, and the ineluctable truth was that until recently this had suited her. If she had had a husband who was more demanding, she might have been unable to finish medical school, and certainly she could not have had two babies along the way. Philip's inattention had been vital to her success, though it seemed cold-blooded to put it that way, even to herself. Yet useful as he had been, she could no longer stand to be around him, much less live with him. She was glad he had left; it was what she had wished for.

Dr. Nygaard seemed interested but not surprised when Sylvia returned and told him that his treatments had alleviated some of Mrs. Lindstrom's pain. "Ah, yes," he said. "Usually there's some improvement, at least at first."

"You mean it doesn't last?"

"Nothing lasts forever," Nygaard said. "There are just new treatments, new approaches, you know that, doctor. But this is only helpful if you continue in the lab."

"But she's coming back," Sylvia said. "She's going to call you." She was uncertain why she was so invested in this relationship's continuing.

Nygaard seemed skeptical. He ran his hand over his scalp and smiled. "Really? I didn't expect to see her again. She seemed put off by all this." He gestured at the disheveled office, the table piled high with papers. "I think she wanted me to have a nurse and perhaps wear a white coat."

Sylvia laughed. "Patients find those things either frightening or reassuring, sometimes both." Then she said, "She did find you a little unusual. She said that."

This appeared to surprise Nygaard, but he was not displeased. He seemed curious about his effect on people. "In what way?"

"Actually, she said you were weird. I have no idea why I'm telling you this."

Nygaard laughed out loud. "Ah, yes. Excellent," he said. "You see, the mad scientist, just as I told you. That's wonderful, superb. And yet you think she's coming back for more?"

Sylvia nodded. "I'm here, aren't I?"

Now Nygaard's eyes seemed to glow with new understanding. "Ah, yes," he said. He waited a moment, then said, "Shall we go into the lab?"

Sylvia thought his manner was charming, even seductive. It was as if he had invited her to bed, and this time there was no hesitation on her part. She wanted to feel that warmth, that heaviness again. She took her seat with alacrity and waited impatiently while Nygaard attached the leads to her arms and forehead. Then she was alone in the little room, waiting for contact with her most intimate impulses, the clicks and whirs of her every thought and impulse.

"Everything okay?" she heard Nygaard say into the earphones.

Without turning around, she waved at him in irritation. She closed her eyes and waited—now the clicking was fast and furious and she rode the intensity of her brainwaves, inside them now, excited and stimulated by the excesses of thought. Then, almost imperceptibly at first, they began to slow, and she felt warmth spread through her fingers and forearms again. It seemed as if they had melted into the leather chair, but she wasn't the least bit concerned. She was one with the chair, the small room, the headphones, the metronomic clicking in her ears. Eyes closed, she was aware of colors, red, green, gold. It was surprising that her brain waves would be colored; she hadn't expected that. Then there was only the occasional click in her ears and the creeping warmth in her extremities. She was in a cocoon, a womb, everything was all mixed-up together, nothing was separate. There was no body, no extremities. Just the slowed clicking and the all-enveloping warmth. It was all extreme. She was vaguely aware of herself slipping away but it didn't alarm her. She was not asleep, not unconscious, just somewhere else. Now the clicking had almost disappeared. There was one and silence, then another and more silence. Then another. And then there was nothing.

Peeled Grapes

Sharon Olds

When I call my mother on Mother's Day
 I thank her again for making me, and for
lamb chops, for smocked dresses, for Buster Brown
Mary Janes, my metatarsals
blue in the radiation box. She laughs, she loves this,
she says, I hope you haven't forgotten
that I peeled you grapes, when you were sick.
You what?! When you were sick, I would give you
a bowl of peeled, chilled grapes.
She giggles. I cannot see it, my mother
giving me a cold bowl
of eyeball glitter, and then I can see
it is a Pyrex dish, there is chill and light and
time and work all over the place,
ovals of pallid mesh, flay
to cheer me up, her labor turned
to my little joy. It is true she tied me
to a chair one day, but she brought me alphabet
soup. It is true she was hairbrush-wild
and lay on top of me poor dotty
soul, for me to pray for her
while she cried on me, but my mother with her long
entranced erotic fingernails
peeled grapes for me, she did not mean it
but she said it: Be yourself.

Lily of the Valley

Emma Wunsch

*L*ILY WANTS SNEAKERS. SHE COMES INTO THE DEN WHILE HENRY'S WATCH-
ing the Mariners get slaughtered for the third night in a row. When
Lily walks in, Boston gets another run, making the score 9–1.

"Dad?"

"Yeah?" Henry turns off the game and the porous blue wall between
them turns gray.

"I think I want sneakers. You know, for my birthday."

"Sneakers," Henry repeats robotically. "You want sneakers."

He asked her three nights ago at dinner. They were eating—or rather Henry
was eating, and watching as Lily wound and unwound the spaghetti. She
wasn't going to eat. He recently realized that this winding-unwinding had
been going on, right in front of him, for weeks.

"Lily," he said sternly.

"What?" Her fork, empty, froze above her plate.

He wanted to say, "Eat it." Eat the spaghetti, the bread, the salad. Long
ago, when she didn't like something, Henry remembered, her mother would
sing a silly rhyme—*three more bites is so nice come now Lily eat your rice*—and
Lily would eat. What rhymed with spaghetti, he wondered before he caught
himself. She was too old for that. Practically fifteen. "I wanted to know what
you'd like for your birthday," he said, surprising them both.

She shrugged.

"Fifteen. That's something."

But Lily just shrugged again. Watching her shoulders move up and
down, Henry wondered, again, how long this had been happening. How had
he not noticed?

"Nottabigdeal," Lily said. She didn't seem to care or need presents.

"Think about it," Henry said, watching her dump her dinner in the
trash. "You should—"

"What?"

"Put that in the compost. That can be composted."

"Next time," she said, walking out.

But now she has come to tell him what she would like for her birthday,
which is tomorrow.

"Sneakers would be cool. Mine are stretched out."

"I need to work in the morning," Henry says. "We could get them after
lunch."

"I can't. I'll be with Alex-Yang."

Alex-Yang is a seven-year-old boy who Mrs. Woolf, a woman down the block, arranged to bring to Seattle from China in order for him to have several operations to fix the hole in his cheek. The orphanage said the boy's name was Alex, but the Chinese doctors who have come to learn from the surgeons at the university hospital call him Yang. Mrs. Woolf pays Lily to help her take care of Alex-Yang a few days a week. Even though Alex-Yang is only four houses away, Henry has never seen him.

Lily says that the hole in Alex-Yang's cheek is shaped like a diamond.

"When you come back then," Henry tells her. "We'll get them before dinner."

He turns the game on when she leaves, just in time to see the Red Sox score on a two-run double making the final score 12–1. He watches the replay on the local news so he doesn't have to think about Lily's sunken stomach, how little she ate at dinner, or children from China with holes in their cheeks. Henry doesn't want to think about the implications of what he has done, what he has agreed to: sneakers. Mostly, he doesn't want to think about how Beth has been dead for six years and that he now must be both mother and father to Lily.

In the morning, Lily's birthday, they both get up early. Henry pauses by his bathroom window and watches his daughter stretch on the porch. Right leg up, left leg up, bend forward, hold. In 55, 65, 75 minutes, when she returns to the house, her shirt will cling to her back and sweat will pour from her temples. When Lily comes in, Henry will be drinking coffee in the kitchen.

"Lily," he will say as a combination of sweet teenage sweat and perfumed deodorant cloud him. "Lily," Henry will repeat firmly, "don't you want . . ." He will trail off here, watching his reflection on the wrong side of a spoon. His face will look inverted, out of alignment. "A piece of toast," he'll say, as Lily runs upstairs.

His daughter has become a runner this summer.

She has been running this strangely hot and humid summer up and down Seattle's hills. Down along the canal, past the espresso stands, under the bridge, and beyond the boats and into the park where she'll run laps around the track, four or fifteen or twenty-eight times before she runs out of the park, past the tennis courts, up all the hills, and into the house where Henry will be waiting, twisting his spoon in his coffee, chewing burnt toast until he remembers to swallow.

Henry swallows now. "Happy Birthday," he says when she comes in. "Don't you want breakfast?" After Lily runs, the vein on the right side of her temple pulses in and out. Henry directs his question to the vein. "Have breakfast." He tries to make this sound like an order. "You should eat," he yells at the stairs Lily has jogged up. "You have to eat," he says softly. "You're not eating. You're doing that terrible thing that teenage girls do, Lily." He swallows the remaining coffee, which is burnt and hollow. "Not eating," he says, as if she were right in front of him. "All this running," he says, even although he knows Lily hasn't heard him, that she's forcing her body under the powerful blasts of hot steamy water, as she pokes the non-existent mounds of flesh on her belly, calves, and thighs.

After breakfast he goes into his study. He's supposed to be writing study guide questions for a physics textbook that will be used at Seattle Central Community College where he teaches. The questions are the last part of the book and should be the easiest to write. Henry sits at his desk and looks at the picture of Beth at a table covered with wine glasses and ashtrays. The picture was taken on their honeymoon. Henry likes it not so much because it's of his now-dead young wife, but because he likes knowing that he knew her at that moment, that he'd been there too, tipsy, in love, taking pictures. How is it that he was once on a honeymoon and is now wondering about the sounds from Lily's bedroom?

He turns on the radio. "Nice day if you like the heat," the DJ says. "Another scorcher in Seattle."

Vibrations echo from the ceiling. What's she doing? Don't think about it. Lily is in her room. Nothing wrong with that. What's wrong is that for the past few days he hasn't been able to come up with a single question for the book. It has to be at the printers by October. October, he thinks, seems crazy. From here, at the end of July, October is blurry and impossible. But supposedly he and Lily will both be back in school. If the surgeries are successful, Alex-Yang will be back in China. Considering the last three nights' games, the Mariners will probably not make it to the playoffs. But heat, he has to think about heat, which is the chapter he should be working on now. The chapter begins with a quote from Francis Bacon:

> Heat is a motion of expansion, not uniformly of the whole body together, but in smaller parts of it, and at the same checked, repelled, and beaten back, so that the body acquires a motion alternative, perpetually quivering, striving and irritated by repercussion, whence spring the fury of fire and heat.

Think of questions the students should answer about heat, Henry tells himself. But Francis Bacon makes him think of bacon, which makes him remember breakfast and Lily and how Lily did not eat breakfast this morning or yesterday morning. He doubts that she will eat anything for lunch. He doesn't want to think about dinner and sitting across from Lily while she stares at her plate, a scowl folding across her face.

Last year, for her fourteenth birthday, they had steak, potatoes, and homemade strawberry shortcake with ice cream. But last year was before Lily started keeping her door closed and jogging every morning. Shit, he's not getting anything done. Worrying about Lily has made him lose concentration. This is not who he is. Henry is organized and controlled.

When his wife got sick, he organized to make her well by creating computerized charts about medicine, weights, and temperatures. He researched until it was clear that despite his organization, Beth would still die.

And after she died, he made sure that Lily was okay, and dutifully took her to meet other kids who'd also lost a parent to cancer. He did this until seven months after the funeral when Lily asked one night that, if Henry didn't mind, if he thought it might be okay, could she go to Girl Scouts instead?

Yes, he said. That would be fine.

Good, Lily said, swallowing her dinner. And things were good. They were sad of course, they missed Beth, but they still talked and did things together. Whatever it was Lily had been eating the night she asked if she could join Girl Scouts, that had been good too, because after Beth died Henry learned to cook. It was important that they have good meals, so after the funeral Henry went from someone who had spent his life making soup and sandwiches to a widower who was an even better cook than his dead wife. Even though he was middle-aged when his wife died, Henry started to read cookbooks and watch cooking shows so he could learn to make roast loin of pork with squash and walnut butter, and sautéed mushrooms with fresh peas on sorrel fettuccine. Lily had tried it all, even the curries and fish dishes, and she said even though they weren't her favorite that they were okay. They were okay, Henry and Lily. Weren't they?

"Okay, Dad?" Lily says impatiently.

"Huh?" How did she just appear?

"I'm going to Alex-Yang. Mrs. Woolf wants me early."

"Fine. I'll walk you over."

She makes a face. "It's practically next door, Dad."

"I just thought, well I'm going out. For coffee."

She shrugs.

"You want something?" Henry asks as they walk down the porch and onto the sidewalk. He knows he sounds too eager, but he can't stop. "I could bring you a croissant or muffin. Get one for Alex-Yang too."

"Alex-Yang can't eat muffins, Dad." Lily sounds annoyed. "He's got, like, a hole in his cheek."

"Right." Henry walks faster to keep up with her. But you don't have a hole in your cheek. You could have a muffin. And a scone. "Suicide Dream?" He points to her shirt. He intends to be light about it, but isn't.

"A band. Suicide Dream is a band," she says, turning up the stone path to Alex-Yang's.

But Henry's got to get out of this dream, this humid reverie of unproductiveness, and come up with the study guide questions. First he'll get coffee. He told Lily that's what he was doing and even though it's over ninety degrees, he'll walk. It's less than two miles. People much older than Henry run marathons, hike Mount Rainier, bike hundreds of miles to fight breast cancer, which is what killed Beth. Every year Henry sponsors two secretaries in his department who run to prevent breast cancer. Would Henry sponsor Lily? How could he not? He's going to buy her sneakers. Maybe the sneakers that she will wear when she runs in the race to stop breast cancer. Shit. He's going to have to do something. Otherwise the problem will just get bigger and bigger. Worse and worse. Like Alex-Yang's hole. Except that, according to Lily, the hole is smaller. It's still there, she told him, you can still see it. But you try not to. I try not to look, she told him. But Henry can see what Lily's doing. It's clear now. But before? Was he trying not to see, not to look?

Henry runs his tongue over his cheek. The coffee shop is ahead of him, but he doesn't want it. Caffeine is making him edgy. He needs to get home and work. Work, he thinks. Force acting upon an object to cause displacement. And he feels out of place all of a sudden, walking on the same streets he has walked for nearly twenty years. He knows it's because it's so hot, but he feels so old and achy suddenly that he wonders if he has the flu. If he's sick, he'll cancel with Lily. Sorry, he'd say, no shoes today. And the summer would end and they'd return to school and everything would be back to normal. But he's not sick. Just hot. All of Seattle is sweltering under an unforgiving sun.

Everything is wrong this summer. Seattle doesn't get this hot. How can Lily run in such heat? That's the real question. She is no longer her whole body. But he's not going to think about that right now. He's going to keep moving. He's going to walk past the coffee shop as he makes his way down the second hill that his daughter has jogged up and down this morning. But unlike Lily, Henry is going to climb this second hill to the store. To buy steak. He's not thinking of Bacon; he's thinking about Newton and steaks because Newton's third law is Opposite and Equal Reaction. For every action there is an equal and opposite reaction. Before he buys Lily sneakers, he will buy steak. After sneakers, they'll eat steak. Both of them. Together.

The blasting air-conditioning in the grocery store makes Henry feel more confident in his decision. He picks up a steak that doesn't contain hormones. Should he get a cheaper one? Would Lily rather have chicken? Screw it. He puts the expensive steak into his basket. He deserves it. He's a middle-aged widower who has to write questions about physics problems and decide what do with his anorexic fifteen-year-old.

Anorexic.

The word has been so loud in his mind, so symphonic and neon, that he thinks he must have said it aloud, but no one in the aisle stops or stares.

What's he supposed to tell her? He walks quickly out of the store, swinging his plastic bag of meat. Should he say: Why aren't you eating? Why don't you eat? What's eating you? He walks faster and faster, thinking of question after question, until he's completely out of breath. He pauses in front of a house where a young woman is lying out on the lawn. It's dangerous to lie under the sun, Henry thinks. She's burning. Sun is powerful. It causes cancer. And cancer is hard to battle. As hard as you try, you can't always win. But everyone is battling their bodies this summer. Alex-Yang and the woman here who is trying to make her white skin brown. And Lily. Beneath her Suicide Dream shirt, her body has become smaller and smaller; even her ear lobes, which sport silver earrings, seem small. Lily is trying to beat back her body. That's why she runs. She is perpetually striving. His daughter is inverting, disappearing into old T-shirts and complicated layers of tank tops and sports bras.

Lily has become a physics problem.

Henry understands this, but he has no idea how he's supposed to solve it.

When he gets home, he drinks a bottle of water before wandering into the living room, where he sees Lily's CD cases on the table. "Ungod," it says on the cover. God, his child listens to a group called "Ungod." He has become a parent of that kind of child. How did this happen? Way back when he and Beth were on their honeymoon, was it destined that their child would listen to "Ungod" and "Suicide Dream" and jog in the merciless sun? He sinks into the couch.

And then he dreams. He dreams Beth is back, Lily is a baby, and the three of them are dancing in the kitchen. Everyone is smiling and laughing and Henry's body feels so airy that he puts Lily in her highchair and leans to embrace them both. But his wife starts screaming and a strange studio audience boos.

What's wrong? Henry asks. What's the matter?

He stands frozen and helpless until Beth points to Lily who has green, red, yellow, brown substances flowing out of a diamond-shaped hole in her head.

You did this, Beth says. You did this.

He wakes, jolted and guilty for napping in the day, sleeping when he should be working. He turns off the stereo and walks into the kitchen where Lily is peeling an apple.

When did she come in? He watches her deft, slow turns of the apple peel. It is a large apple and the peel drapes down alongside it in spiraling swirls.

"I'm only back for a minute. Alex-Yang is napping."

What does Alex-Yang dream about, Henry wonders, watching her cut the skinless apple into little cubes. Smaller and smaller cubes until the pieces are so small that she uses a butter knife. What's she doing?

"You probably wonder what I'm doing." Lily looks at him.

He nods, trying not to seem eager.

She slides the million cubes of apple into a baggie. "Alex-Yang doesn't eat like normal foods."

Neither do you, he thinks.

"If anything is like the littlest bit too hot or cold it will fuck up his cheek. All the operations."

"Poor guy."

"Yeah, well. It sucks 'cuz he really can't eat anything. Apples have to be really small pieces and he has to suck them so they disintegrate. He can't chew them. Anything too big will knock out the stitches."

"That's for Alex-Yang?" Henry's heart sinks. The apple is not for Lily. It's for a small Chinese boy with a diamond-shaped hole in his cheek.

"No," Lily tells him, "it's for me."

He smiles.

She shrugs. "They only had one apple at the Woolf's, and Alex-Yang only eats if other people are eating exactly what he's eating. It's strange."

More than ever Henry wants to meet this little boy.

"Mrs. Woolf says that Alex-Yang likes to eat only when I'm with him. She says he must feel more comfortable around me than other people."

"That's great."

"I mean he likes other people okay, but he eats on his own when I'm with him, though. When I'm not, Mrs. Woolf has to force him. She says it's a lot more work when I'm not there."

"Oh."

"She says she didn't realize how hard it would be to, you know, have him. You could..." Lily walks to the door. "You could say that I'm kind of keeping him alive, in a way. You know, because he only eats when I'm there."

"Wow," Henry says. "That's great, Lil. That's really great."

But three hours later, it's far from great. It seems like they might never get to the mall to buy Lily's new sneakers.

"There's so much traffic," she whines. "Can't we go tomorrow?"

"Today's your birthday," he says, seriously. "Look—Mount Rainier," he continues, as if the mountain, which is starting to come into view, is an unusual landmark for someone who has lived all of her life in Seattle.

Lily pulls the bottom part of her sneaker. The rubber is loose and minute particles fall to the floor. Henry almost tells her to stop ruining her sneakers, that pulling them is making them worse, but there's no point. They're ruined anyway. That's why he will buy her new ones. Which is crazy. Taking I-5 at 5:30 is crazy too. He knows better. They're barely five miles from their house, but haven't moved in twenty minutes. There are too many cars on this stretch of freeway; it is weighted down and soon the road will buckle and the earth will swallow them up, everything in the car, sneakers and all.

"Did you know that Washington, D.C., has the worst traffic?" he says.

Lily shrugs.

"Seattle is third." He counts eight red cars, seven blue cars, three white ones, seven black, and a foreign one somewhere between yellow and green. Henry should have known better than to drive to the mall. He shouldn't have asked what she wanted for her birthday. He stares at a family in a large blue minivan, wonders what they will make for dinner, then looks at the shoulder blades jabbing through his daughter's shirt.

What if he doesn't buy them? Lily would have to glue the rubber back to her shoe. The glue would bubble when it dried and Lily's shoes would be uneven and she wouldn't be able to run. Except she'd probably buy sneakers herself. She has enough money to buy the sneakers herself. She has gotten rich this summer from chewing apple bits with a Chinese boy who has a hole in his cheek.

"You know what's weird?" she asks, five minutes later.

"No. What?"

"Alex-Yang isn't supposed to chew on his left side, right? That's where the hole is, was. He's supposed to chew on the right side, but he doesn't. It hurts when he chews on the left and the food drips out of the hole. You'd think it'd be easier to chew on the right side."

"Sounds complex."

"His Chinese doctors yell at him for it. I mean I think that's what they're saying. I don't know for sure."

Henry keeps driving. All he wants to do is get to the mall. Once they get there, he'll know what to do, know what to say. For now, he'll keep driving.

But when they finally arrive there, he has no idea what to do. The mall feels complicated and he has no choice but to follow Lily as she weaves through the web of large people with large shopping bags to the store where she will pick out sneakers she wants her father to buy her.

Blue ones.

Blue ones with orange stripes. Henry hands the woman at the register his credit card. His hands feel heavy as he scrawls his name across the receipt. He doesn't want to do this, any of it, but he has to.

"Let's eat," he says after he hands her the bag. The steaks can stay in the freezer. That's the good thing about being frozen. Things don't go bad in the cold. It's heat that spoils things, causes problems like cancer.

He chooses Uncle Chang's Express because it's the first restaurant he sees and it seems impossibly easy to point at the dried yellow rice and gelatinous chicken and say "two please, two Cokes," and pay for them and slide a tray over to Lily. It's easier to do this here and now rather than later, when they are home and she's cutting her steak into cubes and dropping them into her lap while Henry pretends not to look.

He looks at her, inches forward in his chair.

"I'm not hungry."

"Lily," he says sternly, not moving his eyes from her, "it's after six. You didn't eat breakfast. You had maybe one one-hundredth of an apple for lunch. You must be absolutely starving. Unless," he lifts his chopstick and points it at her, "unless, there's something wrong."

She looks away.

"Lily," Henry says, "what's wrong?"

She closes, and then opens one eye. Left, right, left. Open, close, open.

Perception. He showed her this when she was Alex-Yang's age. The way your little finger can move from side to side without really moving.

"Lily. I'll help you. We'll find people to help you through this," he says.

"You. Can't. Make. Me. Eat. This."

"No. I can't." Why is he doing this now? Why didn't he say this last night? Last week? Why now?

"It's disgusting, this food."

Henry takes a bite. She's right. The chicken is thickly sweet, sticky. But still, in an odd way, in a way that doesn't fit into any laws of physics or rules of science, it makes sense to be here, to eat this.

"I'll eat at home."

"I don't believe you," he says. He has a bad taste in his mouth and even if he wanted to, he doesn't think he could stand up now.

"I hate you," she says.

"Fine. But it doesn't solve this problem."

"I don't have a problem." Lily bolts up. "Nothing is wrong. Everything is fine."

"Really? You're fine?"

"I'm just not hungry. Let's go."

"After you eat."

"Fuck you!" Lily picks up a handful of chicken and rice and throws it at him before running off.

He imagines running after her, but she's too fast. He brushes the rice from his chest and shoulders onto the floor. Calmly, he removes the cubes of chicken from his hair and lap. He sets them in a neat row on his tray. Then he eats one. A piece for Lil, he thinks. A piece for Alex-Yang. He chews on the left side of his mouth. Maybe later, he'll go meet Alex-Yang. He should do it sooner rather than later because soon the skin over the hole in his cheek will grow thick and strong, and Alex-Yang will return to China.

Alex-Yang, Henry will say as they chew on the wrong sides of their mouths, what do you think I should do about Lily?

Alex-Yang, Henry will say, I miss my wife and I miss my daughter and sometimes it feels like the walls of my life are closing in on me.

Henry keeps eating. He chews and swallows in a unified syncopated rhythm until fifteen minutes have gone by and Lily returns, sitting across from him in the food court, scowling. "You ruined my birthday."

"Sorry," he tells her, even though he's not. He closes his eyes and thinks about all the problems he's going to have to deal with, all the answers he'll have to write. "Lily? What do you think you're going to do?"

"I'm only starting tenth grade, Dad." When she rolls her eyes, her hunger rolls between them like waves. "I don't have to worry about my career now."

"I mean, where do you think this will get you? Do you see that it's not any place good? You have so much going for you. I don't know why you want to do this…this terrible thing." He catches her eye. "Because it *is* terrible, Lily. It hurts me to watch you hurt yourself."

"I'm not hurting myself." She stabs one piece, then another piece of chicken onto her chopstick. Henry watches it bob up and down. Will she eat it? They both stare at it.

"What I'm going to do is…" She puts down the chopstick. "When I graduate," she spits out, "when I'm eighteen and don't live in your house, I'm going to move to L.A. With my friends. And start a band." She scowls, dares him to argue.

"Really? I didn't know you played an instrument."

She gives him an incredulous stare. "Well, not yet. But I could sing or learn how to play the bass or something. It's not hard. I *could* do it."

"I'm sure you could. If that's what you want."

"It is," she says stubbornly. "My friend's brother lives in L.A. and knows all these musicians. He says L.A. is like becoming the number one city for industrial and Goth."

L.A. is the second worst for traffic, Henry almost says. He didn't mention that in the car but now he wants to tell her not to go to L.A. or D.C. The traffic is so much worse there. He needs her to stay here. But of course, she won't. She's going to grow up and go away. He tries to imagine her—at 19, 21, and 32. Living in L.A. At 32 she will be eight years older than Beth in the picture on his desk. At 40 she will be the age Beth was when she died. In 38 years Lily will be Henry's age, the age he is at this very moment sitting with his teenage daughter on her birthday, two plates of greasy Chinese food between them. He can't imagine her so far, so old. He eats a piece of her chicken. Then another. And another. She watches him chew and swallow.

"Well," he says after several long minutes. "If you make it to L.A. you really will be Lily of the Valley."

"What are you talking about?" She sounds angry. "What valley?"

And in an instant Henry realizes that she's still so young. Fifteen is nothing. His daughter is so young that she doesn't even know that Los Angeles is called the Valley. And it's this—the idea that he still knows infinitely more than she does that makes the problem, her not eating, all of a sudden, manageable. Henry is Lily's father, no matter what she says to him or what she wears or what music she listens to. And as her father, Henry understands with an almost startling clarity that he can help her. He *will* help her, he thinks. When they get home, he'll call doctors, other parents, and everyone else he can think of who might be able to tell him what he can do with a fifteen-year-old who doesn't want to eat. He can call people, and research, and work day and night to help. There is nothing between them except the here and now, and Henry understands that soon they will dump their plates in the trash, stack their trays on top of one another, and go home.

"Nothing," he says gently. He stands up. "You want to get going? You want to go home?"

Lily scowls, but a moment later stands up and follows him through the food court, back through the mall, and into the parking lot. Henry links her arm through his, and for that moment she doesn't protest. He imagines he and Lily will go to see Alex-Yang together, where she will eat the food the boy eats. Lily will eat everything then, and Henry will lightly touch the fresh skin on Alex-Yang's cheek, reassured that the boy is healthy and strong. That everyone is.

Above the Angels

Philip Levine

for Strempek

A row of corrugated gray huts
   hunkering down in the November rain.
Across the way the fire burns night and day
though unseen now in first light. Bernard
wakens to the bouquet of warming milk
and burned coffee. It will be said later
he had the bearing of an angel
with clear eyes, a wide untroubled brow,
thick golden curls. His mother's home now
from the night shift to prepare his day,
so he rises and stands as a man
on the cold linoleum. The Rouge plant,
where she works, goes on burning and banging,
but neither mother nor son notices.
It's their life. Nonsense, we say,
how can the life of an angel abide
a Ford plant where the treasures
of the earth are blasted and beaten
into items? In an empty church
in Genoa two years ago, we saw
the girl Mary in a rose gown shyly
bowing before a dazzling Gabriel,
the painting stained but recognizable.
That was an angel, bathed in his own light,
bearing the gift of a God, a terrifying
presence from an unknown world!
When Bernard bows to dip his bread
into the coffee, his mother lays a hand
on the pale nape as though she knows
he will die eleven years from now
in a fiery crash on U.S. 24
on his way home and thus leave
an orphaned son behind. In this world
the actual occurs. In November
the cold rain streams skyward in sheets,
the dawn passes, the day shift arrives,
the houses grip down, separate and scared.

The Liver Nephew

Susan Ito

*P*ARKER KATAMI HAD JUST COME BACK FROM A FOUR-MILE RUN WHEN HE opened his mail—a photocopied article from the *New England Journal of Medicine* tucked into an envelope. He pulled it out with hot, damp hands. There were a few lines, in his uncle's trembling, miniscule print, scribbled in the margin. *Dear Nephew,* it said, *I must ask you for a rather large favor.* The article was about a groundbreaking medical procedure called Living Donor Transplant. The favor, it turned out, was for Parker to donate half of his liver to Uncle Min.

Parker leaned against his front door for several minutes, panting and staring at the brass mail slot through which the envelope had been spat. Thin rivulets of sweat streaked down his neck and forked around his clavicle like transparent veins. He put his hand to his stomach, and then around toward his ribs, patting the skin. He wasn't even quite sure where his liver was located.

Contact with his uncle had been infrequent recently—not much beyond the chipper, generic holiday cards that his Auntie Reiko sent out every year, signed with both their names—but Parker's childhood memories of Uncle Min were tinged with comfort. Parker seemed to remember some mention of Uncle's being ill, but this was to be expected with people of their age, wasn't it? His own parents were both dead, his father of a brain tumor some years ago, his mother from emphysema. Did his uncle really expect to trick Nature, and gain new life from having a younger person's liver? It sounded hopeful and naïve, like cryogenics. Parker squinted at the medical article again, clotted with words he didn't understand, and then tossed it onto the coffee table.

He didn't like the idea of going to a hospital, much less letting them open up his body and take something out. He had seen enough of hospitals with his parents: his father's wrists tied to the metal bedrails with cotton gauze rope, his mother straining to pull in air through bluish lips.

He went into the kitchen and snapped the metal ring from a can of ginger ale, took a long noisy gulp. After rummaging through a junk drawer for a ballpoint pen, he studied the article and then slapped it face down on the table. *Uncle M,* he printed on the back of the page, *wish I could help but I can't. Sorry.* As he contemplated whether or not to write "Love," before signing his name, the phone rang.

"Hello."

"Paka-chan!" The high, breathy voice of Auntie Reiko, who always sounded on the edge of hysterical giggles.

"Hi, Auntie." He scribbled a little star shape on the paper, and then wrote *Love, Parker.*

"Parker, tell me, did you get Uncle's letter? It should be there by now." A rumbling voice in the background, Uncle Min saying something. Muffle muffle, and then a hard click as her wedding ring hit the receiver.

"Auntie? Yeah, it came today."

"Oh, Parker . . ." Her voice rose even higher, tightening and shrinking, until it squeezed into the corner between the ceiling and walls. "Your uncle is so sick, he's suffering so, *kawai soh,* poor thing."

"I'm sorry. I didn't realize." He chewed a bit of skin away from his thumbnail, and closed his eyes. Uncle suffering? He didn't want to know.

She sniffled loudly. "So you'll help him, neh? Your papa's *o toto?*"

"What about Patty and George, Auntie?" His cousins.

"Oh, Parker, they couldn't. So you the last hope. Doctor says he can't last long like this, maybe two months. Parker-chan, please!" Her voice was broken and wet.

"Auntie, I don't know, my job . . ." Perhaps this was something they could understand, his career. He had recently been promoted to editor of a slick but faltering Denver-area magazine, targeted toward urban athletes.

She was now weeping uncontrollably.

Parker's blood thumped so loudly in his ears that he could barely hear her voice. Uncle Min was talking in the background beyond her sobs, and he sounded just like Parker's father, the way Parker remembered his voice from long ago. He looked out the window, at a woman on the sidewalk in a red raincoat. A black dog was pulling away from her, nosing at a paper cup in the gutter. "Let me talk to him," he said.

He paced in his apartment for two days before he gave way to his desperate confusion and dialed Joel's number. They had agreed there would be no phone calls, but this constituted an emergency, didn't it?

Joel picked up on the first ring. There was jazz playing in the background, and more than one person talking.

"Joel. It's me."

There was a pause, and then, "Hey. Hey, what's up?" A strained kind of casual.

"Listen, Joel, sorry to call so late, but something really freaky is happening and . . ."

"Wait a sec, let me go in the other room." The sound of a door closing, and the music abruptly stopped. "What? You're not sick, are you?"

"No, it isn't me. It's my uncle."

"Your uncle? What uncle?" Parker realized that he'd never mentioned his remaining family to Joel, nor Joel to them.

"My dad's brother. Min. Well, he's got some medical problem, something serious, and they're asking me to donate my liver."

"What? You mean if you get in a car wreck?"

"No, Joel, that's the thing. They want me to donate half of it, *now*. They call it a living transplant."

Parker heard water running, and the squeaky sound of the medicine cabinet door. He hadn't been in Joel's apartment in a month, and suddenly he was sick with longing. "Joel? You still there?"

"Wait. He wants *half* of your *liver*?" Parker gripped the phone hopefully. Maybe Joel was understanding how important this was, how impossible it was to make this decision alone.

"Yeah. It's this new thing, this experimental . . ." Parker was rushing his words into the phone.

"And what are you supposed to do with just half a liver?"

"Supposedly it grows back." It sounded insane now, telling it to Joel.

"Huh. That's . . . interesting." The sound of running water.

"So what do you think? Do you think I should do it?" Parker ached to say, *Please come with me,* but he couldn't.

"I don't know what to tell you, Park. Listen, man . . ." The bathroom door swung open, and the receiver filled with partying sounds again. "Hey, it's your decision."

"But I'm asking *you*. Do you think you could come over? Maybe later?"

"I'm sorry, Park. I've got people here." The voices and the music began mixing with Joel's voice, growing louder—he was probably walking into the kitchen now—and Parker knew that his five minutes of privacy was up, that he was being firmly led to the door.

"Yeah, I know," he said in a low voice, and hung up.

And so Parker didn't say no, but he didn't say yes. He had conversations with his uncle's physicians, both the primary-care doctor and the hotshot guy in charge of the transplant team, who spoke rapidly and repeated himself, a verbal twitching. The only clear thing that Parker recalled from the conversation was the number two: two percent mortality rate among living donors. He repeated that to the doctor to make sure he understood. "Mortality rate: that means dead, right?"

"Right, right."

"And you don't think I'm too . . . old for this? I'm thirty-eight, almost." His birthday less than a month away.

"No, not at all. It's a good age, a good, good age."

Parker thought of a morning when he was seven or eight, bouncing on the edge of his father's bed. *It's my birthday, Papa. Say Happy Birthday.* He bounced and chanted until his father rose up from his pillow and smacked him above the ear. *Here's something for your birthday!*

There was one present he remembered vividly: a kite that Uncle Min had brought him for his birthday, a tiger on red silk. Uncle had taken him and Patty and George to a park in Berkeley, a lonely place that was empty of trees, just grassy hills with a wind that tore at their clothes and set the tiger pouncing against the sky.

He agreed to the blood test, and when it came up a match, he packed his suitcase. A thick envelope arrived in the mail from his aunt and uncle, containing a first-class airplane ticket to San Francisco. He had never flown first class in his life. *I'm the fatted calf,* he thought, *being led to slaughter.* He notified his publisher that he'd be out of town, saying that the associate editor would handle things while he was gone. He wrote a note to Joel and left it prominently on the coffee table, in case Joel should happen to stop by. He still had Parker's key.

He boarded the airplane ahead of everyone else, along with the wealthy, the infirm, and the parents traveling with small children. When the flight attendant led him to the wide leather seat, his eyes darted about momentarily, as if he was going to be thrown out. Parker sat down gingerly. How inexpressibly more comfortable the first-class seat was, how delicious the food, how reassuring the heavy thick silverware, the actual china plates. They brought him ice water in a glass goblet, and a steaming towel to press against his face. He tried not to think of the Last Supper.

Uncle Min opened the front door as soon as the taxi pulled up to the curb. "Take a cab, not the shuttle van," they had told him. The house, outer Sunset district, was the same as he remembered—pale pink, unremarkable in the rows and rows of minty little houses all lined up together. Parker remembered wishing, when he was small, that he could lick them, thinking they would taste like the candies next to the cash register at the Ocean Diner.

Uncle Min was wearing his bathrobe and slippers, even though it was four in the afternoon. His skin was a frightening amber color, and his eyes golden, like a cat's. They glossed over with tears as he took Parker's hands in both of his. Auntie Reiko was right behind him, shaking her head with emotion, her hand covering her mouth. Parker reached past his uncle to embrace her, her dyed-black hair smelling like onions and Pond's lotion.

"Dinner ready soon," she said. "You go, go, lie down and rest. Bring your suitcase to George's room. And wash your hands, those planes are so *kitanai*."

"I don't need to rest, Auntie," Parker said. "It wasn't that long a flight." He carried his bag up the half-flight of steps to his cousin's room. The room had been preserved as a kind of shrine to George's boyhood: posters of punk bands, the electric bass on its stand, the rows and rows of sci-fi novels on the shelf. Nothing had been tampered with since George, the prized son, had graduated from high school. Parker's own childhood home didn't even exist anymore; the year he'd gone to college, his parents had moved into a small townhouse in another state.

When Parker returned to the living room, Uncle Min shuffled past him and collapsed in the red easy chair in the living room. It had dishtowels on either arm to cover up the bald spots. "Come on, sit down then. You want a beer? Reiko, get him a beer."

Parker sat on the piano bench, half covered in unopened mail and catalogs. The television was tuned to a tennis match. A gray band of dialogue scrolled up the screen. AND IT'S LOVE NOTHING.

"How come the volume's off?" Parker asked.

"Ah, those announcers, their voices give me a headache." Uncle Min waved his hand disgustedly at the screen. The stereo was on, a scratchy LP of "Man of La Mancha." Parker and Uncle Min sat and watched the yellow ball silently plunking back and forth. *To dream the impossible dream.* By the time Aunt Reiko brought a tray with a bottle of beer and a bowl of rice crackers, Uncle Min was slumped in the chair, snoring.

Parker watched the soundless game until his eyes came to rest on the lacquer box on top of the television set: his uncle's Go game. He lifted it down, and a rush of remembered anticipation filled his throat as he opened it: the same smooth black and white pebbles he'd played with when he was small, their cool weight, the clicking sound they made in his palm. He laid them out on the wooden board, rows of ten. Parker had never actually learned how to play; he just loved making patterns of the smooth stone on wood. He counted out ninety-eight of the blacks. They nearly filled the board, solid, dark. Then he plucked two white from the box and considered their small stark forms against the black field. That was two percent.

"Parker! Baby cousin!" His cousin Patty arrived just as the tennis match was finishing. Her Minnie Mouse voice was a younger version of her mother's. She was only a year and a half older than he, and it annoyed him that she still called him Baby.

Parker awkwardly draped his arm around her. "Hi, Patty."

"Look at you!" She squeezed his upper arm. "You're in such good shape, Parker. Are you still running?"

Patty was twenty pounds heavier than he remembered, and her bangs and round black haircut made her cheeks even plumper. He wondered if she remembered kissing him under the ping-pong table one teenaged Thanksgiving, her mouth tasting like cherry lifesavers, his hands clutching the black rope of her hair. It was so long it had brushed the floor. She was the only girl he had ever kissed.

Brad, Patty's *hakujin* husband, gave him a high-five. "How you doing, man." Brad was the kind of guy who bounced on the balls of his feet, who wore athletic shoes all the time, and who would want to play touch football on the lawn after dinner. Their two-year-old *hapa* kid wouldn't look at him when Brad held him up. "Say hello to Uncle Parker."

"I'm not his uncle," said Parker; he didn't like joining Brad in false joviality. "We're first cousins once-removed." He reached out to tickle the boy under the chin, but it turned into more of a poke. The boy treaded air and started to cry.

Aunt Reiko came into the living room and held up her hands, red and chapped, as if she had just finished building a snowman without mittens on. Parker wondered if she had the kind of illness that makes a person scrub their hands every five minutes.

"*Itadakimasu*," she called out cheerily. "Please come eat. Everyone wash hands first."

"What about George?" Parker said.

Everyone's face suddenly fell flat, and Parker looked out the window. A teenager from the pale yellow house across the street was hauling a black trash bag down the steps. The last thing he'd remembered hearing about George was that he had started up his own computer-graphics business. Maybe it had gone bust.

"George has important things to do." Patty's voice was sharp and she had a tight, odd smile on her face. "Maybe he'll grace us with his presence, and maybe not."

Parker saw Auntie Reiko trying to exchange a look with Uncle Min, but his uncle wouldn't look up from the tablecloth. "*Itadakimasu*," he said firmly, and everyone took their seats and responded in dutiful chorus, even Brad, "*Dozo*."

There was sukiyaki in an electric skillet, the orange extension cord snaking across the dining room table, just as Parker remembered from Sunday dinners after church. Auntie Reiko leaned over the pan, poking at the meat and the clear glossy noodles with extra-long chopsticks. Parker remembered a plastic plate with a duck on it that they had kept in the cabinet just for him. The blue hinged kiddie-chopsticks. He tried to remember how many years it had been since they had all sat around the table like this, his mother and father, aunt and uncle and cousins, lifting the curled meat out of the communal skillet, while the windows around them grew moist with steam.

Uncle Min's nose was the same shape as his own father's, a soft, short beak. They had the same wedge-shaped eyebrows too. Parker thought about the final months of his father's life: a chaotic seesawing between raging incoherence and disturbing, childlike affections. Parker never knew when his father might hurl his dinner to the floor or when he would hold out his jittering hand and whine, "Kiss."

His father had never kissed Parker before, not in his living memory. He had been gruff and distant, communicating mostly in disgusted grunts and a furious tossing of his head. "*Baka!*" he used to shout. *Stupid idiot.* There was not a sliver of kindness that Parker could dredge up from his childhood. All gifts, all warmth, every kiss was only from his mother. Or from Uncle.

Uncle Min was pouring sake into small white cups. Auntie had warmed it in the microwave. "I want to say toast for Parker," he said, his voice husky.

His aunt and Patty and Brad all lifted their little cups. The little boy waved a plastic cup of apple juice. "*Kampai*, Parker." *Kampai!* The heated sake coursed, clean and bright, through Parker's chest.

"Thank you, Uncle," Parker said, the heat of the drink strengthening his resolve. "I'm glad I can do this." This is my purpose, he thought. This is why I am here. He reached down, as had now become a habit, and rubbed his side.

He wondered if he would have been able to do this for his own father.

Parker slept in his cousin George's room that night, surrounded by teenaged posters whose edges had begun to curl. There was no trace of the adult George, the slick guy who produced special-effects graphics for high-end clients like Pepsi and IBM. Parker lay between the clean, faded plaid bedsheets and wondered what his aunt and uncle's favored son had done. Nobody had mentioned his name again during dinner.

Parker slipped out of bed and walked to the kitchen in bare feet. There was a night-light glowing yellow over the stove. He dialed Joel's number, not caring that it was three in the morning in Denver. Joel didn't pick up, so Parker mumbled into the receiver, "Just wanted to let you know, I decided to do it. I'm at my uncle's in San Francisco. We check into the hospital tomorrow." He paused, wanting to say more, but he couldn't think of how to say it to a machine.

Parker woke up to the sound of Auntie Reiko's tapping on the doorframe. "*Ohayo gozaimasu,* Paka-chan. Big day today." Parker and Uncle were going to the hospital for a week of tests and hi-tech photographs, a careful mapping of their veins, the mysterious terrain of their livers' lobes. Before the first slice into flesh, they would see it all on computers, the plan of the entire medical procedure. Parker imagined the click of the mouse over his uncle's darkened liver, how it would lift and float into the little trashcan.

They ate breakfast in silence, bowls of *ochazuke,* hot tea over cold rice, with scrambled eggs on paper plates, and raisin toast. A soft wet grain of rice stuck to his Uncle's chin. As they listened to the drone of weather and traffic on the radio, a buzzer ripped through the kitchen. Auntie Reiko leapt to her feet. "Who—so early?"

And then her pained exclamation from the front door, "George!" Parker looked up to see a familiar face, but with a shining bald head and something sparkling and black in one earlobe. It was his cousin, but nearly unrecognizable. George wore a long black overcoat with delicate shoes and an expensive suit. Parker wondered for an instant, seeing the smooth bald head, if George had cancer, or a brain tumor, but he looked too healthy. He was carrying an armful of lilies wrapped in green waxed paper.

"Hi, Dad." George spoke to his father without looking at him, and then scraped a chair across the floor, straddling it backward. "Hey there, cuz." He narrowed his eyes for a second, and then flashed a brilliant, tooth-whitened smile. "You're a better man than I, Gunga Din."

Parker shrugged. "It worked out. Just luck that my blood matched and yours didn't."

A strange look passed over George's face—a microsecond of pity in his eyebrows. "Yeah."

Parker nodded toward his cousin's outfit. "Well, look at you, George. I guess life's been treating you fine." He hoped that George wouldn't ask about his job, shoestring editor at a monthly that was probably going to fold in a year.

"Well, yeah, the company is really taking off. We did twenty mil this quarter." George spoke with a distracted formality, and his eyes roamed from the ceiling to the floor and walls while he tilted back and forth on the kitchen chair.

"Is that right?" Parker had the urge to reach out and hold George still.

Auntie Reiko dug into the rice cooker with a wooden paddle. Her voice was high and wound up. "George, you want some *ochazuke*? Plenty here."

"No Ma, I already ate."

"So! Parker, are you seeing anyone? Got a girlfriend?" George looked pointedly at his parents. Uncle Min had put his head in his hands and Auntie was rubbing her fingers, shaking her head. George opened his wallet and showed Parker a photograph of a smiling young Asian woman in a ski jacket. The background was brilliant blue sky. "This is Nancy, Nancy Chu. You'll get an invitation to the wedding, next summer." George laughed. "*Shinajin*. Big banquet wedding, lots of good food." He folded the wallet into his coat. "You'll get an invitation. And you can bring a date." George stared at Parker with piercing eyes, the color of strong coffee.

Parker shrugged and dropped his gaze to the table. "I'm not seeing any-one right now." Joel had only been half a year, not long enough to introduce, just like all the others before him. He hadn't come out to his relatives, not really, not after his father had foamed and shouted, *baka* boy! *Kitanai!* Filthy.

George clapped his hands together. "So, Dad, you lucked out, didn't you?" There was steel in his voice. "Got old Parker here to give it up for you."

Auntie Reiko had backed away into the hallway with the telephone. She was calling the taxi company with a high urgency in her voice. "We need a ride to hospital."

Uncle Min lifted his head wiped his mouth with a paper towel. "Parker is a good boy. Good nephew." He grunted and smiled with watery eyes at Parker.

"Yeah. He's the greatest." The two front legs of George's chair hit the floor with a sharp crack. "Only you know what, Dad? I would've done it for you." George leapt to his feet and was pacing the room now, his fine leather shoes slapping on the linoleum.

Uncle Min let out a small cry. "No."

Parker felt something slipping from him, his sense of understanding, his connectedness with the elderly man across the table. His being useful. Here he had been ready, ready for sacrifice, in his mind he was already stripped down and laid flat on a rock, his limbs bound with strips of leather. The hawks would be coming any day now, to tear his liver from his side, and deliver it, dripping, to his uncle. He was ready.

Uncle Min was shaking his head. "George. *Enough*."

"No, Dad, I don't think it's enough. I don't think Cousin Parker here has heard enough. Not until you tell him that you wouldn't let Patty or me get our blood tested, wouldn't even let us talk to the doctors. And so now you've got this poor sucker here, and God help you both."

Parker blinked but still the room would not clear, would not slow its spinning. The sunlight from the glass suddenly hurt. His face twisted into a confused, helpless smile. "Wouldn't let you?" It was an enormous task to form each word.

George paced back and forth, his long black coat flapping like the wings of a bat. "That's right, cousin. That's right. We wanted to, Patty and I, because who *wouldn't* want to be able to do this for their very own father? But he said no. NO, he said, what about Patty's husband, what about Patty's child. Can't do this to them. And even me, I have this fi-an-cée, and I have this business; no, no, too much risk. Huh, Dad? So why don't we call Parker instead? He's healthy! He's athletic! As long as his blood checks out, he's the perfect candidate! He doesn't have any..." George abruptly stopped.

Uncle Min's face was nearly drained of its considerable color. He had turned his face to the window, his shoulders hunched around him.

George's face softened as he looked at Parker. He lifted his empty hands. "I had to tell you, cousin."

So that was why he had been chosen: not for being the favored nephew, for being beloved kin, but for being dispensable. For being alone. For being different.

Auntie Reiko stood in the kitchen doorway, her face wet, her mouth crumpled behind her hand. The bouquet that George had brought lay on the counter. The petals were soft and limp, drooping against the green paper.

Parker's mouth tried to say "Thank you," to George but his tongue lay fat and dense against his teeth. Was that the thing to say? Thank you? He stood up uncertainly.

His aunt's anguished voice ripped across the room. "Paka-chan! No! Not like George say!"

Parker drew a ragged breath and walked to where his uncle sat. He put his hand out, lightly, uncertainly, and touched the thin shoulder. He felt a faint ripple of pity pass through his fingers, and for a moment he thought of changing his mind, of saying *it's all right, it doesn't matter, I'll do it anyway*. But it wouldn't help things: wouldn't make Joel stay, wouldn't make Parker any less alone. The tiger kite had snapped its string and smashed to earth.

"Goodbye, Uncle."

He walked quickly to the hallway, to where his bag was already packed, ready for the hospital. The taxi was idling outside. He passed by his cousin on his way out, and saw that George's brown eyes were wet and bright. George bowed deeply, the front edges of his black overcoat brushing the floor. Parker leaned forward in return, and their two heads—one smooth and golden, one dark—touched briefly, then parted.

The Golden Hour

Sue Ellen Thompson

*T*hose final weeks, there was an hour
　each afternoon when stillness would conspire
with the autumn light. They would embrace

my mother in her sickbed
and my father with his book spread-eagled
on his chest beside her, dozing.

I'd stand outside their bedroom door
and know that nothing bad would happen for an hour—
that I could leave the house, return to find

the cat still curled between the shapes
that were my parents and the same
staccato puffs of air escaping from my mother's

lips. I'd walk the fields behind
their house, the endless avenues of dry
golden cornstalks leading nowhere and away,

and think of those first few weeks at home
with my infant daughter, how the world I'd known
before, the world of books and men and dinner

parties, had abandoned me. The phone calls
from my friends at work dropped off
and what remained of my life gazed at me with slate

blue eyes. Once, after nursing, she fell
into a sleep so bottomless the cell
door opened briefly and I thought

of slipping out, but her hold on me was already
too fierce. Pausing mid-field, I'd turn instinctively
back toward that slowly stirring maelstrom

of grief. My mother would awaken to the sound
of a November wind quickening around
the corners of the house and the sun dropping into

its coinbox. Sometimes her eyes
would flutter briefly, and I'd remember why
I kept that child so close to me for years

and how relinquishing her came hard.
The hour would end. I'd put my mother's arms
around my neck and lift her to the commode.

I'd rent a Katharine Hepburn video
and re-heat leftovers. If it was cold,
I'd swaddle her in afghans on the sofa.

So Much in the World Is Waiting to Be Found Out

Sariah Dorbin

A RAILROAD OF STAPLES TRAVERSES MY MOTHER'S HEAD. WHEN MY EYES travel south I realize my mistake in seeking a better view; from her bed hang pouches filled with fluids the color of illness.

They have shaved the right side where the staples are, but the red hair on the other side has been left alone. My mother looks like Bozo the Clown only worse, Bozo with just half the wig and the bald part in the wrong place. Also the face is no good; I'd understood that the surgery was to relieve the swelling. By appearances, I gather they have simply taken the swelling from inside her skull and transferred it to the outside. They have also, I can see, replaced her makeup with a smear of purple across her cheekbone and temple. What the hell is wrong with these doctors?

Of my mother's talents, makeup ranked high on a rather short list, particularly that most difficult job—eyeliner. More than once she tried to show me the way, but to no avail. Ever since her first eye job, she herself had been blessed with that concavity above the eyelid typical of beautiful women: Sophia Loren, Audrey Hepburn, Catherine Deneuve. With this sort of eyelid, smudging was never a problem. But after arranging me and my frothy prom dress at her vanity and attempting to paint my eyelids for the first time, my mother had clucked with dismay over the way my lids rubbed up against themselves at the crease. "Just try not to blink," she said, and I wondered whether she might be serious.

Leaning against the cold metal rails of her bed, I look down at my mother's swollen eyelids, closed but somehow glaring at me. Even if I were able, I could not paint them for her now.

All I can do, it seems, is try to calm my breathing to match the ordered pace of her ventilator, and reach out my hand to stroke hers. It is limp from drugs or coma, I'm not sure which, and pale and crinkled next to mine, but our fingernails are identical: short, filed into careful ovals, and painted from the same bottle of milky-pink polish we share at our appointment each Saturday, which is always followed by a pair of decaf lattés—hers with Sweet & Low, mine with three sugars. This weekly manicure is one of the few pursuits my mother has shown interest in over the years. Since retiring from the Chanel counter at Neiman's, she has rarely left her condo except to trace a familiar route through Westwood on foot, seeking variety and friendship only in the formal, protracted chats she charms strangers into during their wait for dry cleaning or fresh baguette.

Life, it seems to me, never ponied up for my mother. But then, she stopped wanting things thirty-six years ago, when her agent stopped sending her out, her boyfriend stopped taking her out, and she went to the hospital instead, to begin my life as her own seemed to end.

Here we are, together in a hospital, again. It is the kind of place that makes it clear who is in your life. It is good for that. It is bad for that.

A man named David called me yesterday, while I was casting cats for a cat-food commercial. You'd be surprised how few cats are up to the job, which is simply to eat cat food with the lights on. David's job is to carry a very fancy cellular phone and to call people whose loved ones wind up in the UCLA emergency room. He must deal with noisy freakouts of all kinds in his ear, as well as abrupt silences, as he explains to multiple family members what happened to the loved ones and what the doctors have to say. I cannot believe how well he performed these duties when it was my turn—but then, he only had the one call to make.

Calmly, and with just the right amount of detail, David explained about the truck in the crosswalk, the various head and leg injuries and the not talking. After that, when I'd found my way to him after wandering through the labyrinthine halls of the hospital, he explained about the bleed in the speech center of my mother's brain. It was then that we made the joint discovery of my own legs not working anymore, at which point he gently took my arm and led me to a bank of plastic seats. His palm was remarkably dry.

Today, post-surgery, my mother has been moved to the Neuro ICU, a ward of twisted, twitching people who look as though they will be asleep for the rest of their lives. Most are young men, and though I cannot believe it of them in their current state, these are studly specimens, caught unlucky amidst acts of great daring. All around me lies compelling evidence against the wisdom of bungee jumping, motocross racing, extreme skiing. Also I cannot leave out walking to the hairdresser, the latest calamity sport.

At home, my three dogs follow me around until I remember to put on their leashes and walk them past the sad, chalky houses on my block. It is true that dogs save me in ways people cannot. Right now, for instance, I find myself hoping that all three dogs will shit on the lawn in front of number 2731 so that I can do something with my shaking hands.

Later, the dogs follow me into the bathroom. When they sit on the floor next to me, I place my hands under their wishbone-shaped jaws and feel the heaviness of their heads as they relax.

As I walk down the ramp that slices through the hangar-like space of the ad agency where I work, I see beneath me the tilted, furrowed face of Sean, my 24-year-old assistant.

"How is she?" he asks when I get to his desk. He holds the tension in his face while waiting for my answer. But I can't think of any words that would add up to an accurate description.

Much to my dismay, Sean has told me at regular intervals over the last year that he is in love with me, something I cannot accept as fact, given his youth and how far I feel from my own.

"Millsy," he says now, a riff on my last name. "Sweetie. Lunch?" He touches my forearm; I cringe at the moisture of his fingertips, which reminds me of the more awkward moments between us. No matter which reason I have offered him—the difference in our ages, our positions—he refuses to accept or believe it. "What's twelve years?" he said once. He thinks love is enough; that's how young he is.

I step back, and his arm falls from mine. I've discussed with him several times my need to not have it look as though we are sleeping together. Because we are not. "Messages?"

He hands me a stack of black-lined pink slips, which I flip through as I walk through the office. I feel about this place the way I feel about Manhattan or Chicago—nice places to visit, but I wouldn't want to live there. Sadly, I do live here, sixty hours a week at an orange desk inside a lime green cage, surrounded by other lime green cages housing orange desks. The agency produces crappy advertising everyone is embarrassed about. To make up for this, its founders have spent a large amount of money making the place look *happening* and *creative*, even when it is not. In this way, the agency itself is a kind of lie, much like the product it manufactures.

In fact, I do not actually *work* here. Other people, younger people in my group, do the work. I just look at the work and say *yes* or *no*. This is harder than it sounds, because even when I say *yes* a loud voice inside my head screams *No!* No, this will not win an award, the esteem of my colleagues, a ticket out of this schlock-factory. No, this will not lift me back onto the track from which I derailed somewhere along the line, who knows where. No, this cannot possibly be the sum total of my contribution to society.

Two guys are standing now in my lime-green doorway. The art director is holding oniony pieces of marker paper covered with little black boxes in which dumb things are happening involving a new kind of hair gel. He peers at me through his black stringy bangs.

"The Holdilocks thing?" his tall, beaky partner reminds me, in the questioning way that is supposed to sound hip. "We were supposed to show you yesterday?"

"We're going to play a game," I tell them. "For the next while—I don't know how long—we're going to pretend that I'm blind." I explain that they are to present their ideas to me over the phone, that I will be at the hospital most of the time instead of at the office.

On their way out, I hear the art director mutter to his partner, "Pretend?"

An hour later Sean follows me through the bright sunshine to my car. He stands still, holding my gear for the shoot in his arms, while I lift things away one by one: laptop, cables, casting tapes, production notebooks, and directories.

"I could quit," he says. "To help you."

"No," I say.

"You have a lot of important decisions to make. You'll need someone to talk to."

I don't like that he sounds grown up. Even in the parking lot, this place produces lies.

At the hospital, teams of people with advanced degrees have asked my permission for several procedures each day that I have been here. These encounters are a lot like those in the rest of my life—all I have to do is say *yes* or *no*, and though I always say *yes* here, it is not what I mean. *No*, says that other voice, the soundless one that is perhaps my real voice. No, this can't be happening. No, this is not my fault.

Only weeks before the accident, my mother had asked me to accompany her to the supermarket. There had been a scene involving a lack of artichokes and she'd been asked not to come back. Fortified by my presence, she'd apologized to the manager who, flicking uncomfortable glances my way, reinstated her privileges. This incident clearly pointed to some sort of slippage, a recent, insidious slide from her always-perfect manners. Now, sifting through my mother's bills—many of them apparently months overdue—I do not wish to consider my inattention, my lack of action on her behalf. You're on it *now*, I nearly convince myself. What can be done now?

Ortho wants to re-break the ankle before setting it. Plastics wants to insert a pump in the other leg to drain the wound. Neuro, concerned still with pressure in her brain, wants to operate again. Neuro also wants a g-tube, antibiotics, a trach for better suctioning. Neuro is very demanding.

In between the permission-seeking, I try to eat cafeteria soup that smells like the hallways, and attend to my ringing cell phone. Today the Account Person has played the commercial for the client without me, and the client is unhappy. "The first 28 seconds are fine," she tells me. In the last two seconds of the commercial, the cat was supposed to run into frame and pounce on a bowl of the client's kibble.

"What's the problem?" I ask. "He *pounced.*"

"Yes," she says. "But Jerry says the cat's not smiling."

The doctors' representatives approach me, wearing white coats and effortless composure, but the doctors themselves do not stop and talk; they do not have time.

When I finally demand to meet with a doctor, the conference room pulses with empty chairs and absences—relatives long dead or denounced; acquaintances un-nudged toward friendship; men retreated as from a bad smell (my father, the first of these, who perhaps led the way, held the light, posted the signs).

The woman from Neuro sits quietly but is somehow breathless, as if to say, "I'm here for you, but it's costing someone somewhere something." Her face is blank, feigning patience at my questions.

"We just don't know," she says for the fourth time. My mother may never speak again, or she may fully recover. The longer she stays in bed now, the longer she may be in a wheelchair later.

"Like forever?" I ask. "Is forever a possibility?" The doctor explains something about atrophy and muscle contraction that I can't quite follow. I watch her mouth move, try to square those pretty lips with the ugliness of her words.

"A likelihood?" I ask. "Or a possibility?" I try to imagine my mother with bad legs. Instead, I conjure a crisp March night a few years ago. My mother, striding well ahead of me along Wilshire Boulevard after a movie, kicked her still beautiful seventy-one-year-old legs nearly as high as a chorus girl's while singing *"On the Sunny Side of the Street."* She sang all the words without stopping her legs, even after the sky broke open and dumped sheets of rain.

The point of this meeting is a document I have read and until now have ignored. Drafted by my mother's attorney years ago, this document is a dinosaur of contingency, its wording vague and insubstantial where it should be intricate as lace.

Catastrophic is the word I am stuck on, the word I have come here today to define with the help of an expert. What, exactly, did my mother mean? Couldn't she—a woman who insisted upon butter knives and fish forks—have been more specific?

The doctor straightens her shoulders. "Most people," she informs me, "indicate specifically which treatments they do and do not want. Some draw the line at heroic measures."

"Heroic. You mean like emergency brain surgery?" My go-ahead on that seemed like a given at the time.

The doctor is speaking now in sympathetic tones about the burden of responsibility, even as she leads into yet another request, this time for something called a central line. They want to quit stabbing my mother with needles, to pump in her numerous medications through a single catheter. But this procedure has some risk.

It is like dealing with a crafty mechanic, when I know nothing about cars, but with the stakes significantly higher. I look around the room, my eyes resting on all those empty chairs. "Yes," I say. "Yes."

Each morning I rise out of bed with a sense of purpose that was never inspired by cat food or hair gel. Mired in insurance tasks and the beginnings of a lawsuit against the truck driver, I keep office hours in the hospital's 7th floor lounge. I sit in one chair, pile paperwork in another. I wonder how people ever got through things like this before cell phones.

The other people in the lounge seem happy to have the distraction of watching me lose my shit with the HMO my mother had apparently switched to only months ago. Today a grandmotherly African-American woman watches me as though I were a television show.

"You can't just go to any hospital you feel like," the insurance lady recites into my ear.

"I really don't think my mother *felt* like coming here." My voice sounds as though it has teeth. "But it was six blocks from where she was *hit by a truck.*"

"That was unfortunate," says the lady.

"Yeah, thanks…"

"Because UCLA is not in our network. So she needs to select a hospital that is."

"That's kind of hard to do when you're unconscious," I say, before I hang up.

My next call is from the lawyer I've retained, who requests proof that my mother's medical costs will exceed the driver's insurance coverage of $15,000. The bill for the first week is $73,875. This seems an extraordinary amount of money until I remember that the commercial with the unsmiling cat, which will never appear on the air, cost the Frisky Whiskers people $425,000.

Sean calls. He wants to know what I'm eating for dinner.

"She's not dead," I tell him. "You can stop being my mother."

We both take a breath.

"I'm sorry," I say.

"Are you getting any exercise?" he asks.

My mother, even after three weeks, continues to warrant a steady stream of nurses who care for her in 12-hour shifts. Each tends to her in a flurry of constant, small movements, as though my mother were a complicated gourmet dish. I like today's nurse better than the others; her taut body lends her actions a kind of precision lacking in the others. I sit in a chair against the wall and track her movements: suctioning my mother's lungs; replacing the bag of jade green paste that is her food; monitoring the numbers on the machines whose continuous, mysterious bleeps and clicks I cannot distinguish from the sounds of real emergency.

"Do you want to know what it means?" The nurse has seen me staring blankly at the screen of one of the machines and is offering to help. Each new nurse I've encountered has offered me a miracle, a story of recovery and resurrection that I find unbelievable. This one explains the numbers, shows me which one measures the pressure in the brain, which one reports how many breaths each minute my mother is able to gulp on her own, without the assistance of the ventilator.

"Seven," I say. "That's good, right?"

The nurse nods at the pink sponge lollipop she's breaking out of sealed plastic. I watch her as she holds the white stick and rubs the sponge part around inside my mother's mouth to clean it. Only after she's finished, will I lean over my mother for our daily, whispered, one-way conversation; if I don't time this right, as I haven't on previous visits, my stomach will lurch at the sight of green mucus worming its way along the corner of her mouth.

And my stomach is already lurching at the sight of my mother's eyes, still clamped shut to what is left of her life.

When I leave for lunch, the too-tan head of Pink corners me at the elevators. He wants to increase my mother's antibiotics. The catastrophe of the accident is beside the point; all the places where they have stuck things into her are infected; there's still the pneumonia from too much lying down and now two different infections in her colon.

"So what you're telling me is that this hospital is killing my mother."

"We'll need your permission..." Pink says.

I laugh, but it comes out like metal scraping. "To kill her?"

He explains that the drugs *might* save her. Withhold them, he tells me, and I'll need to prepare myself.

This is my mother's life in the air between us, balanced there while I decide how to answer.

It is my life, too. Once again, I say *yes*.

I have been summoned to a conference room for an emergency meeting. The man at the head of the table clears his throat. "We have a serious problem," he says. "The Frisky Whiskers people have decided to contribute an idea: talking cats. They like this idea very much." This man is my boss, and so I have to listen to him.

"They would like it even more if the cats had British accents. They think one should sound like Michael Caine and the other, and here I quote Jerry himself, 'like one of those veddy propuh butluh types.'"

My boss rests his icy blue eyes on my face. "You have forty-eight hours. Go."

By the end of the fourth week, with still no sign of life from my mother, I spend my time at the window beside her bed, watching people steer their cars in circles around the top floor of the parking garage below. I listen to the cadenced vacuum collapse of the ventilator and eventually look down at my mother, at her hair, now—without her weekly Tuesday appointment—the color and texture of steel wool. Her mouth, which she cannot use to speak or eat or even to breathe, gapes in a kind of permanent disbelief.

My mother is fatally allergic to aspartame, which you can buy in bulk at supermarkets for diabetic baking. Later, when I go downstairs for coffee, I hesitate in front of the little packets that sit next to the plastic stirrers. Aside from the white sugar packets, there are two others, blue and pink. My mother's allergy has always led her to the pink ones, given her necessary allegiance to saccharine. I hesitate, and then slip five of the blue ones into my purse.

In my talking-cat commercial, the Michael Caine cat—a ginger-colored tabby—chases his silver-tipped housemate away from their shared bowl of Frisky Whiskers with a switchblade. "Touch my grub," he says, "and I'll pop a cap in your arse."

* * *

After I present the storyboard to my boss, he asks if I'd like to take a leave of absence.

In the bed next to my mother's lies a young man whose beeping machines alarm me. On a window ledge bright with sunlight sits his father, who occupies this perch, no matter what time of day or night I visit the ward. I wonder why no one else visits. I wonder whether the son is allergic to anything, whether the father ever fondles the fatal substance the way I do the blue packets hidden in my pocket, as though they were sacred religious objects.

Hunched and shaking in my bed, the dogs' heads bent over me in contemplation and concern, I grieve my mother's death for weeks but it never comes. At the end of the seventh week, when the hospital is through curing, then causing, then curing again infections in her colon and urethra and lungs, after I have hissed at and fawned over its various doctors in involuntary fits of frustration and gratitude, my mother is pronounced recovered enough to be discharged. I ride along in the ambulance that will deliver her to the rehab facility. Her eyes, having opened, finally, just days before, bounce off me and roam around the white metal cavity carrying us through the speeding traffic. She looks at me and at the gleaming white interior with the same blank expression.

Walking down the bright hall of the rehab facility, I keep my eyes averted, for fear of seeing something I wish I hadn't. There is already plenty to not look at in Room 31, I keep my eyes down, focused on the sparkle of the linoleum. How can a place so full of illness look so clean?

My mother's roommate is an old woman whose mouth has collapsed from a lack of infrastructure. This does not stop her from screaming over and over three words that I cannot understand.

I would like for this woman's vocal cords to snap and for my mother's to stitch themselves back together. I would like to see before me a sort of speeded-up film version of events in reverse; I would like to see the metal tube slip out of my mother's neck, for the hole it leaves to become unmarked skin again; I would like her hair to grow and regain its color and for her mouth to move and have sound come out; I would like her to stop worrying at the fold of the sheet. I would like more than anything to leave this place right now.

In the interest of moving toward the door, I decide that my mother is in dire need of fresh flowers. Outside, after perusing whatever growth I can find along the borders of the patio, I pick one stem from each plant. Then, bracing myself, I return to my mother's room. I reach out to her once beautiful hands, now dry and gnarled, the nails chipped and yellowing. She looks up at me, her eyes blank, yet I somehow know she feels confused: *What are you, and who do you want?* After some effort I am able to pry open one of her hands and clamp it around a bouquet of rose, geranium, dandelion. By the time lunch arrives, the stems lie scattered in her lap.

* * *

After several weeks of work with the speech therapist, my mother regains some function with her hands. This does not seem quite right, but I'll take what I can get. When I watch one of the sessions, my mother gestures toward cards bearing pictures of everyday objects. She's asked to point to the thing that tells time, and her hand flicks backwards against the card with a picture of a watch. She raises her eyes upwards—*morons,* she seems to say. But when she's asked which one is something to eat, she chooses the hairbrush over the banana. I try not to make this mean anything except that perhaps my mother's eyesight is going. She's *seventy-three*, I remind myself.

The speech therapist is also working on my mother's eyelids. One blink means *no*. Two, *yes*. According to this system, my mother understands what happened to her, she knows where she is, and I am her ostrich.

After the session, I wheel my mother into the dining room. Three women sit at my mother's table. Lunch has not been brought in yet, and through the glass window I can see the attendants standing next to the cart, gabbing away. The youngest of the women—she can't be more than twenty—is swearing about this. The force of her words is at odds with her inert body, collapsed in the wheelchair like a question mark. A long strand of drool hangs from her mouth. *Motherfuckingbitches,* she says to her lap. *Fuckinggoddamnbullshit.* When I look down, away from her face, I see long, dark hairs covering her legs. This sight unfurls a heavy feeling I have kept folded up inside me for weeks.

One of the older women, wearing a dainty pink shirt, sits up straighter in her chair. She thrusts her shoulders back and opens her mouth. "Don't talk like that," she screeches. "I don't want to hear that kind of talk."

Neither do I. My eyes wander to my mother, who is staring at the comics lying on the table. What I want to hear is the kind of talk I was raised on; I want to hear about the significance of beauty, hear it made manifest in the peaks and dips of my mother's trilling voice.

They are on the fourth round of talking-cat presentations when I go back to work. I sit in the meeting while my team presents work I have not seen; the client is silent until the last presentation, which features the cats as hosts of a cooking show. They are making a *ragoût* with all the different meats in the cat food. The one the writer describes as the Anthony Hopkins cat is doing all the work, while the Michael Caine cat sits on the sidelines handing him ingredients and hassling him. In one of the little boxes, the writer points to him holding a rubber chicken between his paws.

"The chicken's a little chewy," he says.

The writer, in performing this line, sounds more like Groucho Marx than Michael Caine. After this, the only sound in the room is my boss's pencil eraser tapping against the conference table.

The client's face crumples as if he just smelled a fart. "A cat wouldn't say that," he finally yelps.

I stand up and lean over the conference table. "No," I say. "No it wouldn't." My hands twist up like claws. "Because a cat wouldn't say any-thing, except maybe, *I can't talk because I'm a CAT*."

At the coffee shop near my headhunter's office I sit with a latté and the clas-sified ads. I have Sean's voice in my ear, reaching like fingers through my cell phone. "I walked out on those bastards," he's saying. "I'm at the market near your house. Chicken or steak?" Sean wants to know. "Beer or wine?"

"Yes," I say. "Yes."

I realize I am qualified to do nothing except tell people my opinion about things I would rather not think about. Just for kicks, I try to find an ad for this. Along the way I realize that I've never understood what exactly a keypunch operator *does*. Sure, operates a keypunch. But what is that?

So much in the world is waiting to be found out.

After letting him grill me chicken and stroke my back before booting him out with an apology and a peck on the cheek, I lie in bed with thoughts about Sean. None seem the kind of thoughts that would make him happy. What does he want to do with his life, besides follow me around and hand me message slips or flowers? I imagine a future for the two of us, one in which he does the laundry and I take him shopping for new cargo pants. Such fantasies seem obscene, but not in the right way.

My mother grasps my hand when I offer it to her, strokes my fingernails. Later, while swallowing the pureed lumps of meat and peas I spoon into her mouth, she lifts her hand, fingers curled against her palm. She studies her nails, lets her hand fall to her lap.

At the bottom of my purse, next to the blue packets I have carried around these five months, is the bottle of nail polish I bring to the weekly manicure appointment we used to share. I pull it out, and in my hand it hov-ers in the air like a question.

My mother's eyes blink twice in succession. Maybe it's a speck of dust. Maybe it's *yes*.

Socks

Meg Kearney

*M*y father's body has ceased to shock me.
His skin runs over his bones like a slow
river, rippling where belly meets hip. We've
learned how to hold him: one arm each around
his back, a hand braced under a thigh; Mom
and I stand on opposite sides of his
bed and, on the count of three, lift him
onto the bedpan. We close our eyes:
Dad, then me. Oh, he pants, it's so damn cold
as I tell myself, *I am not the first*
daughter to do this. Afterward, Mom pulls
his gown down over the stones of his hips
while I train my eyes on the Gold Toe Socks
I'll later steal, when Mom gives away his suits.

Stubborn

Meg Kearney

My sister and I take turns shaving Dad's
face. We're terrified we'll cut him; his
blood's thinner than the soup at school.
I'm more confident with his right cheek,
she with his left, and as we work he
teases, *I knew there was some purpose*
for left-handers in this world. Watch out,
I say, or I'll let the night nurse do this,
and he gives my sister a wink. His wife
and daughters are like bull dogs on
a meat wagon, he tells the nurses: even
after he is dead, we won't let go.

PART III

DENOUEMENT

Living Will

Holly Posner

At doctor dinners the talk sometimes turns
to death. The dilemma tonight:
Better to stroke out fast in the A & P
or suffer a longer, gentler loosening of screws?
Like Iris Murdoch, the spine man says.
Brutal, his wife adds. (They've just seen the film.)
twenty-six novels, no warning signs . . .
In the end, we agree, it's less about losing the keys
than remembering what a key was for.

Ah, but if we're lucky, we'll see it coming, I say,
Look at Virginia Woolf—she made a choice.
The table counters with research stats,
new meds, and protocols, burying me politely
with indisputable data as once again
First do no harm circles its wagons.
But merlot's fueled my metaphysics.
It takes courage to drown yourself, I insist.
Shoot me before I'm thorazined to my chair,
name tag slung round my neck, all hollow-socket and drool.
The brain's a traitor, my husband counters,
it won't announce the if or when.

We ride home in silence,
wondering how we'll manage not to die
too soon, not to live too long.
Although he loves me I understand
he'll not be the one to whisper, *It's time,*
help me load my pockets down with stone.

Studies in the Subjunctive

Ruthann Robson

*I*F I WERE TO WRITE YOU A LETTER ON A CARD FROM A COLLECTION ENTITLED "Autumn Leaves," this is what I would say: *Today is Anne Sexton's birthday.* Would you wonder how I knew? Would you remember, even in November, the calendar you gave me? She would have been 73 today. Or would not be. She could be dead of cancer (all those cigarettes! all that alcohol! her mother's painful extinction at 58). The subjunctive's sharp blade can cut in more ways than suicide.

If I try to imagine the knife, I cannot. It must have been steel and sharp, but was it serrated? It must have been accompanied by others, some smaller, some longer. How odd to feel the serious effects of an event for which I have no memory. Which is the purpose of anesthesia after all. The surgeon warned I might not survive. But after eight hours of cutting, I was still alive. The tumor was not.

Though all care be exercised, the letter could be fatal. Once my worry was that my card would contain some embarrassing grammatical error. Or at the most severe, that it would not arrive, having been trapped in the labyrinth of the postal service with no Ariadne to guide it to liberation. But now I imagine my creme-colored and rust-lined but still porous envelope nestled next to some cheaply porous envelope which just happens to be poisonous. It might be that I have sent spores to you when I meant to send a cheery greeting. Anthrax is now a part of our vocabulary.

Live life normally! The imperative from public officials. From my doctors. And so I try to continue my letter to you on Anne Sexton's birthday. Deciding to forgo her conditional age in favor of her unconditional poetry, I consult my bookshelves, brimming with what my mother once cursed as my vanity. My twenty-five-year-old paperbacks are infested with microscopic organisms: mold or even paper mites. I sneeze (could this be a symptom of something else?) as I look for an appropriate quote with which to begin. Something to serve as an epigraph. We are nothing if not literary; even our letters have inscriptions, like tombs. But my inspection of the book is distracted by underlining. In ink!

What a pompous college student I must have been. Thank goodness you didn't know me then. I often wondered whether, if my family had believed in poetry or the rules of grammar or that language could solve or soothe or be useful, I might have continued a career in literature. I might have not been so intimidated by the professors with their perfect accents and syntax. I might not have been mortified when I was directed to Fowler's A DICTIONARY OF MODERN ENGLISH USAGE *(and make sure you get the third edition)* after I handed in my paper on *The Uses of Ocean Metaphors in the Poetry of Anne Sexton.*

Now that the subjunctive is dying... This from the third edition, 1938. Anne Sexton would have been ten years old and my mother would have been one year old and the renowned H.W. Fowler would have been delighted about his work's immortality if he were still alive. *The subjunctive is, except in isolated uses, no longer alive.* Isolated in a suburban house seems better than being isolated in poverty. What if my mother had had the privilege of Anne Sexton? She probably still would have been depressed, but she would have been smarter about it. Or at least she could have driven a convertible bought by her father, the wool-factory owner, rather than walking to her job in the garment factory as a pregnant teenager.

Anne Sexton's psychiatrists thought it was only a matter of time. Isn't that what they always say, these doctors who chose the mind over getting their hands dirty? Before I found the surgeon who would agree to operate, other doctors recommended a psychiatrist who would assist me in accepting my death. I did not come from a family that believed that money should be wasted on a luxury like therapy. Wasn't that lucky?

In THE AWFUL ROWING TOWARDS GOD, this is what I have underlined: *wounding tides, the surf biting the shore, the sea that bangs in my throat, the sea without which there is no mother, the surf pushes their cries back.* There is the kind of reader who feels compelled to decorate her books with her own comments, little notes to the writer as if the author could read them, as if the author would be interested. I have not been her kind. But in this book, there exists one phrase of marginalia: *extended metaphor.* My handwriting is careful. Just as it must have been on my paper, *The Uses of Ocean Metaphors in the Poetry of Anne Sexton,* produced before the age of personal computers and at an age when I was too poor to purchase a typewriter. Somewhere in the universe, if only in the past, this paper still exists, echoing on the envelopes I would grace with my return address: *Ocean Avenue, North Sea Drive, Tidewater Lane, Shore Blvd.* Sexton's poem *At the Beach House* made me cry for what I did not have, would never have. Sexton's poem *Doctors (They are not Gods/though they would like to be),* I had ignored.

Today, at the inland post office, the postwoman comments on the beautiful calligraphy that graces my envelope, announcing my prosaic return address. Now that all mail is suspicious, that it could wind its way through the body in ways that could be incurable, I find her compliments comforting, talismanic. I would hope my doctors would be her kind.

Fowler classifies the uses of the subjunctive into four categories: alives, revivals, survivals, and arrivals. The alives consist of imperatives and conditionals in which no one could suspect the writer of *pedantry or artificiality*. (*I wish it were over* is the example provided by Fowler, the exemplar provided by Sexton, in life if not writing). The revivals are the province of poets and poetic writers, to be eschewed by the ordinary writer, who cannot but sound *antiquated* should he write *If ladies be but young and fair.* The survivals are not incorrect grammatically, but they *diffuse an atmosphere of dullness and formalism over the writing in which they occur.* Most objectionable, the arrivals are the best proof that the subjunctive should be put to rest: infected as it is with the illnesses of mixed mood, sequences of tenses, indirect questions, and the dangerous miscellaneous, risking pretentiousness. A risk Sexton avoided with her direct accessible language. Too direct, some critics declared.

If it were fall and it were 1974, Anne Sexton would be newly dead, and I'd be in college, and H.W. Fowler would still be dead, and I'd be drinking vodka in water glasses, and my mother would be threatening suicide, but my girlfriend would actually commit it. Not neatly in the garage, like Ms. Sexton in her cherished red car, but as colorfully daring as the dying leaves in New England. Blood splattered on the sidewalk in front of her house. In autumn, the sea doesn't dry up, but it might as well.

Were, in the subjunctive sense, is *applicable not to past facts, but to present or future non-facts* which belong to *utopia*. Fowler is quite precise on this. But to understand the exactitudes of grammar, one has to have an acquaintance with the basics. Before I went to school, the word *were* was a place of mystery to me, a utopian *where*. The past, present, and future were not tenses of verbs, but the captives of then, now, maybe someday. Listen to my mother talk: *We was going to get there then, but they was late and so we go nowhere.* No were.

Where you were that morning: in the CT machine at the cancer center; stopping for a bagel, cream cheese, no butter please; sleeping late with a former lover, sweaty with regrets that will soon dry small; on the plane you almost didn't make, feeling lucky to be going from Boston to L.A. for an interview; finishing the carpeting job in Queens before heading to the project downtown; at the Pentagon cookie shop, selling the last macadamia and chocolate chip; in the student lounge, looking up from the television set to see the same smoke, the same absence; at the veterinarian's office, picking up the dog's ashes; on the ledge, holding his hand, considering a choiceless choice; in the cockpit, between the sky and the ocean, aiming for the skyscraper's promise; on Chambers Street, using a briefcase as a shield; cradled in the stairwell, counting the flights, coughing and crying, dialing the cell phone, battery dead; in a place that will never be forgotten, never remembered, in heaven, in hell, in shock, in pieces, in tears, in a rage, incomprehensible, inarticulate.

Having revived.
    Having arrived on the other side of some deep but invisible ocean, on the

continent of those about whom the word *miracle* is whispered, I am still possessed of my Fowler's and my mother and my handwriting and my longing for a beach house.

Only now I don't understand suicide.

Only now I am suspicious of Anne Sexton (and the others, the others) for their deception: that death is romantic and not full of dullness and formalism; that death is literary and survivable.

Only now I wonder if Sexton (or Plath or Virginia Woolf...not to mention Hemingway) would have been diagnosed with a rare and almost always fatal cancer instead of depression; would she have fought her way into the clinical trials, past the doubting doctors, screaming *I am but young and fair; too young to die, I am only* 45, 30, 59, or 42 *like me*; or would she have succumbed, welcoming the morphine the doctors would provide in excess, as if they are gods and this is mercy.

If I were to continue my letter to you on Anne Sexton's birthday, inside the card with the images of the yellow gingko leaves and red maple leaves and the towering trees we once would have described as aflame but can no longer since we have seen what we have seen, I might still insist on trying to turn lines from Sexton into aphorisms with my careful inscriptions. *In November counting the stars / gives you boils. Be careful of words / even the miraculous ones. Many humans die. / They die like the tender, palpitating berries / in November.* I would not write you how my abdomen still twists, a labyrinth constructed by my surgeon, my Ariadne, my rowing god with his oars of knives. Or of the dangerous miscellany of my side-effects, seeming to mimic the symptoms of anthrax poisoning, now that we know what the symptoms would be. I cannot but sound antiquated should I write: if oceans be but metaphors, then what is this salt that clings to my scars? And I would not but sound too much the poetic writer rather than the ordinary one, should I write you, my dear, that I struggle to get past the subjunctive *(what if? if not?)* every day, including this brilliant November day when the waves twist from a far off hurricane and we still strive in our boats hewn of grammar to arrive at utopia, or at least survive into some future.

To a Child Contemplating Suicide

Helen Klein Ross

Your grandfather outlined
Ghosts of awl, hammer,

Wrench on a pegboard
In permanent ink—

So certain was he that
What was essential to him

Could not be improved upon,
Lost or replaced. Would that

I could make vivid
The void

You'd make upon leaving
The place you belong.

Art

Eric Nelson

O ctober, a woman and a boy, a tumor
overtaking his brain, draw pictures
in the waiting room.

She makes a red apple as round
as a face. Then from her hand a cloud
grows and darkens over the apple

until the crayon breaks inside
its wrapper and hangs like a snapped
neck from her bloodless fingertips.

He's drawn two stick-figures
up to their necks in falling gold
leaves, their heads all smiles.

It's you and daddy, he tells her.
Above them a flock of m's
fly toward a grinning sun.

When she doesn't answer
he says on Halloween he'd like
to be a horse with orange wings.

Staring at his picture, she says
It looks like Thanksgiving.
Where are you?

He taps the sun. *I'm shining on you.*
She hugs him as if trying
to press him back inside her.

I'm not crying, she whispers.
He looks over her shoulder.
I'm not crying, too.

A Roomful of Christmas

Scott Temple

*T*HE CORNER ROOM IN THE CARDIAC INTENSIVE CARE UNIT WAS TOO TINY for the woman in the hospital bed. She lay staring into a single square of light that entered her room from the hall window. The bed sheets were twisted about her bloated belly, which rose and quivered like a jellyfish as she breathed. I looked at the clutter of technology in the room, the winking lights, the numbers flashing in electric greens and reds, the beeping monitors. Medications dripped from clear plastic bags on an IV stand, into tubes connected to more tubes, before finally draining through a needle into the back of her hand. A small bathroom, the size of a closet, opened to her right. The room had the cold, remote feel of a lunar landing module, tucked deep inside the university medical center. It was not a place where a woman should wait indefinitely for a new heart.

The TV was loud when I walked into the room. An afternoon game show barely distracted her from whatever it was that preoccupied her. Nothing cut the unremitting gloom that emanated from this little corner of the university hospital.

The electrical activity in Roberta Keane's heart registered in long, loping lines that bounced across a monitor next to her bed. Numbers shone on another monitor. The left-hand number registered systolic blood pressure; right was for diastolic. Both numbers edged up when she saw me walk in.

She stared at me and said, "You must be the psychologist they wanted me to see."

I felt like an intruder whose visit she must have feared.

"They think I'm going crazy, don't they?"

"No," I said. "The head of cardiology asked me to come by. He said you're getting discouraged. If he or I spent six weeks in this room waiting for a heart, they'd be saying that about us, too."

She smiled.

Roberta Keane's heart was giving out under a double load of congenital damage and repeated viral infections. At thirty-eight, there wasn't enough heart muscle left to pump blood through her big frame. She was too sick to leave the bed without help, and when she did leave, a coil of tubes and wires followed. Roberta Keane would either leave this room with a new heart, or she would die here.

She reached for the remote control clipped onto the bed beside her, and she turned off the volume on the television. Tears brimmed in her eyes.

"That's me, before I got sick," she said, pointing to a photograph on the nightstand by the bed. I picked it up. She looked like a different woman. Before the viral infection uncorked her spiraling heart disease, she had been robust and healthy, even beautiful. Cascading waves of blonde hair, straight posture, and a full bust showed proudly in the picture. Now, her skin looked sallow and slack. Her eyes were still a brilliant blue, but they were sunk into dark orbits that spread like puddles under her eyes. Gray streaks ran through partly combed hair.

"It doesn't look like me any more."

I set the photograph back onto the nightstand. A silver balloon, tied to the bed by a string, drifted in the stale air. The wall by the bathroom was covered with get-well cards. Another photo, pinned to the wall, caught my eye.

"Is this your family?" I pointed to another photograph. A younger, healthier Roberta Keane had an arm around a tall wisp of a man, his face as thin as the edge of a butter knife. Three teenage girls, each of them plump, stood by their sides, smiling into the camera.

"That's Elvin. My husband. My rock. And those are my girls. One of them just left." She cried and turned away from me.

"I'm not going to get a heart," she whispered.

"Is that what you sit here thinking? Day after day?"

She nodded and turned toward me. Over the foot of the bed another game show played on the now silenced TV.

I pulled my chair closer to her.

"You just had a look on your face almost like you were watching something in your mind's eye."

"I see the same thing, over and over. I'm in this room, and I'm dying. A helicopter touches down outside, with a new heart. And the flight crew hands off the heart to a nurse. She runs into the hospital. But I die before I get my heart."

It was an image that made tears burn in my eyes. "Is that what you really believe will happen?"

"I still have some hope. But the longer I wait, the weaker I get."

"That picture must be awfully believable when it takes over your mind."

"It sort of takes over like that at night, when I'm alone."

"A lot of things feel different at night, don't they?"

She tilted her head and looked at me. "I used to say that to my girls when they were little, and they got scared at night. It'll seem different in the morning light. And it does."

"What happens to your mood when that scene goes through your mind?"

"I sink. Way down."

"Suppose you pictured yourself at home, with a new heart, laughing with your daughters? How would you feel?"

"I wish I could believe that's what's going to happen."

"Do you think that's possible?"

"*Now,* I do. It's daylight." She smiled. "By the way, my friends call me Bobbie."

She agreed to make some notes on a pad of paper she kept by her bed, and I agreed to come back the next morning. Whenever her mind drifted to the helicopter scene, she would write down her mood, give it a name and a number for intensity, from zero to a hundred. I hoped that she might see the connection between the images and her mood, and that these images were just one story among many, but one that stirred up only fear and despair. Then, if she could accept that this was only one among many possible outcomes, maybe we could find something to replace the story of her death that kept replaying in her mind. If we can't read the future, why not pick the story that helps us cope until the future comes?

A nurse popped into the room to change bottles of IV saline and to help Bobbie into the bathroom. My cue to leave.

I walked beneath long double rows of fluorescent tubes, hall after hall, toward the elevators. I never told the truth when colleagues asked me why I spent so much time doing consultations on medical units. Instead, I gave an answer that made me look noble and intellectually curious. The latter, at least, contained a grain of truth; there wasn't much literature on treating heart transplant patients and I liked extending psychotherapy into new domains. What I didn't tell colleagues was that people like Bobbie Keane put a bone-deep scare into me. The distance between Bobbie and all the rest of us can be traversed by a single virus. Like her, I had a picture in my head. I saw myself in that hospital bed one day, scared and despondent, and not as strong as she was. I wanted to learn through Bobbie to cope, if and when my time comes to have serious medical problems.

I learned later that it isn't just a question of how you cope; it's also a question of where you're hospitalized. The transplant program had taken a downward arc to disaster, but I didn't know it that morning. I'd find out, months later, on the front page of the morning paper.

Next morning when I arrived, Bobbie was knitting away under the bright bar of a single fluorescent tube that glowed behind her head. When she saw me, she laid down the yarn and needles and peered at me over the tops of her reading glasses. She reached for the remote control, and turned off the sound. While she was fiddling with the remote, I noticed her blood pressure readings. They weren't jumping as they had in my first meeting with her.

"I did it," she said, reaching for a blue spiral binder on the tray where her lunch sat untouched. "I've been looking forward to talking with you about this."

She flipped to the first page of her notes and handed it to me. Sure enough, when the images of her death played, her mood plummeted. When she focused on going home with a new heart, her mood improved. She had talked with her husband, and he was pleased.

"Last night was pretty rough, though. I just lay here, thinking. But I also thought about that morning thing we talked about. It doesn't make sense to lie there thinking about that helicopter getting here too late. But they're afraid to give me any more medicine. What else can I do?"

While I was thinking, I could hear a wheezing in her breath that I would swear was not there yesterday. Her lips were slightly blue, and her eyes sank deeper in the orbits of her skull.

"Bobbie," I said. "If you could imagine for a moment that you get a heart, leave this place, and go home, into your everyday life again, what would you be doing? Say in six months?"

She answered quickly.

"I love Christmas. I always told Elvin I want to build a room onto our house. I'd fill it with Christmas decorations. We love to go to little shops all over the city, looking for ornaments and lights. I look for them all year long. I have little handmade angels, and Russian eggs that dangle from hoops. I have hundreds of Christmas tree ornaments and strings of lights. If we built that room, I'd have five or six artificial trees that I'd keep lit up all year. In winter, I'd put up natural trees. And I'd sit in that room with Elvin and the girls and we'd just look at all the trees and lights, any time we wanted, all year long."

"Bobbie. Can you picture yourself sitting in the room full of Christmas, you, Elvin, your girls, just looking out at all those lights, blue and red and green, blinking on and off, and all those colorful, delicate ornaments, spheres and stars and candy canes on the trees? Can you picture all five of you together in that room?"

She thought it was pretty funny imagining a room like that in the middle of a hot July day. But we did picture it for almost thirty minutes. We had a good time.

"If that other picture pops into your mind, can you just gently bring your mind right back to that room?" I asked.

"I think so. There's a chance it might just actually turn out this way. That it'll be okay after all."

"Keep the faith," I said.

The corners of her mouth turned upward, and she flashed me a V-sign with her fingers. When she breathed through her parted lips, I noticed that her breathing was shallower and more rapid than the last time I'd seen her. Her heart and lungs were working harder, and with less efficiency, just like the transplant program.

Bobbie Keane died on a Monday afternoon. That morning, the head of cardiology had called to tell me that if I wanted to see her again, this would be my last chance.

When I got there, her husband was holding her hand. His hands were soft for a laborer. And he delicately brushed a sweat-soaked curl back over her forehead. Bobbie was panting short, rapid, ineffectual breaths through blue lips and a pinched nose. Her eyes were wild with fear. An oxygen bottle pumped gas into a cup over her face. When she saw me, she reached for the blue spiral notebook we used for our work. It lay in front of her, on the tray. She flipped to a blank page with her free hand, and picked up a yellow pencil from the tray. She drew a zero and made a slashing line through it.

"No talk," her husband said. "She's saying no talk."

I took her free hand and looked at her eyes. I just stood there. Her husband was on her left. I was on her right. We just held hands. I squeezed tight. When I left the room, her husband followed me.

"Bobbie told me about how you helped her," he said. "About how she'd think of that room we wanted to build, instead of lying in bed being scared when she was alone at night. Thank you. Thank all of you; the transplant surgeon, the cardiologist; all of you. You've done everything you possibly could, and I'm grateful."

Then he went back to his wife.

An hour later, she was dead.

I walked fast, trying hard not to cry until I got to my office.

When I crossed the long, windowed ramp to the psychiatry building, I saw a helicopter drifting down toward the heliport outside. I wondered if it was bearing a heart torn from a breast at a distant hospital and packed in ice, arriving too late for Bobbie.

One morning, months later, the story was splayed across the front pages of the newspaper. A war had broken out for control of the heart transplant program. The chest surgeon and the hospital nursing department were the principal combatants. The surgeon wanted things done his way; nursing wouldn't accommodate. The chest surgeon went on strike. The cardiologists would later claim they didn't know that the chest surgeon was refusing to transplant their patients; they kept admitting patients, expecting them to get hearts.

People stopped getting hearts. Patients died.

Nobody was providing oversight, not the dean's office, the executive vice chancellor's office, or the hospital CEO.

When the last of the lawsuits was finally settled, a court order forbade the litigants from ever talking about what happened. The state attorney general called a press conference and issued a blistering public attack on the university medical center's leadership. The executive vice chancellor, the dean, the CEO, and the chest surgeon all resigned. I never did another transplant consultation at that medical center.

Despite the gag order, I probed to find out what happened. I wanted to know if Bobbie Keane died because of this. I desperately wanted to believe she would have died no matter how well run the service. But I could never get a clear statement about this.

That fall, I got a letter from Elvin Keane. He thought I might want a photograph of his wife, "just something to remember her by. This was Bobbie's smile when stable and healthy," he wrote in blue ink across the back of the picture.

A pretty blonde woman with lively eyes sits at a kitchen table and smiles into the camera. She is holding a little black and tan puppy in her arms. The puppy is looking into the camera, too. A darkened house looms in the background, now missing a mother and a wife and a room that she hoped one day to add.

"Silence = Death"

Rafael Campo

*H*is worn-out T-shirt, black as mourning, black
as countless deaths, surprises me—it screams
a phrase I've heard so many countless times
before, in words hot pink as countless
fevers—heat of language, demonstrations,
why does it still threaten me, I who held
my patient's hand who died his wordless death,
the respirator hissing in my ear
the countless breaths he couldn't take himself.
That was years ago, almost decades now.
Today, I see his T-shirt and I think
he isn't taking all his antiviral meds,
the countless pills he piled on my desk
to silence me, my T-cell counts and viral loads
detectable at greater than one hundred thousand,
the silent viral particles that swell
to numbers more than even we will count—
I pause, and shift a moment in my chair;
I ask, "How many loved ones did you lose?"
"I can't count them" is his response. "But one
left me this stupid T-shirt when he died."
Then, we're silent, counting moments, death
counting us in all its infiniteness,
in all we know that words cannot explain.

The Raft

Toni Mirosevich

*T*HEY ARE ALL ON THE RAFT AT THE BEGINNING, EVERYONE WHO EVER counted in your life, along with those who didn't count, the resolved and the unresolved, every true blue friend, every nemesis, every good neighbor, every bad, your kindergarten teacher, the school bully, swim instructors, car mechanics of honest and ill repute, the quiet man you saw every morning at the coffee shop who nodded as you entered, your favorite checker who rounded down the total more than once, the shifty tax accountant, the girl who gave you your first kiss, the one who chose another, every inconsequential affair, and on there too, everyone of consequence, the inner circle, family, blood, those you call your loved ones, your one and only.

If you have evidence—credible, irrefutable—that the end is coming, if you have been given a timeline, then you have time to gather up everyone, see that they get on board, which isn't possible for those who are taken from this life without notice, off guard, quickly, in a flash, an instant, in the plane going down, or the car crash, the gunshot, the heart that bursts without warning; not possible for those who drop dead in their tracks, right there on the sidewalk, for no apparent reason, nothing to indicate today was the day of reckoning for them, the day of sorrow for those who didn't see it coming and therefore weren't able to go along for the ride. Their loved ones will never be able to make a case in their defense, propose a bargain, *take me instead*, not like all those people on your raft who propose and propose and propose to no avail, who know full well that getting on board with you means somewhere, sometime, in the not too distant future, the ride will end.

So in the beginning it's like a party or a convention of everyone you know or knew and you've even invited; the estranged, the long gone, the ones you've banished from your life; the grudge that never ended, the betrayal that never healed, that resulted in years of absence, in not calling, though, lord knows, nowadays we always have the means within reach, you can ask the person in the grocery line, right in front of you, if they wouldn't mind, can you use their phone, and you can call because you remember the number, be honest, you remember, and when they answer, say, "I just wanted to hear your voice again," without initially telling them the kicker, that your days are numbered, are being tallied by someone with an abacus in hand and each day, week, month, the hand reaches out and moves a bead over to the other side, and each time you hear the click of the wooden bead: loud, sharp, final.

* * *

You float down the river and soon learn this isn't a joy ride, you're not free yet, of duty, of care, of what binds you to the earth; there's one more job to do. It's your task to turf the unessential cargo. Certain people must go, and even though it was you who invited them along it is now you who decides the ones who don't matter so: the one night stand, the members of the PTA, the odd relations you had to stomach but could just as well have done without, the convict nephew, the viperous aunt, all the coworkers who came back late from their breaks and didn't care that you had to work overtime, and you were robbed of those minutes, precious minutes you could use now. How many minutes are wasted in waiting, in stewing, in unhappiness, and there are others who don't deserve a second thought, all the bosses who were, well, bosses, and therefore expendable when the time comes, for this is the one time the rank and file rise up and turn the tables, here's the real revolution, so you can say Supervisor, and hey, you, CEO, you go first, and you give them a little push.

Now there's more room to move, not exactly a dance floor but a little more elbow room, and you begin to enjoy this spaciousness, this range of motion, now you can see the point of letting go, of getting rid of all that encumbers, and like a circus carney with his finger on the flip switch that, once flipped, sends the clown into the dunking tank, you are the one who gets to say when, and you laugh, not at the surprised look on the clown's face, or the way he flails underwater, *glub, glub, glub*, not at others' misfortune but at your own meager power, this little bit of say so, that's delicious and spiteful and then strangely sad; see it's not meanness really, it's just that your body's getting weaker and you're less able to maneuver the raft with all that weight, so there goes the good friend who fed your dogs when you went on vacation, there goes the couple you played poker with, now a favorite schoolteacher who taught you the wonders of the Pleistocene age, now a childhood priest.

You must jettison them one by one in order to stay longer, that's how it is, either or; you aren't able to carry them though, ironically, when they signed on they thought they were carrying you, they thought you were the one who needed help. They joined up to be there for your every need, to fluff a pillow, run errands, bring a tuna casserole, *eat, eat,* they say, *you need to build your strength*, and you, who hate tuna, take a bite. All these people, well meaning, telling you what to do, and it dawns on you that there's always a flip side: while they think they are the strong ones, the support, it's the other fucking way around, and you want to shout, *I am carrying you*, but instead of wasting your voice you pretend like you need to stretch and you make a grand sweep with your right arm and six go in at once, and because it's so easy, and ultimately economical, you do the same with your left arm and the raft almost tips over as one entire side falls off. (And you think to yourself: this is a new form of triage, and then continue.)

So it's you and you and you and you. With quick speed you decide, you whittle and reduce and bring the number down. Now you can count the ones who are left on one hand. You've been efficient, and they stand before you, staring your way: your mother, your sister, your father, who is dead, your one and only. Push your father over first, you'll see him soon, he's already on the other side, so you explain the deal: it's kind he came, but let's meet up later, and he gives a knowing smile as he was the first to teach you how to leave, and then does a swan dive and hardly makes a splash. Now whose turn, it's harder to decide, but you choose your mother, who bore you and raised you, who failed you as you failed her. *I'm sorry*, you tell her, *sorry we were never able to ford the distance but even so I've been meaning to tell you thank you for all you did, but on the other hand, why did it have to be so hard*, and before she goes she holds your hand for a moment and because you are diminished, because you have been getting smaller all this time, your hand feels small in hers, like it must have felt when you were young, and you feel the warmth of her body pressed into the flesh, into the palm of her hand, pressed into you, and then, without warning, you let go.

Your sister is next, whom you only came to know, to really know, late in life, whom you'll never know, not like when you were young: an older sister who looked after you, who put her hands on your shoulders like you were a pet and steered you through tall crowds, who handed you down her outgrown clothes, her red blazer with the gold buttons, the blazer you coveted, that had her smell, her power. She's been there the whole trip, with her cheery stories and Hallmark cards and stupid gifts that you cherish—the cat holding on in the TGIF poster, the pop psychology books on how to create your own destiny—each gift as precious as a handmade basket or a requiem. It will be hard for her, for she will have no one left, for even though there is her husband, her children, they aren't first blood; a father, long gone from this world into another, a mother long gone in this life, and you are her only link, and that's why you push her, tenderly over the side, for you cannot lift her any longer, and she, even though she never knew it, she, for so long, by her pluck and belief and good heart has lifted you.

There's only one left. The one. Your one. You decide, right then, to never let go. You will take her with you, you'll strap her on board and you can go together, it will be like a weekend away, you tell her, a chance for a little break, a trip up the Mendocino coast, a drive to the country. You were lucky, so very lucky: you loved her and she loved you, and face it, she is the one whose hands built this very raft, with her knowledge of tools and craft, she was always the practical one, and it was she who packed the picnic basket and looked after provisions, she told the doctors when to intervene and when to go to hell, she made the passenger list and rowed when your arms were too tired. She took care of everything so you could save your strength, so you could push them over, she made it all possible for you to leave like this, in full command, possible to leave this life without regret, for you felt loved by her. You're not sure if she can swim without you. Someone else can teach her, it's high time she learned. And, when her back is turned, you give her the most loving, the firmest push and she falls into the waves.

There is no one left; there's room to stretch and move. Room for a game of foursquare or calisthenics, room for cartwheels, forward rolls, pirouettes. Funny this lightness you feel, this expansive body, no one to bump into, no burden to carry. They're gone, all your loved ones and not so loved, they're gone and what's odd is you don't miss them, for you are past that, with them went all feeling: blame, regret, love, sorrow, anger. Once the bodies left so did the pain. Every bead on the abacus is carried over to the one side, except one. There's one more thing that needs to go. You have to jettison this, even this, the raft, sturdy raft, life raft, and in an instant it breaks in two, so flimsy, like a cardboard box, it falls away. How did it ever stand your weight, how did it ever hold you?

A Widow at 93

Andrew Merton

S he says she's surviving,
by which she means she's dying

slowly. As a precaution,
every night she tells her pillow

goodbye. *Survive* is a sharp word;
The *v*'s cut like shivs.

A ruthless transitive verb,
indifferent to the objects

it has taken:
father, mother,

husband, brother,
son

Morning at Fifty

Alan L. Steinberg

> *"Let us go and make our visit."*
> —T.S. ELIOT

T HE DRIVE TO THE NURSING HOME ALWAYS OCCURRED IN THREE STAGES. The first, which took Ebstein past the confines of the city, Ebstein experienced in a purely mechanical way—as if he were a taxi driver. He focused on the workings of the car, how the engine sounded, how responsive were the brakes. He scanned the instrument panel, noting the oil pressure, the engine revolutions, the gas level. He felt like a race-car driver on the morning of a race, or a jet pilot just before takeoff. He was all business, all concentration.

The second stage, which took him from the outskirts of the city to the nursing home, was the worst, the one he dreaded the most. His absorption in the mechanical details of the automobile gave out, and he was left face to face with the horror of what lay ahead: the building of the zombies, where the dead lay waiting to die again. His heart would race, and he would feel weak and hollow. Sometimes, he would break out in a cold, seeping, sweat that chilled both his body and his soul. He had to fight the impulse to suddenly turn the car around—or into the oncoming lane of traffic.

The last stage, as he neared the actual building, was one of preparation. The panic subsided as quickly as it had arisen. He took a deep breath, composed himself. He checked to see that he had the chocolate, or the flowers, or the miscellaneous items that his father needed, or that Ebstein thought his father needed. He took his last sweet breaths of untainted air, aimed the car at the parking lot, and began the ordeal.

As Ebstein climbed the cracked stone steps of the nursing home, which the rain had darkened and dampened but had not scoured clean, he armed himself with kindness, wore his smile like a surgical mask to protect him from the contamination of decay. He knew many of the residents by name—like Achilles in Hades. He could decipher their moans, translate their shrieks into desires. Willy, the curved man, who had been a backhoe operator for fifty years, sitting hunched over the levers in his cell-like cab till his back had rounded into the shape of a cup hook, and who walked now with his eyes closed, crying out in perfect iambs, "I want my pipe and tobacco," till an aide fetched him and brought him blind and shuffling to the smoking room. Agnes, the scowler, who would say with perfect reasonableness, "I've got to get out of here. Help me get out of here," but who was too frightened to take a step beyond the front door. And the lady-with-no-legs who always smiled and who patted his father's hand, saying, "Look who's here. Look who's come to visit," though she herself hadn't had visitors for years.

His father was where he almost always was—in his room, in his stuffed chair, looking out the window at the walled-in garden beyond. Whatever he saw there through his cataract-dimmed eyes seemed to make no impression on him. He never spoke of it, not even when Ebstein called his attention to some detail—a squirrel or a bird, or even someone walking. What he saw when he looked, or if he saw anything, Ebstein would never know. It would be just one more blank space in his father's life, another chasm that lay between them that he would never cross.

Ebstein's father shared his room with Sam. Sam was a big man, with thick arms and a thick neck, but soft now and clumsy, muscle turning into fat unevenly; it took two or three of the young female aides to maneuver him around. Even though he could see, he almost always kept his eyes shut so that Ebstein thought of him as a blind man. Watching the aides struggling to lift him and guide him to the bathroom or the dining room always made Ebstein think of Samson at Gaza. Mostly Sam was silent, but periodically he would start shouting, saying things over and over, stuttering almost, the words never quite complete, never quite making sense.

Today Sam was in his chair, tied to it, really. The aides had devised a system whereby they wrapped the long belt of his robe around the back of the chair and fastened it, so that he wouldn't suddenly get up and crash into something. Rubbing his big, dry hands together over and over, Sam sat quietly for the moment, for which Ebstein was grateful.

Ebstein took a deep breath and walked over to his father, touching him on the shoulder. His father seemed to him so small now, so frail and shrunken that he wondered how he could ever have seemed so vast, so threatening. Is this what life does to you, Ebstein wondered, take you and drain you and leave you like the dry stiff husks of flies dangling in spider webs? Or was it only that his father's anger and disappointments had taken a toll inside, hollowed him out, as it were? Each time he touched his father, Ebstein had that momentary dread that his father would just shrivel into nothingness, disintegrate into a small heap of dust at his feet. He could almost picture himself standing there while the aides in their white uniforms swept up the dust, saying, "What have you done to your father?"

But the dread passed, and his father merely looked up at Ebstein with those watery-dull eyes that neither rejoiced nor condemned, recognized nor greeted. Ebstein had seen eyes like those, hundreds, thousands. They were the eyes of those who had given up hope or had hope wrung from them—those standing in lines waiting for something, anything, to happen; those standing behind the bars or fences looking out at the world they could never reach; those left barely alive after the war or the revolution or the hurricane had moved on. They were the eyes of those who had passed beyond hope or hate; who had passed beyond even resignation to something more primitive, less human. They reminded Ebstein of the bulbous-eyed look of dead fish. Every time Ebstein saw that look, he said a silent prayer inside his head—to the Universe at large, to whatever forces created it or guided it: "Please let me die before I look like that."

Ebstein could not understand why his father did not die, did not will himself out of this terrible existence. Sometimes, Ebstein felt a tremendous anger well up within him. For a moment, he felt like screaming at his father, shaking him violently the way his father used to shake him and his sister. "Don't you know it's time?" he felt like shouting. "Don't you have any sense of shame?"

But that rage, too, passed and was replaced by a quiet sadness—a general sympathy for all that was living and dying, himself included.

"Good morning," Ebstein said, the old ritual beginning.

"Good morning," Ebstein's father answered, sitting there patiently, head upturned slightly, fish-eyes full of translucent light.

Ebstein never knew how things would go. Sometimes, it seemed his father knew exactly who he was. "You're my son," he would answer when Ebstein asked. Sometimes, he would turn to an aide who chanced by. "That's my son," he would say. Sometimes he seemed pleased to see Ebstein, as if Ebstein's presence, his flesh and blood, his forced smile, his words, all were a kind of comfort to him, like a warm blanket on a cold day. Sometimes, he seemed to Ebstein to be resentful, angry because Ebstein was there, or because Ebstein didn't come often enough, or because he couldn't make his eyes clear again, or his hair grow or his strength come back, or because he wasn't going to stay long enough. And there were times, it seemed to Ebstein, that his father didn't even know he was there, or care; that Ebstein was just one more shape floating indistinctly past him, one more vague and threatening shape before his great bulging fish-eyes. Ebstein himself felt insubstantial then, as if he were without weight and substance, as if he himself and his father and all his life were but a mist the next good wind could blow away. On those days, Ebstein could barely stay half an hour, looking every minute at his watch, hearing his own words echoing hollowly off the white walls, aching to get outside before he evaporated into nothingness, desperate to get into the car and hear the comforting roar of its engine and glide down the highway, the wind warm or cold against his face, stinging him or cooling him with the comforting molecules of existence.

"Do you know who I am?" Ebstein asked hopefully.

A smile, barely, formed on his father's dry lips, but the cataracts clouded the eyes so that no human expression registered there, just round, dull pupils floating in a gray primordial sea.

"You're my son."

"Do you know what day it is?"

"The day my son comes," Ebstein's father intoned, but already the voice was beginning to disengage, Ebstein sensed, to break off again, as it were, from the reality of the moment.

"I did. I did. I did. What a goddamn time. What a goddamn time . . ."

It was Sam, his voice booming, as if he were talking to someone across the room, across the street, even. He was rocking back and forth in his chair, still rubbing his hands together. His eyes were clamped shut.

"It's my birthday," Ebstein said, bending closer to his father, trying to be heard above Sam shouting, "You know that. You know that. You know that."

"Your birthday?" Ebstein's father asked, as if he could really understand.

"What a goddamn time. What a goddamn time."

"Do you know which one?" Ebstein implored. "Do you know how old I am? Guess."

"It's my son's birthday," Ebstein's father said, but whether it was a question or a statement or just mindless repetition, Ebstein could not say.

"Everybody said so. Said so. Said so."

"I'm fifty today," Ebstein said. "Fifty. Half a century." Ebstein hoped against hope that putting it that way would break through the fog he could almost feel thickening and settling between them.

"Fifty?"

"The people don't know. The people don't know," Sam shouted, rubbing his hands more vigorously. "The people don't know a goddamn thing."

"Yes. Can you remember when I was born? Fifty years ago. Can you remember that long?"

"Yes," Ebstein's father said.

"I did. I did. I did that time."

Ebstein looked at his father, tried to put the word together with his father's expression, the gray fish-eyes. "You do?"

"No matter how it happens. No matter how it happens. No matter how," Sam bellowed, his hand rubbing reaching a furious pace.

"Can you tell me?" Ebstein said, afraid to hope; afraid not to. "Can you tell me what you remember?"

"Not a goddamn thing. Not a goddamn thing."

Ebstein waited, looking at his father sitting there, small and frail, also waiting. Patiently waiting. But waiting for what? For the aide to come? For night? For tomorrow? For death? Ebstein bent even closer, took his father's chin in his hand, lifted his father's face to his.

"Do you know what I'm asking? Can you understand me?"

Ebstein's father said nothing.

"I did. I did. I did," Sam said, his shouting beginning to subside.

Ebstein sighed, removed his hand from his father's face. The road home is never easy, he thought. There are no shortcuts. History is never complete, not even your own.

"Yes." Ebstein's father said into the silence, his voice steady, firm.

Ebstein bent close again, hope flickering. "Yes, what? You remember? You understand? Tell me what." There was urgency in Ebstein's voice. But already he felt the moment slipping away, the room darkening. Ebstein's father, like Sam, had closed his eyes.

"Do you know what day it is?" Ebstein asked softly.

Silence.

"I had a time. I had a time. I had a time," Sam said, his voice soft now, almost a whisper. And then he, too, was quiet.

Ebstein took out the chocolate that had nearly melted in his pocket, broke off a small piece and put the rest of it in his father's hand, gently folding his stiff fingers around the sticky wrapper. Then he walked over to Sam and touched him on the shoulder.

"Here's a piece of chocolate for you," Ebstein said.

Silence. Silence. Silence.

His Own Time

John Thompson

THERE'S SOMETHING ABOUT THIS WAITRESS THAT KEEPS ME COMING BACK here. Part of the draw is obvious: it's her hair. I've never seen anything like it. It's braided into a ponytail that hangs like an auburn rope along her back. I'm hoping to get up the nerve to ask her out. She wipes a table, straightens up, and whips the braid of hair over her shoulder. From where I sit, it appears to come dangerously close to the blades of the ceiling fan. It's an illusion. I know that. Even so, an image ambushes me, her hair snarled in the blades and her body yanked off the floor, her pretty legs flopping as she hangs from the makeshift gallows. I turn back to the bar to try to clear my head.

I did a little time once. It wasn't a long bit, but that doesn't matter much. Time is time. One day a new guy on the block, Lenny, decides he can't take it anymore. Some men are playing cards, and some are walking in circles around the perimeter of the cellblock. You'd be surprised how much time you can kill walking in circles. Most guys walk with somebody. I think it's so they don't look crazy. You hear guys say how they walked with so and so for seven years at some joint or another. That's what "walking with" means. And there's a certain stride and pace. It's not for exercise; it's to kill time. I can spot a man on the street with the stride and know he's done time. It's a sort of shuffle that keeps you moving, but there's no hurry because there's no destination.

Me, on this day, I'm reading a book. I'm thinking it was *Zorba the Greek,* but I'm not so sure. Some guys walk away the months; I read away the minutes. I'd read anything I could get my hands on just to lose myself in something. Anyway, I'm reading and the last thing I have on my mind is Lenny and his problems. There's a saying, "Do your own time," and that's exactly what I intend to do.

Only this guy Lenny makes it hard to ignore what he's up to, which is to off himself. I don't know why he wants to exactly, there could be a hundred reasons, or no reason at all other than you're in a place like this, but it ought to be a private thing, at the very least done at nighttime. Lenny's got a sheet all twisted up into a rope and he's dragging his desk from his cell to the end of the block where there's a pipe. When he passes by my cell he's mumbling something to himself about how he'd be better off dead, or maybe I'd have never noticed. Then he gets in place and spends a minute or two checking the layout. He climbs on the desk and drapes the sheet over the pipe. It's funny what I remember next. The normal roar of the cellblock starts to quiet a little at a time now. It was like a factory I worked in once. At break time you could hear the plant wind down incrementally as each machine shut off, only on the cellblock the roar winds down as each con notices Lenny and shuts up to watch the show.

Lenny is in place. He throws the sheet rope over the pipe, and then pulls a snug knot to the drainpipe. I'm thinking that if he does wrap the noose end around his neck and jumps off the desk, the sewer pipe will break and shit will pour onto the block and stink it up worse than normal, because I can't really believe that Lenny will succeed at this anymore than he's succeeded at anything else in his sorry life.

He isn't even a decent criminal. Lenny is in prison for stealing copper wire. He and a cousin would go into the woods and pull down the wire to hunting camps and cabins. They'd cut down hundreds of feet of wire at a time, roll the mess up through the woods, over rough mountainous terrain that was filled with poison ivy and other shit. Then they'd drag the coils of wire into a truck. They'd drive it home, burn the insulation off in their backyard, and then haul it another fifty miles to a scrap yard to sell it for 39 stinking cents a pound. A real fucking job would have been less work. Even so, they'd managed to get busted because they helped themselves to the liquor in the hunting camp and passed out on the front stoop of the lodge. To top it off, the hunting lodge belonged to a politician so Lenny got the maximum sentence. I can't think of Lenny without thinking of *Cool Hand Luke* and Paul Newman breaking into parking meters to get himself locked up. Only Lenny is no cool hand anything. Lenny is a fuck-up, pure and simple. A likeable fuck-up, sure, but a fuck-up nonetheless.

Lenny's got the noose around his neck and he's poised on the edge of the desk. I put my book down and sit up in my bunk. He hesitates and readjusts the noose so the knot is on the side of his head. I'm not sure what difference it makes, but it seems important to him. He reaches up and checks the knot at the pipe, which seems okay. Then he turns his head back and forth like he's getting comfortable in a dentist chair headrest. Finally, somebody from the other end of the block yells, "What the fuck do you think you're doing?"

Lenny ignores this and tugs on the sheet again, checking the strength of the pipe. He seems satisfied and moves back to the edge of the desk. He's in position and seems ready.

I wait. The whole cellblock waits. I'm getting angry, though I'm not exactly sure why. Lenny just pisses me off. He readjusts the sheet again at the pipe. I don't want this to happen; mostly I don't want to think about it. I get more pissed off the more he stalls, and apparently I'm not the only one. Morgan slams his cards down, "Jesus Christ."

Every cellblock in every prison has a con who runs the show. Morgan runs this one. It's not that he's the toughest dude on the block; I doubt that he is, but the toughest dudes look to him and do what he says. He's a career criminal and proud of it. Morgan's smart, too. He talks to me because I read more than comic books. Morgan has given himself quite an education here; during his times of incarceration he's read most of the classics. It's all part of the life in the can. Morgan claims he'd take a year on the inside if he had to, for every ten on the street living the way he wants. That is, by his own rules.

Morgan's also got a mean streak. He lists the aluminum baseball bat as one of the century's greatest inventions. A man can hear the whistle from the bat before it hits the kneecap, he told me. So even if the man he's punishing closes his eyes, he can still hear it coming, and Morgan likes that.

Morgan gets up from the card game. "Get the fuck down from there asshole. You're not going to do anything." I'm glad Morgan is going to put an end to this charade.

Lenny, his voice a little gargled from the constriction of the bed sheet around his throat, says, "I am, too."

"Well then what's the holdup?" says Morgan. "You're fucking up my game here."

Lenny doesn't seem to have a response, but his eyes grow more doe-like.

"Well?" Morgan starts to amble toward Lenny, reaching into his shirt pocket for his Marlboros.

"Leave me alone," says Lenny.

Morgan holds the cigarette pack out in a friendly gesture. "Relax," he says. "I'm not going to stop you. I'm just offering you a last smoke. That's all."

Lenny is shaking now. Facing Morgan is worse than facing death.

"Here." Morgan offers the pack with a cigarette tapped out and easy to grab.

Lenny takes the cigarette and Morgan lights his own and then holds the match up high enough so Lenny can get a light, which is pretty high, since Lenny's head is tethered to the pipe. Lenny inhales. I figured maybe everything is going to be okay and we can go back to doing our time in peace. That's when Morgan asks Lenny if he really wants to die and Lenny says, "Yeah."

Morgan steps back a little and as calmly as could be says, "Then die you pussy motherfucker," and kicks the desk out from under Lenny. Lenny's body drops the few inches of slack in his makeshift rope. Morgan turns away after the kick and starts back to the card game without looking at Lenny who, as it turns out, didn't really want to die and is flopping and kicking while grabbing onto the rope with both hands, fighting for life. The cellblock is as quiet as I'd ever heard it as Morgan gets to the table and says, "Deal."

Nobody looks at Lenny as he fights the fight of his life, trying not to choke. But we all hear him gurgle and kick, his feet banging at the wall trying to get a toehold. It's as if Lenny had never existed and isn't at the end of his rope in the back of the cellblock.

The next sound I hear is the cards shuffle then slap to the table for some-body to cut. Nobody even looks in Lenny's direction. Me, I'm no better than anybody else. I hate Lenny's guts. I go back to my book. I don't watch and I don't help. What does it matter really?

The waitress's hip brushes against my arm, and I pull away as if her touch had cut like a shiv. I shake it off and come back to the present. When she puts in her drink order, I lean back to look at that tantalizing rope of hair and I know I'm never going to ask her out as I had planned. I mean, who am I kidding? I couldn't look at her without thinking of that place and Lenny. Always pushing away that image. When she turns to take the drinks to a table, I throw a buck on the bar and walk beside her stride for stride. Then she stops to serve a drink, and I keep on walking. After all, a man has to do his own time.

The Accident

Gray Jacobik

Never having died before, the panic-stricken are at once
realistic and incredulous: *So this is dying,*
and *This can't be happening* entwined
in the thread's final knot.

The great unknown is suddenly, unstoppably, onto you.

Do you hold your breath or scream, let go into
a widening darkness
like the aperture of a camera rolling
its metal petals closed, a pinhead of light, then nothing?

And the immense pity of it; wasted time
never to be salvaged, the unsaid never to be spoken.

You may believe in black tunnels that open onto fields of light,
or imagine, come to escort you home, a smiling robe-clad guide,

but suppose it is so much less than this?

So nearly nothing the drama is lost even on you,
less than an afterthought in your oxygen-starved brain,
your final urge a flashbulb's pop.

The unexpected comes preceded by its irreversibility,
the way a bride comes down the aisle
behind a procession begun with flowergirls.

But death's no wedding; not a word of promise is required of you,
although an absolute union is.

Helicopters

Elinor Benedict

PORONUI FISHING RANCH, NEW ZEALAND

*F*rom the meadow pool we watch
the helicopter come and go, carrying
from lodge to more distant streams
other couples in leather and canvas
who pay dearly to catch rare trout
none of us will keep.
                              The land rolls out
its green carpet, checkered with tree farms,
threaded with rivers and wooly fields
that Kiwi people call the bush, where
bees hum in white *tamuka* blooms
to make a honey so fine that
hospitals here swear by
its healing.
                     But how long will it take
even in this valley of pleasure to hear
a chopper's blasting rattle without
seeing fire, red gape of wounds,
desperate hurry, life wasting?
Even here, sounds and images
of war endure.
                      I stop untangling my line
from tamuka, drop my rod and hold
my ears against the noise, trying to
think instead of luckiness—old age
escorting my husband and me
with all honeyed comfort and delay
to a death just as certain as the one
that casts war's helicopters
into air, fishing for men.

Breathing

Cortney Davis

S OMETIME DURING THE EERIE, DISORGANIZED HALF-HOUR BEFORE MIDNIGHT, Peter Locke, a medical intern, arrived to see James Harris, his eighty-four-year old patient, whose condition was rapidly deteriorating. The patient's private duty nurse, Irene, had paged Peter just as he was hurrying toward his dreary, cell-like call room, hoping to catch a few moments of sleep before the next wave of admissions from the ER started rolling in. His head ached, his stomach felt vaguely upset—perhaps it was the hasty dinner of French fries and a greasy cheeseburger—and he didn't have any idea what he could possibly do to help Mr. Harris. Peter had admitted this patient ten days before—just two weeks into internship. He saw Mr. Harris every day on rounds and even tried to cram in some reading about end-of-life care and the importance of doctor-patient bonding during a terminal illness. But now, as Peter's first rotation of internship was about to end, he was, frankly, tapped out. Part of him hoped that Mr. Harris would die quietly and agreeably during the night, when some other intern was on call, but now it seemed that he might have to be the one to pronounce Mr. Harris after all. He would be the one to pretend, in front of a grieving family, to listen for the heart beat that he already knew wouldn't be there, to shine his penlight into the dead man's fixed, pinpoint pupils, then turn away from the body and say the words his chief resident had drilled into him, words he had yet to actually say aloud: *I'm sorry. Your (insert here grandfather, grandmother, father, mother, husband, wife, son, daughter, companion, friend) is gone. Please let us know if we can be of any help.*

Peter wondered about the implications of the word, *gone*. Couldn't he simply say *dead*, which seemed more truthful, more final? And why not ask if there was something *he* could do, rather than something *we* could do? Was that purposeful evasion meant to derail any possible requests, to keep the family at arm's length just when they might have innumerable needs and questions? This avoidance of precise, personal words suggested to Peter that the bonding he read about wasn't, after all, such a good idea. A patient who'd been pronounced gone instead of dead might sneak back, reappearing unexpectedly, just when everyone had been convinced of his absence. Such incongruities floated into Peter's mind when he was particularly tired, when the mountain of technical information he tried to digest was overwhelming, giving him heartburn more profound than anything caused by cheeseburgers and fries.

Entering room 23B, anticipating Mr. Harris's demise, Peter felt mortally fragile himself, as if his skin had peeled away to expose the network of nerves beneath. If there was one more attack, if a nurse chided him, accused him, or demanded of him one more thing he couldn't do, Peter thought he might just explode. If Mr. Harris were dead, lying there as inert and vulnerable as the cadaver Peter had dissected in the anatomy lab years earlier, Peter knew he was in danger of crying, something he hadn't allowed himself to do in four years of college, four years of medical school, and three and a half weeks of internship.

Mrs. Irene McNamara stood up when Peter entered and walked part way across the room to greet him.

"Dr. Locke? I'm Irene." She looked, Peter thought, fifty-ish, maybe less, with reddish hair tinged with gray, and light eyes that were framed by fine crow's feet when she smiled. Good, Peter thought. She's smiling. Mr. Harris isn't dead—a crude thought, but he didn't regret it. Knowing the patient was alive gave him a feeling of relief. He smiled back.

"I didn't know they made private duty nurses anymore," Peter said.

"Cherry Ames, Private Duty Nurse," Irene said. "Once upon a time one of my favorite books."

Irene looked, Peter thought, both kind and tired, nevertheless crisp in her patterned scrubs and white nurses' shoes. Standing next to her, he felt rumpled and sweaty. He turned to look at Mr. Harris. A day or so before the patient had been in a semi-private room, bloated and noisily in pain, yelping every time a nurse touched him. Even when no one was prodding him, Mr. Harris would groan with each breath, annoying his roommate, who complained to the head nurse. Peter had ordered Mr. Harris moved to a private room, a dying room, although no one called it that. Seeing their father alone in a room far away from the wards and also from the nurse's station, Mr. Harris's daughters worried. Supposing he called for help? What if the nurses didn't hear, and he died alone? Peter agreed with the daughters' request for a private duty nurse, and the nursing office assigned Irene McNamara.

Mr. Harris was lying on his back in the middle of the narrow hospital bed. His hip bones, like two shark fins, tented up the white sheet and green thermal blanket draped over him. His mouth was open, the red, dry ridges of his hard palate visible, his forehead waxy with sweat. Peter looked back at Irene.

"He's actively dying," she said, matter-of-factly, as she shifted Mr. Harris's pillow. "Sometimes this phase can take hours. Or days." The activity of her body, as she moved around Mr. Harris's bed, tucking and soothing him, seemed almost incongruous in this room of death.

"I haven't seen you here before," Peter replied. "Maybe I haven't been on call the nights you've been here."

Irene moved to the other end of the bed and adjusted Mr. Harris's feet. She nodded as she worked. "Of course I read your notes on the chart."

"Glad to hear someone does," Peter said, stuffing loose papers back into his clipboard. "Usually the nurses don't pay much attention to an intern's notes."

Irene murmured slightly in response but didn't look up at Peter. "I'm concerned that my patient's pain control isn't adequate. I'd like you to increase his morphine. And I wonder if you'd take a look at that one spot on his hip that's breaking down. I just can't seem to—"

"How much morphine is he getting now?" Peter interrupted, his voice sharper than he'd meant it to be.

Irene picked up the flow sheet and handed it to Peter. She had written each time she had pushed a few milligrams of morphine into Mr. Harris's IV. Next to each dose were numbers indicating his blood pressure and his respirations, both of which were steadily dropping. His last blood pressure had been 70/40. His respirations, though they were noisy and deep, were now only eight per minute. A few times, Peter saw, the respirations had shot up to 25 or 30 a minute. Irene's notations indicated that shortly after the morphine was delivered, the breathing had slowed. All this he'd have known, had he stopped to check Mr. Harris's chart before coming in. Handing the sheet back to Irene, he felt foolish.

How he hated being among the dying! He couldn't stand to look at Mr. Harris, not because he lacked empathy or pity, but because he was tired and cranky, and he'd rather be doing something instead of simply standing around and watching. Still, he felt no desire to leave the room. Here, at least, there were no alarm bells or chief residents barking orders, no nurses laughing in the hallway or calling him at three a.m., just when he had fallen asleep, for an aspirin order.

"My grandfather died at home when I was ten," Peter said, the words surprising him, coming as they did from a distant memory. "I'm not sure what he died of. I can't remember much about him, only what my mother tells me."

Mr. Harris suddenly reminded him a bit of his grandfather. Something about the thin mouth or the ears, the fleshy lobes. When Peter first met Mr. Harris, the chief resident had stood back and motioned Peter forward to the semi-conscious old man's bedside. "Okay, Sherlock Holmes," the resident said. "Go ahead and examine Mr. Harris. He's got a fascinating murmur. Makes you think his heart should kill him, but it'll probably be pneumonia. He had a small rectal carcinoma, got a stroke after the colostomy. Now a hospital-acquired pneumonia." Peter had examined Mr. Harris while the resident scribbled in the chart.

This time, it was Irene standing guard as Peter unraveled his stethoscope, wearily pushed up Mr. Harris's gown and listened, for the twentieth time this week, to the muffled lub-dub of his heart. Then Peter pressed the stethoscope tight against the chest and listened as the patient's raspy breaths came in fits and starts. He tucked the stethoscope under Mr. Harris's back. "The poor guy's drowning," he said. Listening, Peter felt a little short of breath himself.

Irene slipped on latex gloves and wiped inside Mr. Harris's mouth with a glycerin swab. The swab came out glistening, loops of mucus hanging from it, like strands of lights strung along holiday roof tops. Peter's stomach turned.

"Yes," said Irene. "I know. Anything we can give him to dry up these secretions?"

Peter looked away, pretending to study the IV bag and the plastic tubing, all the familiar, clean equipment surrounding the bed. The acid burning a hole in his stomach felt like fire. He expected to see, any minute now, a puff of smoke rise from his scrubs, followed by a flame that would leap out, igniting his lab coat. Maybe the nurse would come to his rescue, throwing a glass of water on him or wrapping him in a blanket. Maybe she would tell him what medications helped to dry up secretions. Maybe he would push Mr. Harris over the edge of the bed, disposing of him so he could lie down himself and go to sleep, while Irene watched over him, checking his blood pressure every so often to make sure he was still alive. Peter said, "I'll up the morphine."

Irene tied the patient's gown. "And for the secretions?" She folded the blanket under Mr. Harris's chin and readjusted the nasal oxygen.

Peter sighed. Suddenly a part of him wanted to bolt from the room. Another part of him felt pity for Mr. Harris, a rush of empathy that surprised him.

"Why don't we turn off the IV," Irene said, blotting Mr. Harris's forehead with a washcloth. "He doesn't really need the fluids now, does he?"

Peter flipped the pages of his clipboard. "Sure. D/C the IV fluids." His stomach churned.

"And before you leave," Irene said, "can you help me give him a boost up?"

Peter looked at her.

"Just go around to the other side, and we'll hoist him up a bit. He's sliding."

Irene motioned Peter to the other side of the bed, which had been raised up almost waist high. "Just hook your arm under his and grab the draw sheet." She positioned her body on Mr. Harris's left. "On the count of three, hoist him up, but make sure you pull the draw sheet at the same time."

Peter put his clipboard on the bedside table and leaned over Mr. Harris's right side. Together at her count of three, their heads almost touching, Irene and Peter hauled Mr. Harris up toward the head of the bed like two farmers heaving a bale of hay off the tailgate of a truck. Then they both stood. Irene rubbed the small of her back with both hands. Peter grabbed his clipboard and held it tight under one arm.

"So, you're on call tonight," Irene said.

"Yes. My luck." Peter shoved his other hand into his lab coat pocket. His arms were too long, his frame too tall, his knees too knobby, his short hair too unruly. Every part of him seemed ill at ease and out of place. He wondered if the nurse was married, if she had children. She could be my mother, he thought, and that realization both unsettled and intrigued him. He wondered where she lived and what she did when she wasn't at the hospital, as he sometimes tried to imagine his patients' private lives. He hugged the clipboard until its hard surface pressed against the buttons of his white coat.

"Do you think he'll die tonight?" he asked. "I've never pronounced anyone before."

"What'll happen is just when you're finally asleep, I'll call to wake you up," Irene said, without a trace of irony in her voice. "Then you can call your resident, so he won't get any sleep either."

Peter wanted to protest that he wasn't worried about sleep, he was worried about death. About how it would be to stand alone in the room in death's presence, to touch its cold skin and rest his warm hands upon its sunken chest. Instead he said, a bit too loudly, "Call me if you need me, okay?" and walked out of the room.

At two a.m., Peter Locke poked his head back into room 23B. Irene had balanced Mr. Harris on his left side. The sheets were pulled down and she was washing his back. Mr. Harris's breathing was hoarse but audible. "He's still with us?" Peter asked.

Irene looked up. "And you? You're still awake?"

"I had to admit an elderly woman with a fever. Frankly, she looks as bad as Mr. Harris. I thought maybe I could swing by before I tried to catch some sleep . . . just in case."

"Just in case you could pronounce him before you went to bed?"

Peter shifted in his spot. Why did his words sometimes sound so stupid? "Well, I'm not actually going to get any sleep tonight," he blurted out. For a moment he considered telling Irene the real truth—that if Mr. Harris did die tonight, he didn't know if he could stand it. He had too many things to deal with and he didn't feel able to control any of them: pneumonia, death, internship.

"Here," Irene said. "Put this in the drawer, would you?" She tossed Peter a small white bottle and, bending over the patient, began to massage his back, kneading and smoothing his bare skin, which had, Peter noticed, turned the color of Silly Putty.

Why does she even bother, he wondered. Why doesn't she just sit down in the chair next to the bed and read or doze, as he'd seen some of the night nurses do?

"Peripheral circulation closes down when patients are near death," Irene said, as if reading his mind. "The skin gets clammy and that makes them feel cold. Massage helps. Even if it doesn't, it lets Mr. Harris know I'm here."

She finished the back rub and guided Mr. Harris down flat again, balancing the slight weight of him and settling him gently. "There you go, Jim," she said. Irene smoothed a wisp of his hair back into place.

Peter's feet were aching. Even his most comfortable sneakers felt like vises after twenty hours. The plastic-covered visitor's chair at the bedside looked tempting. He turned his gaze back to the patient, trying to think of something clinical to say. "His breathing seems easier. More regular."

"Thank you for increasing the morphine," Irene said. She pulled up the bed rails, and they snapped into place with an authoritative click.

"You're welcome," said Peter.

"If we were in Mr. Harris's home," Irene said, "I'd open a window."

Peter flopped down in the chair and hooked his heels onto the bottom rung of the bed rail. Immediately the pressure on his toes eased.

"When my grandfather was dying," Peter said, before he even knew what he was thinking, "my mother opened his bedroom windows. It was May, and the air smelled like my grandmother's garden." He swiveled his feet on the rail. "I can still remember the smell of peat moss and gardenias."

"How old was he?"

"About eighty-four, I think. Same age as Mr. Harris here."

"Mr. Harris owned a series of grocery stores," Irene said. "He started with one little mom and pop store about the size of this room. By the time he turned the business over to his son-in-law, he had a chain of supermarkets all over the northeast. His wife died four years ago of a brain tumor."

"How do you know all that?" Peter asked.

"One of his daughters told me. It was hard for him to give up the business, but he felt he was getting too old to compete."

"Scary to get old," Peter said.

"It's certainly not for the faint of heart," Irene said with a sad smile. "What did your grandfather do?"

"He was a tailor. I used to hang out in his shop while he fitted customers or made suits. He'd hang the measuring tape around my neck and I'd be in charge of the pins. He'd be sewing with his machine, come to a pin and, without stopping, take it out and hand it to me to stick into the pincushion. It was our ritual. Then he'd take me out for ice cream."

"You said you didn't remember much about him."

"I don't really, not much. I remember the night he died."

"You were there?"

Peter nodded. He was vaguely aware that the circulation had returned to his feet. "After dinner my mother told me to go in to say good-bye to him—she thought it wouldn't be long. Then she made me go upstairs to bed. I couldn't sleep. I kept hearing him make these choking noises. When he died, I could hear everyone crying. I stayed in my bed and stared at the ceiling, imagining what awful things were going on downstairs. I tried to cry too, but I couldn't. To me, he wasn't dead, he was still my grandfather sewing in his shop and buying me ice cream."

"Have you ever seen anyone die?" Irene asked.

Peter put his elbows on his knees and ran his hands through his hair. It felt greasy, uncombed. His belly still burned and grumbled. "Not really. I saw one guy who didn't survive a code, but that wasn't like a natural death."

"It's funny," Irene said. "I gave a talk about death and dying once, and when I asked people to raise their hands if they'd ever been with someone at the moment of death, the exact moment that death occurred, almost all the nurses and nurses' aides raised their hands. Not many doctors did."

Irene walked around the bed, stepping over Peter's feet. She lifted the sheet from Mr. Harris's legs, slipped in a bed cradle, then settled the sheets over the cradle. "His feet and legs seem more sensitive to pressure now," she said, sitting in the chair next to Peter's and moving it closer to the bed. She took Mr. Harris's hand and put her other hand a little higher up on his arm. "Jim?" she said. "Are you more comfortable now? I'm here with you."

Peter watched her. She looked tired before, and now she looked as exhausted as Peter felt.

"Judging by his breathing and his skin color," she said, "we're going to get really busy in a couple of hours." Irene turned to him with a look on her face that was almost sly. "If you're up to it."

At 4:35 a.m., Peter returned. Classical music was playing on the radio, and the lights were dim. Irene was reading something to Mr. Harris.

"You still up, Peter?" She didn't seem surprised to see him.

"Actually, I got to lie down for a few minutes. The woman with the fever stabilized." Yawning, he plopped down in the chair. Its plastic cushion deflated under him with a hiss of air. "I can't sleep when I'm on call anyway. I keep waiting for the beeper to go off. What are you reading to Mr. Harris?"

"A letter from his daughter. She writes every day, something about their lives, her memories of her childhood."

"You seem pretty close to the family."

"I suppose I've become a connection to their father, but I don't know that I'm really close to them. The older I get," Irene said, "the more I find myself pulling back from getting too involved." She shook her head. "Maybe it's time to go on vacation."

"Strange how patients move in and out of our lives, isn't it?" Peter asked, although he had not yet been really close to any of his patients.

Mr. Harris's irregular breathing filled the silence. Then Irene said, "I don't know. I find that I remember them. Your grandfather—he was your mother's father?"

"Yup. Poppy, we called him."

Raising her voice, Irene said, "Jim, your doctor, Peter, is here with us again. He called *his* grandfather Poppy." She looked at Peter as if to say, your turn.

Peter cleared his throat. "Hello, Mr. Harris," he said. "I've been working with your internist for the last few weeks. I admitted you to the hospital." He looked at Irene for some signal that he had said the right thing. She stroked Mr. Harris's hand.

"You're doing great, Jim," she said. "Don't worry. We're here with you."

Peter stood up and walked to the small corkboard where Mr. Harris's daughter had pinned family photographs. There was a photo of Mr. Harris as a young man, gaunt and serious, with a white grocery apron around his waist. In another, he had his arm around a stunning young woman, tiny and small boned. The other photos showed Mr. Harris and his wife with one or both of their daughters, a series in which each of them aged until Mr. Harris was an old man, holding grandchildren on his hip or cradling them in his arms. His wife was gray and fading, then absent, and his daughters became women, their faces a reflection of their parents.

Peter tapped one of the pictures. "It's too bad we never really know who our patients are. They come in sick or out of it, like Mr. Harris here, at the end of their lives." He sat down again, pulling his chair a little closer to the bed rails. "I don't know if it helps or hurts to see them as whole people. It makes all this even harder."

He reached through the bed rails to squeeze Mr. Harris's arm. "What a great family you have," he said. "Your wife was beautiful."

He sat there in the dim light with Irene and Mr. Harris. Between the back and forth sawing of Mr. Harris's breathing, Peter heard the loud ticking of the wall clock. Through the hospital window, a faint glow rose from the parking lot. In the hallway, the night nurses walked back and forth on squishy soles, whispering.

"Do you have any kids?" Peter asked.

"I have three boys and one girl. All of them grown up, three engaged. I'm preparing to look in the mirror one day and see a grandmother staring back at me." She paused. "What about you?"

Peter shrugged. "Not a whole lot of time for social life these days." He nodded toward Mr. Harris. "How are his vital signs?"

"I've stopped taking them," Irene said. "Help me pull him up again, would you?"

They bent together over Mr. Harris, hooked their arms under his, and slid him higher in the bed.

"He's got a lot of hair for an old guy," Peter said. "My grandfather was totally bald, except for a mustache."

"It's funny," Irene said. "But after a while, all my patients remind me of someone in my family."

"Really?" said Peter.

"Or maybe I pretend that they do." She stood by the window for a moment. "All the young women seem like my mother. She died from ovarian cancer when she was thirty-nine. And all the old ones remind me of my grandparents. Or my father, who's getting old now too."

Peter's heart started pounding. He noticed this clinically, as if he were his own physician. He'd never talked about death before, not like this. Talking about death openly made him feel odd, but oddly alive.

At 6:15 a.m., after he'd been to 3-East to see about a post-op lady who'd pulled out her IV and to 7-South to write a Percocet order, Peter returned again to room 23B.

A deep fuchsia seeped through the window. The bed rail was down and

Irene was sitting on the bed next to Mr. Harris, who was propped almost upright on his pillows. She held his hand and chanted "ahhh" along with each of his exhalations. Peter listened from the doorway. It sounded to him as if they were singing together, or praying.

Irene didn't seem to notice Peter entering. And Peter—seeing Mr. Harris's eyes open, rolled back in his head, and the nurse, leaning in close toward her patient—stopped several yards short of the bed. Mr. Harris's breathing was harsh and deep as he fought to pull each breath into the depths of his frail body. With each shudder, Irene leaned farther forward. As each breath squeezed out of the patient's lungs with a prolonged groan, Irene joined in, her *ah* a controlled, musical harmony. When Mr. Harris's breathing slowed, Irene followed his lead.

Peter stepped closer.

"You're just in time," Irene said, motioning for him to sit on the other side of the bed. "I called his daughter, but I don't think she'll make it. He doesn't seem to want to wait."

Peter put down the bed rail and sat next to the patient, whose body was barely a sunken disturbance in the sheets. "Put your hand on his arm," Irene said. "Let him know you're here." Then, more loudly, "Peter and I are here with you, Jim. I'll take care of Carly when she gets here. Everything will be all right."

Mr. Harris stared up at the ceiling, his eyes filmed over and dull, his mouth opening, then falling shut with every breath.

"Are you okay?" Peter asked.

"Not really," Irene said without looking away from Mr. Harris. "Are you?"

They heard a commotion in another room. Someone dropped something metallic that clanged and bounced. Voices rose and fell. An aide came into the room with a breakfast tray and Irene waved her away.

"What was that sound you were making?" Peter asked.

"It's called breathing with a patient," Irene said. "It's like going part of the way with them, a way of letting your life and their death overlap." She glanced at him. " Do you want to try?"

Peter didn't know what to say.

"It's easy. You don't have to do anything," she said. "Watch Jim's chest rise and fall and just breathe along with him."

In the hall, the day shift nurses were arriving. Peter could smell coffee brewing. The voices of residents, debating some lab value, moved close to the door and then down the hall. Mr. Harris sucked in another deep breath, then— with a harsh, terrible groan—let it out. Irene joined in with her *ah*, sustaining her note, then letting it fade away with Mr. Harris's breath. Peter leaned closer; before he thought about it, his lips parted as he offered his own *ah*, a whisper that was as involuntary as one person's yawn in response to another's.

"Good," Irene said to Peter. Then to the patient she said, "It's okay, Jim. We're both here with you."

She held her arm fast around Mr. Harris's shoulders, her hair frizzy in the morning light.

"This is it," she whispered, and Peter felt a sudden grip of anxiety. But as Mr. Harris let go a final, slow moan of air, Peter found himself joining in, his deeper *ah* blending with Mr. Harris's and Irene's, the three notes braiding around one another. Mr. Harris's lips paled, his eyes darkened, and together their three breaths rose into the room, fading out in unison.

Cemetery Plums

Jim Tolan

*O*ne who would offer ripe fruit to the dead
as if knowing their desires, as if believing
desires still lived in them, would know
how tangible remains the memory of its juice

across the mouth and chin and sliding
along the tongue. Do not be misled.
The dead miss life more than we miss them,
their loss more than equal to our forgetting

and our grief. And a bowl of fruit offered
in their name returns to them as the memory
of a mouth rapt in joy around moist and living
flesh. Who among the dead does not long

for the sun-wet meat of smooth-skinned plums,
the bitter sweetness of each pitted heart?

The Long Journey Home

James Tate

Jeannie had worked as a waitress at the Duck Pond
Cafe for the past eight years, and, during that time, she
had met some pretty strange characters. But, last week,
there was one who beat them all. He was a dead man. He
shuffled in and collapsed in a booth, barely able to hold
his head up. She brought him a glass of water and a menu.
He grasped the glass of water with both hands, and brought
it slowly to his parched lips. Half the water spilled down
his dirty, blue suit, but he didn't seem to mind. "My god,
that's good," he said in a thin, raspy voice. Jeannie poured
him another glass, which he drank immediately. Though his
eyes were almost vacant, he stared at Jeannie's with deep
gratitude. Then he studied the menu excitedly. "I'd like
a double cheeseburger and extra large fries," he said. She
handed the order to Dennis the cook, but said nothing to him
about the deceased customer. She went back and filled his
glass several times, and each time he thanked her and tried
to smile. When his food was finally ready, she delivered it
and he stared at it in awe. "Enjoy," she said, and he replied,
"Yes, yes, I certainly will." She went back to the counter
and watched him devour all of it in several minutes. When
she went to clear his table, he said, "I'd like more of the
same. Is that possible? Are there any rules against that?"
"Certainly not," she said. "Coming right up." She delivered
the order to Dennis, then waited on a family of five who had
just sat down. She was happy that they didn't have a view
of the dead man. After he had finished his second meal, she
asked him if he would care for some dessert. "Oh, yes, indeed,
that would be excellent," he said. He wanted a piece of
apple pie and three scoops of vanilla ice cream. His voice
was coming back to him, and there was even a little gleam in
his eyes. When she delivered his dessert, he thanked her
profusely, and reached out and touched her hand. She started
to freeze, but then caught herself, and grabbed his hand in
hers. "What's your name?" she said. He smiled at her. "Do
you mind if I eat?" he said. "Of course not. That was rude
of me," she said, and walked back to the counter. She delivered

the food to the family of five. They suddenly seemed very loud
and annoying. She much preferred the company of the dead man
who was so quiet and grateful. When he had finished his dessert,
she brought him his check, which he stared at for a long time.
He searched all his pockets to no avail. "That's okay," Jeannie
said. "Don't worry about it." "I was so hungry, I never thought
about the money. That was bad of me," he said. "No, no, it
was an honor to have given you this food. You needed it. I
could see," she said. "But do you have anywhere to go?" His face
looked pained as he thought that over. "Everyone has a place
to go. I'll find one. I don't know how, but, maybe, something
will occur to me. I'll just keep walking. Someone might recognize me,"
he said. "You just needed to get your strength back,"
Jeannie said. He stood up. "I can't thank you enough," he said,
and shook her hand. She stood at the window and watched him walk
down the street, staring into people's faces as they passed.
He was somebody's father or husband or something, but he might
as well be invisible.

The Weight of Absence

Judy Katz

When you died our house sank deeper into the earth,
  pressing on the roots of trees.
I could feel it sinking
as each visitor pushed open the front door,
laden with cakes and casseroles, the full weight
of their bodies—every muscle and tendon,
shinbone   pelvis   hips   moving
down the hallway, moving   past the closet
where your dresses hung, still with your smell,
moving into the living room where our father
sat low to the ground.

I had watched you grow smaller and smaller,
ice chips on your tongue.
And as the morphine took you
here and there, Paris and summer camp,
the lake at night—
I thought I understood:
lighter and lighter
you would become,
a lightness leading
to nothing.

But the house did not rise that day;
it sank.
No mass   no matter
no thing   in the bed
in the blankets
in your place.

. . . Divorced, Beheaded, Survived

Robin Black

WITHOUT QUESTION, ANNE BOLEYN WAS THE PLUM ROLE.
    Day after day, dusk really, in the time between school and dinner, in the small, untended yard behind my childhood home, there were fights over who would get to play her. Even the boys loved everything about being the Lady Anne—the tell-tale pillow under your shirt, long before the elaborate royal marriage. "Henry dear, I have wonderful news!" The twigs you could tape to your hands, just next to your pinkies, to show those extra fingers that she had. The fact that we all knew there had been extra breasts as well. The simple, distant weirdness of it all. "Ooooh, I'm a witch. I'm a sexy pregnant witch. And I want to be queen of all England!!"

My older brother Terry was undoubtedly the most convincing. Once, he stole a dress from our mother's closet—a red and white Diane von Furstenberg wraparound so he could use the belt-like part to hold the couch pillow baby, the future Queen Elizabeth, in place. "Oh Hal," he cooed to Ben Mandelbaum from next door. "You don't need that old Spanish cow of a wife of yours! With her sour little daughter. You just wait! I'll give you that son you want and deserve. Right here, my sire." With a pat to his lumpy middle.

Almost nothing beat watching him sidle up to Ben, who was always our Henry, due to his heft, to the early growth of unattended facial hair across his heavy jaw and to the fact that he was the only one of the neighborhood boys who steadfastly refused to play a wife. "Oh Harry, let's go frolic in the meadow and leave these nasty courtiers all behind!" Then Terry would bump his swollen front against the damask tablecloth Ben wore draped across his back, knotted in a bow beneath his chin.

It was almost worth giving up the role yourself just to watch Terry give it his all, and it might have been worth it if it weren't for the execution scene. But the beheading was just too good not to fight over. Katy Denham, from the house behind ours, both of whose parents were Jungian psychologists, usually asked to be the anonymous executioner.

"Do you forgive me, my grace?" she would intone, from behind an old Batman Halloween mask, her voice as deep as she could make it, her straight yellow hair hanging to her waist.

"I do, Sir. I do forgive you."

And when I was Anne, I would then offer her my hand, to kiss and to hold as I knelt. Looking up to the sky, I would press my palms together, as if in prayer—or as I imagined people praying might do. Raising my own long hair up above the nape of my neck, I'd lean my head down over the chopping block—a white, enameled lobster pot, turned upside down—and await the mortal blow from the black rubber axe that Katy swung.

It was all Johnny Sanderson's idea. His father was a professor in the medical school and had started up at the university the same year my father joined the history department. Those were the days when there were still teas and formal dinner parties for new faculty, and my parents and the Sandersons had struck up a friendship of sorts.

Johnny was a year younger than Terry, a year older than me and he was one of those kids who seemed to know a lot about himself before any of the rest of us had much of a clue of who we were. By that spring, when he was eleven, he knew for sure that he wanted to be a history professor, like my father. But instead of American history his thing was Europe. He was a short, skinny boy who usually wore brown corduroy pants and a gray sweatshirt. And he looked young for his age. People were always thinking he must be in my class—sometimes even younger than that.

I don't know exactly what satisfaction Johnny got from having us act the thing out in my backyard time and time again, over those several weeks. I think it must have been something greater than what the rest of us enjoyed, hamming it up as we lay our heads down on the lobster pot or moaned while giving birth to another of Henry's brats. There was more to it than playacting for Johnny, a kind of intensity that crept into his voice when we all gathered after school, had some juice and fruit or crackers, whatever my mother had around. A kind of edgy tension as he said, "Hey, anyone want to act out the thing again?" And he knew how to hook us all too, every time, rotating which kid would play Anne, having the good sense to hurry through the more boring wives—though he never let us wholly skip a single one.

"Off with her head!" Ben Mandelbaum would shout at the afternoon's Jane Seymour. "Off with her head!"

"Divorced, beheaded, *died*," Johnny would correct. "The third wife died. No beheading. Jane Seymour died a natural death."

He was the first of the many obsessive, bossy intellectuals I have loved and have lived to impress. Nothing pleased me more those afternoons, than when, as Katy's axe head hit my neck, Johnny Sanderson would burst into spontaneous applause or even sometimes say "Great, Sarah. Really, really great."

That was the spring of fourth grade for me, 1973—the last months before Terry got sick, and then sicker, and then got better for a little bit, but then died in '74, which shocked me when it happened; but now, thirty years later seems to have been as inevitable a conclusion as the strike of Katy's axe.

To my own children, that long neglected backyard is only part of Grandma's and Grandpa's house, where we go for Thanksgiving, for the Christmases we don't spend with Lyle's folks in California, for occasional weekend escapes from Manhattan, into Massachusetts. To see the leaves changing color. To celebrate a birthday. My mother's seventy-fifth. My father's eightieth. Events that for me carry an inevitably muted quality. My mother's eyes damp, with what she swears are tears of joy, as she opens her gifts. My father softly talking to himself, after the candles have been blown out, after his wish has been silently made, all alone on the back porch swing.

The children are too old now to play out there much when we go up, though I used to watch them dart around the wild, thorny rose bushes in games of tag, and hide unsuccessfully from one another behind the lean Japanese maple. Sixteen and twelve now, Mark and Coco are four years apart—we had been two apart, Terry and I. And maybe it was superstition that made me wait that extra stretch of time before getting pregnant again. I don't know. Lyle would have liked our children to be closer in age: "Keep the parenting years compressed." But I put our second child off, and so my boy and girl were always just a little different from the pair we used to be.

I've been thinking a lot lately about all the ways we try to protect our children. And ourselves. Three weeks ago, Mark's best friend Jason was killed on the Long Island Expressway. That Sunday morning, I was making a special breakfast—French toast and bacon—because Coco had a friend sleeping over. The girls were still in her room, and Mark was lying on the couch, reading. Lyle was grading some papers on the kitchen table, complaining about them as he did. "How can these children be in college and still be so close to functionally illiterate?" I had just pulled the eggs out from the fridge and held the carton in my hand when the telephone rang. It was close to ten o'clock.

"Can I talk to Mark?"

The voice on the line was a kid, but not a voice I recognized.

"Who's calling?"

It turned out to be a boy I'd known for years.

"What's the matter, Nick? You sound terrible."

As he told me, I turned my back on Lyle who was suddenly alert, watching me. I opened the fridge and put the eggs away. "There was this party . . ." I'd known about the party. Mark had thought of going, but had decided he had too much work. "I don't even think they were drinking or anything . . . or not much anyway . . . the way I heard it, the other guy, I don't know, I think someone said it was a truck, he might've been stoned or something. Nobody else was even hurt . . . ."

The bacon on my stove crackled as Nick spoke. My back still to Lyle, I reached for a fork and turned over the strips. Lowered the heat.

"Are your parents there?" I asked.

They were.

"We'll call a little later, Nick. Let me talk to Mark first. We'll be back in touch."

"Who died?" Lyle asked, before I even hung up the phone. I told him.

"Jesus Christ."

"Car accident."

"Holy shit."

"Yeah. Holy shit."

I turned off the bacon. And kissed my husband's motionless head before going in to talk to Mark.

"This is the part where Anne learns for certain that she's going to die," Johnny Sanderson had coached us, every afternoon. "No more chances. She's doomed. You should show a little emotion at this point."

And Terry would hold his face in both his hands, his shoulders heaving in enormous, wracking, make-believe sobs.

But in real life, it was all silent hours. Vacant stares.

As soon as we learned Terry was sick, my house stopped being the daily gathering place. Everyone but me seemed to have known what was coming. He stopped being the boy who would throw himself into anything that seemed like fun. And one by one the other children began avoiding us. We had played together all our lives and then it ended. There was no more ease between us. Not even between my brother and me. I didn't know how to speak to the quiet, solemn boy he had become. And he didn't seem to need me, anymore. Not as a companion. Not to confide in.

I sat next to my son where he lay stretched on the couch. "Hey, bud." I took the book from his hand as I spoke, and lay it open on the tabletop. "Something's happened, sweetheart. Something bad." His face was still unwashed from sleep, his brown hair a little messy on his head.

I don't know. Maybe Ben Mandelbaum's mother saw a different side of her son after my brother died. Could detect a new thoughtfulness in his eyes. Maybe Katy Denham cried herself to sleep for weeks. Maybe Johnny Sanderson's heart was broken. I never knew. They never told me. Johnny did go on to be a history professor, like he always said he would. Made a name for himself at the same university where our fathers had taught. But maybe his life wasn't exactly the way he'd always imagined it, because of what happened to my brother when we were kids.

My son's face changed as he took in the news.

"He's dead?"

I nodded. He shook his head.

"No. That's impossible. Just yesterday..."

I nodded again; and he still shook his head. Coco had come into the room in her nightshirt. Just behind her, I could see her friend in pajamas holding a hairbrush in her hand.

"What's going on?" Coco asked.

"Nothing," Mark said. "Go away."

"Dad's in the kitchen, hun. Go on—he'll talk to you." And grasping my urgency, she left; but for a moment her friend just stood there staring at us, the brush caught halfway through her hair. Then she too turned and walked away.

"Mom, he can't be dead."

I didn't speak.

Can't be. I know that feeling.
Can't be.
But is.

I don't think about Terry every day, anymore. And sometimes I'm stunned by that fact. It isn't only the discomfort of disloyalty I feel; it's the fact of utter disappearance after death. The idea that as loved as we may be, we may also be forgotten. If only for a day here and there.

More than a decade ago, as soon as I thought Mark was old enough to ask me questions, I made the decision to put away the picture of my brother that I had carried from my parents' home to college, in and out of my first brief marriage, in and out of the first apartment Lyle and I shared and finally into our family home. I took it down off the bookshelf where it sat between my old books—all the orange spined Penguin classics, Shakespeare, Woolf, all that—and Lyle's many chemistry texts. It just seemed to me to be too hard on the children, too hard on Mark particularly to have that happy boy face smiling down, and to know what had happened to that other boy. The lines between him and my own son were too easily drawn. And I was afraid my brother's face would become a fearful thing for them. And maybe for me as well—now that I had kids of my own. So I put him in the dresser drawer I use for the few really fine scarves and gloves I possess, the softest place for storage I could find.

But of course the children have always known that I had a brother and that he died. A brother named Terrance, Terry. They know about him without my ever having had to tell either of them. Uncle Terry, he would have been. It's family information. The kind that travels in the air that children breathe.

At Jason's funeral, we lined up in a row. My husband, my two children and I. Mark and Coco wore the dress clothes I had bought for Thanksgiving, which is fast upon us, now. Another drive to Massachusetts. A family visit home. I'll have to phone my parents, I know, and tell them what happened. I haven't done that yet.

We never did call Nick back, the morning that we heard. And I don't think Mark's spoken very much to any of his friends since then. Not about Jason. He goes off to school, and comes right home. Heads straight for his room and closes the door. Coco's asked me if he's going to be okay; and I tell her that he will. And I know that he will. It just takes time, I tell her. It's only been a few weeks. It'll take some more time.

I forced myself to go up to Jason's parents as they stood beside their son's casket, and to say the things you say. Lyle came too, of course, and shook their hands. Mumbled something. Bit his lip. Stepped away so another family friend could do the same. I didn't force the kids, but eventually Mark made his way over. The mother and father both hugged him, hard, and Jason's kid brother shook his hand, with an empty, numb expression on his face. Mark didn't come back to us, right away. He just wandered to a corner of the church and stood by himself for a while.

The truth is that sometimes more than a day goes by before I remember to think of my brother. It's only natural, I've told myself, time and time again. It's human nature, I've thought—as though there's consolation to be found in that. And maybe there is. Maybe it's a gift to be able to let go of the remembering. Some times. Some things.

"What was it like, Mom?" Mark asked me for the first time ever, yesterday. "What was it like when Uncle Terry died?"

Uncle Terry.

I took my son by the hand, into my room, and I opened the dresser drawer. And there he was, smiling out from above the softly folded scarves, the empty fingers of my own gloves seeming to want to hold him there.

"It was hard," I said to Mark, as he lifted the picture toward his face. "There is no secret answer. It was terribly, terribly hard."

When I got to Henry VIII in high school—European history, 10th grade— Katy Denham and I were in the same section. She still had that long, straight hair to her waist and she wore overalls most days. The rap on her was that she smoked a little dope, but not more than most kids. We weren't really friends, anymore. And neither of us said a word, not a single word to each other about the subject when it was raised. It was as though we had never spent those hours together. As though she had never held and kissed my hand. Never asked for my forgiveness, which I so freely gave. And neither of us had watched my brother in that dress, pregnant and cooing seductively to his sire.

There are things that go on, I believe, important things that make only an intuitive kind of sense. Silences, agreed to. Intimacies, put away.

"Divorced, beheaded, died, divorced, beheaded, survived."

Miss Rafferty wrote the rhyme out on the board, and Katy Denham and I dutifully copied it into our notebooks, as though we might otherwise forget.

In Suicide's Tracks

Lisa Rosen

*A*fter solstice
every day more light to miss you in
more time for shadows
wherever we turn. What if
I'd called with a beam of before?

Mount Lemmon where we sat on a pine log
talking toward some truth
with a weight of mothers behind us
the world ahead a swirl
of risks we felt ready to jump into.

That time you were craving stars
you walked up into the Rincons
without a tent. The clouds moved
and those distant white blessings
said yes to every wish.
And you came back out with wilder hair
and a hunger you had every reason
to believe you would always be able to feed.

Luminarias line a path it's too late to walk.
But whenever you said my name
I heard a history of friendship in your voice
calling me back to my most natural self.
I would give anything to duck back into November now
and sound out the syllables that root you.
I'd bring a message from your guitar,
it misses the press of your song.

And I would sidle in wherever I found you
emptying of light, lift
your head, stroke out worry
or hold on beside you, saying
We'll double our grip, make
darkness be the first to let go.

Apartment 1-A

Amy Mehringer

S HE DRINKS MERLOT. TWO BOTTLES SIT ON HER BUTCHER-BLOCK COUNTER, one open and half-empty, its cork stuck crooked in the top. An avocado, two over-ripe bananas, an unwashed knife, a small bowl filled with matches. An unplugged toaster, some potholders, unopened mail, a few votive candles, a Mr. Coffee, pictures of kids stuck to the fridge, and a bottle of Triple Sec standing with rolls of paper towels on top of the freezer. That's everything of hers I can see without opening a cupboard or a drawer.

I could really start going through her things, but I shouldn't even be doing this. I've already finished fixing her disposal, and there are other jobs to do in other apartments, but still I linger in her kitchen, under the weak yellow light that seeps out of the fixture overhead. I imagine her walking around this morning before leaving for work. Maybe half-dressed—a slip and stockings and a blouse, but no skirt—she stood here using this knife on a piece of fruit or to butter toast. Maybe she had a headache from drinking that half-bottle of Merlot. She rushed out, I'm almost certain of that, forgetting that I would be coming in with my master key to fix her garbage disposal. When she comes home, there will be no sign that another person was in her apartment, and only when she turns on the disposal tonight will she remember me.

We came here twelve years ago, Jane and I, and we planned on staying the rest of our lives. For Jane, that was sooner than we expected. It took her thirteen months to die, and in that time, it seemed I never slept, but only cared for her constantly, in addition to doing the repairs and the standard maintenance that comes with being the manager of these apartments. When she finally died, 5-D sent flowers, and I received cards from almost every occupant, but only this tenant, the woman in 1-A, came to the church service and then later to the memorial garden where Jane is buried. She came over to me afterward. She was a distant mourner, not close to Jane and me, not like our families and the friends we'd built up after we got married. But she came over after the coffin had been lowered into the ground. She's a tall woman, taller than I, and her graying hair blew in her face as she pressed my hand and said, "I am so sorry, Mr. Alessandro." Since then, we have not spoken, not unless you include the nods we've exchanged in the parking lot when I am shoveling snow and she is hurrying to her car.

We've had a rough winter. Twenty-five inches of snow already and it's not even Christmas yet. Almost every morning, I chip away the ice that has formed overnight on the front stoops of the buildings. When I have time, I help shovel out cars, but there's always something else to do when it's cold.

Someone's heat is always going out. Most people get crabby when it's not fixed within a few hours. You've got to do whatever you can to stay warm in this kind of weather. I don't blame her for the Merlot. Let her curl up with it at night. Let it sink her into sleep so she doesn't even notice the cold.

I'm curious about her, so I start leafing through her unopened mail. A religious brochure, something from a hospital, an offer from a credit card company, and a donation request from the Muscular Dystrophy Foundation. Then I look at the pictures stuck beneath magnets on her refrigerator. Some photo Christmas cards, many showing children with adult handwriting scrawled on the bottom, reading "To Aunt Jenny" and then the cookie-cutter graphics: *Peace on Earth* or *Season's Greetings*. There are other pictures—someone's wedding and the tenant herself, 1-A, holding a very tiny baby. One faded black-and-white photograph of a young girl, bangs cut too short, smiling beneath a Christmas tree, her fingers already ripping open a wrapped present. *1976* is stamped in black on the thin white border.

1976 was the year after Jane and I were married. That same Christmas, Jane and I were living over in Lockport, where she was a waitress at the Howard Johnson's and I was the night desk clerk at one of the hotels in town. For all I know, the cancer that killed her could have been growing back then, all those years ago, when we were too poor to afford Christmas gifts and fell into bed at night holding each other, which was gift enough. We laughed about it later, once we landed this job, moved in here, and had enough money to buy each other almost whatever we wanted.

A daughter, a younger sister, a niece, a family friend. The girl in the faded photograph could be anyone. Her almost dumb-faced smile and egg-shaped head and the too-short bangs make her seem pale and sad.

I have been here far too long and, though it's still too early for her to come home from work, any one of the other tenants on this floor could have seen me come in here, and they may be aware that I haven't left yet.

"Mr. Alessandro was in your apartment today," one of these tenants could say to 1-A.

"Oh, yes," she'd say, remembering. "My garbage disposal is broken. He was probably fixing it."

"He was there the entire afternoon."

But I have not been here that long, and I won't be. Before I go, though, there are other things I want to see.

1-A is one of just a few tenants who have been here longer than Jane and I. Nowadays, this area has become transient. It used to be that if you were born here, you died here. Jane and I were both born in Buffalo, at Millard Fillmore Hospital, three years apart, and neither of us ever ventured further than a half hour's drive over the Canadian border, except for the week we spent in Albany on our honeymoon. But these days, most of the young people are leaving for bigger cities and better opportunities. If they go to college, they never come back, and if they don't go to college, they work at drugstores or gas stations and live in apartments only until they can afford a down payment on a starter home somewhere on the south side of town.

The people who stay and make lives for themselves in these apartments are divorcées or older folks who can't afford mortgage payments anymore. 1-A is a divorcée or a widow, I don't know which. When Jane and I landed the job here and moved from Lockport, 1-A was working as a receptionist in the admissions department at the university. She's worked her way up to director of administration in the School of Science. I've seen her coming and going enough to know she's got to be there Monday through Friday around 8:30 in the morning, and she doesn't come home until after 5:00. I imagine she comes home tired and flicks her shoes off, settles on the couch, maybe pours herself the first glass of the night's Merlot.

Her couch is plush yellow with matching throw pillows that have rope tassels on each corner. 1-A is just around my age, just around the age Jane would be—48—and I wonder what heartbreaks and joys she has lived through. What was it that made her come over to me afterwards, squeeze my hand, as if she understood what it felt like to lose someone close to you, when she barely knew us? There are many kind people in the world, but near-strangers usually don't show up at your wife's funeral unless they've felt a similar pain.

There are many kind people in the world. Jane was the kindest. This time of year, when I was out before sunrise shoveling snow so my tenants could get to work on time, Jane always joined me. Bundled up in scarves, she'd shovel next to me, until she got sick, and even then she'd make sure something hot was waiting for me when I finally got home. But Jane couldn't cook worth a damn, so it was never something I really looked forward to. And then she got too sick even to make watery hot chocolate and burnt scrambled eggs, and by then it was summer anyway, and there was no snow to shovel, though it felt that there should be. All summer, I felt ice-cold, frozen, waiting to thaw.

1-A has a nice layout: a one-bedroom with a balcony that overlooks the sloping hill in back. In the summer, kids play soccer and kickball there, but now that it's covered in snow, there are sled paths instead—trails two feet wide that lead down the hill and almost onto the road. 1-A must be able to hear the kids' laughter and yelps of excitement from her windows, if she listens. I listen. Jane loved watching the kids play. That summer, the second to last thing she asked me to do for her was to prop her up near the windows so she could see the children playing on the hill.

"That's the last thing I want to hear," she told me. "The sound of children."
Jane and I never had children.

I've ended up in 1-A's hallway where her bedroom is. The door is closed. I stand in front of it looking down at the knob as if it'll open by itself if I stare long enough. Finally, I try it. The knob turns easily. I almost feel guilty as the door opens and I'm left standing in the entrance of 1-A's bedroom. A queen-sized bed, neatly made with a flowered comforter and matching curtains. The shades are drawn, making the room dark, so I step in to get a better look. A large dresser with matching mirror, pictures stuck in the sides. A photograph of the same dumb-faced girl on a bicycle, and then another of her in front of a birthday cake. On the wall above the bed, a crucifix, and on the opposite wall, a framed embroidery that reads, "May you be in heaven a half hour before the devil knows you're dead."

I open her closet. Her shoes are lined up neatly on the floor and her clothes are hung in a tight row. I just graze my fingers against them at first, feeling their soft material and the way they move against one another, but then I lean in close and smell them. 1-A wears perfume. It's all over her clothes, a flowery scent that smells like the cosmetics department at J.C. Penney. Jane wore White Shoulders and she only wore it once in a while so that it was fresh and surprising every time I smelled it. When I went through Jane's clothes, they did not smell of White Shoulders, but of soap and a fainter scent that I cannot name but that was unmistakably hers. I smelled it on our sheets for months after she died. Sometimes, I smell it still.

It has been such a long time since I have touched women's clothing. I grab fistfuls of material and smell it, rubbing it against the side of my face. I embrace 1-A's clothes. I hug the weightless bodies that hang in her closet. I hold them as if they are in need of support, and then I straighten them. I feel almost guilty, as if by touching her clothes, I have touched 1-A herself. But my needs are simpler than that. And no one will ever know. I shut the closet door.

On the table next to her bed are the Bible and a Sidney Sheldon novel. A lamp. An alarm clock, the kind that runs on batteries, not on electricity. A funeral card. I sit on the edge of her bed and page through the Sidney Sheldon novel. It's full of white wine and sunshine and a man named Roland. I pick up the funeral card, half expecting it to be Jane's. *Stephanie Marie D'Angelo*, it reads in script. *1968-1976.* And then a prayer: *For it is in giving that we receive; It is in pardoning that we are pardoned; And it is in dying that we are born to eternal life.*

The blessed Mary is on the card's front and for a second, I stare at her serene and ageless face. Then, I lean the funeral card back up against the lamp in what I think is the exact same spot.

After I propped her up near the open windows so she could hear the children, the last thing Jane asked me to do was feed her. And I did. I sat on a straight-backed chair next to our bed and I fed her the pills she asked for and when they were all gone, she smiled at me and said she wasn't in pain any longer. She closed her eyes and I opened the window wider so the sounds of children playing on the hill out back could fill our bedroom, and then I climbed into bed next to her and I held her until well after she was no longer there for me to hold.

There's a broken stove in 7-C to take care of, and someone's heater died on the third floor, and there's always more snow to shovel. I smooth the flowered comforter on 1-A's bed and I straighten the pictures tucked into her mirror. The dumb-faced girl stares out at me. It's as if she knows. Then I close 1-A's bedroom door and walk down the hallway, back into the kitchen where I turn off the dim overhead light. Everything has remained in place. I close the door and step out into the winter that seems as if it will last forever.

First Anniversary

Joan Michelson

I have to fight your death. Already a year
nearly. All this month of darkening, nearly
never-ending, a year. Nearly a year
of battle lost, this other year we took

no holiday, again went nowhere. Next week
I see you hand-to-mouth in mocking gasp
at my leg stuck in plaster,—you, in the glass
behind the house plants, watching how I hop.

After a year, my ankle merely swells.
A year like no year; and you again nearly,
last night in the window looking well.
Incredible, poised to win. *Well stop!*

I say, *A truce until I'm cold, out, down
beside you, nearly victor, nearly gone.*

Her Last Week in Their Paradise

Elaine Schear

FRIDAY

S HE IS NOT SURE WHERE TO BEGIN: THE BANK, THE REALTORS, THE LEAKS IN the sink and the ceiling. She needs to decide what to pack and ship. She needs to call her 92-year-old aunt. She should see her father's friend Sonny, one of the old guard who still lives at Springlake. She should make a visit to the cemetery. Make sure they carved the right dates into the stone under her father's name. She feels like a dog chasing its tail, pawing the Florida crab grass. At last she lies down, but her eyes won't shut. She gets up to lock her bedroom door. She thinks about the robbery, ten years ago, at this house—her parents' retirement paradise—on the night her mother died. She thinks about Dad lying on the bedroom floor after the third and final stroke (for how long before his caretaker, Phyllis, arrived the next morning?). When the funeral was over, she left Dad's house key with Sonny and flew home to Boston. Two years ago.

SATURDAY

The large bathroom mirror shows too much. Dark circles, lines. Outside it's raining and cold. The house is filled with bubble wrap and Styrofoam peanuts. As promised two years ago, her mother-in-law, Rhoda, flies down from Connecticut to help. She's grateful for Rhoda's cheerful nature, her generosity, the Brooklyn stories and raunchy jokes she used to share with Dad. Rhoda says take the porcelain earth-toned Lladros with their breakable fingers, the Hummel figurines of children with their rose-cheeked faces.

She signs papers to list the house. Goes to a movie alone and stands in line behind pre-teens on cell phones. She misses her daughters, ages seven and eleven, back at home in Massachusetts. She returns to the house and takes down the zippered satchel wedged into the corner of her parents' bedroom closet. She has waited a long time for this. When she was a teenager, her mother had walked in on her wide-eyed discovery of the canvas bag of love letters her parents wrote to each other when Dad was still in the army. Now, reading them slowly, she is fascinated by the beauty of her mother's blue script, her father's crammed black type, their unrestrained desire.

SUNDAY

Rhoda guts the walk-in closet in her parents' bedroom and makes fun of her father's sport shirt collection arranged by pastel color on wooden hangers.

She feels sensitive about these comments, even though she herself used to ridicule his humdrum taste in clothes, his penchant for wearing stained shirts. Rhoda packs green plastic bags of polyester slacks and brand-new shoes still in their boxes. They drag them to the front door in hopes that someone will pick them up. She remembers how her father scuffed his way to this door for the *Sun Sentinel* in the dark mornings. She can see him sitting at the end of the couch, hard at work on the crossword puzzle, his jeweler's loupe in one eye, three duct-taped dictionaries at his side.

MONDAY

The carpet cleaners take out bloodstains. It feels less her parents' house now with its new smell of cleaning fluids. Rhoda flies back to her teaching job in Connecticut. She wishes there were someone else, a sister or brother, to help her stay focused on the tasks ahead or just to fill the emptiness of the house. She can manage being there during the day, but the night is intolerable. She arranges to stay at a nearby motel. The cell phone bleeps out a tinny salsa. Roofers come and go with estimates. She hires the one who can come the next morning. Phyllis arrives with Chinese takeout. They sit in the kitchen and reminisce about her father, who Phyllis started working for after his first stroke. She understands how Dad must have appreciated her calm presence, the musical Jamaican lift in her voice. She spoon-fed him pills in applesauce, cleaned up drool, stood by in case he slipped in the shower or set fire to the house while making spaghetti sauce. She drove him to the library, Home Depot, grocery stores, doctors' appointments. She gives Phyllis the big TV and the good set of dishes and they load them into her little car. Before she drives away, Phyllis says, "You gave me the best. Now I know you really love me."

TUESDAY

She brings eighteen bags of clothes to the Goodwill, but they're too busy to accept them. A Haitian woman approaches her on the way into the parking lot and offers to take them all. She is grateful to give them to a real person. As they load the bags into the woman's large van, she imagines skinny Haitian men wearing her father's oversized shirts and heavy E-width shoes.

WEDNESDAY

A man named Jed, sporting a greasy ponytail, comes to the house to look over the furniture. After a walk-through of no more than a minute, Jed says the stuff is too "Florida" and assures her no one will buy it. She is puzzled because, after all, this *is* Florida. He has taken a silver basket out of a glass cabinet, swings it on his thumb, and waves a hundred-dollar bill. He glares into her face and says, "Hey, *schwartz gelt.*" Black money? She's not sure what he means with this Yiddish phrase, but it doesn't sound good. She wants him out of the house. He keeps swinging the basket. She takes the cash.

She gets lost on the way to the cemetery and arrives in the dusk and rain. Even at close range the cemetery resembles a vast, barren field. Gravestones lay close to each other, flat on their backs, level with the grass. Just steps from the parking lot she finds the modest granite marker, water beading on its shining surface. She stands at the stone, stares at their engraved names, and imagines her parents under there, together, the way they'd always planned it. It is starkly clear how apart they are, her dead parents, and she, the adult surviving child, the orphan. She's dreaded this moment, yet there is relief in facing all that she had put off. She knows she may never come back. She wanders nearby and finds herself at the gravestones of children. Her mind shifts to her family, the daily pleas of her girls for her to come home, the patience of her partner. Impossibly, she looks up to find herself at the center of the arc of a rainbow in the darkening sky. Once back at her parents' house, she knows what to keep, what to get rid of. She cleans out the bathroom cabinets and the fridge. She finds one remaining jar of Dad's homemade sauce in the freezer. She goes out to buy the kind of spaghetti he liked, cooks it *al dente* the way he taught her many years ago, and sits down to eat in the stillness of her parents' kitchen.

How Snow Arrives

Michael Collier

*T*he pine trees stood without snow,
   though snow was in the air,
a day or two away, forming in the place
where singing forms the air.

"Mother?" is what I heard my mother say
said in such a way she knew her mother
didn't know her, as if they stood
beneath the trees and breathed the singing air.

How frail the weather when its face
is blank or, startled, turns to find
its startled self in a child's voice,
flake by flake of the arriving snow.

"Mother?" is what I say, as if
I didn't know her, standing blank
and startled where she stands beneath
the trees among the singing air.

Medicine Chest

Amanda Auchter

Your face is an old wound.
  Yesterday, it stood behind
me while we combed our hair.

Today, nothing, stripped from
the cracked glass. My cage of bone
is hollow, all broken sinews

and valves, stopped dead. I empty
you here—clear the residue
of your skin, wipe the mirror

clean of fingerprints. What is left?
A razor, aftershave, bottle of pills,
tube of toothpaste, your broken watch.

First Steps

Floyd Skloot

After fifteen years
my first steps
without a cane
are quick and stiff.

I am dizzy with freedom
and not the tottering child
or Frankenstein I'd imagined.

Wild in the torso but a little prim
in the hips, I still have a long way to go
before calling this a walk and I'm not sure
if I dare look away from the ground before me
because wind rippling through leaves makes me dizzy
and the last thing I need at this point is to fall on my face.

I didn't plan for this. If there's one thing my damaged brain
has learned by now, it's to make no plans, have no expectations
and accept whatever the new day brings. Today I forgot to take my
cane with me when I left home for a walk. As soon as the door closed
I realized I was empty-handed and stopped dead. I had to smile. Freud!
Forgetting Intentions and Bungled Actions! Maybe I did plan this but did
not know. Which would be consistent not only with Freudian interpretation
but with brain damage as well. All right, I would follow through and see where
this led me because another thing I've learned since getting sick is that the body
knows things that the mind does not. It was time to look up. To gaze at the road
ahead.

Another Life

Susan Varon

I doubt whether picking my way
down the sidewalk with Betty Schack
(another cripple)
will lead either of us to glory,

we might as well sit on the side
drawing with sticks in the dirt,

Betty meticulous and careful,
I slashing and cutting the earth
with my expressionism,

our canes lying forgotten, rolling
their eyes at each other, imagining

they remember when they were new sticks
with the hope of being used for a gun or a doorjamb.

In my drawing I imagine being new, too,
demanding loudly of the world, kicking up clouds,
lustily calling for another life. Over our heads,

people are talking on cell phones
till the air is buzzing, we hardly dare
stand up into it, straighten our stiff joints,
look around for our canes and be startled
when they come dancing to us,
not knowing they've decided

they lucked out to be what they are,
to be allowed to stand upright and accompany us,
taking lessons in fortitude and grace,

in this city so difficult to walk in,
this city so worth it anyway.

Sleeping on the Perimeter

Gaynell Gavin

M OST U.S. SOLDIERS HAD LEFT VIETNAM BY THE SPRING OF 1973. The war continues, however, in the psyches and bodies of not only those who were there but also of those who love them.

My cousin's legs, chest, and hands were blown up, requiring more than thirty general anesthesia surgeries, but we did get him back alive. It was the end of 1968; he was a twenty-one-year-old infantry sergeant, and I was a high school sophomore.

My ex-husband's brother, who was in military intelligence, agrees with my cousin's view that the war was about profit, "about food contracts, building contracts, weapons contracts—about keeping all that going." He and my cousin have never met and know virtually nothing about each other. My cousin is a rather brawny, rural Midwesterner of Irish Catholic descent. My brother-in-law is a tall, skinny African-American from urban Massachusetts. Although from very different backgrounds, they share similar conclusions about Vietnam.

I do not recall how my brother-in-law and I came to be alone in his mother's Roxbury kitchen one Sunday afternoon in early 1972 when her house was full of people. But he sat across the Formica table from me and said of his Vietnamese wife, who was expecting their first child, "My home is where she is. She is my home." His wife is smart, energetic, pretty—a former U.S. embassy secretary with a pale scar on one cheek, cut by a plate glass window when the embassy was blown up. By the end of 1993, they have worn wedding rings inscribed with their marriage date for over twenty-five years. For over twenty-five years, my brother-in-law has also worn a bracelet made from spent casings and given to him by Montagnards who worked with him. He holds his wrist out so that I can see the brass circling it more closely. "A gift to me," he says, "from the black people of Vietnam." Despite the sadness in his voice, it seems to me now that, for a moment, I felt the surge of contentment which surely must have been happiness to have him here, alive.

In late 1998, while visiting Colorado, I ride from Golden to Boulder with a friend—a tall, rangy former infantryman who has lots of gray in his dark hair. He alternates between obliterating himself with alcohol and fighting to save himself. An engineer for thirty years, he "crashed and burned," as he put it, after his children were raised.

The war, he says, was about fear, "about being so scared you shit all over yourself, about having your buddy standing next to you one second and pieces of what used to be him all over you the next. You're trying to pick these little pieces of him out of your teeth, thinking, *Why him and not me?*"

The man is chain-smoking, while driving his 'Cowboy Cadillac,' a very large and old white pickup. "The part I couldn't take of what the Army crammed down my throat was demonizing the enemy, dehumanizing them. I understood it was our job to kill them and theirs to kill us, but pretending they weren't human, that it wasn't human beings we were killing—that was the part I couldn't do.

"Vietnam was beautiful. You'd look out across the land; you'd see some little girl leading a huge water buffalo. It was beautiful. And green. A peaceful picture. Then the picture would blow up. Literally. It happened to me within twenty-four hours of the time I got there. And I realized, *Holy shit, there are people all over the place here who are trying to kill me. I mean these people are seriously trying to kill me.*"

I do not know whether this man will win or lose his long fight, but of course, I hope he will win. He appears in and disappears from my life intermittently. He apologized to me once for his alcohol and unreliability. I was visiting his sister while he, too, was staying there, making repairs to her house. No matter how late into the night he drank, by dawn he was working, and every morning he fixed coffee for me. So, when he handed me a cup of coffee while apologizing for drinking and talking about Vietnam the previous night, I said, "Don't apologize. You're still standing, and in my book, you get about ten thousand extra points for that. I doubt you could ever do anything that would use up all those points." And I meant it.

He has disappeared, and I do not know if I will see him or hear from him again.

It was also in 1998 that "an overweight, broken-down soldier," to use his own description, told me that he didn't know what I could possibly see in him. We had been introduced at a party several months earlier. With gray hair and a neatly trimmed beard, he was not unattractive, but neither was he a man I would have otherwise noticed in a crowd. As I chatted with him, our conversation struck me as mildly pleasant but unremarkable. Eventually, it was the way he spoke, as a single parent, of his son and daughter, and his animals—a houseful of rescued stray cats and a dog—that caught my attention.

Like my cousin, my brother-in-law, and my Colorado friend, this man had served in Vietnam. "Don't hold it against me," he said. "I was there three times."

"Why?" I asked. "Why were you there three times?"

"The first two, I thought we were doing the right thing. By the third time I knew better." He added that if we hadn't tried to help France continue colonizing Vietnam, Communism would not have become an issue there. "By my third time, I knew we were in the right war, at the wrong time, on the wrong side. But I was a captain by then, a career officer, and I'd learned to take pretty good care of my people, to help keep as many of them alive as possible, as long as possible, against the odds. I didn't want to leave them."

Later, I saw the scars: first the barely-visible one just above his mustache where the rifle sights pressed into his face as his helicopter was shot down, then gradually the other scars, far too many to keep track of which ones came from which battles. I also saw the pile of medals, gotten, he said, at the cost of too many lives.

A long purple-red scar which runs the length of his sternum is the largest, and one night, lying next to him, my head pressed to the beat of his heart, I traced the scar with my fingers, as I'd done before. "Tell me how you got this one," I said.

They'd been fighting on a hill. After he was hit, he said, he was the only one left alive. He pulled a body over him and fell asleep, expecting never to wake up. When he did awaken, it was to the prodding of an enemy soldier's bayonet cutting his chest, but the soldier either thought he was dead or decided he was close enough to death not to bother with, and went on to other bodies. Again, he drifted into sleep, expecting not to wake up, and again he was awakened, this time by rain, the following day. The rain felt good, he said, cool and cleansing. The third time he fell asleep he did not yet realize the rain had probably saved him and he still did not expect to wake up. For another day, he drifted in and out of consciousness as American rein-forcements arrived, and fighting raged around him. On the third day, Americans took the hill and found him among the bodies piled there.

When he has finished telling me, my head still pressed to his heart, my fingers still on the scar, I tell him it is a sign to me—this scar—a reminder to say thank you for his life, my brother-in-law's and my cousin's. But, how-ever much I would like gratitude and love to be enough, they won't be.

His dreams are bad and getting worse, he says; he's trained himself to wake up when he dreams. He awakens twice most nights to walk through the house. Securing his perimeter.

A psychologist once told me that, no matter how tired they become, sol-diers in a combat zone report an inability to sleep. Now, when I can sleep, my dreams are also mostly bad. In one, I stand grounded in a panic of sorrow, as my soldier flies away from me in a helicopter. It flies between telephone wires above me and becomes smaller with distance until it is a lonely black speck. Finally, when I can no longer see the helicopter at all, I wake up crying.

We start to fight, infrequently at first. The soldier accuses me of looking down on him for having served in the military, of not supporting the war, of disloyalty.

"How can you say that to me? You're the same man who said that your medals cost too many lives, the man who said it was the right war, at the wrong time, on the wrong side."

I realize that, as I've become afraid of his anger, my own fear has begun turning to anger. And what is anger but alchemy: grief encoded and loss transformed?

I hear the struggle in his voice as it starts to rise; he forces himself to lower it. "Those are only my personal opinions. But combat replaced everyday life for me. I like crisis, love it. In fact, it's fun. Don't even try to understand because you can't and never will.

"All that matters in a war is keeping the people with you alive. That's the only thing worth fighting for. It was a better high than anything else I've ever experienced or can imagine, and it made me feel more alive than anything else ever has or ever will. Anyway, personal opinions don't matter in a war."

"They matter to me," I say. "How can you tell me it shouldn't hurt me that you've been hurt? That I should make myself feel nothing about it? How can you even think that's possible?"

"If life hands you lemons, make lemonade," he says, and I have to wonder if he's intentionally trying to make me crazy. "People in this country want us when they need us, and then they want us out of sight, so they don't have to think about us or look at our scars."

It is a Sunday afternoon, and we are sitting on the edge of his bed. "You're talking in clichés and *non sequiturs*," I say. "I'm not 'people,' and I've never flinched from looking at your scars." I smear tears across my face with my fists. "I'm not the one in this relationship who's too afraid to look at scars."

"I am a behaviorist," he snaps. "I refuse to live in the past. I've put it behind me. I refuse to wallow in pain and self-pity with you."

I want to tell him, "If you don't listen to the part of you that's screaming, *Take care of me*, that part will scream louder and louder until it drowns out everything else in your life," but I can't get the words out. I want to tell this soldier he can stand down now, it's his turn to stand down, but instead I manage to say something about having to leave before his children come home from their mother's because I don't want them to see me this way. He puts his arm around me, and I sob into his shoulder, crying too hard to speak, too hard to make him know that he is my country—and my war—the country inside of me, that civil war of love and fear.

In the spring of 1999, my cousin visits. I have made the poor man listen to me rave, which he, accustomed to the women in our family, has done kindly and patiently. As he prepares to leave, do I let up? No, I do not. "How can an otherwise reasonably intelligent man say such a stupid thing to me as 'personal opinions don't matter in a war'?"

"Trying to secure his perimeter, emotionally speaking," my cousin says. "In a war you try not to let yourself love anyone, but he's started to let you in, and now you're too close for comfort. He's closing the gate on you, reinforcing it with a row of concertina wire, and mining it. Did you hear what I said? Because this is important: *He's booby-trapping the gate.*"

I listen carefully, knowing these two soldiers have hit it off because the previous night, after dinner, they shared a codger bonding ritual: smoking cigars together in the garage, an occasion which lacked brandy only because my cousin had given it up for Lent. I look at him: finishing his coffee, putting on his leg brace, closing a suitcase, picking up the cane he hates using but needs more frequently these days. Then, as he stands beside his van with the purple heart license plates, my bearded and burly cousin pulls me to him, and in the moment that we hold each other tight, I tell him that I love him, and he tells me that he knows. He smoothes my hair and says, "I can try to help him get the help he needs. I talked to him about it. I'm yours by blood. But in a different way, I'm also his by blood. He'll be all right."

I know my cousin wants to believe that. So do I.

In 1971, when a neighbor died in Vietnam, I found his death shocking, not because he was a terribly close friend, but because of his irrevocable, sudden disappearance from among those individuals with whom the landscape of my childhood and adolescence had been peopled. Without giving it conscious thought, I'd wrongly assumed they'd always be there. My neighbor had become a medic and, like the medic who cared for my cousin, had died trying to help someone else.

My soldier who lay on a hill during his third tour in Vietnam was—like my cousin when the land mine got him, like my neighbor about whose death I know little, like most of the boys among whose bodies he lay for three days, like most of the boys who fought in that war—considerably younger than my twenty-eight-year-old son is now.

It is with the memory of a close friend who died that *In Pharaoh's Army*, Tobias Wolff's memoir of his time in Vietnam, ends. "[Hugh] loved to jump…I always take the position behind him, hand on his back, according to the drill we've been taught. I do not love to jump, to tell the truth, but I feel better about it when I'm connected to Hugh. Men are disappearing out the door ahead of us, the sound of the engine is getting louder. Hugh is singing in falsetto, doing a goofy routine with his hands…He yells, *Are we having fun?* He laughs at the look on my face, then turns and takes his place in the door, and jumps, and is gone."

My soldier tells me he, too, loved to jump. I can hardly imagine jumping from a plane, and I certainly cannot imagine wanting to do it. Still, I wonder if I absolutely had to do it, could I? Maybe there are a few individuals in the world from whom, if connected to one of them, I could borrow the nerve. Maybe this soldier is among them.

Sometimes, while my soldier, who has not slept deeply since Vietnam, stirs restlessly beside me, I cannot sleep at all. He is turned away from me and, afraid to disturb him by touching him, but more afraid not to, I put my hand on his back, which is thickly and solidly muscled. I lie awake wondering if he too will turn and jump and be gone.

He does turn, toward me, but does not quite wake up. Instead, he reaches for me in sleep and pulls my hand to his chest. This is not one of the times when I pull him to me fiercely, into me as if he could keep me here, connected to the world. Instead, I rest my fingers gently against the scar—my sign, my reminder to say thank you. So, I say it silently. And then silently, knowing its implausibility, I ask one thing: that we be saved—that this war end at last.

Survivor

Eamon Grennan

*L*ike another heart against your hand, the bee you've captured in your hankie
Buzzes and shudders between your fingers before you set it free to curl away
On the bright, breeze-ruffled air, all its eye-facets blurred by the sudden dark
You caused to come down on it, its pollen sac gleaming a dusty gold like the rim
Of the cloud you saw last evening covering the sun at dusk, that jagged outline
An electric unlikely colour—of this world and yet beyond it, a quickened fact that
Simply happens and is gone, the way the bee you release is gone in one swift
Whipswerve so you wonder was that streak of eye-blazing strange gold really there
At all: a piece of the ordinary puzzle of the world, something to silence you
As the beat of another heart tapping its Morse against your hand would.

Whatever Is Left

Cortney Davis

*M*y patient miscarried
this week in the ER.
A nurse took the 16-week
conceptus, slipped it
into a cup, hurried
it away. Today,
the woman asks if she
can have it back—
Lo que quede, she says,
Whatever is left.

Permits must be signed.
Come back tomorrow.

Now, it's tomorrow;
I hand her a plastic cup
wrapped and taped so
no one can see
what's inside. She presses it
to her belly. *Boy,* she asks, *or Girl?*
If I open the cup, what will I see?

Boy, I say.
Blood and small bones.

I walk her to the elevator.
She says, *Thank you.*
Marco, she adds, raising
the cup. *My son's name.*

Visual Anguish and Looking at Art

Carol Zoref

*H*AVE YOU SEEN IT?
'It.' The question comes easier this way, or perhaps with less difficulty than finding the words to name an absence instead of a presence. The question is tucked between the detailing of deadlines, news reports, and the practicalities of living in a city that has been bombed. My verb of choice: bombed. Neither 'event' nor 'tragedy' sounds right, though nouns will come soon enough. For now, here at the beginning, only verbs will do.

I understand these were commercial jetliners, not ICBMs, that split the steel and glass of the World Trade Center. But these were missiles nonetheless, guided to their targets by hand, by eye. Someone, a person, had a long-standing vision, intentions, imagined the explosions and death that would follow. The relationship of this action to seeing, including my seeing, is one of the things I cannot get out of my mind.

Have you seen it?
The question is whispered because of the magnitude of pain surrounding the subject of the wondering. It is a wondering inhabited by solemnity, sorrow, and an inference, I think, of shame. To have seen suggests a desire to look, and desire itself, in these first few weeks, is a feeling regarded with misgiving.

I live in Manhattan but I work in a suburb. The colleagues who also make this short trip each day are the ones who ask the question in the early weeks of our grieving. The others, the non-city dwellers, offer a beautiful meal from autumn's bounty; a bedroom quiet even with the windows wide open, a comforting press of a hand. They are kind and generous and, above all, sincere, wanting to know how we urbanites are holding up.

They are glad they are not us.

This is the sentiment I am certain they are harboring, though I do not have concrete evidence supporting this thought. I am generalizing with unfairly broad brushstrokes (are there any other kind?) because what I saw on September 11th was so abominable, so obscene. The usual and more exacting particularities of experience with which I navigate the world—the sound that something makes, the finer points of how it appear—have been eclipsed by a numbing of the senses that can accompany shock.

The relationship of apprehending the world through the impression of things, versus feeling the world through emotions and understandings, is always a fluid composition. Whatever balance I characteristically strike has been thrown askew. I am also fearful that my observing such wretchedness only blocks from where we live, not shielded as most people were by the framing of the bombings by a TV screen, will somehow render me disgusting, as well; that people will look at me and be reminded of the day's horror to the exclusion of anything else. This suggests more about the limitations of my own thinking of the moment than about the psyche of anyone else.

I did not ever want to know first-hand the *thwump* of a jet flying into a skyscraper, its cacophony resembling an empty construction bin being brusquely dropped at night onto a deserted street, all the people in the neighborhood busy sleeping. Or the sirens that commenced their wailing minutes later and did not stop for days. I did not want this information reinforced when a second hijacked jet created the sound again eighteen minutes later. As if I might have already forgotten or disbelieved and my eardrums, those compilers of sensory accuracy, were seeking verification. I did not want to hear the roar rising from the thousands of workers walking uptown as the first tower collapsed and then the second. Their shouting was like the cry of a stadium crowd watching football, but an anguished aggregation of screaming rather than cheers. I did not want the sounds of my own screaming, either, or the feel of my fisted fingers pulling the hair at the back of my neck, or the grotesque taste of fear-laced breakfast in my mouth when I threw up.

I did not want my skin saturated by the viscid smell, like a scummy swamp fire into which someone kept tossing radios and telephones which shorted out as they hit the water. The number here reaches thousands, too. I did not want the fine, gray powder that turned to a mucilage of soot on our windowsills, a residue of everything that once was and now was not.

The very worst are images of people falling off and jumping from the burning buildings, though I kept saying at the time this could not be possible. I did not want to see what I was seeing; did not want to believe in the accuracy of my senses, though they are always where I start knowing what I know. These images of people, unlike the sounds or the smells of that day, are a series of agonies for which I will offer no simile. There is a time when only the thing itself must do: a moral decision, not a technical one. The suffering of those people was their suffering; it was neither a metaphor for something else nor something that can be more meaningfully depicted by simile. At least not yet, not so soon. Perhaps these, like the nouns I avoid to describe the bombings, will come later on, when my relationship to that day is altered by the promise of perspective and understanding that comes with time.

I do not want to be a detail in this mural I am rendering. I wish I were not among those of us who live closer and closer and closer, still. Meaning we who, having witnessed the horror through our living room windows and then on the streets, as my partner and I did, continue seeing *it*, the unfolding of *it* over and over, until even with eyes closed, *it* is all that we see.

The dogged persistence of these unassimilated images creates its own particular terror, all the while serving as a reminder—re-staging might be more accurate—of the experience as originally encountered.

This, I am told by a psychologist friend, is the predictable pattern of trauma. The brain, having been asked to understand faster than it can absorb, replays the unprocessed stimuli again and again. This yet-to-be comprehended information appears repeatedly on the surface of the mind's eye, the place where new information waits its turn to be digested.

What does one do, then, with this backlog of awful images, the ones for which the brain finds no place because it is slow in making room for what is unbearable? The brain continues to process new images, other less terrifying pieces of stimuli, but not these. There is no way to attend to them faster without disengaging from the painful discourse of processing, from the communion between the heart and mind that is consciousness. One would have to disengage from the testimony of the senses; deny them out of a delusion that the processing is complete. An invitation, for sure, for the pain to re-emerge sometime later where it will hurt most, a location that won't announce itself until it is bloodied. Does this mean I should abandon hope of finding some form of relief? And what about the senses: have they been irreparably damaged by a bombing I could taste and feel and smell, hear and see? I ache for something greater for my senses, which are not intended solely for witnessing grief. I want them to feed once more my longing to understand, my desire—there is that troublesome word again—to know even what is painful.

What I find is that my brain, still so over-stimulated, cannot focus. I am incapable of doing what I want to do most. I pick up only those books I must read for work. I think about writing but am unable to write, which is as close to writing as I get. Almost three weeks pass. I am wondering if and when I will ever feel anything else. I realize I am waiting to feel different, and waiting itself makes me feel out of control, as out of control as I felt watching those flame-engulfed towers collapse. The waiting, because there is no end in sight, feels unbearable.

Then I notice in *The New York Times,* where every article now reads like an obituary, a review of an exhibit nearby in SoHo, photographs by Kenro Izu titled *Sacred Places.* For as drawn as I might be to the notion of the sanctified, it is the idea of place itself that compels me to lay the review in a prominent spot on my desk, confirm the hours, block out time in my schedule so I might go. The physical world, perceived through vision, often activates my processes of wondering and contemplation. In the absence of my own imagining—one of the means by which I navigate what I am wanting to understand—I intuitively turn to the inventiveness of others. I am preparing now to venture into a singular world in which, according to *The Times* review, sensory perception is central. It is a realm that promises not people—and therefore the potential for the interpersonal landscape that always triggers the deepest of my upsets—but the eminence of place.

The photos in the gallery on Wooster Street are of sacred sites in Tibet and China and Cambodia. They are of temples and shrines and sanctuaries.

The photos are exquisitely detailed, exposed as they were with the 300-pound, large format camera that Izu carried over one range of mountains to the next.

Some twenty years worth of beautiful work and what I get stuck on are the political consequences for those who believe in the sacred. Tibetan monasteries have been shuttered for decades by the occupying forces of the Chinese government; Buddhist temples in China itself, after years of desecration by Maoists, have been restored and converted into attractions for western tourists; the ancient ruins of the city of Angkor Wat have been bruised and battered by the neighboring armies of Asia, by the colonial armies of the west, by the Khmer Rouge cadres of Cambodia itself. What gets lost again, as I consider these photos, is what is hallowed, obscured this time not by governments but by my own impalpable thinking. I am deliberating what I know from the histories, rather than turning to my wounded, weary senses in order to see.

This kind of perceiving—my information-driven knowing of the moment—seems far removed from the work's intentions, when I consider each photograph on its own terms.

I start again.

In the opening photo, a jewel of a mountain is showered by sunlight no other nearby peak receives. The other mountains are not diminished by this, though the undeniable fact is that they are in shadow. And I, unable to shake the chill that has invaded my bones these recent weeks, become as keenly aware as I am of anything that day of my wishing to be embraced by the sunlight, too. The eminence of place, as rendered so artfully in these contact printed, platinum-palladium photos, provokes in me the desire for an elation of being. This is one of the things art does when we permit ourselves to absorb it by allowing it to absorb us as well. It reveals to us a quality of feeling; makes us recognize the feeling as if it is something we had previously known somehow, though we had never before imagined its existence in this way. It is because Izu has envisioned *his* intentions so masterfully that I become able to feel this at all: through his mindfulness of dimension, both tactile and conceptual; through his patient exposures of many minutes rather than the usual fractions of seconds, therefore casting that distinction into further relief; through the belabored use of 14 x 20-inch sheets of film to better register detail, and by doing so preventing the distortion that might result from immense enlargements. Each photograph is an invitation to a reciprocity of experience, rather than something done *to* the viewer, as with the bombings.

With this image of Kailash in Tibet, I begin reacquainting myself—albeit self-consciously, clumsily—with the act of beholding. For the first time in weeks, I am able to look at something closely; I can regard, receive, discern, and apprehend an impression of things fully and purposefully through visual reception. I am aware of having a visceral response as well. I feel a euphoric flush on my face in addition to a touch of vertigo from looking down and up, left and right, again and again, as if I, like Kenro Izu, am standing at the foot of that very mountain. All this, in conjunction with a willingness to work mindfully with the accumulation of experience, enables me to understand something in a way I had not known it before, something relating to states of awe. It is the experience of coming to know in this way, however haltingly, which is central to my feeling alive.

A week passes and I am attending a conference on the Upper East Side. When my meeting ends, I head down the block to the Metropolitan Museum of Art. I have resolved to see the newly opened exhibit of drawings by Bruegel the Elder, a heavy-handed decision. Why heavy-handed? *It will be good,* I keep telling myself as I climb to the second floor galleries, *a way to embrace the world.* It is as much an instruction as a thought.

I've got to get out of here, is what I am soon thinking, en route from the first print to the second, trying unsuccessfully to persuade myself to stay. The problem lies not in Bruegel, but in me. I am unable to contemplate these images of people eating and scavenging and playing and torturing and making love or engaging in brutal and unloving sex; unable to find room in myself for the twisted faces and twisted bodies that are the human heart of Bruegel's drawings. They are too brutal, look too much like the colorless and still smoldering steel and broken glass of lower Manhattan.

Anyone observing me hastily leaving the exhibit might have thought I was disinterested. But the problem, which is always the problem in the face of trauma, is that I care too much; I care so much that I am unable to distinguish between a drawing and the three-dimensional world. My relationship to metaphor is missing, misplaced; the people in Bruegel's drawings are as tangible as the jumpers from the Twin Towers, their agonies actual and literal, not representational nor metaphorical. My capacity to receive an impression of things, to allow myself to absorb art and allow it to absorb me in a thoughtful, edifying or enlightening way is at the mercy of the reflexes seeking to protect me from further anguish. My brain, without my conscious participation, has established newly circumscribed boundaries: The un-peopled, exalted worlds of Kenro Izu, yes. The overpopulated and suffering worlds of Bruegel, no.

What I have also learned about trauma is that any severe shock can trigger a re-experiencing of an episode from the past. So I am feeling assaulted, abandoned, unable to untangle the threat of harm from harm itself, though the sensation of being threatened is a category of trauma, as well. I am having an anxiety attack in the Metropolitan Museum, despite my being long past having these attacks with regularity and being well practiced at not letting them show. There is a difference, though, between what I am feeling at this moment and those archetypal, Ur-traumas of long ago: I can remove myself from the Bruegel exhibit because, over time, I have learned how to do that, too.

The past knocks on my door again. I walk the corridor to the 19th century paintings, home to the Met's collection of the Impressionists, just as I did when I was 16 years old and in love for the first time in a way that caused me more anguish than elation. That troubled yearning, in combination with other elements particular to my adolescence, left me feeling like an inexpressible mess. I often went then, as I go now, to the Impressionists for their unembarrassed lushness, for their light. So much light, so much color. And beauty. Degas' dancers, Seurat's strollers, Matisse's women. Except, for now, too many people. Cezanne's still lifes. Better.

I am standing before Van Gogh's *Green Vase With White Roses*, though the white of those roses is created with most anything but white. And the roses *are* beautiful. And the green vase is beautiful too, green with lots of blue in it suggesting a balance against the green backdrop, a yellow infused green and therefore the opposite of blue. The same yet different, an irresistible harmony.

And why should I resist?

At the opposite end of the museum are 17th century Dutch still lifes, works painted two hundred years prior to Van Gogh's. I am reminded of Mark Doty's book-length essay *Still Life With Oysters and Lemons,* which I recently read and then read again. My level of anxiety spikes, then passes. A revelation! I will visit the painting by Jan Davidsz de Heem that inspired Doty's rapturous exploration of the relationship of the object world to memory and the imagination. Perhaps this is why I have been drawn to the Met, to finally see this painting that is so much in the back of my mind. As if I truly need a reason. Yet it feels good to have a purpose, however humble, this organizing principle for my time in the museum. What are organizing principles if not challenges to chaos, if not providers of even modest degrees of control?

Still Life With Oysters and Lemons is the smallest painting in a room filled with still lifes; an abundance of grapes and lobsters and lemons and snipe and, in one by Jan Van Huysum, minute yet precisely rendered ants, contributing as they must to the decay of a setting of fruit. Still life does not mean no life; it suggests a devoted concentration to the abundance of a moment. The observer, however, needs to keep company with that moment, as envisioned by the artist, for much longer than a true moment. That is when the wondrous relationship of reciprocity—being absorbed, absorbing in return—can begin taking place. Even when the vision is one of death.

I picture the many others who have looked at these paintings too, some in ways that I perceive them and some in ways I would never consider, all of which reminds me that it is not I alone beholding them. I am, as Mark Doty writes of us, a member of a community of attention givers. Which is probably the place I have been wrenched from these lost weeks and for which I have been yearning; the place where I live with a keen mindfulness of the world as initially received through the senses.

There is another term I learned from my psychologist friend that I find appealing as well, though I stretch its application so far as to render it somewhat inaccurate. Still, it reflects something acute to my sense of injury. The phrase is "counter-trauma," used for describing a person who returns to the site of his or her ordeal as a means of asserting authority over the experience. That is precisely what I was seeking when I found my way to the Impressionists, to the Dutch still lifes, to Izu's spirit-filled photographs. I was seeking to counter my sense of trauma through a part of me still hurting. Not through the category of image offered by Bruegel, which comes closer to my actual experience of visual anguish; which might, in the future, serve as a metaphorical vehicle for my revisiting that day. I was seeking to counteract the experience of visual trauma through the act of seeing itself, only made possible again by looking at beauty.

What I had seen of the World Trade Center bombing and could not stop seeing had traumatized my mind's eye, continued taking place in the here and now. I had to coax my literal eyes into looking around again carefully and faithfully before I could try once more to absorb what my mind's eye was still refusing.

I was tending to my heretofore inconsolable eyes on that visit to the Met and to Izu's "Sacred Places." I was introducing exquisite and sublime images to my traumatized consciousness not as replacements for the horrors I had seen, but as additions. The Izu exhibit was the first step: the stillness of place in steadfast images, their quietude suggesting preconditions of tranquility and potentiality of relief. The Impressionists, later on, were a way to absorb the beauty of a more internalized, personalized world, at the same time as my mind was struggling still with the awful images it continued rejecting. That was the necessary order of experience before the aestheticized anguish of Bruegel could again be considered. And why not? This is how we ideally begin our infant relationship to the world: through fundamental, beautiful sensation. It is how we start preparing for the more complex and ambiguous forms of beauty that will follow.

Powerless as I was, I had found a way, long after it ended in lower Manhattan, to stop the bombing in my mind's eye.

The assault on my sensory capacity, so central to my being, impelled me in conscious and unconscious ways to get it back. Should I feel shameful for that? That would mean feeling shame about being alive, survivor's guilt. The dead, I imagine, would think this a waste. The dead, I imagine, would think of better uses for living time.

What I am doing now is reasoning, and shame and guilt do not always have their origins in reason. Which is why the shame I felt as I walked to the remains of the World Trade Center between my visits to the Izu exhibit and the Met was pointless, though I felt it nonetheless. Perception does not convert as fast as we would like into active understanding. What I was doing downtown in those weeks when our sidewalks were still empty but for those of us who live here, when our streets were open only to emergency vehicles, was paying a condolence call. I was also engaging in a more exacting act of counter-trauma, though I did not know it at the time because I was acting out of an impulse for which I am grateful. And yet, it was not enough.

My visit to the Met, it turns out, was the more correcting form of reparative mastery. Perhaps this was the case because of the sequencing of events. But it was in the museum that I finally consciously identified the location of a particular injury and a means by which to tend to it. Not that this diminishes or annuls my other efforts. Understanding takes place in stages, not all at once. This is a fact I know well, but one I lost sight of in the depths of my anguish. Then, an evidently irrepressible desire to absorb and understand enabled a new sensibility to ferment, to emerge, to contribute to the long undertaking of a restoration of self.

It is through the senses that the exterior world is made palpable, and through our thoughtful attention, such as engaging with or making art, that this knowledge accumulates meaning. Events in their verb-states often resist our predilection to comprehend because they feature action and reaction ahead of reflection, analysis, and insight. The legacy of inconsolable grief and, potentially, despair come when life's arbitrary horrors are fixed in the moments of their happening. Unlike the elongated moment of a still life, these frozen images and feelings are unyielding; they can wield as much destructive force as the initial trauma itself. It is by discovering a means through which to begin our reckoning, by extracting from the experiences themselves whatever it is we need in order to drive ourselves forward, that we make room within for that which is otherwise unbearable.

So to those who ask, *Have you seen it?* I answer, *Yes.*

Autumn, 2001

Strategy

Samuel Menashe

*T*he strategy
   Of crook and cranny
Is to persist
The tottering granny
May outlive
A man riveted
To his task —
We are given
What we did not ask

Bereavement and Beyond

Joan Kip

> *It is not night when*
> *I do see your face*
> —WILLIAM SHAKESPEARE,
> *A Midsummer-Night's Dream*

*I*T'S NOW EIGHTEEN MONTHS SINCE ART DIED, AND WHILE HE CONTINUES to inhabit the depths of my house, that place where our souls meet, the upper stories still feel his absence. Existing within two overlapping levels, two distinct wavelengths, I float untethered between his reality and mine. While in his reality, I feel we are joined in communion and I'm back living a remembered sublimity. But within my own reality, that of the temporal with its day-to-day practicalities of taking care of the house, the garden, the finances, there are moments when I am overwhelmed with a recurring sense of desolation, the aloneness of a solo performer.

Before I was widowed, I facilitated bereavement groups and I remember pronouncing to the grieving members—with the comfortable conviction of the uninitiated—that our most abiding relationships never leave us, that we simply internalize them much as we internalize our parents. We hear their voices, see their faces, may even sense their hands in ours. They are impressions we cannot erase. Now, as I wander the house Art and I shared for forty years, the house in which we raised our children, I wonder if I could still make such a pronouncement.

My job, I tell myself, is to recognize the different wavelengths within which I exist, knowing that while I'm in my practical mode, there is another deeper wavelength that I see with my inner eye. It is there, while meditating in the quiet of my room, that I meet my internalized "other" within an alliance fashioned beyond time. Endowed with a questing imagination, if I can free my mind from its usual constraints and enlarge my conditioned perception of but one reality, I am able to find that other realm: the realm in which Art is with me, touching my face with his hand, hugging me when I return from the store, holding me close as we fall asleep.

Each morning I step back and observe myself in my new life as a widow. I carry on with my usual exercise routine of dancing to Reggae or to Scott Joplin—oiling the bearings, loosening the joints. It is a routine that comforts me, enabling me to move threatening sadness to a lighter level. Times past, Art would remain in bed, watching me, relieved that he wasn't as compulsive as I. Some mornings, I sense that Art is still in that bed watching me, and when I have finished dancing, we stay with each other for a while, connecting with intention across our two realities.

Recently, however, I began to feel as if an unseen enemy was unraveling my slim defenses, a throwback to those early days just after Art died. I realized that I'd been thinking about him less often, had written him fewer letters. Sometimes an hour or two passed when I didn't think about him at all, didn't see his bearded face or hear his resonant voice. Later that morning, washing dishes, I looked out the window onto the garden Art had made, and had a vision of him there in his old gardening slacks and even older white shirt. I realized then that my panic was about my fear of losing him, of letting him go. Were I to relax my passionate concentration on Art, might he slip out of my life and fade away like a forgotten photograph, blurred and lifeless, a darkened shadow of the original?

In my day-to-day existence, time imposes its own reality and I know that no matter how much I try to cling to Art, his image will ultimately blur and gradually diminish. Sometimes, as I lunch with friends or attend a concert, my tears are forgotten for a magic moment, and I am hugged by my old happiness. But the curtain falls, the lights go on, and then, driving home alone, I'm back clinging to the sad, empty space alongside me. Eventually, after hours, days, weeks, I remember what I've always known: my love for Art lives in my heart, unchanged, unchangeable.

I don't believe that bereavement is a straight path to a beckoning shore. Rather, it is a capricious zig-zagging journey, one with Sisyphian overtones. And as I move along this unfamiliar rocky path, feeling more centered—time and again I find myself jerked back to my earliest grief: the grief I thought I had "dealt with."

It happens whenever I find myself staring at an elderly couple holding hands, whenever I hear a certain piece of music or look at a particular photograph. It happens when I touch Art's watch, his worn-out wallet, his keys—so much of him still around the house, waiting to capture my attention. Museum pieces from our youth together through our old age, his possessions conspire to catch me off guard and, for a while, I land right back on square one. At this point I have found the best thing—perhaps the only thing—to do is to shake hands with grief, as I would with an old respected friend, then turn around and walk right back to the present. For I can never go back entirely to that which has left me, that which I have left.

I am thinking that there should be a Catechism According to the Bereaved, some gentle-bound truths to counter the many mistaken notions about bereavement, both for those living with their bereavement and for the still apprehensive observers.

One of these notions is that after one year, we are presumed to be all mourned out. People, kind friends even, will imply that one is now ready to close the door on sorrow and resume a life unattended by grief and by tears. I am sure they mean well; it's just that they are entirely mistaken. It is true that time softens the initial blow, but I don't think I could ever completely seal up that door—and perhaps I shouldn't—for the act of mourning inspires my healing and incubates my sorrow, allowing for its gradual transformation.

Maybe tears are a natural antidote to the anguish of an otherwise inexpressible grief. In the early days, I would not weep. But my body would soon shake from the withholding and eventually break down. Occasionally there are still mornings when I wake up from a night's sleep with a deep sense of heaviness and restraint, and I know this feeling to be one of tears struggling to escape. One of my musings is that we humans are born with an endless reservoir of tears and joy—complementary twins—into which we dip or plunge, as the occasion arises, and that when I am with one, the other is not far away.

Another mistaken notion is that once a person has died, he or she has become an unmentionable, someone to be dropped from the roster, wiped off the slate and filed under Departed. To give voice to their name is somehow to commit an indelicate social blunder. Shortly after Art died, I was invited to a dinner party and decided to face this baptism by fire—my first time out alone. I hardly knew the other guests around the table, but they had known Art for many years as his colleagues. The evening passed slowly, the conversation distant from my interests, but I hoped to be an attentive guest. I was surprised, however, that no one mentioned Art's recent death or offered me a word of sympathy. After a while, I brought Art's name into the conversation, which resulted in an uneasy silence and a swift move to another subject. Later, and somewhat belligerently, I again offered up Art's name, and again the same uneasy silence followed. I left that dinner early and am sure the other guests must have been relieved. I don't fault them for what I assume to be their own fears of mortality, but it made me realize how tender our culture is, how fearful of death so many of us are. And how needy we bereaved can be in the early months of our loss.

There are also those godsent others: friends, acquaintances, even strangers who, by a miracle of innate empathy, manage to convey a compassion that warms my coldest parts. I am ever grateful when I am asked directly how I am doing. Facing someone's avoidance only denigrates my sadness, as though all those yesterdays with Art had never happened.

Events tend to happen in clusters and death is no exception. Around the time of Art's death, many of my closest friends were also dealing with the loss of partners; vigorous people suddenly faded and died. It felt as though some kind of hex had descended upon us all. In the mutuality of our grief, we sad ones rallied around each other and supported each other as we fled into the solace of feverish domesticity: one old friend remodeled her entire living area, another added a large studio onto her house. After Art's death, like a butterfly emerging from its chrysalis, I had every room in my house repainted in bright colors. It was an audacious act, tinged with guilt, as if I was celebrating a too early thaw, yet it yielded a momentary liberation from the darkness of grief.

In some ways, grieving the loss of Art has cut through my emotional complexities, opening me to the core so that, in all manner of things, I feel a new freedom. Shortly after Art died, a physicist friend of his visited from England. John and I share a deep friendship and he asked me if I had ever written about my feeling of being loved by loving. It's a question that has stuck in my mind. But the more I ponder, the less clear is my thinking—shades of the chicken-and-egg enigma cloud my thinking. Is my feeling of being loved by Art dependent on my first having loved him? Is it possible to love without the assurance of having been loved? It's a philosophical round-about which confuses my mind.

Yet my heart seems to understand. I have an abiding sense of Art's love moving through my sorrow and comforting my soul. And alongside his love for me is my own expansive love for him, as we move in concert with one another across the illusion of separateness, embraced within a spiral of light, which has no beginning, no end. The world assumes a softer glow now—my corners having weathered into roundness; I've lost much of my former sharpness, and I don't think it has anything to do with the possible lassitude of old age. It has more to do with love becoming visible.

In The End

Robert Nazarene

*I*n the end

    (if this is

       the end)

I will meet

you at the

end of what

you think is

the end

About the Contributors

Dannie Abse published his first book of poems while a medical student at Westminster Hospital. He was the Writer in Residence at Princeton University before returning to England to run a chest clinic. He is a Fellow of the Royal Society and President of the Welsh Academy of Letters.

Julia Alvarez is the author of three collections of poetry, a book of essays, books for children and highly acclaimed novels, including most recently, *Saving the World*. Her latest book is *Once Upon a Quinceañera: Coming of Age in the USA*. She is a writer-in-residence at Middlebury College.

Amanda Auchter is the editor of *Pebble Lake Review* and author of *Light Under Skin*. She received poetry awards from *BOMB Magazine, Mid-American Review*, and *Harpur Palate*. Her poems appear in *AGNI, Barrow Street, Crab Orchard Review, The Iowa Review*, and *The Marlboro Review*.

Charles Barber teaches psychiatry at Yale University. The essay *Songs from the Black Chair*, from his memoir of the same name, won a Pushcart Prize. Excerpts of the book have appeared in the *New York Times*, and on NPR. His newest book is *The Numbing of America: How Psychiatry Medicated a Nation*.

Elinor Benedict has published several chapbooks of poetry and a collection, *All That Divides Us*, that won the May Swenson Poetry Award. Her work has appeared in *Poetry, Indiana Review, Shenandoah, Image,* and online *Blackbird*.

Robin Black is currently completing a novel as well as a memoir, *Belongings*, about her father, the late Charles Black. She won the 2005 Pirate's Alley Faulkner/Wisdom Writing Competition, and has twice received Special Mention from the Pushcart Prize. Her latest book is *Immortalizing John Parker and Other Stories*.

Jan Bottiglieri's poetry has appeared in literary journals including *Margie, Oyez Review, After Hours*, and the anthology *Illinois Poets: Where We Live*. A communications professional living in Schaumburg, Illinois, Jan is also an associate editor for the poetry annual *Rhino*.

William Bradley is an assistant professor of English at Florida Atlantic University, where he specializes in creative nonfiction, and literature and medicine. His work has appeared in *The Chronicle of Higher Education, College English, Ars Medica*, and *The Missouri Review*.

Melisa Cahnmann-Taylor is associate professor of Language and Literacy Education at the University of Georgia. She has published in *APR, Quarterly West, Puerto del Sol, Barrow Street*, and won prizes from Leeway and Rosenberg Foundations. Her latest book is *Arts-Based Inquiry in Diverse Learning Communities: Foundations for Practice*.

Rafael Campo practices medicine at Beth Israel Deaconess/Harvard Medical School. Recent books include *Diva*, *Landscape with Human Figure*, and *The Healing Art: A Doctor's Black Bag of Poetry*. New writings have appeared in *Commonweal*, *The Georgia Review*, *The Nation*, *Prairie Schooner*, *The Progressive*, and *Virginia Quarterly Review*. His latest collection of poetry is *The Enemy*. www.rafaelcampo.com

Seth Carey was born on Cape Cod. He loved the water and enjoyed taking friends on fishing trips, followed by his famous sushi parties. ALS did not dim his zest for life. He died in his boyhood home in August, 2005. This essay is his sole published piece.

Michael Collier is a professor of English at the University of Maryland and the director of the Bread Loaf Writers' Conference, Middlebury College. He is the author of five books of poems, most recently, *Dark Wild Realm*. He is a former Poet Laureate of Maryland.

Cortney Davis, a nurse practitioner, is author of three poetry collections, a memoir about her work in women's health, and co-editor of two anthologies of poetry and prose by nurses. Her most recent collection, *Leopold's Maneuvers*, won the Prairie Schooner Book Prize. www.cortneydavis.com

Debra Anne Davis is a freelance writer whose work has appeared in *Utne, Massachusetts Review,* and *Sonora Review*. She holds an MFA degree from the University of Iowa. www.debraannedavis.com

Stephen Dixon is the author of 15 novels and 12 collections of stories. His latest novel, *Meyer,* was published by Melville House. Dixon retired after 26 years teaching at Johns Hopkins, and is currently working on a new novel. He lives in Baltimore and New York City.

Sariah Dorbin is a freelance writer in Los Angeles. Her short stories have appeared in *The Antioch Review*. She holds an MFA from the Bennington Writing Seminars, and is currently writing a collection of essays about failure.

Arlene Eager's poems have appeared in *Hudson Review, Atlanta Review, Southern Review, Gettysburg Review, Critical Quarterly,* and numerous anthologies. She leads the advanced poetry workshop in the Round Table Program at SUNY, Stony Brook. She lives in New York and Maine.

Gaynell Gavin is the author of *Intersections*, a poetry chapbook. Her prose and poetry have appeared in *The Chronicle of Higher Education, Fourth Genre, Prairie Schooner,* and the anthology, *Best New Poets 2006*. Her memoir, *What I Did Not Say*, was a finalist for the AWP Award Series in Creative Nonfiction.

Eamon Grennan is the Dexter M. Ferry Professor of English at Vassar College, and teaches in the graduate creative writing programs at Columbia and NYU. His most recent poetry collections are *Still Life with Waterfall* and *The Quick of It,* and a translation (with Rachel Kitzinger) of *Oedipus at Colonus*.

John Grey is an Australian-born poet, playwright, and musician. His latest book is *What Else Is There* from Main Street Rag. His work has appeared in *The English Journal, Northeast, Pearl,* and the *Journal of the American Medical Association.*

Rachel Hadas is Board of Governors Professor of English at Rutgers University. Her recent books include *Laws* and *The River of Forgetfulness* (both poetry collections), and *Classics* (selected prose). She teaches seminars on literature and medicine at the University of Medicine and Dentistry, New Jersey.

Amy Hempel is the author of five short-story collections. *The Collected Stories of Amy Hempel* was named one of the Ten Best Books of the Year by the *New York Times.* Her stories have appeared in *Harper's, Vanity Fair, GQ,* and *The Quarterly.* She teaches creative writing at Bennington College.

Susan Ito co-edited the anthology *A Ghost At Heart's Edge: Stories & Poems of Adoption.* Her work has appeared in *Growing Up Asian American, Making More Waves, Hip Mama,* and *CHOICE.* She is a fiction editor and columnist at the online journal *Literary Mama.*

Gray Jacobik is a painter and poet who lives in Deep River, Connecticut. Her collections include *Brave Disguises* (AWP Poetry Prize), *The Surface of Last Scattering* (X. J. Kennedy Prize) and *The Double Task* (Juniper Prize). She is on the faculty of The Stonecoast MFA.

Roy Jacobstein's *A Form of Optimism* won the Morse Poetry Prize. His previous book, *Ripe,* won the Pollak Prize. His poetry is included in *LITERATURE: Reading Fiction, Poetry & Drama.* He works in Africa and Asia on women's reproductive health.

Miriam Karmel's writing has appeared in *Dust & Fire, Sidewalks, An Intricate Weave: Women Write About Girls and Girlhood,* and *Jewish Women's Literary Annual.* She received the *Minnesota Monthly's* Tamarack Award, and has just completed *Nora's Story,* a collection of short stories about the effect of illness on one family.

Judy Katz's work has appeared in the *New York Times Book Review, Salamander,* and the *Women's Review of Books.* She works as a producer in public television and documentary film, and lives in New York City.

John Kay is an education counselor in Heidelberg, Germany and taught writing for the University of Maryland in its European Division for many years. His poems have appeared in *Kayak,* the *New York Quarterly,* the *Wormwood Review, Chiron Review, Pearl,* and *Jewish Currents.* His most recent chapbook is *Further Evidence of Someone.*

Meg Kearney is the author of *An Unkindness of Ravens, The Secret of Me,* and *Home By Now.* Former Associate Director of the National Book Foundation in Manhattan, she is now Director of the Solstice Creative Writing Programs of Pine Manor College in Massachusetts.

Joan Kip was a hospice counselor and now writes about aging and matters of the heart. Her work has been published in the *San Jose Mercury News, Rockhurst Review, Tiferet,* and several anthologies. She lives in Berkeley, California, and, at age 89, is currently finishing a memoir

Caroline Leavitt is the author of eight novels, most recently *Girls in Trouble.* A book critic for *The Boston Globe, People* magazine, and *Cookie* magazine, her work has appeared in *Salon, Psychology Today, More,* and *Redbook.* She lives in Hoboken, New Jersey.

Barbara F. Lefcowitz has published nine collections of poetry, most recently *The Blue Train to America,* and many articles and short stories. She has won fellowships and prizes from the National Endowment for the Arts, the Rockefeller Foundation, and the Maryland State Arts Council.

David Lehman's most recent book of poems is *When a Woman Loves a Man.* He edited the new edition of *The Oxford Book of American Poetry.* He teaches in the graduate writing program at the New School in New York City.

Philip Levine's most recent book of poems is *Breath,* published by Knopf in 2004. He has received many awards, among them the National Book Award for *What Work Is* and the Pulitzer Prize for Poetry for *The Simple Truth.*

Lou Lipsitz is a psychotherapist in Chapel Hill, North Carolina. He is working on one book of poems about being a therapist and another about men's issues. He remains committed to learning the flute and harmonica despite many failures. www.loulipsitz.com

Joan Malerba-Foran is a high school teacher in New Haven, Connecticut. Her poetry has appeared in *JAMA*. She has received scholarships, most notably from the *English Speaking Union,* to study Shakespeare at Oxford. *The Little Things* is her first short story publication.

Thomas McCall is a physician who lives in Chicago. He has published two mystery novels, *A Wide and Capable Revenge* and *Beyond Ice, Beyond Death.* His short fiction has appeared in *The Missouri Review.*

Amy Mehringer was a Peace Corps volunteer in Cape Verde, West Africa. Her stories have been published in *River City, Kiosk, Folio, The Baltimore Review, The Washington Review, So to Speak,* and *Koktejl.* She has won awards from *River City* and *Folio.* She lives in Syracuse, New York.

Samuel Menashe served in the U.S. Army in World War II, and in 1950 was awarded a *Doctorat d'Universite* by the Sorbonne. His poetry collections include *The Many Named Beloved* and *The Niche Narrows.* He received the Neglected Masters Prize from the Poetry Foundation, which included publication of *New and Selected Poems.*

Andrew Merton turned to poetry after 25 years as a journalist. His work has appeared in *Alaska Quarterly Review, Comstock Review, Cranky Literary Journal, Powhatan Review, Paper Street,* and *American Journal of Nursing.* He teaches at the University of New Hampshire.

Joan Michelson lectures in creative writing and literature at Birkbeck College, London University. Her writing has been included in the 2006 British Council anthology of new writing, *NW14,* and the anthology *Loffing Matters*. Her collection of poetry is entitled *Towards the Heliopause*.

David Milofsky is the author of four novels and many short stories. His writing has appeared in the *Chicago Tribune*, the *New York Times* and the *New York Times Magazine*. He has received fellowships from the National Endowment for the Arts, the Colorado Council on the Arts and Humanities, and the MacDowell Colony.

Toni Mirosevich's new nonfiction collection, *Pink Harvest,* received the First Series in Creative Nonfiction Award from Mid-List Press. Poetry collections include *Queer Street* and *My Oblique Strategies,* winner of the Frank O'Hara Chapbook Award. She teaches creative writing at San Francisco State University.

Rick Moody's most recent publication is a collection of three novellas, *Right Livelihoods*.

Nikki Moustaki is the author of *The Complete Idiot's Guide to Writing Poetry* and is a recipient of a National Endowment for the Arts grant. She has taught at New Yorik University, Indiana University, and the New School.

Madeleine Mysko is a nurse whose poems, short stories, and essays have appeared widely. She has published a novel, *Bringing Vincent Home,* and a poetry collection, *Crucial Blue*.

Robert Nazarene is founding editor of *Margie/The American Journal of Poetry* and of *MARGIE/IntuiT House Poetry Series*. Mr. Nazarene's collection of poems is titled *CHURCH*.

Eric Nelson's most recent poetry collection is *Terrestrials*. Previous books include *The Interpretation of Waking Life* and *The Light Bringers*. He teaches in the Writing and Linguistics Department at Georgia Southern University.

Sharon Olds' books include *Strike Sparks, Selected Poems 1980–2002, The Unswept Room, The Wellspring,* and *The Dead and the Living,* which received the National Book Critics Circle Award. She teaches in the Graduate Creative Writing Program at New York University, and twenty-two years ago helped found the ongoing writing workshop at Goldwater Memorial Hospital, a 900-bed state hospital for the severely physically challenged. From 1998–2000 she was the New York State Poet Laureate. She is a member of the American Academy of Arts and Sciences and a Chancellor of The Academy of American Poets.

Robert Oldshue is a med/peds physician in Boston.

Alicia Ostriker is the author of eleven volumes of poetry, most recently *No Heaven*. Her most recent volume of criticism is *Dancing at the Devil's Party: Essays on Poetry, Politics, and the Erotic*.

Linda Tomol Pennisi's books of poems are *Seamless* and *Suddenly, Fruit*. She directs the creative writing program at Le Moyne College in Syracuse, New York.

Holly Posner is the author of *Explorations in American Culture* and winner of the 2005 Greenburgh Poetry Competition. She received her MFA from Sarah Lawrence, and has taught at the New School, Hunter College, and New York University. She currently edits *Line*, a journal for the Hadar Foundation, which sponsors scholarships in the creative arts.

Sharon Pretti's work has appeared in *MARGIE, Healing Muse, Marin Poetry Center Anthology,* and *Manzanita*. She is a medical social worker in San Francisco and runs Age of Expression, poetry workshops for senior citizens in long-term care.

Mark Rigney is the author of *Deaf Side Story: Deaf Sharks, Hearing Jets and a Classic American Musical*, and won two national playwriting contests. His plays have been staged in six states, including Indiana, where he lives with his wife, two boys, and far too many mosquitoes.

Ruthann Robson is Professor of Law at the City University of New York School of Law. She is the author of novels, short fiction collections, and books of legal theory. Her essays include "Notes on My Dying" and "Notes on a Difficult Case."

Lisa Rosen's poems have appeared in *Poetry East, Kaleidoscope, Gertrude*, and the anthology, *A Chaos of Angels*. Her chapbook is *Bright Omens*. She teaches at a community college in Eugene, Oregon.

Helen Klein Ross is a former advertising copywriter who lives in Manhattan. She has published in *Mid-American Review, Hunger Mountain*, the *New York Times*, and mrbellersneighborhood.com. She is at work on a collection of poems and a novel.

Harriet Rzetelny is a clinical social worker. Her fiction has been published in *Alfred Hitchcock's Mystery Magazine* and she has produced film scripts for the American Cancer Society and the Food and Drug Administration. She lives on Cape Cod and is working on her third novel.

Elaine Schear is a high school tutor, former teacher educator, and fund-raiser for public high schools in Cambridge, Massachusetts. Her poetry has appeared in the *Boston Globe, the Carquinez Poetry Review, Blueline, Rive Gauche, Spare Change News,* and *Sojourner: A Women's Forum*. She is at work on her first collection of poems.

Peter Schmitt is the author of three collections of poems: *Renewing the Vows, Country Airport* and *Hazard Duty*, and a chapbook, *To Disappear*. He teaches in Miami, Florida.

Hollis Seamon is the author of *Flesh: A Suzanne LaFleshe Mystery* and *Body Work: Stories*. She teaches writing and literature at the College of Saint Rose in Albany, New York. http://members.authorsguild.net/hollis

David Shine's poems have appeared in *Poetry East, Georgetown Review, Saranac Review,* and *Paper Street*. He works as a mergers-and-acquisitions lawyer in New York City.

Hal Sirowitz is the former Poet Laureate of Queens. He has been published in *Tiferet,* and wrote the preface for *Broken Land: Poems of Brooklyn.* He recently performed in Jerusalem, at the Kisufim Conference for Jewish Writers.

Floyd Skloot's books include the novel *Patient 002,* about human medical research from the patient's point of view; two memoirs of living with brain damage, *In the Shadow of Memory* and *A World of Light*; and the poetry collections *The End of Dreams* and the forthcoming *The Snow's Music.* He lives in Portland, Oregon.

Clarence Smith is a resident in radiology at Vanderbilt University. His fiction has appeared in *Rosebud.*

Alan Steinberg teaches at SUNY Potsdam and has a doctorate in English from Carnegie Mellon University. He has published fiction (*Cry of the Leopard, Divided*), poetry (*Fathering, Ebstein on Reflection,*), and drama (*The Road to Corinth*).

John Stone's fifth book of poetry is *Music from Apartment 8: New and Selected Poems.* Dr. Stone is Professor of Medicine (Cardiology), Emeritus, at Emory University School of Medicine. He has often taught for the English Department.

Sandy Suminski lives in Brussels and is working on *Shining Wings,* a memoir about her experiences with mental illness.

James Tate won the Pulitzer Prize in 1994 for his *Selected Poems.* His most recent book is *The Ghost Soldiers.* He teaches at the University of Massachusetts, Amherst. His other awards include a National Book Award, the William Carlos Williams Prize and the Wallace Stevens Award.

Scott Temple is a clinical psychologist and a professor of psychiatry at the University of Iowa, where he specializes in the treatment of mood and anxiety disorders, and psychosis. He is at work on a novel, in hopes that the fourth time is a charm.

John Thompson's story earned Special Mention from the Pushcart Prize. His work has appeared in *Raven Chronicles, Bayou, Northeast Corridor, Piedmont Literary Review, Widener Review* and the anthology *Working Hard for the Money: America's Working Poor.* Philadelphia's InterAct Theatre Company's "Writing Aloud" has read his work.

Sue Ellen Thompson is the author of four books of poetry, most recently *The Golden Hour.* She is the editor of *The Autumn House Anthology of Contemporary American Poetry* and was Visiting Writer at SUNY Binghamton. She lives in Maryland.

Jim Tolan has published poems in *American Literary Review, Fulcrum, Louisiana Literature, Many Mountains Moving, Margie,* and *Rock & Sling.* He lives in New York City and teaches at the Borough of Manhattan Community College, where he co-chairs the Writing and Literature Program.

Pat Tompkins is an editor in the San Francisco Bay area. Her fiction has appeared in *flashquake, Mslexia,* and *Cicada.*

Susan Varon recently relocated to Taos, New Mexico, from New York City. She began writing poetry in 1992, after suffering a severe stroke. Her work has appeared in over 40 publications, and she has won fellowships to the MacDowell Colony and other residencies. She is an ordained Interfaith Minister.

Abraham Verghese's memoir, *My Own Country,* was a finalist for the National Book Critics Circle Award. *The Tennis Partner* was a *New York Times* notable book. His newest book is *Cutting for Stone.* His writing has appeared in the *New Yorker, Atlantic Monthly, Granta,* and the *New York Times Magazine.*

David Watts is a poet, physician, and commentator on NPR's *All Things Considered.* He has published three books of poetry and organizes the Writing the Medical Experience workshops at Sarah Lawrence College. He lives in Mill Valley, California.

Angela Wheelock has worked as a journalist, teacher, and archivist, and now is an editor and writer. Her essays have appeared in *Notre Dame Magazine, Shenandoah,* and *Geist.* She lived in the Yukon for more than a decade.

Emma Wunsch has published fiction in *Passages North, Lit, Brooklyn Review, Fugue,* and *Inkwell.* She teaches English at Brooklyn College.

Carol Zoref teaches at Sarah Lawrence College. She won the I.O.W.W. Emerging Artist Award, and has been honored by the Virginia Center for Creative Arts, Hall Farm Center for Arts, and In Our Own Write. She is now writing about the intersections of the arts and society.

Sherwin B. Nuland is Clinical Professor of Surgery at Yale. He is the author of *How We Die,* which won the National Book Award. His other books include *Doctors, How We Live, The Mysteries Within, Maimonides, Leonardo da Vinci, Lost in America,* and, most recently, *The Art of Aging.*

Danielle Ofri is co-founder and Editor-in-Chief of the *Bellevue Literary Review.* She is the author of two books about life in medicine: *Incidental Findings* and *Singular Intimacies.* Her writings have appeared in *Best American Essays, Best American Science Writing,* the *New York Times,* and on *National Public Radio.* She teaches and practices medicine at Bellevue Hospital.